MW01038188

Cannot put it dow

It's so readable that ___ in Margaret's world, & going through the emotions with her. Just cannot wait for book 3 to find out what will happen to her. If you like historical novels , based on real research, then this trilogy is a must. I highly recommend it.

—NSK

Read this series!

I have just finished Lady Margaret's Challenge. I was transported back in time. The description of the weather, the crops, and the Keep were so detailed. I am an avid reader and these books have captivated me. I am so looking forward to the next book.

—JILL OLSON REIL

Fantastic Book!

This book is a treasure. In Lady Margaret's Challenge she transforms her estate, faces dangerous attacks, contends with three suiters, deals with King Henry, and improves the lives of many. Best of all, you feel you are there and totally experiencing life in 1102 A.D.

—KINDLE CUSTOMER

Read, Enjoy, Learn!!!

As I've finished each book in this series, I've eagerly awaited the next book. Her characters are dynamic. The plot is enticing. Ms. Sportelli's voice is a welcome addition to this genre.

—AMAZON CUSTOMER

Note: This novel includes beheadings, a sexual assault, and a hanging, which may be triggers for some readers.

LADY MARGARET'S
CHALLENGE

V. C. SPORTELLI

Creazzo Publishing
Sioux Falls, South Dakota

Creazzo Publishing
401 E. 8th Street Suite 214-1194
Sioux Falls, South Dakota 57104
USA

Published by Creazzo Publishing
www.CreazzoPublishing.com

First Edition: 2019

ISBN 978-1-952849-03-9 (paperback)
ISBN 978-1-952849-04-6 (mobi)
ISBN 978-1-952849-05-3 (ePub)

Credits:
Cover Design: Jennifer D. Quinlan
Interior Design: *wordzworth.com*
Map and Illustration: Lindsey A. Grassmid
Editor: Margaret K. Diehl

Publisher's Cataloging-In-Publication Data
(Prepared by The Donohue Group, Inc.)
Names: Sportelli, Victoria, author. | Grassmid, Lindsey A., illustrator.
Title: Lady Margaret's challenge / Victoria Sportelli ; [map and illustration: Lindsey A. Grassmid].

Description: [Second edition]. | Sioux Falls, South Dakota : Creazzo Publishing, [2020] | Series: Henry's spare queen trilogy ; book 2 | The second edition of this work has a new cover design and revised front matter but no changes to the text or descriptive portions of the bibliographic record. | Interest age level: 016-018. | Summary: "Henry I, King of England awards Lady Margaret an estate and coins for a dowry. As she waits for the King to send her a husband, she repairs the estate and her knights defend it. After Henry sends her unsuitable men, she reappears at court then flees to hide in her estate. Ill, Margaret almost dies, but recovers and helps others to marry"--Provided by publisher.

Identifiers: ISBN 9781952849039 (paperback) | ISBN 9781952849046 (mobi) | ISBN 9781952849053 (ePub)

Subjects: LCSH: Henry I, King of England, 1068-1135–Juvenile fiction. | Ladies-in-waiting–England–History–To 1500–Juvenile fiction. | Marriage–England–History–To 1500–Juvenile fiction. | Great Britain–History–1066-1687–Juvenile fiction. | CYAC: Henry I, King of England, 1068-1135–Fiction. | Ladies-in-waiting–England–History–To 1500–Fiction. | Marriage–England–History–To 1500–Fiction. | Great Britain–History–1066-1687–Fiction. | LCGFT: Historical fiction.

Classification: LCC PZ7.1.S7174 Lac 2020 (print) | LCC PZ7.1.S7174 (ebook) | DDC [Fic]–dc23

For
Eric and Dawn

Each of you is unique and wonderful.
I am so grateful you are in my life.

Contents

England, 1099 A.D.   viii

Lady Margaret's Estate   ix

A Royal Family   x

A Noble Family   xi

Characters   xii

Preface   xviii

Chapter 1   Demoted   1

Chapter 2   Sunday   11

Chapter 3   Market Day   23

Chapter 4   The Road   35

Chapter 5   Ash Wednesday 1102 A.D.   43

Chapter 6   Almost There   53

Chapter 7   Rough Start   65

Chapter 8   Mine   79

Chapter 9   Creating Order   95

Chapter 10   Father Manntun   107

Chapter 11   Fear and Fire   121

Chapter 12   Eastertide   139

Chapter 13   Visitors   147

Chapter 14   Twin Troubles   167

Chapter 15	An Addition	177
Chapter 16	New Sister	185
Chapter 17	Tithe and Tax	199
Chapter 18	An Attack	213
Chapter 19	Court	223
Chapter 20	An Execution	249
Chapter 21	Aftermath	259
Chapter 22	Home	269
Chapter 23	Another Suitor	279
Chapter 24	Departure	299
Chapter 25	Christmas Court	305
Chapter 26	Return	317
Chapter 27	January 1103 A.D.	331
Chapter 28	Fever	343
Chapter 29	Lent	351
Chapter 30	April	359
Chapter 31	May	371
Chapter 32	June	385
Chapter 33	July	399
Chapter 34	Royal Arrival	411
Author's Notes		422
About Early 12th Century England		423
Preview of *Lady Margaret's Future, Book Three*		427
Acknowledgments		436
Glossary		438
About the Author		449

England, 1099 A.D.

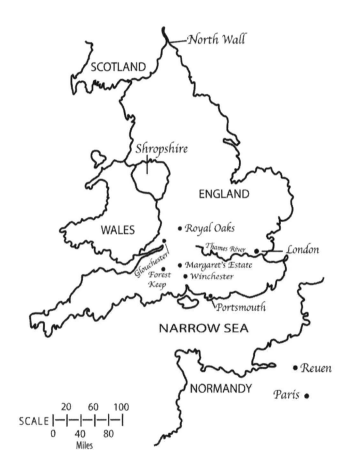

North Wall

SCOTLAND

Shropshire

ENGLAND

Royal Oaks

WALES

Thames River

London

Glouchester

Margaret's Estate

Forest
Keep

Winchester

Portsmouth

NARROW SEA

Reuen

NORMANDY

Paris

SCALE

20   60   100

0   40   80
Miles

Lady Margaret's Estate

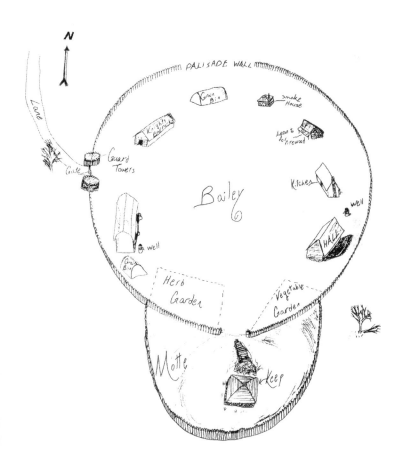

A Royal Family

<u>William I (the Conqueror)</u>   m.   <u>Matilda of Flanders</u>
b. 1028 - d. 1087 A.D.   b. 1031 - d. 1083 A.D.
King of England 1066 - 1087 A.D.

Children:

Richard (Deceased)

Robert, Duke of Normandy

William II
b. 1056 - d. 1100 A.D.
King of England 1088 - 1100 A.D.

<u>Henry</u>   m.   <u>Matilda of Scotland</u>
b. 1068 A.D.   b. 1080 A.D.
King of England 1100 A.D. -

Child:

Princess Matilda
b. 1102 A.D.

A Noble Family

Charles   m.   **Rosamonde**

b. 1064 A.D.   b. 1069 - d. 1099 A.D.

Lord, Royal Oaks Estate-1086 A.D.

Children:

Margaret

Charles

(called Young Charles)

Raymond

Cecily

Characters

Normans

Eustace. A scribe and lover of books, son of a knight landed.

King William I (the Conqueror), formerly Duke of Normandy. Married Matilda of Flanders. He invaded England in 1066 A.D., had himself crowned king and ruled England until he died in 1087.

Children: **Richard** died in a hunting accident.

Robert was passed over for the English crown and accepted the Dukedom of Normandy. In 1097 he joined the Grand Crusade to the Holy Land in search of wealth. In 1100 he returned to Normandy.

William II (Rufus) was his father's favorite son. He was King of England from 1088 until his death in 1100 in a hunting accident.

Henry holds land and great wealth in Normandy inherited from his mother.

King Henry. Became King of England 3 August 1100 after his brother King William II died in a hunting accident. He renamed Aegdyth, Princess of Scotland, Matilda and married her on 11 November 1100. They have a daughter Matilda, born 5 February 1102.

Lady Cecily. Fourth child of Lord Charles of Royal Oaks and the late Lady Rosamonde.

Lady Claire de Clerkx. Lady in service to Queen Matilda.

Lady Cleanthe. A young lady living in Normandy.

Lady Margaret. First-born child of Lord Charles of Royal Oaks and the late Lady Rosamonde.

Lord Bedwin. King Henry assigned him to guard Lord William de Warenne's former estate.

Lord Cai of the Fens. A former squire to King William I of England, who awarded him a knighthood, made him a lord, and gave him an estate.

Lord Charles of Royal Oaks. His estate lies three days' ride southeast of Gloucester in Worcestershire.

Lord Henry de Beaumont, 1st Earl of Warwick. Holds the most lands for the Crown and is the most powerful earl in England. His immediate support of Henry helped to make him King of England.

Lord Robert de Belleme, 3rd Earl of Shropshire and Shrewsbury. Holder of those and several other estates; the second most powerful lord in England after Henry de Beaumont, Earl of Warwick.

Lord Thibaud de Reims. The eldest brother of Lord Charles of Royal Oaks.

Lord William of Avondale. A widower with two small sons. He is a strong supporter of King Henry and is Lady Margaret's undeclared champion.

Lord William de Warenne. 2nd Earl of Surrey, but was most often called the Earl de Warenne. He lost his English title and lands in 1101. King Henry reinstated him, but gave de Warenne several tests to prove his loyalty, which he completed in 1106.

Princess Matilda. The first-born child of Henry, King of England and Queen Matilda.

Sir Andre. Suitor to Lady Margaret.

Sir Cachier. Member of King Henry's corp d' elite assigned to protect Lady Margaret.

Sir Cavel. Suitor to Lady Margaret.

Sir Charles, called **Young Charles.** Second child of Lord Charles of Royal Oak and the late Lady Rosamone. He is his father's heir.

Sir Gailard. Member of King Henry's corp d' elite assigned to protect Lady Margaret.

Sir Raymond. The third child of Lord Charles of Royal Oaks and the late Lady Rosamonde.

Sir Ricardo de Campo. A knight from the Iberian peninsula who fought with King William I, who awarded de Campo an estate and the management of the King's Inn at an important crossroads.

Sir Roger. Constable of the new castle in Winchester. He moved from the same position in the small castle after it burned.

Sir Roussel. Member of King Henry's corp d' elite assigned to protect Lady Margaret.

Lady Margaret's Knights Errant

Sir Claude	**Sir Demetre**
Sir Giraud	**Sir Hughes**
Sir Masselin	**Sir Roulin**
Sir Sauville	**Sir Verel**

Clergy

Anselm, Archbishop of Canterbury. An important monk and theologian. In England he defended the Church's interests. He was exiled by King William II in 1097 and called back by Henry before he was crowned king. He and King Henry are in disagreement as to how much power the Church will have in England.

Father Gregory. Saxon. Priest for Queen Matilda while she was in Forest Keep. Friend and confidant of Lady Margaret.

Father Manntun. Served Lord William de Warenne. Now resides on de Warenne's former estate and serves Lady Margaret.

Father Simeon. Head Priest of Church of the Blessed Mary, Suindune.

Gabriel de Chanoise. Bishop of Oxford.

Others

Cormac mac Cennedig, Scot. He has known Queen Matilda since her birth and had served her brothers, Donald III and Edgar, Kings of Scotland. He now serves Lady Margaret as her seneschal.

Caitlin. Irish. Brought to London to be sold as a slave and bought by Lord Charles as a wedding gift for his bride. She had been the nursemaid to Lady Margaret since her birth. Freed upon the birth of Margaret's first brother, Young Charles, Caitlin is now Lady Margaret's friend and helper.

Matilda, Queen of England. Half Scot and half Saxon. Princess of Scotland and sister to King Edgar of Scotland. She was born Aegdyth and renamed Matilda, after King Henry's mother, when she married King Henry in 1100 A.D. and became his queen. Henry often called her Aegdyth in private.

Syghelm. Dane. He fights with an axe and has spent his adult life as a mercenary.

Saxons on Lady Margaret's Estate

Hus.: **Felamaere.** Reeve
Wife: **Erwina**
Son: **Ainemaere**
Son: **Denemaere**

Hus: **Linton Elder**, Aleman
Wife: **Gytha**
Son: **Linton Younger**
Son: **Lindene**
Dau.: **Goscelyn**

Hus.: **Scirburne.** Farmer
Wife: **Ifig**
Dau.: **Leoma**
Dau.: **Willa**
Son: **Scirwode**

Hus.: **Rammeg Elder.** Carpenter
Wife: **Hugiet.** Cook's Helper
Son: **Rammeg Younger**
Son: **Rammethan**
Dau.: **Haesel**

Hus.: **Scelfdune.** Farmer
Wife: **Raedaelf**
Son: **Scandy.** Page
Dau.: **Cleva**

Hus.: **Jorgon.** Hostler
Wife: **Dena**

Hus.: **Aldcot.** Farmer
Wife: **Beornia.** Cook's Helper
Dau.: **Alura**

Hus.: **Hloetun.** Farmer
Wife: **Berthtilde**
Dau.: **Cleva**

Dau.: **Aeda**
Son: **Haelum**

Son: **Hludaelf**

Margaret's Servants/Maids:
Cleva
Midryth
Haesel
Cyne
Alura

Hus.: **Haraleah.** Farmer
Wife: **Cadda.** Cook's Helper
Son: **Hartun.** Page
Dau.: **Carlia**
Son : **Haraford**

Daelton. Jorgan's Helper
Duone. Kitchen Worker
Elstan. Serves Lady Margaret
Garwig. Blacksmith
Neara. Head Cook

Hus.: **Saegar.** Farmer
Wife: **Meagth**

Other Saxons

Heardwine. Farms outside Suindune.
Saebroc. A tanner who lives just outside Suindune.

Preface

On 5 August 1100 A.D. Henry, son of William the Conqueror (William I), was crowned King of England. All was not well. Several barons and earls wanted the kingship. His brother Robert raced home from the Grand Crusade to claim the crown he thought was his right as the elder brother. The Church expected to rule over whoever was king. To keep his crown, King Henry had several fights on his hand.

In March 1101, Queen Matilda miscarried the heir Henry needed to help him secure his throne. When next she was with child, Henry sought a better Norman midwife and found Lady Margaret, who agreed to help his queen bear a healthy child. After Margaret revealed the rumors someone may have poisoned the queen and caused her miscarriage, Henry secreted both women in a fortress deep in the forest. Driven out by persistent rumors and to prove the queen really was with child, Henry took the women and their guards to the small castle in Winchester.

Matilda birthed a daughter and was so desperate to provide an heir she switched her daughter for a Saxon's son. The queen's actions devastated Henry. Queen Matilda blamed Margaret for the plan; Margaret was certain the king would execute her.

Instead, Henry amazed everyone by granting Margaret the three boons for which she had previously bargained. In open Court and with his queen at his side, Henry awarded Margaret more money, land, and property than she had ever dreamed might be hers and much more than Matilda or the courtiers expected. Matilda observed how her husband gazed at the girl and knew her own future. If she did not produce an heir immediately, Henry would replace her. He made Margaret wealthy to raise her rank. If need be, she was going to become his next queen.

Margaret announced her third and final boon, the right to sign her own marriage contract rather than to have her estranged father do so. Her request was so outrageous the king refused to grant it. Matilda seconded his disapproval and uttered a subtle threat to the girl. Margaret did not understand why Queen Matilda had suddenly turned on her. Margaret was also totally unaware of King Henry's intentions toward her. Dismissed from Court, Margaret decided she must prepare her new estate well to attract a prospective husband as soon as possible.

1

Demoted

15 February 1102 A.D.

Margaret backed four steps before turning away from Queen Matilda and King Henry, who, in an angry voice, had dismissed her—no, ordered her to leave. She passed curtained sleeping bays within the hall while she walked an aisle the couriers left for her. As Margaret advanced, they showed first their frowns and then their backs.

No privileged screened area for me. Stop shuffling. Pick up your feet. Look up. Up! Smile as if all is well. Shoulders back. March.

She strode toward the main doors and gray daylight. From the entrance steps, Sir Roussel directed her around the building's right corner. A bitter wind slapped her in the face and tore at her clothes. The thin-soled slippers the queen had provided were no protection from the pebbles covering the courtyard dirt. Within two yards, Margaret limped toward the distant stone outer wall and a wooden structure. Winter continued its attack, whipping her skirt tightly around her legs as she fought to take steps. Her hair flew over her face, blocking her sight. Margaret shook her head to free her locks, crossed her hands over her chest and shivered.

Winter is attacking me as if it is the royals' ally. Have they sent me out into the cold to die? May I have mine mantle, mine things? Margaret stumbled on a hole in the stones. *Purchase sturdy boots with thick soles.* At the end of the hall wall, another wintery blast rounded the corner, pushed Margaret's hair left and tried to freeze her right cheek and ear. She blinked and squinted to protect her eyes. *Two doors, no windows. Servants' quarters? Such a loss of rank in so short a time!*

Sir Roussel opt the right door.

Women's side. Cots. Clothing on pegs. Where goes that back door? Margaret strode through the double line of cots and opt the door at the end of the room. She smelled midden from a single, slim window slit. She grimaced and forced herself not to pinch closed her nostrils. Pieces of bark and splinters of wood in the corners proved the room lately had held firewood for the braziers in the dormitory. A cot, a chamber pot, a stool, and one lit, fat candle on a small table filled the tiny space. *A message. I can bear it. I must. Oh, Mother, what have I done? Your voice rings inside mine head. 'Too bold, too bold. Be a lady.'* Margaret sighed. *Too late.*

At the outer door Sir Roussel turned to see no one had followed; the wind slammed the door shut. Gailard and Cachier carried the money chest through the second doorway. They lifted the trunk over the table and the cot to deposit it in the far corner. Margaret almost tasted the rotting onions fouling the air.

Their breaths or outside? Ask not.

"We did not choose this place, my lady."

"Of course not, Sir Cachier. You may depart."

"We stand guard at all times. That chest will draw thieves and murderers."

"Sir Roussel, Sir Gailard, Sir Cachier, make a show, but promise me."

"My lady?" they replied in unison.

"If someone attacks you, die not. You are more valuable than either the chest or I am." Margaret's gesture halted their objections. "Promise."

"I promise," they replied in half-hearted tones.

Probably mean it not. The king's charge is more important. Oh well, I tried.

All four turned at hearing the outer door open and close. Sir Roger, the king's constable, approached. He stopped halfway into the building, wrinkled his nose and coughed twice. "You will attend Mass elsewhere but not in the cathedral. Dine and sup in your room. Enter not the hall, the keep nor any other part of the castle. Stay in this room unless you are leaving the grounds. The king orders you to depart before Ash Wednesday."

"Please inform His Royal Highness I obey. I must hire men and wagons and purchase what I need. As the morrow is Sunday, I will confine me to this room as soon as I return from Mass. I plan to leave Winchester Tuesday morn."

Sir Roger nodded as he turned to flee the odors assailing him. The group watched him wrap his cloak around his body and slip through the doorway. Again the wind slammed the door shut, but Sir Roger opt the door for a moment to free a corner of his cloak.

Next to march to Margaret's door was the Lady Claire de Clerkx, resplendent in a mink-fur-lined and edged mantle and matching scarf also mink-edged. She glowered at each of them. The knights stepped aside, but she refused to enter the room.

"A fitting place for you," sneered the woman.

Pretend this is the best room in the palace. Thwart her. Margaret's smile seemed genuine. She curtsied. "God give you a good day, my lady." Margaret's cheerful tone hid the dismay she felt at her loss of station. *Smile for real.* She relaxed her forced grin.

The woman gestured servants forward. The first deposited her bedding on the cot, the second her personal belongs and her clothing. Margaret's eyes widened when the final servant held out her sword in its scabbard. As Lady Claire talked, Margaret took it from the man.

"Her Highness says you are to keep that thing until His Highness calls for it." She made a rude noise. "Why she would trust you with a weapon is beyond me. She has no need of you or it."

"Did you protect Her Royal Highness during her first child bearing?"

"I have served Queen Matilda since her coronation."

"You failed to protect her first babe, and the heir died. I served her and her second babe lived." Margaret lifted her scabbard so the sword's hilt and guard were upright, and the sword was but inches from Lady Claire's nose. The weapon was now a cross, the kind men at arms used to make oaths. In a hard voice, Margaret threatened, "I swear by this cross before you. Fail her again and you will answer to me." Margaret's eyes dared the woman to speak; Margaret blinked not, moved not. *Speak and I might smack your face.*

The woman turned on her heel and marched away.

"Are you going to wear that?" asked Sir Roussel.

"No need." Margaret smiled at him. "I have you." She turned and placed the weapon on the table. "Two to guard, one to escort me? Or the opposite?"

"Two to guard. Where are you bound?

"I need wagons and oxen. I will order them today, fill them Monday to be ready Tuesday dawn."

"Whatever you purchase or rent will cost you dear, my lady. Everyone knows your wealth."

Margaret leaned toward Sir Roussel as if sharing a secret. "But they know not how well I bargain." *Not cert about that among city folk. Distract them.* "Sirs, please tell me of yourselves."

Sir Roussel answered for the other two. "We are of His Royal Highness's corps d' elite. An inner circle among his knights."

"Have you lands? Are you married?"

"We are not yet knights landed. I have served in His Royal Highness's corps for two years. Sir Gailard one. Sir Cachier since last month. If we do well during our five years of service, the king will award us our own mail, sword, horse, lance, land and lord. Then we may marry."

"You are from a special group. I am honored to have your protection."

At that moment, a knock on the outer door put the men on alert. The men drew swords as Margaret stepped over the cot and backed into a corner to stand before her chest; she looked toward her sword. *Should I have grabbed it? No, insult them not. I need their good will.*

"Who goes there?" demanded Sir Roussel as he strode to the door.

"Cormac mac Cennedig. Unarmed. Alone. Me lady, may I speak wi' ya?"

"Of course! Of course!" called out Margaret.

Beside the entry door, Sir Gailard put his back to the wall as Sir Roussel, sword in his right hand, opt the door with his left. Cormac stayed outside until Roussel motioned him forward. Half afraid he would be cut down from behind, the Scot glanced over each shoulder as he approached Margaret. He wrinkled his nose while he pulled his forelock. Margaret stepped back over the cot to meet Cormac at her door.

"We can talk here, with the door open to protect mine reputation. Have you come from Her Royal Highness?"

"Nay, me lady. I have not. I have come for meself."

"Oh." Margaret's manner drooped. "What want you?"

"Well. Tis this, me lady. I like the warmer weather here. I have no real reason to return to Scotland and reason to stay. I am older than some, but I am an experienced seneschal. Might ye need one? Hopefully me?"

Margaret looked to Roussel.

"He went with the traitor."

Eager to be accepted, Cormac listed his abilities. "I speak Norman, Saxon, Scots and a little Latin. I read and write and figure, so I can keep track of things for you. I gain people's confidence. They like to talk to me and often tell me more than they realize. I can turn away those ye want not to see without 'em gettin' angry. In Scotland I ran a smooth household for more than one king."

"What reason to stay? Why mine household?" *Do you also spy for the royals? Better one I know than one I know not.*

Cormac blurted, "Where ye are Caitlin is cert to be, soon or late. Me lady, she has been missin' four days. Where is she?"

"Cormac! After the teasing you have done? After she purposely ladled hot soup onto your lap?" Cormac's expression betrayed him. Margaret teased more, "Cormac, why did you not tell me!"

"She stopped whackin' me with her cookin' spoon. She even smiled at me once or twice. I take that as a hopeful sign. If I am at ye new home, she may come round." Cormac added, "She will return to ye, will she not?"

"I hope so." Margaret smiled at seeing relief spread over his face. "But if you stay, or how long is Caitlin's choice. I will not have her upset. If she makes a fit at seeing you, I will tell you to leave."

"Agreed." Cormac rubbed his hands together in pleasure. "Now I am in ye employ, what may I do for ye?"

"Tell me what you have heard." Margaret waved toward the outer door. "Has anyone asked for me?"

Cormac saw her men look away. "Not that I know, me lady. Talk is His Royal Highness is still peaked at ye. Talk is any interested family will wait until ye leave and he is calmer."

"Peaked? Calmer? You are a diplomat, Cormac." *Do something. Prepare to leave. Not seeing me may calm him.* Margaret turned to her first step toward reaching her new home. "I need wagons and oxen to haul goods, gear and small livestock. Will you accompany me to market? I want to purchase two and rent the rest today to order them ready for departure Tuesday dawn."

"Gladly, me lady. May I suggest ye bargain with all the stablemen first? Tell 'em ye will hire the one who costs ye the least. Make 'em work for ye business."

"Good thinking, Cormac. Please wait while I prepare."

After Margaret closed the door to her room, she relieved herself and brushed down her wild locks. She removed the key from her sleeve pocket and knelt. The oak was barely visible for all the metal strapping nailed to it. She ran her hands over the metal bands on the top and body of the chest. Every corner and edge was strapped. Both the metal and the oak varied in color as they seemed to be aging at different rates, though both looked relatively new. Margaret pushed the chest with both hands and could not move it. The locking mechanism was a hole in the center strap, and the key turned hard in the lock. Margaret's eyes widened at the pile of silver coins. She ran her fingers through her wealth.

So many. Thousands and thousands. More than I will ever need. Margaret smiled as she dipped both hands into the chest and brought them together beneath the coins. She lifted her hands, and created a waterfall of tinkling silver that piled up in the center of her treasure. After smoothing the coins and patting them, she ordered, "Now get me a husband." *Lord William? I like him.* Margaret sighed. *Two boons granted, coins and land. King Henry hates the third. Will he ever grant it me? I told him I want no precedent. His power can grant me the right to sign mine own marriage contract. Do I still want that? Wait, as Cormac suggested, until he is calmer and sees the right of honoring mine boon.*

Margaret hid a few coins in each sleeve pocket before she dragged her old leather purse until her treasure filled it. Margaret pulled the strings tight. She closed the lid and locked the box. *If I hang it from mine girdle? No, too easy to snatch. Where?* She looked around. *I must wear the key too.* To make a necklace, she untied the leather thong from around the sword's scabbard. She tied the key in one place and the pouch in another before knotting the leather strip at her nape. She dropped the items between her bliaut and chemise so her girdle would catch it should her makeshift necklace fail. She picked up her mantle and hugged it as images of the queen flashed in her mind. She sighed. *Shoulders back. Head up. Let them think not I am defeated. Go about mine business as if all is well. Ah, Mother, I do remember. Quiet, calm, dignified, pure keeps a lady steadfast and cert.* Margaret gritted her teeth and squinted away her coming tears. She tied her scarf under her chin, swirled her mantle round her shoulders and fastened it with her brooch. *Straight back. Smile.* Margaret opt the door. "I am ready," she announced. Margaret spotted a fifth man talking to the others. "Elstan?"

"My lady," he replied in Saxon. "May I serve you? I have no other place to go," he added in a rush.

Margaret remember the dictum Sir Charles's reeve had taught her. *I wager he can learn about mine estate by asking other Saxons. I need him.* She motioned him forward and whispered, "Someone told me 'Saxon tongues are swifter than Norman hooves.' I go to market Monday. Can you know by then what I need to add to mine estate?"

Elstan whispered back in Saxon, "I promise I shall."

Margaret spoke Norman aloud so the other four heard her, "Then you may serve, Elstan. Cormac and I go to bargain for oxen, wagons and donkeys. Join us."

Sir Cachier led Margaret; the Scot and the Saxon followed her. Everyone outside the hall doors turned away from the group as they crossed the bailey and strode through the barbican.

2

Sunday

16 February

As Margaret walked, she flapped her mantle as if she had wings. Cold deterred her not. *I hope this removes the foul odors. That midden is truly disgusting, but they may remove it not on a Sunday. Pray they do so in the morn.* Margaret strode past the cathedral and took the path toward High Street. Spotting a small church across the way, she approached and opt the outer door only so far as to slip through it. *In this weather, no one of the Court will come here if they can hear Mass inside castle.* Sir Cachier followed. Mass had just begun. While the Church in Rome preached all ranks were brothers and equals in God's eyes, no one followed that expectation. Even within church walls, those of rank stood in front. Margaret chose the back because, when the royals ordered her away, she knew she had become a social outcast. With no kneeling cushion at hand, she folded her outer garment and used it against the cold dirt floor. Margaret smiled at those who moved away and at the space they left around her. After the service and announcements about the week ahead, Margaret stood and waited to leave last. Because she kept her eyes downward, she missed spotting the one man who had looked upon her favorably.

Ten feet beyond the entry he had lingered. "Lady Margaret, how nice to see you again."

Margaret, who had wrapped her mantle close to her body and had covered her mouth and chin with the top edge, stopped. She turned toward the deep voice. She lowered the mantle from her face and curtsied before she responded. "I am glad you speak to me, Lord Cai. Think you it wise?"

"Dear girl, I am too old to give much concern to what happens at Court. Should the king take me to task for spending time with you, I will mutter a few of His Highness's misdeeds as a youth. He would soon close his mouth," Lord Cai added with a wink.

Margaret smiled at the old knight. *I wonder what he knows.*

"My lady, please do me a great honor to join me in breaking your fast. I should be glad for your company. Mine house is but two streets away and within the walls."

Behind her, Sir Cachier cleared his throat.

"I have been remiss, my lord. May I present Sir Cachier, one of the knights His Royal Highness assigned to protect me."

Dropping his left hand to his sword pommel, Lord Cai acknowledged the man. "Sir Cachier."

By also touching his left hand to his sword pommel, Cashier showed he would not follow Lord Cai's words with a challenge. "My Lord Cai."

"If Sir Cachier may join us, I accept your kind invitation."

"Of course, of course." Lord Cai offered his arm, and Margaret set her right hand upon his forearm. "I supposed him to come along. Not that you need a chaperone with one as old as I am." The old man chuckled before he turned serious. "However, my dear, you are a valued person. We do not want you took and ransomed." Cold and wind buffeted the trio as they walked. At the door of a two-storied house, Lord Cai waved Cachier forward. "Please inspect the house and garden so you will know she is safe. Mine men are free this day and not required to return until sunset. All you should meet is mine housekeeper and her daughter. Try not to frighten them."

At Cachier's return from his inspection, Lord Cai gestured Margaret to follow her guardian and asked her permission to lock the door. Margaret nodded. *Am I safe? Why speak of ransom?* She forced herself not to touch her dagger handle.

"This is the great room. The housekeeper and her child sleep in the room behind it. Three sleeping rooms upstairs, small, but sufficient unto mine needs. Dear, let us walk the garden while the table is reset for three."

The housekeeper curtsied to acknowledge his instruction and waved her twelve-year-old daughter toward cupboard shelves holding dishes, ale mugs, and wine goblets.

Margaret stepped aside to let Lord Cai pass before she exited the house. In the garden, she saw a small table and a chair in sunlight. Near the back wall she noted a rope hung between two posts.

"My lord, while we eat, may I air mine mantle and scarf there?"

"A good idea to let the brisk air clean your clothes."

"I smell that bad?"

Lord Cai only smiled.

13

When the housekeeper called them, Lord Cai escorted Margaret inside and sat her to his right, the place of honor. He then waved Cachier to his left. He led a Te Deum before the meal and filled their goblets with white wine. Lord Cai stood not on rank and conversed easily. During the soup course, he asked of Margaret's plans and offered several suggestions how to choose knights errant. When Margaret asked who de Warenne was, Cai explained he was a rich lord, holder of an estate in England and one in Normandy. He had sided with Robert in the invasion of July last and had provided the king's brother with men, arms, and coin. After King Henry had bought off his brother, Henry sieged de Warenne, seized his lands, and banished him.

"Such is the price of choosing the wrong side," warned Cai. He added, "King Henry could have beheaded him. The king was most generous to have just banished him and his family."

"My Lord, know you another story about mine grandparents like the one you told me the first time we met?"

"Alas, dear lady, no. I saw neither of them afterward. I am sorry."

"I thought not, given what you had told me, but I had to ask."

They dined on roasted lamb topped with a sauce of simmered white wine and butter. Turnips and carrots surrounded the meat. Cai turned to Cachier. Margaret learned of Cachier's early life in Normandy, his training, and how he came to serve the king. Lord Cai kept their goblets full as the three dined slowly and chatted. Cai spoke of his life. Margaret was saddened to learn Lord Cai's wife had died, offered her condolences, and promised to pray for the repose of the lady's soul. Lord Cai slowly nodded his thanks. Then Margaret asked him how he came to England. Sir Cai told a long tale of coming as a squire to King William the First and of serving him for five years before King William made him a knight and awarded Cai an earldom. He talked of finding and courting his wife.

"My lady was so brave. She left the comforts of civilized living in Normandy for the wild forests of England. She took mine hand and never looked back. Made a warm, loving home and bore me two sons and two daughters."

"You are a fortunate man to have so much," said Cachier.

Sir Cai set down his goblet and placed his hands upon the table. "Not so fortunate, son. Mine second boy died when he was eight. Mine first-born died in the crusade. My daughters married well. I do have five grandchildren."

Cai looked away so Margaret placed her hand over his.

"And they love you very much," she offered.

Cai smiled wanly. "Thank you."

Margaret changed the subject. "You keep a house in town?"

"During King William Rufus's rule, we lords had to appear three times a year to renew our vows of allegiance. Two fellow lords and I each bought a house to share, they in Gloucester and London and I in Winchester. I use this house when I have business in town. Safer and more comfortable than an inn. I have a residence when I need it and rent income when I let it. The keeper is a widow, who gets a home. A good arrangement for both of us."

"Indeed."

Lord Cai patted Margaret's hand. "If it please you, be mine guest when I am not here, dear lady. Just send a message to 'Lord Cai's house; Winchester is small enough everyone knows it. I will instruct mine housekeeper to save it for you. If I am in town or it is already let, she will find a suitable place nearby for you. Safe and clean, of course."

"Lord Cai, you are a generous man. I am most grateful."

The conversation became desultory comments about the weather. Margaret asked to be excused. Their farewells were warm and long.

"Will you sup with me as well?" Cai requested. "I suggest two men as escort; returning to the castle after dark may be dangerous."

"I thank you for your kind offer, my lord, but I needs be back in time to sup in my room. Principle, you know."

"I understand."

You are a good man, Lord Cai. Would he who sired me be like you. Not even thinking his name. Not after he murdered Mother. "I thank you, my lord, for warming mine heart and filling mine belly with better fare than I will get when I return, but return I must." She curtsied low and departed.

Margaret found Gailard guarding the outside door. "We broke our fasts with Lord Cai in his town home. Did mine meal arrive? I hope one of you ate it."

"We shared, my lady."

"Good. Sir Roussel?"

"Inside guarding your room."

"Thank you."

Margaret opt the door and the women inside went silent and froze. She saw Roussel leaning against the door of her room with his arms crossed over his chest and looking supremely bored. She ignored the women she passed. Roussel opt her door and followed her inside. Cachier took his place and closed the door for them.

"I worried."

Margaret explained. Then she asked, "Who are they?"

"Laundresses, bakers, kitchen help and such. No personal servants."

16

"Of what are they talking?"

"Nothing of consequence."

You, no doubt. I wager they tried to flirt with you. Poor man.

"What knights think you we might gain on the morrow?"

"At Michaelmas, others hired the skilled knights errant for the winter. We will find wanderers and the dregs, I fear."

"Please send word I am looking for men."

"I already have done. They will be outside the walls on the morrow if they are interested."

"Sir Roussel, we need to find the best we can. If you trust them not, neither do I. We need to know whom they last served, why they left, and how long they will stay with me. Please tell them I will pay them for the time they work; but, after I am married, my lord will decide who will stay or go. Either way, I will pay them, first at Easter, and then monthly as long as they meet your standards and mine."

"Your standards?"

Margaret explained them. "What will be the hardest part?"

"They will not obey a woman. Best the three of us give the orders."

Margaret nodded. "I will be at market most of the day. I leave you to select horses, weapons, armor and other gear knights errant and we need. After you have selected a group of men, I want us to make the final choices together."

"As you wish."

"If you have a purse, I will fill it so you may purchase what we need of horses and such and to outfit men who need gear."

"My lady, I will need a large purse to provide all you need for ten knights; they will cost you over one thousand shillings." At seeing Margaret's eyes widen as she frowned, Roussel licked his pointing finger and wrote the math on the table. "Twelve pence per shilling a thousand times is twelve thousand pence."

First, Margaret's jaw dropped. Then she sputtered, "Twelve thousand pence!" Margaret's emitted strangling noises.

Before Roussel could say more, Gailard knocked.

"Your supper has arrived, my lady."

Roussel unsheathed his blade and stood shoulder to the door wall. He nodded for Margaret to op the door. A servant carried in a cloth-covered tray and set it on the table. He turned and gasped.

"Leave," ordered Roussel.

The man fled and dashed toward the outside door. Clusters of serving women watched him fling op the door and slam it.

After the servant left, Roussel motioned Gailard; the three of them filled the room. "You forgot the password," Roussel hissed. "'My lady' first is safe. 'My lady' last means danger."

"Sorry."

"Forget again and someone might die." Roussel continued, "We eat by turns. This time you are last. Relieve Cachier; send him inside."

Roussel shook his head at the man's back. "A good fighter, but no memory." Roussel looked at Margaret. "I will remind him daily." The knight closed the door behind himself.

Margaret found her flint rocks among her things, struck them together several times over the wick and lit her candle. Margaret sat and downed her meal of boiled fish and turnips, bread without butter, and a mug of ale. She knocked twice on the wood to signal Roussel, who carried the tray to the outside door and set it on the floor. *Smart of him. The fewer people near mine chest the better.*

Roussel called out, "My lady, the Saxon Elstan wishes to speak with you."

"He may enter. Please leave the door opt." Margaret stood.

"My lady." Elstan pulled his forelock.

Margaret sat on the cot and motioned to the stool. When Elstan purposed to sit well away from her, she motioned him forward.

Does not flinch at the odors. Good boy. Good man? I wonder his age. They sat almost knees together and with their heads close. From the doorway no one could read their lips or hear their whispers.

"I have come with news of your estate, my lady. Because the king banished de Warenne before Michaelmas, the reeve organized the harvest and paid the Church and the crown's taxes. Over the winter they rebuilt the burned parts of the palisade and the entrance gate. They also rebuilt two burned roofs and repaired scorched homes. The barracks burned in the siege; your men will sleep in the hall until you rebuild the barracks. Your villeins have not the means to built again, but they are a hard-working lot."

"I am glad to hear it. That bodes well."

"Not all is success."

"Why not?"

"The knights who routed the traitor were awarded de Warenne's possessions. They took everything but the trestles, table boards and benches in the hall and the anvil. They took the blacksmith's tools as well as everything in the kitchen, every pot, knife, wooden boards, bread pans. They even yanked out the fireplace arms from the stones and took them.. The conquerors also took beds, bedding and linens. They emptied the smoke house and stole every bite of food from you and the villagers. They took three wagons and six oxen and all your seed for this year's harvest."

Margaret covered her face with her hands. *Dear God, what loss! The king gave me all this coin to favor me not but because he knew the estate had been laid waste.* Then she removed her hands and stiffened her back. "What else?

"They raided the village as well. Only the villeins smart enough to hide seed bags and their things have anything. Frost killed the few Lenten crops the Saxons planted right after Epiphany. They hunger; two old folk and a babe have died. The villeins are eating bark soup."

A euphemism for starving unto death.

When Margaret commented not, Elstan offered his advice. "My lady, I would buy two or three wagons, but no oxen. They are expensive and eat prodigious amounts. Rent them for the journey. Four donkeys—at most six—can do the work at half the expense. Two can haul an empty wagon into place; four or six can haul a full one. Transfer them as needed. If you need more wagons, I suggest you rent them and the oxen to haul them."

"Good advice. Thank you, Elstan." Margaret added, "How know you all this?"

"As soon as I learned which land the king gave you, I made inquiries." Elstan hid his Saxon sources with, "Gossip has been to your advantage."

"I will rent the wagons and oxen. I desire to purchase two wagons and six donkeys. Thank you for your good advice, Elstan. On the morrow will you accompany me to market?"

"I am honored to serve you for as long as you wish."

"Your Norman is good. I may have need of you to translate between the peoples. I need you to help me think a market list."

They worked past bedtime. Margaret watched Elstan tiptoe down the aisle of sleeping women. She bade Gailard good night and closed the door. While wishing for Caitlin's cert hands and good advice, Margaret undressed and brushed her hair for a long time to calm herself. She knelt beside her cot.

I need a double bed. What if I am wed to a large man? Thick ropes between a sturdy frame. Six or eight legs for a heavier person. Oh God, please give me the strength to endure waiting for the royals to forgive me. Please send me a good man, one who will care for me and give me healthy children. Forgive me mine transgressions. Jesus the Christ, remind me the right ways to behave toward others. Mother Mary, help me be a better girl so someone will want me. I beg You to send me a good husband. Your will, Oh God, in all things.

Margaret added Sir Cai's late wife to her litany. She kept the king and queen in her prayers even though she knew she was no longer in theirs.

3

Market Day

Monday, 17 February

"Not as fine as the royals' chairs, but definitely suitable for a lord and his lady. These will age and color nicely," she said to no one in particular. "Are you cert a lord would like this pair of oak armed chairs, Sir Gailard?"

"I am. They are fine chairs. But it is stools you will use daily."

"I thank you for pointing out what we will need on a dais." Margaret bit her lower lip and muttered to herself, "Three for knights, the priest, a lord, me, Caitlin. Cormac? Why not." She said aloud, "We need eight" as she turned toward a stack and purchased ten.

Margaret stood outside the carpenter's shop and lifted her face to the sun. Grateful for its warmth and no wind, she removed her scarf and tied it about her neck. *Hides mine necklace. Harder to cut it loose and run. Not that anyone dare approach from Sir Gailard's side.*

The pair returned to the castle to refill Margaret's coin bag. Back walking High Street, Margaret grinned at how the knight held his sword pommel with his left hand so the scabbard tip tilted outward a good two feet from his ankle. When they walked shoulder to shoulder, they cleared the middle of the street. Every man, woman and child stepped aside or stood with their backs against a building as they passed.

So this is what it is like to walk with a lord beside me. I sense his power. They feel it too and avoid us. I like this! Margaret observed the flow of buyers and heard the hawkers' cries. *How exciting! Having enough coin to purchase whatever I want. Enjoy this day, for I may never return to Winchester. What man wants his wife leaving home? Do they think us a pair? No matter if they do. I pray no Court news has yet reached the streets.*

When the pair came upon the market cross in the center of town, Margaret hired three men, one to follow them and take their purchases to the stable and two to guard the wagons. "Elstan keeps an accounting of every item. Men, know you are responsible for mine goods. If you damage or steal any item, you shall purchase a new one for me. If you cannot, you owe me treble its value." Margaret added with force, "Fail me and I shall enslave you until you pay your debt. Elstan, please go with the guards. Remind the hostler our wagons are to stay inside. We know these men not. I leave you to stay this night alone inside the locked barn. Stay awake. Call out an alarm if need be."

"May I have a few coins for food, my lady?"

Margaret reached inside her right sleeve for five pence and placed them in Elstan's hand with, "No wine. Little ale." Elstan accepted the coins with a smile and a nod before he gestured to the two men. The three Saxons left for the hostler barn near the city's northwest gate. "Now that I have the wagons and animals, I must also choose kitchen wares, bolts of fabric, bedding, and so much more." Margaret smiled in anticipation. "Let us walk High Street both ways to note what is available."

By late morning Margaret had acquired new fireplace arms, pots, pans and other metalware from black smiths. After returning to the castle for more coins, Margaret chose linens, blankets, and ticking for her new beds. She bought bolts of sail cloth after claiming the thicker fabric to be better at keeping out drafts at half the cost of the expensive bed drapery she had been offered. To that, she added summer fabrics for herself, Caitlin, and Dena. *Such Luxury! Enough coin for all I want, not just for what I need.* Next she purchased many bolts of common wool cloth to award fabric to her villeins as required by law. Each year they sewed new clothes and wore them first on Easter Sunday. Margaret purchased already-made simples and a wooden box for them because she feared they too had been taken from de Warenne's estate. Sir Gailard sent the goods to the wagons. Obtaining seed and planting implements was next. Margaret refilled her purse, and returned to High Street. Because Margaret had been her father's chatelaine, she was in her element at the farm end of the town's market. After purchasing implements, she easily counted what kind and how many sacks of grain she needed to feed her people. Margaret deliberately overestimated the amounts. *Better to purchase more seed than not to have enough.* After sending the implements, grain and seed sacks to her wagons, Margaret let Sir Gailard lead her to the smells of cooked food wafting not on High Street but from a side lane. They saw no stalls, just boards on trestles side by side as each vendor called out what he or she had for sale and at what cost.

"Step aside," Sir Gailard ordered the four people ahead of him. They left. Margaret and he stepped forward. The knight looked behind them. Those individuals had also disappeared into the crowd in the square.

"Thank you," whispered Margaret.

Afraid to speak, the seller pointed right to chunks of cooked meats on sticks that lay atop a metal pail with coals on the bottom. Then he pointed to a small barrel of ale to his left.

Margaret asked, "What meats are these, sirrah?" She hoped her used of an honorific loosened his tongue.

"Chicken. Goat. Mutton."

Margaret looked to Sir Gailard to order first.

"Mine parents raised me on goat meat. Not bad if you are hungry. Two mutton."

"One chicken for me."

"And two mugs of ale," added Sir Gailard.

Margaret slipped five pence into Sir Gailard's hand. The knight placed the coins on the wooden slab. Normans did not touch Saxons. The seller let the pair choose the sticks they wanted as he wiped the insides of two pottery mugs, which he filled and set before them. Only then did he pick up four of the pennies. Sir Gailard pocketed the fifth. He and Margaret turned and stepped across the street to lean against a building as they ate.

Wants no one at his back while his hands are full. Good knights think of such things.

"My lady, could you not purchase the rest on the way home and save coins? Reading has an excellent market with less costly prices. It is but a long day's ride east from the intersection where we ride west to your estate. We would be only two or three days more to arrive home."

26

Margaret munched on a bite of chicken before she responded. "Sir Gailard, the longer we are on the road with that chest, the more likely blackguards and thieves will attack us. I would rather use more coin here and go straight home."

"Yes, my lady."

Margaret frowned. *If I am wrong, I will have spent too much and still be attacked on the way. I just made a man-like decision; if I am wrong there is no help for it now.* She finished her ale and dropped her stick into the mug; Sir Gailard did the same. He took her mug in his free hand and gestured with his head they should move together. He deposited the mugs on the corner of the seller's table.

"I smell bread! Want to share a round?" At Sir Gailard's nod, Margaret again followed her nose. She pointed to a round; the knight paid with a penny and received a hapenny, which he dropped into Margaret's hand. She broke off a chunk of bread and handed the rest to Sir Gailard. They munched in companionable silence. Margaret gestured west.

"Tinsmith next. Livestock last. What have I overlooked? Boots for myself!" Margaret wriggled her toes. "I can no longer wear these flimsy slippers. I feel the dirt and cold under me as if I were bare-footed." After more bargaining and buying, Margaret sent the silent worker, who had followed them all day, to deliver both goods and animals to Elstan.

Late in the afternoon, Sir Gailard asked, "Have we all you need, my lady? No rings, necklaces or furs to buy?" he teased.

"Of course not!" Margaret was indignant. "A lady does not pur-chase her own finery. Besides, we may need to send to Reading for more livestock or other necessity."

Gailard roared his laughter. "Finally! I hear something of sense. 'I had better purchase this. We may not see the like elsewhere. Oh, we might need that' is what I have heard all day. I am amazed you still carry coins in your purse," he chided.

"I know very well what I spent, Sirrah. To the hapenny. I can still gain what else I might need with ease." Wistfully, Margaret looked down the street they had just walked. "Never have I experienced this much freedom," Margaret murmured. "I likely never will again." She added aloud, "Please spoil not our day, Sir Gailard."

"I apologize , Lady Margaret." Gailard offered his arm. "Are you ready to return?"

Margaret took a last looked down High Street and its East Gate in the distance; she placed her hand upon Gailard's forearm. "Let us hope Sir Roussel had good fortune in finding men." Margaret's comment was her escort's hint she had forgiven him. The man they had sent to the wagons with goods had returned. Margaret paid him what she owed. "I forgot to feed you this day. Please take these two pence for what I would have paid for a meal."

The man pulled his forelock, took the extra coins and pocketed his wage. Fearful of robbery, the Saxon looked left and right to spot anyone paying attention to him. At the next intersection, he spun left and dashed down an empty lane.

Lady Margaret and Sir Gailard walked toward the wide lane that wound past the cathedral and to the smaller of Winchester's two castles. Outside the castle walls and left of the barbican, Sir Roussel stood talking with fourteen men who varied in age and appearance. The men were of average height to tall; all were lean yet well-muscled. Their thick arms and broad shoulders proved they had wielded swords for years. Only one man's clothes looked new and well kept. The eldest showed gray in his beard and hair, and the youngest looked barely old enough to be squire much less an experienced knight. Mayhap, his lack of beard and unlined face belies his age. *Roussel would not have let him stay if he will not fit.* Margaret crinkled her nose at the odors of animals, manure, sweat. None of the candidates wore metal rings-covered jerkins or swords. The men went silent and still as they appraised the woman approaching them. Margaret scrutinized the men as hard as they did her. *Old clothes. Need mending first or they will fall apart with washing. Some with no cloaks. The axe holder dresses well. Fur jerkin and cap. New boots.*

"These passed mine combat tests."

Looking away from her prospects, Roussel quietly reported the strengths and weaknesses of each man as he pointed at him. He concluded, "The one holding the axe is a Dane. Allowed to wear a beard. Speaks Norman and Saxon."

"He looks frightening."

"An axe scares most knights. Cuts right through metal rings on a leather jerkin. At least breaks bones through chain mail and can kill if the fighter is strong enough, which he is."

Trying to impress Margaret, each man stood tall and puffed his chest. Bed and board was a valued prize when most knights errant wandered and starved while seeking work.

"How much should I pay them?"

"Two pence a day if they stay till Easter. Three shillings a month after that. Normal pay is five, but these are desperate for work and will take what you give. Three is still fair."

"The Saxon Elstan served the queen at Forest Keep. He wants to come with me for a reason. A Scot will be mine seneschal, also from the queen."

"They will tolerate a Scot but not a Saxon. Put him in the hall with Normans and there will be trouble—and blood." Sir Roussel read Margaret's resolve in her eyes.

"Then we need one other not of our people to make a pair of odd ones. The Dane if he will stay."

"Agreed."

Margaret stepped forward. "Thank you for waiting for me. Sir Roussel approves of you. That I approve I have not yet decided. If you will not work for a woman until her lord arrives, leave now. Anyone who will not work agreeably with men of another peoples had best leave as well. A Saxon interpreter and a Scot seneschal are already in mine service."

One man picked up his bedding roll and threw it over his left shoulder. He grumbled. "Not me. Won't sleep with a stinking Saxon."

A second man added, "Any man who works for a Saxon-loving woman deserves what he gets—a knife in the back."

The pair left together.

"I list other requirements for service. On these I am unmovable. I hire you to protect mine villeins, not make victims of them. You will not abuse them; you will not steal from them. Because you hold no land, you cannot court, so you will leave their women alone. You will not get drunk. You will not fight each other off the practice field. Break mine rules or any Norman law, and I will treat you as I do any other transgressor. If you will not abide by mine rules, leave now."

Two men shuffled their feet then stood still, but no one left.

A cold winter makes them only compliant, not agreeable of me or mine conditions. Margaret turned to Roussel. "Have you told them I will clothe them? Do they know any armor, weapons or horse I give them is for use only? They own them not. Did you tell them I will pay them an extra month's wage if mine future husband dismisses them?"

"They have no stomach for serving an un-lorded woman. The only way I got them to stay is to promise them you soon will be married. I told them your lord would give them extra pay if he dismissed them."

Margaret announced the wages she and Sir Roussel had discussed. When no man left the line, Margaret rambled to Sir Roussel as she thought aloud. "Thirteen or more is ill fortune. If one or more leave before I am married, we will be reduced to that ill number and evil will befall us. Will nine do? With you three that is twelve. Will not mine future lord hire men of his own choosing? If we hire more than…" Sir Roussel, "Which do you want not?"

Margaret took pennies from her sleeve. She spoke kindly to the men before her.

"Sir knights, I regret I cannot retain all of you. Thank you for your time. Please take these coins for the day you spent on mine behalf. I wish it could be more, but I must account for every expense to mine future lord."

Thrice, Roussel pointed to a man and shook his head.

With that, Margaret stepped forward and gave a rejected man two pence. The first man said nothing.

The second said, "Thank you. No one has paid me before sending me away."

The third added, "This softens the blow, my lady."

"If in the future my lord wants more men, I hope you will seek him."

Margaret walked the line with Roussel to learn each man's name. At the end stood the Dane with his axe head on the ground between his feet and his hands resting on the handle tip. Margaret looked into warm, smiling, bright-blue eyes. She spoke Norman to him. "Syghelm, welcome to mine service. Tarry you in England long?"

"Yes, my lady. I was working toward way home from Iberia. I decided I like England, so I have worked here almost two years now."

"Have you family to which to return?"

"Sadly, no. Mine parents are dead. I soon will be thirty-nine, my lady."

"And a skilled fighter, I wager."

Syghelm's smile broadened as he nodded once very slowly.

Margaret moved away.

Roussel reported, "I have bought gear, armor, and horses for ten. The Dane says he won't ride. Shall we keep or return the spare? *Night is more than twenty; I may need a new gelding.* "Keep a gelding should I want him. Need I do any more here?"

"No, my lady. I made a first payment for the horses and gear from the coin you gave me. I will accompany you to your room and get the rest we owe. Then I will attend to the preparations I need make before dawn."

On her return, Margaret looked upward at the hall building. She admired the tooth and gum defense at its top and remembered looking between the merlins with drunken eyes. *Seems so long ago. Mayhap if I get safely to mine land and prepare well, a husband will arrive. Please God, let me not make any more mistakes before I leave. Blessed Mary, soften her heart, I beg you.* Margaret was glad the women's room was empty.

A little later Father Gregory came to her door and identified himself. Margaret smiled as she opt the door. "Father, has anyone sent you to me?"

"No, I am sorry. She has not."

Margaret's eyes dropped to the floor.

"She has chosen a new confessor. Your new home is more than halfway to mine bishop's residence. May I travel with you as far as your estate? I can reach Oxford from there. I hope taking me with you will not be a bother."

Margaret looked at the priest. "Would you stay and 'bother' me for a long time. If I have no priest, may I ask your bishop to let you stay?"

"I like that idea."

"We leave at dawn. Please tell Sir Roussel your travel needs. Ride in a wagon and tie your donkey to it if you desire." Margaret thought for a moment and added, "Please, will you say Mass for us on the road so we may depart as soon as the city gate opens? I want to be away…" Margaret's voice caught with emotion so Father Gregory took her hands in his.

"Of course," Father had interrupted her so she did not cry. "Pray with me for a safe journey."

Margaret stiffened her spine and went to her knees beside the priest. Father intoned the words gently. *His voice soothes my nerves.* After he left, Margaret sat on her cot and covered her eyes with her palms. *Cry not. I have coin and lands, and I will get a good husband. Give them not the satisfaction of learning they have brought me to tears.* Margaret repeated these words to herself until she stopped tearing.

In Forest Keep she acted like mine friend. Did she act so only because she needed me? May a queen have a friend? Oh Mother, would that you were here so we could talk. I wonder how Night is faring? I dare not ask one of the knights to leave. I forgot to ask Sir Roussel to see to you, mine friend. I hope you forgive my forgetfulness. At least I will ride you on the morrow.

Just as the night before, a servant brought her meal on a tray but spoke not. Just as the night before, Margaret ate alone. Just as the night before, the king's knights stood rounds guarding her and the chest. Margaret's last prayer was for a safe journey. Her final thought before she fell asleep was gratitude for three brave men's protection. *I am not alone. I only feel so. I am not alone. I have you, Oh Lord.*

4

The Road

18 February

In the morning's grayness, clouds seemed but dark patches in the sky. At first, the road was empty, but it soon filled as the sun rose to burn off the light fog. Behind three wagons of logs that teams of oxen strained to pull, a column of men carried bundles of sticks and limbs. The wood was bound for the market and into the homes of the poor and the wealthy alike. Keeping warm was key to keeping healthy this cold, wet month. Behind them walked the peddlers with sacks on their donkeys. They too headed to Winchester's High Street. Margaret's party commanded the road, so all walkers stepped into the ditch as they passed, and wagons stopped. Soon the sun warmed the travelers even as a cool breeze reminded them spring was still a month away. Clouds drifted eastward as the sky turned a faded blue.

After Father Gregory said Mass from a moving wagon, the party broke their fasts on their horses with bread passed down the line. They drank ale from their personal flagons. At the end of the meal, Margaret turned back to the wagons. Elstan, driver of the fifth wagon, knew what she wanted. By the time she arrived, he had already grabbed her sword and the scabbard lying at his feet and was holding it toward her.

"I thank you," said Margaret as she reached for it. She dropped reins on Night's neck as he did not need them; he walked beside the wagon. While she donned her weapon, she asked in Saxon, "What have you noted?"

"Putting the drovers first was smart. These donkeys follow. Easier driving them. The Dane sits on the chest with his axe visible."

Elstan smiled and leaned toward her. "Please lean in and smile as if we are chatting."

Margaret did so. "I have discovered no treachery."

Margaret laughed as if at a joke. "Speak no Norman before them. If they speak it to you, understand them not. They will be freer the farther we go."

"Well said, my lady." Elstan grinned as if she had spoken a joke.

Margaret smiled back before she nudged Night to ride in front with Sir Roussel.

Pedestrians stood off the road as the party passed. Even wagons pulled aside and waited. Margaret noted the stares of the curious even though she had not perceptibly moved from looking straight ahead as should a proper lady of wealth and position. Two miles from the city they passed the Half Moon, an inn.

Just after midday the company rode to a knoll. They found Sir Verel on a rock beside the road and before a small fire. Large sack in hand, Cormac jumped from the first wagon.

"A regular stopping place, this," Sir Verel reported. "I have replaced the firewood I used." He swept his arm as he talked. "From here we can see a quarter mile of road in both directions and identify anyone sneaking through the bare trees or thrashing through the bushes."

"Good enough," said Roussel.

Cormac set out bread and two large jugs of ale. He removed cooked capons from the bag, put them on sticks and held them over the fire to warm; he then laid each on a wooden serving board. After cutting them apart, he tossed the bones down the backside of the hill, and offered the flesh to Margaret. She accepted choosing first and took a piece of meat with skin. Margaret gestured Cormac to serve her men next. Later she sipped only a little ale. Margaret walked about with her hands pressed against the small of her back.

"My lady, would you rather ride upon a wagon seat? More room to slide on the bench."

"I think not, Sir Cachier. On Night I can see farther and move faster if need be. I will take a private walk. Will you escort me?"

Cashier preceded her into the trees. When she passed him, he turned his back to her. On their return, he asked her to walk ahead of him. At the fire she said, "I thank you Sir Cachier. Cormac, you provided for us well. I appreciate the good meal." All heard her, and a few of her new men nodded in agreement.

A drover approached the party. "We will not move for a while. We watered and fed the oxen; now they will rest. It's nine or ten miles between inns. We have gone four. In three more miles we stop to water and rest the animals again. When we reach the inn, we feed and water them for the night. My lady, I expect us to take three or more days to reach your land. The oxen are hauling heavy wagons and can go no faster."

"How know you when is three miles?" ask Margaret.

The man pointed to a rock beside the road.

"Mile markers, my lady. Every wagon driver and traveler knows them."

Margaret colored at having announced her ignorance and lack of traveling. She nodded and looked away. Gailard and Verel rode ahead to arrange accommodations and to warn them of any dangers. With Roussel, Cachier, and Sauville in front with Margaret, the rest took up the rear.

Attacked from the rear? More likely from the sides. Easy to hide in the ditches.

Margaret looked ahead both left and right. *Will Night warn with nervous behavior or snorts?* Paths and roads wandered through tree trunks still holding barren branches. Their buds were unwilling to expose themselves to the cold. Without the hint of spring, birds sang not. They fluffed themselves and sat in tree notches or pecked the ground in the hope of finding food. A brown dog raced down a path to bark at and harry the animals, but a knight met him, shouted, and drove him off. In a clearing, Margaret spotted workers. In the distance, the top of a stone keep intrigued her, but she asked no one whose it might be because she assumed no one could know. She was wrong. The king's men were cert the road was safe because the local baron hung every thief or cutthroat he caught. The train rounded a bend and found Verel facing left, sword pointing to the forest.

"My lady, switch sides," ordered Cachier as he rode ahead.

Margaret took the right side of the road, switched the reins to her left hand, and placed her right hand on her sword hilt. She watched Cachier stop and converse. Then he too pointed his horse toward the forest. Margaret spotted disheveled women in rags cowering behind barren trees; their hair was matted, their hands and rags were filthy. *Likely, they have fleas. Their shoulder bones show through their skin, and they look starved.* An unseen babe cried. *Why are they dangerous?* Margaret passed as did the wagons. Behind her, knights leered at the women, but spoke not when they realized Margaret was looking back at them. Cashier rejoined her at the head of the column.

"Who are they?"

"Ditch women, my lady." Before Margaret could ask more, he added, "Of no concern to us."

About a mile later, the party again stopped to rest the oxen. Donkeys brayed to each other and stomped their hooves in anticipation of getting water pails placed before them. Winter or not, the animals needed water and time to cool before again pulling the heavily laden wagons.

Shortly before sunset Margaret spotted a palisade and a roof. The painted sign by the gate displayed a lion and a swan. The innkeeper stood under it. Margaret rode through the gate toward Elstan, who was smiling at her approach. At the inn door, Elstan assisted his lady's dismount and took Night to a barn. Margaret noticed the innkeeper's wife had tied a clean apron over her work one. A spot had leaked through. Margaret watched Gailard and Cachier carrying the chest toward her.

"Mine room?"

"My lady, it is a fine room with a lock and clean linens as you required. If you will follow me."

Margaret walked into a modest great room and up the stairs to the right. Past the door to a women's sleeping room, she entered a small room under the eaves barely lit by a tiny window. She bent to get through the low doorway. The knights deposited the chest against the outside wall and left. Margaret smiled at seeing the door's long bolt of thick metal could be set far into the wall.

"I want a basin of hot water, clean cloths for washing, and a lit candle."

"At once, my lady. I will bring it to you myself."

"What is supper?"

"On Shrove Tuesday we serve a hearty meat stew, bread and honey, and all the ale you can drink. With no meat allowed except on Sundays until Easter, we like a feast."

"I look forward to it." Margaret nodded the woman's dismissal.

Soon a girl knocked on the door. "Water and rags, my lady, and food and drink."

Sword and dagger in one hand, Margaret unbolted the door, stepped back and took her sword in her right hand.

"Enter."

The girl opt the door and froze. Tray in hand, the woman stayed outside.

"Just me and mine girl."

"Cachier?"

From around the corner Margret heard, "Only them near."

Margaret lowered her blade and, with it, motioned them forward. The two moved with alacrity, bowl and cloths on the floor and food tray on the table. The girl scuttled out; the innkeeper's wife curtsied.

"Stay, I have questions. Why is your inn so named?"

"They say mine husband's deep voice is a lion's roar when he is angry. When he was courting me, he liked mine long neck so he added the swan to the sign."

"What are ditch women?"

The woman clutched her apron and looked at the floor.

"Explain."

"Women who have fallen so low no one will care for them, feed them, protect them. Anyone can ravage or even kill them without penalty. They beg when they can, steal when they must. You saw them?"

"Far from here. How did they fall?"

"Being a slattern with a man is common. Accused of debauchery. Other things. If fathers or husbands kill them not, they declare them ditch women, strip them naked and toss them out of the family. They are lost to all decent company." The woman looked up. "My lady, please tell me how many."

"I saw four and heard a babe crying." The woman's face radiated pain as she pulled her lips inside her mouth to prevent herself from speaking. "I should have stopped and thrown them coins. They were half naked and freezing."

"Oh no, my lady. They would follow you to your lands, beg on your border and steal from your villeins. You then needs kill them to be rid of them. They are a desperate lot."

"Who buries them? Where?"

"No Christian burial for them. They bury each other in the forest. If they die alone, they become food for animals. Please, my lady, think not of them, speak not of them." The woman curtsied, her face pale, hands twisting. "May I go now?"

Margaret followed her and poked out her head to ask, "Sir Cachier, will who will guard the door all night?"

"We three by turns."

"God give you good rest, Sir Cachier."

41

Margaret closed and bolted the door. After her meal, Margaret knelt bedside. Her prayers ended with her gratitudes: for her father not declaring her a ditch woman as he had threatened, for having escaped her father, for having saved the princess, for her wealth and a possible better future, for having escaped Court and the king's wroth at her last boon request, and, finally, for a day of safe travel.

5

Ash Wednesday 1102 A.D.

19 February

Father Gregory had heard confessions since before dawn. He then set his traveling altar on a table in a corner of the great room. Everyone in the inn and in the area crowded into the room, up the stairs and on the walkway above for Ash Wednesday Mass. After the locals departed, breakfast was a pottage of grains only or bread without butter or honey; they were given not wine, only ale. The Church allowed ale because the fermenting process cleansed water, a drink that often caused illness or death. The fasting season had begun.

The wagons again rumbled over the stone road. Drivers and riders swayed as if aboard a small, heavy ship. Margaret looked left and right, trying to peer into the forest. "What may we expect ahead, Sir Roussel?"

"About nine miles ahead is Rooster's Nest, an inn like the one we just left."

The second day passed much as had the first, but without meat. At Roster's Nest, supper included boiled vegetables and fish, both of which had been overcooked and under-seasoned. The bread was passable, but the cheese tasted too salty. No one drank a second mug of ale. *I am grateful few women traveled in winter so I have the women's sleeping room for myself and mine chest. I am not grateful for that meal. Tasteless. I ate it only to fill mine belly.*

The next morning Margaret asked Gailard, "What may I expect on the road ahead? Where will we stop this night? Might we have better fare?"

"I am cert, my lady. At the crossroads, east is Reading and usually safe. West to Bristol is wild country, mostly forest. Our direction. The greatest danger lies that way. We sent Cachier ahead to hire us space at King's Inn, just eight miles from your land." At Margaret's frown, Gailard added, "Worry not, my lady. We have enough men. Should we be attacked, we will protect you. A short sword will be of no use against armed men."

It will kill anyone who gets through you and close enough. Margaret chose silence. *I have ne'er even struck a person. Dare I wound or try to kill? Have I the stomach to strike to save mine life? Think not on it. If the need arises, decide then. I pray to you, Oh God. Let me harm not one of Your own.*

The caravan of animals, wagons, knights and lady moved north as scheduled., including rest stops for the oxen and donkeys. The party rode for hours and again dined on bread, cheese and ale as they went. At the edge of a village called Newbury, they passed an inn too small for their use. Two miles further their road stopped at another going east and west. Southwest of the crossroads and on a rise stood a formidable palisade of ten-foot poles. The sign bore a large yellow crown.

"The King's Inn," announced Sir Roussel.

"A bold name," replied Margaret as they rode toward it.

At the corner of the palisade they turned and walked a low road with a dirt bank between it and the wall.

"It really is His Royal Highness's inn. The Conqueror had it built to protect the roads. The crown owns it, but an Iberian and his wife earned land south of here because they supervise the compound and keep the accounts book."

"Why is the gate on the backside instead of on the road?"

"Harder to attack or siege. Look above you. Were we attackers, archers could shoot us along this whole wall." Past the wall, they took the winding road to the main gate. Margaret saw a huge complex of buildings, barns, and outbuildings. "See how well protected it is."

"I am impressed." *I wish I needed not such protection. Wealth is indeed a burden. I pray mine palisade walls are tall and the gate is sturdy.*

"Wait until you see your room."

Margaret sat upon an armed chair with her feet on a cushioned footstool. Braziers kept the room warm and wood stacked in the corner would do so for days. Margaret had checked the triple bed at the other end of the room with its green draperies embroidered in blue and gold., two tickings, fine cream-colored linen bedding, blankets and a brown fur covering. *Bear skin mayhap?* At her end of the room stood an oak table with a writing desk upon it and a second, larger table for dining. Margaret was ensconced in the royal chamber at the top of the stone keep. The two floors below were for guards and servants. That the steps permitted only one person on the landings at a time was further proof of her protected status. *Truly fit for the royals. Sitting in warmth within such wealth about me! Is this how she feels living in luxury and comfort? Does the queen always feel so protected and cosseted? No, not even being this protected saved her first babe. Who got so close to her that he secretly poisoned her so she lost his heir? Who had the power to send a second poisoner after she hid her daughter and pretended a Saxon boy was the king's heir. Oh God, I pray you punish him for killing poor Dena's son. He killed two innocents You tried to send into the world.* She glanced at her money chest. *A quarter empty already. How could men, horses, arms and such cost so much! Even the household goods were dear. I must husband the rest with great care.*

A servant had served her a bowl of hot broth when she arrived. The ewer held warm water for washing. She ordered her meal to generously serve two and asked the innkeeper to invite Sir Roussel to join her. At a knock and the announcement of his name, Margaret stepped to the door. *Thick, triple hinges and bolts. No one is getting through that door by force. Even a long time to burn.* Margaret bent to throw back the bolts at her knees. Then threw back the ones waist and shoulder high. *The door ops easily and is well balanced.* "Thank you for joining me, Sir Roussel." She stepped back and curtsied.

"Thank you for inviting me." He bowed and entered.

Margaret noticed his clean hands and pared nails. *Washed, even his hair. Clean shirt. Boots polished.* She smiled at him. *I like he shows me respect. Am I too proud? Nay, it is merely the way things are meant to be.* Servants followed Sir Roussel into the room carrying platters of food, pitchers of ale and dinner ware. They bowed to her and left. Margaret watched Roussel bolt the door without objecting. As was proper, she gestured him to sit before she took her place. She filled a plate with a whole fried fish and boiled vegetables and poured a white wine sauce over it all. She poured a goblet of ale for her guest before she served herself.

"The fish tastes good with this sauce on it," commented Roussel.

"I appreciate fish today, but I will soon tire of it."

"By Easter I will not want to dine on fish for two months."

"Me as well."

They dined in silence. Margaret nibbled at her food while she waited for him to eat half his meal.

"Have you seen mine land?"

"I helped take it."

"Is it true the king's men took de Warenne's property for payment?"

"They sold the goods for chain mail, helmet, and blade."

"How came you to serve the king?"

"His Royal Highness hired me after his coronation." Roussel puffed his chest when he added, "King Henry named me the first man for his five-year plan."

"Five-year plan?"

"On First Day the last three years, His Majesty has announced name of a man for whom he will buy land in a lord's barony. If I serve him faithfully and well for five years, on the sixth First Day I get horse, sword, armor, lance, land and a lord. I will be a knight landed and can marry."

"Congratulations! He must think very highly of you to have named you the first."

Roussel beamed at Margaret before he poured another goblet of ale.

"Gailard was declared First Day last year, and Sir Cachier this year."

You told me this before. I ask to place you in a good humor for I need you on mine side when we arrive at mine new home.

"I am indeed in good company and safe."

"As safe as you can be, given the times."

Margaret took a few bites to give Roussel time to eat as well. After he reached for more boiled carrots, onions, and turnips, she continued. "Sir Roussel, will you describe mine lands to me?" She ate while he talked.

"Imagine a rough square tipped almost south on one point. It is near evenly quartered by two paths, northwest to southeast and northeast to southwest. Your bailey is at the intersection. The north half of your lands and the southeast butt against the king's forest. You are fortunate, my lady; the southwest butts against land once was owned by Bishop Odo, the king's uncle. After he died, the king reclaimed the land. Across the king's road from your property is a holding of Warwick's. He too rules with a hard fist. They protect you all around."

So the king has me surrounded! Why? What is he planning for me? No help for it now. I shall be wary.

"How far from the road is the bailey?"

"The Crown owns the land one hundred feet on both sides of the middle line of all main roads. The lane to your estate is partly on crown land. At the corners of your land are stone markers and mayhap even on some edges." Roussel thought and added, "A quarter mile?"

"So this compound is on royal land."

"It is."

"And the king's father ordered the stone roads built." As he talked, Margaret finished her meal.

"Oh no, my lady. Story is the Ancients built them; no one knows when. Saxons arrived over six hundred years ago, and they say the roads already were here. Some call the builders Giants because of the size of the roads and how intricately they are laid. Ice, snow, nothing moves them. Did you know, when it rains, water runs right off, and the roads dry quickly? They never have growths between the stones. Others believe the Ancients used magic. Many say they also built the North Wall, the one that keeps out the Scots. In some parts of the country, people found huge mosaics of marvelous color and design on the ground or just under it. I believe the builders were giants to build homes so large."

"How know you all this?" asked Margaret after she had swallowed her last bite.

"When we are not fighting, we enjoy storytelling. Just repeating what I have heard."

"A fine tale and a fine mystery." Margaret let the man finish his meal in silence. *Clever. Hazel eyes, sandy hair. Thick neck and arms. Tall and build like a fighter. Washed up but wears mail even to dine, likely sleeps in it. Neither handsome nor ugly. Once landed, he will find a wife with ease.*

With his gold-lined pewter goblet in hand, Roussel sat back. "Our greatest danger lies ahead." He sipped. At Margaret's "How so?" Roussel explained. "The next inn is five miles away and the road to your land almost three miles past that. Few travel toward Bristol or Gloucester this time of year. Wild country with forest right up to the road. Best places from which to ambush us."

"What suggest you?"

"We need more men. Sir Ricardo de Campo, who lives nearby and supervises this inn, may lend us a half dozen—for a price."

"Nine plus you three. Twelve are not enough?"

"Thieves and cutthroats had four days to mass and plan. Logs across the road, archers, fire. If it rains tonight as predicted, the stone road will be passable, but not the dirt road to your bailey. We must get you and the wagons over a dirt road and safely inside your walls."

Margaret pursed her lips as she considered what to do. "Better to pay the man for the use of his knights than to have him set them upon us and take all. How many men, how much?"

"Six knights. Six pounds."

"Six pounds! No. Only two of us to one of them. Bad odds. Four knights for only two pounds. Less if you bargain well. Wait. What if he uses those four to infiltrate and sends the rest to murder us and blame thieves?"

"Possible but not likely. I told him you are under the king's protection. One advantage of using his men is he is then responsible to the king for your safety."

"You have spoken to him." At the man's nod, Margaret asked, "What say you?"

"Two pounds worth, no more. Even if it only buys us two men. Lord Ricardo becomes partly responsible for your safety. Not a bad bargain. And two more swords."

"Very well, two pounds."

Roussel handed Margaret an empty bag. Margaret rose, went to her chest and unlocked it. She turned so she could see Sir Roussel while she worked.

"I recommend you stack the pennies ten high on the floor. Make four and twenty stacks; that is one pound."

From his chair, Roussel watched her count. At one pound counted, Margaret deposited the coins into the leather pouch, set it aside, and began the second pound. She held the heavy, full leather bag with one hand on the bottom to prevent it from breaking open. She placed the bag before Roussel.

"I will speak with Lord de Campo tonight. Please be ready at dawn. We want to arrive before dark."

As Roussel took the pouch, Margaret asked, "When do I pay the innkeeper?"

"On the morrow as we leave. Your use of this room and our dinner were the king's gifts. You must pay for the needs of all your men and animals."

When he estimated the cost, Margaret's eyes popped. *What grain and livestock I could buy with that!* "I will have it ready."

"Remember to give him extra for his good will. You may want to stay again."

"God give you good rest, Sir Roussel."

"And to you, my lady."

Only after Margaret had shut and bolted the door, did she shake her head as she mumbled over the cost of wealth. *Mother never told me any of this. How much coin it takes to live, to travel, to wear nice clothes, to keep up appearances after bad harvests. Oh, she complained about paying the Crown its taxes. Who does not? But I never heard either of them worry about keeping what they already had.* She paced for a while, walked to the table and finished the ale. Then she paced a while more. *Now I know why the king gave me such wealth. And not just because mine estate was stripped bare. It takes this much coin to live well. Will mine future husband come from wealth or have his own? I know Lord William of Avondale does—or appears to. I pray you ask for me soon, Lord William. Being wealthy is harder than I thought it would be.* Her second prayer this night was to request God not to let it rain until she and all else were inside her bailey and behind a sealed gate.

6

Almost There

While still in the great room, Roussel reported he had gained three knights and then laid out his plan. "I sent Gailard, Verel, and a rented knight ahead to spot dangers and report. Cachier and Masselin will ride in front of you. Men will ride beside each wagon. Syghelm will still protect the chest wagon. The last knights and I guard the rear."

Will this plan be good enough? Are they enough? Roussel said they were the leftovers others did wanted not. How well will they protect us when they are only paid fighters—and temporary ones at that? I pray they care enough for their own lives they will fight well and save me in the bargain.

In the morning, the column turned to the road west. Margaret looked up and smiled to see a pair of archers at each corner of the palisade. They were safe for the moment. At the five-mile marker, the inn looked old, rundown and seldom used. A hopeful keeper in a filthy apron stood at the gate, but departed when he saw they were not stopping. The forest continued to encroach on the road with saplings and bramble bushes.

That keeper is lax in keeping the underbrush fifty feet back for a mile each way from his inn. Who makes him do the task?

Another mile and the column stopped when Masselin rode back. "A tree is across the road. Suspicious. The dirt in its roots is still moist. I need two men to remove it while we guard." Elstan volunteered, but Masselin refused his offer with, "By law, you can bear no weapons, so you would be useless."

"I am fast and can run back and warn the party should evil befall you."

"Please take him with you," said Margaret. *That is not a request.* Masselin frowned and then nodded. Elstan tied the reins to his brake stick, jumped down and loped down the road.

Roussel sent the two men guarding the middle wagon. He ordered the rest to draw blades and face the forest as they looked for archers in the trees. Margaret twisted in her seat and leaned against Night's neck to be a smaller target. *That you stand still means you smell not strangers.* One side charged into the trees and, having found no one, returned. The other side did the same.

Might the tree have fallen from a heavy rain? Have we just imagined possible attackers? Never did I think wealth brought such dangers with it. I must be wary, even of the men I hired. Others who covet what I have will fight and kill to get it. What if one of them is already with us to call for his friends when we are the most vulnerable? Breathe. Breathe. Trust the king's men. Run to them if we are attacked. Yes, them. I want walls around me and a locked gate. Please, God, let me reach mine new home.

Horses sidled because they sensed the nervousness of their riders. Donkeys brayed and the goats in the fourth wagon bleated. Roussel sent Giraud and Hughes to see if attackers were behind them. Even having nothing happen made everyone nervous.

While they waited, Roussel dismounted. "Stand," he ordered his war horse as he dropped the reins. That the horse froze even as he watched his master step away surprised Margaret. As Roussel worked, he explained, "An attack will most likely come while we are in the road to your fields." Roussel stepped behind her and double-fastened her sandbag counterweight on her platform. "We are hampered by trees on both sides. The most dangerous place is at the rock marking the south tip of your border." The knight motioned Margaret to shift her feet; he checked the wide straps, which held her leather seat on Night. They were still tight. "The place is barely wide enough for a wagon to pass and the ruts are deep. My lady, please check that the rope attaching you to the saddle is tight." Roussel ordered, "They must not catch you!" Margaret returned her feet to the wooden platform and nodded agreement. "Forget the wagons and all else. At the turn toward your estate, Masselin will ride beside you with two others behind you. The four of you race all the way into the bailey. Stop not for any reason. Not even to help a knight who falls. Leave your sword sheathed, ride low and with a hand full of mane to steady you. Remember, you are riding to save your honor and your life." Margaret undid and refastened the rope around her waist as tight as she dared. *Please God, protect me. Keep the men safe. Oh God, Your will in all things.*

Roulin returned to report they had cleared the barrier as Elstan climbed on his wagon. Roussel remounted, and the column moved with alacrity past the tree now on the side of the road. They rode a mile more, and arrived at the entry to Margaret's property.

We have hours to dark, plenty of time to reach the bailey. Where are the birds? Margaret's chest tightened; Night sidled then stopped. She transferred the reins to her left hand; with her right she grabbed a handful of Night's mane. Masselin, sword in hand, rode up beside her and ordered, "Now." He rode up the right rut to guard her back.

Jaws clenched and leading far forward, Margaret said, "Run!" and followed him in the left rut. Margaret's heart thundered in her ears in rhythm with the four sets of hooves pounding the ground as they sped up the road. With his first steps, Night ran for fun; then he dropped his head and charged forward in earnest. Margaret's tight grip on his mane upset him.

Arrows rained upon the party. Armed men stood and attacked. "Jerusalem!" shouted Roussel.

Everyone sprang into action. Margaret kicked a man who tried to grab her foot to pull her off Night. Margaret's heart raced. Behind her a sword flashed. An attacker lost his hand and screamed. At the rock marking the corner of Margaret's estate, two men jumped up. Both bore the stench of the unwashed, and their clothes reeked of smoke. The one whose face was curled in a snarl, roared as he used the stone to launch himself at Margaret and missed. An attacker had grabbed her mantle and yanked hard. She choked, jolted backward, and gasped for air as the cloth tore at the brooch. Margaret's feet left the platform bottom. Night stumbled at the jolt and dug his hooves deeper into the earth. He struggled to regain his momentum. Terrified, Margaret careened backward from the hard pull. At a shout and a scream behind her, she was free.

An arrow whizzed past Margaret's leg and stuck in the earth ahead of Night's hooves. The pair raced on. Margaret clung to her horse as she bounced on her seat. Night stumbled in the wheel rut;

Margaret fell forward. Her heels slammed against Night's side and knocked the breath from her as she slipped from the platform seat. She dropped the reins as she grabbed with her left hand for more of Night's flying mane. Margaret lifted her right knee against Night's shoulder and pushed against the platform bottom with her left foot to regain her seat. "Run! Run, Night!" she urged. Margaret pulled hard on her handfuls of mane as she righted herself. Margaret's heart pounded so hard in her ears she heard little of the fight behind her. Masselin was gone. Wheezing hard, Night ran on. Margaret cleared the trees. She saw the fields to her left were empty, sunlit, and quiet. She glanced to her right and saw the same. The only knight behind her held his reddened sword aloft. Far behind the pair, swords clashed and rang. They heard unintelligible shouting and distant donkeys braying. Night slowed as his breathing became louder. He panted and wheezed. Margaret breathed hard through her mouth, in, out, in, out. Her heart raced as fear clouded her mind.

"Keep going! For the bailey, my lady. Make haste!" yelled Demetre from behind her. Margaret dug her heels into Night's flanks, and both dashed ahead. Margaret's forehead almost touched Night's neck. *Poor Night, your age is showing. Lathered and breathing hard. Please, mine friend, die not. I need you still.* Even though Demetre rode at her back, Margaret drew her blade in case he was with the attackers. *Trust him not!* They raced ahead. *I must be safe! I must be safe! God keep me safe!*

The fight behind the pair continued. Ducking arrows, Syghelm spun off his seat and crouched in the wagon bed ready to behead anyone who approached the chest. Knights brandished swords and charged. Arrows bounced off chain mail but not ringed leather. Even grazed and bleeding from a neck wound, a rented knight kept fighting. Knights on steeds had the advantage of height, quick-shifting animals and long blades. Swords pierced flesh and hacked limbs. Screams of pain pierced the air. A bodiless voice yelled attack orders from within the trees. Noise and shouting frightened the bellowing animals. The donkeys pulled hard against their harnesses to escape the men attacking the column, but they could not move for the wagons ahead of them. A knight ran down an attacker with a knife ready to cut his horse. The boy screamed as he fell under the war horse's hooves, and the animal stomped on his chest. Knights ran through two archers crouched in tree notches and watched them fall. A knight slashed the arm of a third archer and watched as the man fell one way and his severed limb fell the other. The gray-hair man screamed his agony as he quickly bled to death. A young man with fair hair remained because he was so high in his tree. A knight stood in his stirrups and threatened him with his blade. The archer pulled his bow over his head and through one arm, jumped for a second tree, slid down its trunk and fled into the woods.

Half the knights chased fleeing men; attackers died, blood fountaining from necks or seeping from bellies. Staying with the wagons, the other half of the knights brandished their swords, ready to strike again if need be. Their blades flashed and caught the sunlight still streaming through the trees.

Now well ahead of the fray, Margaret recognized the road bent left of the palisade wall ahead. Her heart still raced and she gasped for air in gulps. *Why is the gate is on the west side? Should I slow Night?*

Sir Demetre reached her and advised, "My lady, stop not. If someone on horse comes out, race left into the trees and hide. I will kill him."

The road gently climbed between the empty fields and Demetre relaxed as he spotted no one beside or behind them. Margaret looked ahead to the knoll and the palisade walls. Above the palisade's pointed tree poles she saw a face. Two armed figures rode out of the gate. As Margaret's heart again raced, she tightened her grip on Night, pulled him left and headed him into that direction. Night kicked up dirt as they fled.

With swords in hand, the knights neared and yelled, "Friend or foe?"

Demetre shouted, "Friend! Enemy behind us. Go!" as he reined in his horse.

The pair dashed past Demetre and into the trees. Margaret stopped Night and turned him back toward the gate. She patted Night's neck as his wheezing slowed. Her breathing and racing heart slowed not as her thoughts raged on. *I feared for mine life! I might have lost Night! And mine hired men! Someone will pay for this. How dare they! How dare they!*

At the bottom of the hill, the road switched left then right before it reached the gate. On the walkway stood a man in a helmet. Fifty yards way, Margaret waited for Demetre.

"I trust no one."

"Nor I." Margaret's tone revealed her rage. "They should have met us at the road. Why were we not warned? Were those two the only knights guarding mine land?"

To the right of the gate a knight silently watched them; on the opposite side, a man waved.

Shocked, Margaret shouted, "Jorgon?"

Jorgon waved again. "Yes, my lady," he yelled.

Thank you, God! Him I trust.

With her sword, Margaret pointed to the knight. "Who is he?"

"Sir Bedwin, the king's man. My lady, you are safe and we are inside."

Margaret rode into a bailey full of people and animals. She turned right toward the walkway ladder. The silent crowd backed away. Mothers clutched their children to them. Men pulled their families into their arms. All watched the proud young woman on the lathered black gelding as she sheathed her sword. The knight only lowered his bloody blade and remained on his horse as well. Behind them three villeins re-closed the gate and dropped two bars into place, one high, the other low. Someone grabbed Night's bridle. Margaret looked down to see who wished to die. She blew out air and some of her anger.

"Thank you, Jorgon. He has labored hard and is wet. I fear for him."

"Fear not, my lady. I will cool him slowly and take good care of him." Jorgon held Night's bridle and spoke softly to him.

"Caitlin?" yelled Margaret.

From behind the crowd, she heard, "Here, my lady." Margaret looked over the villeins toward the sound but could not spot her friend. "Hot water for the wounded. Pokers into flames for burning."

"Yes, my lady."

"If the first wagon gets through, it holds sacks of flour for bread. Choose a bolt of servant cloth for bandages. I will need your simples, needle and threads if you still have them. Mine are in the second wagon." Margaret untied the rope around her waist.

"Yes, my lady."

"And honey for the wounds."

Jorgon reached up as Margaret leaned. She placed her hands upon his shoulders and jumped to the ground. "Is Dena here as well?" Jorgon nodded. "Good."

Margaret patted Night's neck. When he swung his head to her, she kissed his cheek. "Thank you, Night, for saving me. You go with Jorgon." She informed her hostler, "His oats are in the fifth wagon."

Margaret looked upward to the knight for whom she had hard questions. She climbed the ladder to the palisade walkway. "Lord Bedwin? I am the La…"

"I recognize who you are," said the thin old man gruffly.

Ignore his disdain. She noticed his chain mail was missing links as if arrows or blades had broken them. His conical helmet had rusted in the dented places but the nasal, which dipped down from the front edge and covered his nose, was burnished clean. She walked to his side, grabbed the pointed logs and leaned toward the trees from which she had come. She saw no wagons, no knights. *Please God, save them.* She chose not to finish with "Oh God, Your will in all things" because she would not have meant it. "Why were we not warned? What took place here?" Margaret was no more civil than Bedwin.

When Lord Bedwin shrugged, his chain mail clinked. Both of them glared at each other. Margaret tamped down her rising anger. Finally Bedwin spoke. "Two days ago. Caught the villeins leaving Mass. Rounded them up and marched them into the bailey. I let them in and locked the gate. Their leader rode Sir Walter's horse, wore his mail, and brandished his sword. He had been on patrol. They also killed the aleman. They settled into the villeins' houses. This morning they threatened death to any who left the bailey and disappeared."

"How many?"

"I counted twenty-one, mayhap more. How many did you bring?"

"Fifteen knights." To Margaret's great relief, wagons moved out of the trees. *One. Two, Three, four, five. Drivers. Syghelm. Elstan. No*

61

knights. Margaret turned away from Bedwin and faced the bailey. Rank odors of fear, sweat, and human waste assailed her. *Take charge now or lose mine advantage.* "I want mine reeve!"

A tall man with sun-bleached hair stepped forward. He called out "my lady" as he pulled his forelock.

"Manage the bailey. Clear space for the wagons. Assign men to guard them. From the first wagon unload only what we need. Get women to carry flour for bread and the starter to the kitchen and put them to work. Send cloth for bandaging to Caitlin. Clear space for fifteen knights and ready the barn for their horses. Fill the horse troughs with fresh water. Get the stable boys. No one leaves until mine knights report. *Ask him to do something. Let him think he is still in charge.* "Lord Bedwin will say when you may return to your homes." From the corner of her eye, she saw the old knight nod. She faced the crowd. "I smell the remains of ashes and debris in mine bailey. I smell sweat, piss and shit. If any of you has fouled mine wells, I will send you to God. No one leaves until the grounds are cleared and clean. Pick up all your messes and take them with you, even wet dirt." Margaret continued to yell. "When you villeins reach your homes, I need honey. Not for food, for wounds. Any amount, however small, bring to the hall."

"Done, my lady," answered Reeve. He turned to the crowd, pointed and called names and tasks. "Ifig, Leoma, and Willa, to the kitchen. Rammeg and sons, to the wagons. My sons, fill the horse troughs. Farmers, to me!" Moving, talking, doing, the villeins came to life. Three men unbarred the gate and opt the doors. Wagons rumbled in.

Better mend mine way toward him. "Lord Bedwin." Margaret nodded politely to him. "I regret our loss of Sir Walter. We will avenge him. I will pray for the repose of his soul." Margaret watched his pale blue eyes soften. "His Royal Highness sent three men to relieve you and to guard me until His Royal Highness chooses mine husband, Sir Roussel, Sir Gailard, and Sir Cashier. When they arrive, I leave you to talk with them and to do what is necessary. I also hired eight knights errant and rented three others. With your permission, I will tend the wounded."

"You have it," Said Sir Bedwin with a bit of grace.

Margaret bobbed a quick curtsey before she descended the ladder and strode toward the hall. Because she had placed her left hand upon her pommel and thrust her scabbard from her body, everyone moved far from her path. The sun sent shards of light through barren trees as it set.

7

Rough Start

Seated on the edge of the dais, Margaret watched the last wounded knight approach. "Sir Hughes, I believe."

The youngest knight errant sat on the end of the bench nearest her. "My lady."

The hall was full. Saxons lined the walls in hopes they might sleep inside. The last pair of knights was finally eating warm bread and bites of cheese from the wheel Elstan had taken from a wagon. At the other end of the hall Bedwin and Roussel were deep in conference. One large man had heated a poker to red hot in anticipation he still needed it. He turned and turned it in the fire pit coals that warmed the hall.

"How came you by that?"

"I was fighting one man when another attacked. Sir Cachier killed him, but I got nicked."

Margaret lifted the wet, red cloth from his tanned forearm and saw his wound was a long knife gash that still oozed blood. *This is more than nicked. Mayhap he will lose the use of his arm.* Then She lay a clean cloth over the wound and instructed him to press gently on the cloth that soon reddened. She guessed, "And you want not your arm burned?"

"I have heard of stitching up small wounds. Needle and thread. Can you do it?"

Margaret shook her head. "'It is still bleeding too much; it needs burning." She thought a moment. "We might combine the treatments, burn to stop the blood flow and then stitch it closed. Mother and I talked of it, but we never did it. Are you willing to gamble?" Trying to encourage him, she added, "The muscles might bind together."

Hughes nodded. "I must have the use of it to hold a shield."

Cormac approached and set a small covered pot beside her.

"My lady, the priest, Father Manntun, brought this. Tis the only bit of honey."

"Thank you, Cormac. I require a bottle of wine from the third wagon."

Margaret and Hughes waited until she could bear silence no more.

"How you came to be errant?"

"I squired and trained for my lord. When he died two years ago, to save coins, his heir released several of us. Since then I have worked here and there."

Not his fault he is for hire. How many errant knights share the same fate?

Cormac set the opt bottle on the dais floor beside Caitlin's sewing kit.

Margaret offered wine to Hughes. "Drink only three gulps; I need the rest to treat you and the others." As Hughes drank, Margaret asked, "Cormac, who is the knight at the other end of the fire pit, the one with the poker?"

"Sir Claude, my lady."

"Sir Claude," Margaret called. "Sir Hughes needs burning. Here or there?"

"There, my lady."

"Cormac, hold his shoulders steady. I will hold his wrist."

Cachier rose from his place and approached. "My lady, I fear he will buck and strike you without knowing. Best let men do this."

Margaret stood and walked away. She watched Claude approach, but could not look. The smell of burning flesh sickened her. Margaret swallowed against her rising gorge. *Glad mine belly is empty.* She turned back. "Your first scar?" She searched his face.

Holding his lips between his teeth, Hughes nodded.

"That was the easy part. Still want stitching?"

Hughes nodded again.

"I need to get among you to stitch the wound, but I also need you to hold him still." The men moved aside, and she stood between Claude and Cachier, who shifted so as not to touch her. Margaret set down her scissors after she cut a long length of thread. *Would that needles were thinner. Good enough for wool, but not skin.* As she threaded the iron needle, she talked. "Hughes, the men will hold you. I will draw the needle through your flesh four or five times with tails on both sides. Cormac will push your wound together. I will tie the thread ends together. If your flesh holds, I will bandage you. If not, I will cut you free."

67

At the first stitch, Hughes grunted; his eyes popped wide with pain. At the second, he howled. He looked down at his wound as the needle again neared his flesh, and he fainted.

"Poor boy," said Masselin mockingly as he looked on.

"He favored us. Now I can work faster. Keep holding him should he awaken before I finish." Three times more Margaret pushed hard to get needle and thread through the healthy flesh on either side of the wound. With each stitch, she swallowed to tamp down her stomach twisting as if it wanted to disgorge unknown contents as she worked. "Cormac, push his skin close together, only but touching. We need to leave room for pus if it festers."

Cormac did as he was bid. Margaret pulled and tied, first the end stitches, then the center one and finally the two remaining on either side of the middle stitch. Before Hughes roused, Margaret drizzled wine over the wound. The young knight slowly returned to consciousness. Cormac let him lean against him as he roused.

"Well done."

In disgust Hughes moaned, "I fainted—like a girl."

"Which was the best thing to do. Thank you. Look at it before I bandage it."

"Are your stitches holding?"

"Indeed, Sir Hughes."

Margaret dug out the contents of a small jar with a stick inside it; she drizzled honey on a short length of cloth and gently placed it over the wound. "That will seal the wound and keep it clean." She took a long strip and wound it round his arm to cover the patch, tore a length in half and used both ends to tie the bandage together. "Hughes, I need to see this every morning and every night. If you become hot or feverish, see me at once. No hard duty for you until this heals. Guarding only. This experiment is important, and I will not have you tear open the stitching."

"I am right handed."

"Nevertheless. No using your left arm. Place your hand upon your stomach or let your arm hang, whichever feels better. And no sleeping on your left side. On your back with your left hand on your chest. Get cloth from Caitlin and make an arm sling if you like."

"Yes, my lady."

Margaret handed Hughes the wine bottle. "I suggest you share what remains with those who helped you." Margaret walked to Reeve who was standing on the other side of the fire pit. "How fare mine Saxons? Any with wounds that need treating?"

"No wounds, my lady. They will stay in the bailey this night. They are still too frightened to return to their huts. They are cold."

"I will ask the knights to sleep on one side of the fire pit. The Saxons may have the other side. Or the kitchen. Or whatever place they can find." Margaret thought a moment and added, "The stable will be warm. Mayhap there."

"Already full, my lady."

"How long have you been the reeve?"

"This is mine second year."

They like him enough to have re-elected him. Glad he is experienced. "I would like a bucket of water and a large rag by the church door. I expect everyone to have cleaned hands before entering church."

"Yes, my lady."

"Please come with me," instructed Margaret as she walked to the other end of the fire pit. Margaret stood still beside the seated knights until Bedwin looked up. She gave a short bouncy curtsey.

"Lord Bedwin, Sir Roussel, may I speak with you?"

At Bedwin's curt nod, Roussel made room beside him on the bench. Reeve stood at her right shoulder. Margaret looked to the king's man.

"With your permission, Lord Bedwin?" At the man's nod, she gazed at Roussel.

"Sirrah, at the start of the attack I saw a knight wounded in the neck. I did not treat him. Where is he?"

"He fought heroically but soon fell. He bled to death, my lady."

In a hushed voice Margaret asked, "Whom did we lose?"

"One of de Campo's men."

"His name?"

"Sir Richard."

"We must bury his body and say Mass for him. Sir Roussel, what say the other two rented men? Bury him here?"

"They will return to Lord de Campo and take his body with them."

"Reeve, tell the Saxons Sir Richard died. I ask them to pray for the repose of his soul. I will ask Father Manntun to remember Sir Richard in the Mass on the morrow, record his name for us and to say Mass for him on this date for a decade."

"What will you do?" asked Lord Bedwin.

"I shall pray for him every morning and night for a year and a day." Margaret dropped her head a moment and then raised it. "Lord Bedwin, have we found Sir Walter's body?"

"The priest wrapped Sir Walter in a shroud as he did the rented knight. Their bodies lie inside the church."

"We will say Masses and pray for Sir Walter." *Mayhap they will think better of me because I said softly what a woman should at a time like this. Keep using a soft voice, nod as if asking for their approval. Act the lord only if they challenge my authority.*

Bedwin, Roussel and Reeve nodded their approval. Her acting a lord's role had startled them. She had made commands as no woman should. By praying for the dead, Margaret showed that she really was female. For the moment.

"Sir Roussel, were all our attackers killed?

"Not all. Some fled into the woods. Their leader also disappeared."

"What know we of them?"

Bedwin nodded to Roussel, who answered. "The leader came from Winchester. He heard we three were to accompany you and believed we were all the protection you had. Most likely, he left Sunday after gathering a few others. Picked up more on the way. They were not seen on the road, so they must have come on forest paths."

"How know you this?"

"The bowman high in the trees agreed to trade knowledge for his life."

"First you ran him down, got the information, and then you killed him?"

"Yes."

"Well done." *I care not if they think me bloodthirsty. Someone will pay for this attack, for these deaths.* "What did they here?"

Bedwin replied, "They attacked Tuesday morning as we left Mass. They killed the aleman."

"Why?"

"A man grabbed his wife. He came to her rescue and died." Margaret gave no reaction so he added, "The leader stopped it, ordered the women left alone, and herded us into the bailey. They occupied the village and pillaged."

71

"Reeve?"

"Lord Bedwin tells it as it happened."

"We are still in great danger." It was not a question.

"Until you are wed," Roussel added. "Every time you leave the compound. Even if you lock yourself inside, an army could attack while our men are guarding your land. Someone may round up your villeins and kill them one by one, until you come out. What happened today will happen again. Mayhap more than once unless His Royal Highness acts fast."

He is right. We put down this attack hard. Now we must stop more. "How do we prevent more attacks?"

From the other side of the fire pit, Masselin set the wine bottle on the table boards and spoke up. "When I was last in London, I saw heads on pikes on a bridge. Thieves, murderers and such beheaded for their crimes. Some were fresh, some old. After the birds picked their bones clean, boys knocked the skulls into the river or kicked them in a game. A grisly sight and a dire warning against wrongdoing."

"Sir Roussel, how many did our men kill?" After he said "eleven," she began. "I have instructions." When he did not refuse her, she continued. "On the morrow after Mass, I want the attackers' corpses." Margaret saw Bedwin glowering at her. She looked to her head Saxon. "Reeve, you will instruct Saxon men to strip the bodies bare and stack their goods. Sir Roussel, choose what you and the other knights want. Reeve, distribute what remains among the Saxons, fair and even. Burn the rest. "

"Is that all?"

Without looking Lord Bedwin's way, she responded, "No, Lord Bedwin." She continued, "Reeve, while some attend the bodies, order a group of Saxons to the forest to cut poles, long enough a man on a horse cannot touch the top plus three feet for burial into the earth. Taper the tops as needed and stand the poles along the king's road on either side of our entry lane. I want as many as there are bodies plus one to remain empty as a warning. Sir Roussel, you will behead the bodies and place their severed heads atop the poles. Reeve, mine Saxons will dig graves behind the poles. Be cert each body matches the head it is missing." Margaret ignored the men's shocked faces by looking away. *I care not what they think. I must make the shock of what we do so great, no one else will even think of encroaching on us again. Be strong. A man would do this, so I must, no matter how I feel. Hide. Make mine face a mask. Sound hard, heartless.*

"A warning against any who might think to attack?" surmised Roussel.

Margaret looked back and nodded. "Exactly. Everyone who travels the road will see our deed and know, 'Attack this land and die.' Word will pass swiftly. Let us pray heads on pikes will be enough to warn others away."

"You will do no such thing. I forbid it!" said a voice behind Roussel.

The reeve bent and whispered in Margaret's ear, "Father Manntun."

"Ah-h-h, Father Manntun, do step around to Lord Bedwin's side and join us."

The priest did so. "It is sacrilege to defile a body. We will say Mass and have proper burials in the church graveyard."

Margaret began in a compliant voice, "Indeed, Father we will bury them and say Mass." Then her voice turned cold and hard. "Only after birds have eaten the flesh from their heads and their bones are bleached will we will bury their skulls with their bodies. They killed a Norman knight, a death sentence. They murdered one of mine people. As the attackers died un-shriven, I treat them as the Church does ditch women. They will not be buried among good Christian people." Margaret gave the estate priest a hard look. "The sun should have bleached the skulls by Michaelmas."

"My child..."

Margaret heard not the rest he said. *I am no child and cert not yours!* "They murdered Sir Walter. Well you know the law: kill a Norman and all involved die."

"I challenge that not, but as a Christian you should..."

"Protect mine Saxons and keep mine land safe." Margaret still faced the priest. "If we do as you propose, others will think us soft. We will be attacked again and again. For the coin. To ransom me. Because we look weak. To force me to marry my attacker. We will not be safe in the church, in the fields, anywhere. No, Father, we will do as I say and give such a warning no one else dare attack again."

"Only a lord can order what you have ordered," warned Father Manntun.

"Until His Majesty sends me a husband, I stand in his place. I act however I must to hold this land and keep its people safe." *Dear God, let that be enough to gain their agreement.*

"Lady Margaret, you cannot..."

"Father Manntun!" Margaret barked.

Sir Roussel interrupted the pair with, "We must demonstrate ruthlessness or be attacked repeatedly. I agree with Lady Margaret, but, my lady, you dare not order it. Others will consider you a bloodthirsty, unnatural woman. Then what man, what family will want you?"

"Who will say it was his idea? Who will order it done?" In the silence that followed her words, Margaret prayed. *Please God, one strong man among them.*

"I am a lord. I order what we have discussed be done. It is mine idea, is it not?"

"Oh, yes, Lord Bedwin!" came three voices.

Father Manntun started to sputter, but Lord Bedwin's glare stopped him.

"Furthermore, I will inform King Henry of mine wise decision to forestall more possible attacks," added Bedwin.

Margaret leaned forward and grinned at the old knight. She clasped her hands together at her breast. In a small, sweet voice, she said, "Oh dear, Lord Bedwin, this decision is harsh, indeed. I fear it will hurt my heart."

Lord Bedwin's eyebrows lifted as he dropped his chin. "Lady Margaret, harsh as this punishment may appear so to such a … gentle one … as you, it still must be done. I do it for your protection, my lady."

"Ah well," Margaret sighed. "If this be your decision, then all I can do is to accept your good judgment. I thank you for your strength and wisdom." Margaret modestly lowered her eyes and her hands.

Roussel and the reeve silently looked upon this charade in utter disbelief. Father Manntun harrumphed and left without excusing himself. In the shadows, Elstan smiled to himself as he slunk away.

"Lord Bedwin, I am grateful for how the Saxons repaired the ramparts and the gate and for the other work they did. What are your instructions as to what we are to do after we plant our crops?" Margaret asked. "They are already late."

"Your first task should be to put the keep in good repair and for you to live there. Sleeping under the same roof as your men is unseemly. Even if you pull up the ladder every night onto the visitor's platform. As for them, they needs live in the hall until you rebuild the barracks. You must complete it before Michaelmas. The hall already bears human stink from the Saxons sleeping in this place. Also, you will need the stalls to store the harvest."

"Thank you, Lord Bedwin. You give good counsel." *Despite how we began, glad I am he sent you here.*

Bedwin informed Margaret he and his two remaining men would leave to report to the king after Monday Mass. Roussel reported his assigning the guard rotation. She requested her knights leave one side of the fire pit for Saxons. After the knights departed the bench, only Reeve remained.

"Reeve, what have I overlooked?"

"Nothing save one. You need to eat."

"God give you good rest, Reeve."

"God give you good rest, my lady."

I mistrusted Sir Demetre. How shall I make amends?

"Sir Demetre?" she called. When he approached, Margaret stood as a sign of respect. "I thank you, good sir, for protecting me and for getting me safely into the bailey."

Surprised at such kind words, Demetre nodded. "You have mine word. I will always have your back, my lady."

"Again, I thank you, Sir Demetre." *I hope I sound warm enough, grateful enough.* She remained standing until Demetre returned to the rest of the men at the other end of the hall. Then she sat. Exhausted, Margaret placed her elbows on the table and put her head in her hands. *Is it proper I put down mine head and sleep here?*

Will I still appear strong? A small bread round torn in half appeared between her elbows.

"Eat," ordered a familiar voice.

"Caitlin!" Margaret raised her head and grinned. She grabbed Caitlin's hand and clutched it. Caitlin looked tired, but she was still herself, a twenty-one-year old Irish maiden. Her skin still milky white with a light dusting of freckles across her nose. Her eyes still bright blue under a cap of rusty red hair pulled back into a single braid that stopped her waist. Still dressed in a Saxon gunna because she was a foreigner and not allowed to wear Norman garb.

"Eat." Caitlin smiled back. She set down a mug of half hot water and half wine beside the round of warm bread.

"I have missed you so! I have questions." Margaret released her friend.

"Eat while I talk."

Margaret sipped the mug and dug out the middle of the round and chewed small bites.

Caitlin sat and reported only the basics. "You have seen Jorgon. Dena is here. We are fine. For now, they were staying in the village with a widow. The keep is shambles. Chinks gone. Fireplace stack needs cleaning. Unusable for now. Before the attack I only had time to clean the hall. I made a bed of blankets on the sleeping platform above the storage rooms behind the dais. We can raise the ladder after we climb it. Leave the mug. Time for bed."

Worried Margaret had so exhausted herself she might fall off the ladder, Caitlin followed close behind her. Margaret knelt before a straw bed covered by a blanket and prayed. She ended with *Thank you, God, for keeping Caitlin safe and bringing us back together.* So exhausted was she, Margaret fell into a deep sleep as soon as she rolled onto makeshift bed. Ever Margaret's chaperone, Caitlin lay down next to her and covered them both with two more blankets she had also taken from a wagon.

8

Mine

Saturday passed in a flurry of work. The Saxons returned to their homes, assessed the damage, and lamented the loss of their food-stuffs, including every item in their gardens. While the men followed Lady Margaret's orders, women and children scoured the forest for acorns, weeds, and tore bark from the few birch trees not already stripped. Their findings, thrown into a pot for a soup would be given to the youngest and the sickest. Three knights guarded the Saxons; a few prepared the hall as a living and sleeping space. More ranged the land seeking intruders.

To placate Father Manntun, Margaret went to the priest instead of her sending for him. *He meant well yesterday. But I could not be forgiving, or I will be considered too soft to rule. Roussel already commands the knights. He commands from God. I must be obedient to God's representative on earth, on this estate. On Church matters and customs, I will defer to Father. Yet I cannot let him take power over the estate from me. Obedient to God's will and Father's commands whenever I can be. Do what I must when I cannot. Balance, that is what I need with him. I needs find a balance. I hope this is a start.* She espied the shack attached to the church and knocked on its door. Despite the priest's diffidence at meeting her outside his door, she was reverential. Margaret even curtsied before she made her need known.

"Father Manntun, I have inspected the bailey and counted what we have. Our people were hungry. Now they will starve. I brought what I thought was twice the seed I need to plant. I now know I need more. I must provide food and more seed. If you would be so good as to write a letter of permission for a Saxon or two to take a wagon to Reading, I will send coin and knights to guard them. They need to leave immediately after Monday Mass if they are to reach Reading in a day."

"Their names, my child?"

Margaret smiled to hide her back was up at his belittling tone.

"Before dark, I will consult with Reeve, and he will send you word of whom he recommends. I know you will want to write the letter well before midnight."

"Sunday is inviolate. You will do no work, no inspecting the village, no conducting meetings."

"Of course not, Father. Sundays are inviolate." *Mother worked on Sundays when we went midwifing. She even cooked. Defy him not. Give in. Besides, we need the rest, and sitting requires less food.*

"You will confess your sins; you will start with your actions of yesterday. Now."

"Yes, Father," replied Margaret with a meekness she felt not.

Afterward, Margaret turned to the barn to see to the milch cow. *Glad the barn is still standing.* Margaret admired its length and width.

She looked up to a large, square door under the roof. *It will hold enough hay and fodder for a whole winter. Glad no one thought to look up, or the conquering knights might also have taken the pulley for pulling up the platform used to store feed. This barn will hold a half dozen cows and even more oxen, plus pigs, goats, and chickens in winter. Good outside pens. Someone built well.* She petted and stroked the animal as she prayed part of her penance. Her hushed tones soothed the beast who had been so badly frightened by the attack she would not release her milk. Margaret filled the cow's trough with fresh water and fed her the scraps of hay found in the corners on the floor above. The cow swung her buttocks from side to side in her distress at her bulging udder.

"Sorry I am. No oats," said Margaret as she stroked the animal's side. "Do with hay for now. New grass should be up in three weeks. Mayhap sooner, God willing."

"It is a hard day if you are talking to a cow."

"Please talk in soft, soothing tones. I am trying to calm her. Cormac, please seek a stool and pail for me."

Continuing to speak gently, Margaret asked him to take her place beside the cow and to pet her. Margaret hummed a random tune as she moved into position. Margaret's first effort failed, but her second pull on a different teat resulted in a squirt of milk hitting the inside of the pail. The cow's mooing changed from pained to relieved. *Relief for us both, girl. You get relief. I get milk for the children.* "Good girl! I promise to feed you well. Just keep giving milk," requested Margaret as she patted the cow's flank before she returned to filling the pail. Margaret's seneschal continued to soothe the cow with a gentle tone. "You are a woman of many talents, my lady. From ordering knights and defying a priest to having heads impaled on posts and now milking a cow."

"I do what I must. What have you learned?" As Margaret worked, Cormac filled her ears with information and gossip. Jorgon arrived.

"How fare you and Dena?"

"I am fine. She is still grieving over her lost son."

Margaret nodded her understanding as she continued to milk the cow. "Jorgon, will you and Dena stay for a time? Will you still be mine hostler?" At his nod, she added, "Do you wish to live in the widow's house or have one of your own?"

"That will do for now, but I think it better if we have our own home in the village."

Given what happened in Winchester, I can well understand your desire to be away from me. Living with me would be too hard for Dena.

At Margaret's request, Jorgon left to fetch a spoon from the kitchen. He returned to the hall to report Lady Margaret was going into the village.

"Not alone," answered Gailard.

He assigned three men. They met Margaret and Cormac at the gate and escorted them to the Reeve's wattle and daub house. It needed whitewashing, but the thatched roof looked sound. As Reeve and Margaret conferred about what to obtain in Reading and whom to send, Cormac went from house to house announcing fresh milk was available.

"This is mine wife Erwina and mine sons Ainemaere and Denemaere."

The whole family was slim. Erwina looked to be about thirty with sandy hair and blue-grey eyes she hooded with a furrowed brow as if she oft worried. The boys looked sideways to their father before pulling their forelocks. Each was as light-haired as their mother, but had brown eyes like their father. Margaret nodded recognition after Erwina curtsied and the boys pulled their forelocks.

"I know not your Christian name."

"I am Felamaere. Most call me Fela."

"I shall call you Reeve while you are so."

"As you wish, my lady."

"How old are your sons, Reeve?"

"Ainemaere is eight and Denemaere is six, my lady. They are good at guarding animals grazing in the meadows."

"While I serve milk, please think of a good milkmaid for the cows."

Cormac had placed the two women with child first in line. The first looked ready to birth, but Meagth informed Margaret she was not due for another three months. The second woman reported her babe had not yet kicked, so it was not yet alive. Behind them, Cormac had lined up the children from youngest to twelve. The women drank two spoonfuls of milk. He instructed them to go to the end of the line should there be enough for another portion. When a new mother carried in a tiny babe entered, she looked both proud and worried. She curtsied and whispered said shyly, "He is but a week old and mine milk is drying up, my lady." Margaret stood and served the infant a tiny sip. She offered the mother three spoonfuls of milk with the instruction to drink as much ale as she could to bring back her milk. To win the children to her, Margaret held the spoon for each one. Eager for more, several little ones bit the spoon as if to keep it. Mothers smiled and Margaret giggled. Mothers held the hands of their youngest and led them into the house.

"My lady, he has not eaten this day."

Margaret saw the toddler's distended belly. *If the children are faring this badly, how much hungrier must be their parents!* Margaret shook her head in disbelief and was aghast when the woman cowered.

"You are safe. I was thinking of de Warenne. How could he! Were he here, I would tie him to a tree and not feed him for a month."

"The cows were his. The knights took them."

"Well, this cow is mine and I share."

"Thank you, my lady."

The woman took the boy outside.

Before the next child entered the house, Margaret called out, "Cormac!"

"Yes, my lady?"

"Explain they are to get in this same line and in the same order each time we have milk. Wherever I stop, the next person is the front of the line for the next pail of milk we have. Please send in the next person."

The pregnant women and two mothers with babes drank a second time.

"Erwina?"

"Yes, my lady?"

"I wish to pass out milk on the morrow, but I lack the time to do so every day. May I send the milk for you to hand out for me?"

"I would be honored, my lady." The woman stood a bit taller as her mouth moved into the tiniest of smiles.

"As the reeve's wife, you are an important person. I expect you to be fair and even to all when you portion out the milk. Please start with small portions as I did today. I want no one to sicken because their stomachs are so weak. I trust you to increase the portion of milk as they become stronger. Remember fair and even."

"I promise. Fair and even."

"Good. Thank you for performing this task, Erwina. I appreciate your help."

Erwina curtsied and smiled.

Well pleased with herself, Margaret swung the empty pail beside her as she returned to the bailey. The spoon clinking inside the pail cheered her.

"Good politic, my lady. Be good to the children and the adults will favor you."

"You saw their bellies, bloated but empty. Gray skin. I started with sips so their stomachs would not toss the milk. If the cow gives more milk, they will get more. Not politic, Cormac. Just doing mine Christian duty."

"Yes, my lady."

Knights in the hall, kitchen workers and the servants supped on a bread roll and water that had been boiled and blessed in the hope it would kill no one. Those seated on the dais: Fathers Gregory and Manntun, Sirs Bedwin, Robert, William, Roussel, Gailard, Cachier, and Lady Margaret ate the same meal.

"Knights can not fight on bread and water, Lady Margaret. If this is all the food you have, I fear they will revolt or bolt."

"Sir Roussel, I agree. As we have been apart all day, I must tell you I have arranged for a wagon to leave Monday morn for Reading. The Saxons will bargain for food, barrels of dried cod, and grain. Do we have the men to escort the wagon and protect our supplies?"

"I will see to it."

"We cannot eat meat the First Sunday of Lent, but the Saxons have caught a few fish. Only enough for a stew. Caitlin saved our remaining vegetables for it." Margaret's forced her smile and her cheerfulness about the morrow's main meal was met with a frown.

"Fish stew. What joy."

"Then we fast again until the wagon arrives. Wednesday eve?" she guessed.

Roussel shrugged.

Margaret leaned toward the knight and said in a hushed tone, "Please warn the men not to hunt and eat meat while on patrol. They needs confess, and Father Manntun is not a kind priest; he will not forgive them. His penance might be no eating meat the five Sundays before Easter when doing so is permitted. Plus he may add even harder penances."

Roussel looked surprised she knew of what the men had said only among themselves. Margaret added, "I am tempted to tell you mine penance for mine deeds yesterday. Suffice it to say the prayers are the easiest part."

"Was ordering poles, beheadings, and un-Christian burials worth the penance?"

"Yes."

"My lady, is it wise to defy a priest? He can make your life a hell on earth."

I dare not respond. What might Father Manntun do if he hears? "I see Sir Hughes has returned from guarding the gate. After he sups, I need to examine his wound."

"I will send him to you, my lady," intoned Roussel as he stood.

The knights departed as did Father Manntun. Only Father Gregory remained.

"Father," began Margaret, "please tell me of your day." After he did so, Margaret made her request. "Father, I have forgot how to write mine name. Would you be so kind as to teach me again?"

"Who taught you?"

"No one, Father. Several years ago I discovered it writ on a parchment and struggled to copy it in dirt. Now I remember but the big first part."

"Why do you want to write it?"

"I want to surprise King Henry when I sign mine marriage contract with more than just a mark."

"Margaret, for your own protection, I will not teach you. It is against the laws of nature for a woman to read much less to write her own name or to be able to write at all." Father Gregory paused. "Most high-born men cannot do it. Only priests, and so it must remain. Risk it not, or you will suffer. Someone might even name you a witch and get you burned. Forget what you saw and never attempt to copy it. I am only warning you, not trying to be cruel. Truth is, I would suffer great punishment if I taught you." Father Gregory placed his hand over hers, "Swear you will ask no one else. I want you to live."

A witch! Is burning what men do to keep women in their places? Shaken, Margaret swore a holy oath as Father dictated it. *Do as he says. Forget even what little I recall. Not safe. I have already been in trouble with a priest for bathing and washing too much. Now I wear a sword. Even if it is by the king's command, doing so makes me an unnatural woman. That I can use it is even worse. Never challenge priests. They can have me excommunicated, or worse. Burned as a witch! Please, God, protect me. Make me forget how to write that tiny part of mine name.*

Father patted her hand. "Good girl. Sir Hughes has eaten and awaits your aid." Father stood, put his hand on her head as he blessed her, and left the hall. *Do a woman's duty now. Remember to pray to God to heal him. Aloud. I forgot that part yesterday. Overstep mine bounds as a woman only when I must or suffer the consequences. Father Manntun will see to it. Of that, I am cert.*

Sunday passed quietly. After Mass and breaking her fast, again with bread and boiled water, Margaret stayed on the dais. She looked down the hall much bigger than her father's. Though a single door, the main entrance was on the left side at the other end of the building so winds did not extinguish the fire in the pit down the center of the room. The far end warmed those entering. The near end warmed the feet of those on the dais as the length warmed those at the tables on both side of the fire pit. Margaret watched smoke rise and disappear out three small ceiling holes. *A better design than one big one. Better chance to prevent rain from extinguishing the fire.* She grieved the stalls on either side were empty of grain sacks. The knights had taken the left-side stalls for their clothing and gear. Servants had scrubbed clean the tables and benches on either side of the long fire pit. At night they became the platforms for sleeping, one or two on a trestle table, one on each bench. No one slept on the rushes walked on with muddy boots; they were full of food debris and were homes for critters. On her dais twenty inches above the floor, she could see and be seen. The firelight created shadows behind the men. The roof supports created stalls behind them, which were so dark they seemed to disappear. *Empty, except for the men's weapons and gear. Please God, may we fill them to the roof with sacks of grain come harvest time, so all live.* The hall smelled more of sweat and human odors than of what little food had been consumed. *Too gray and brown. We need more color, more liveliness in here. Better food, and more of it, will help everyone. Remember to order the Saxons to burn more firewood. That should brighten the place and help it to feel more cheerful.*

On the dais, two tables sat eight across and two on the ends. Behind her, two storage rooms were divided by an aisle that led to a back door. A sleeping platform for male guests topped the rooms and back aisle. The side door to her right led to the kitchen and the outdoor baking oven. Fearful of fire, no builder put the those in the hall or even near it.

She checked three knights' slight wounds before calling Hughes forward. "Your skin is still pink and only a little warm. The swelling around the stitches has declined. Your forehead is still cool. I am hopeful of your healing." Margaret changed the inner bandage. She used the honey sparingly.

"Must you do this?" Hughes asked. "Will you have to confess working on Sunday?"

"Treating the sick and safeguarding the land never stops, Sir Hughes. Besides, I am just looking and visiting. Nothing to confess." *Oh God, I am only helping your own. I seek Your forgiveness, not his.* Margaret excused herself and took to her bed on the guest platform. Norman and Saxon alike lazed away the day. Not moving or napping saved energy. The Normans and the few called to be servants supped on fish stew.

When Roussel noticed Margaret only betook of bread and water, he asked, "How long?"

Margaret shrugged. "Until after Mass Sunday next."

Roussel pushed his round to her. "Take this. We have much to do on the morrow, and you need your strength."

"Thank you, sirrah."

Margaret's using the less formal address was her first effort at friendship. That he did not ask her to say "Sir Roussel" informed her he accepted her gesture. *Use it only when no one else could hear.* "What think you of mine people?"

"No slaves or freemen and only one sokemen. All villeins. Cormac said they supported de Warenne—or seemed to—until

His Royal Highness defeated him. Now they 'appear' to be loyal to the king. I trust them not. They are Saxons."

Margaret quoted what Caitlin had taught her. "They are farmers, who want protection for their families and crops. Leave them to their own ends, and they will be loyal to whoever defends them and keeps the laws. If we let them hold mainly to their Saxon laws, they will tolerate our Norman ones."

Roussel repeated an old saying. "Until they can find a Saxon leader who promises to rid the land of Normans."

"They have not found one in thirty-five years. They are not likely to now. I remember Sir Charles' Saxons preferred King Henry over his brother Robert over a year ago. Saxon leaders wrested that agreement of Prince Henry, then supported him. His Royal Highness has given them no reason for them to change to Robert, a weak wastrel. His Royal Highness's defeat of his brother, de Belleme, and de Warenne last July proves he is his father's rightful heir. Anyone who even thinks of rising against the king will die or face banishment. What he needs now is an heir." Margaret's mind flashed as she saw the face of the infant princess. *First a son, poisoned and now a girl. Please God, an heir.*

"God willing, the next babe. And soon."

"God willing," she said as she thought a quick prayer to support her words. Margaret spoke her "God give you good rest" to each at the table and went abed.

After Mass Monday everyone stood outside the church. Lord Bedwin, Sir Robert and the rented knights left with Sir Richard's shrouded body fastened to his horse. Gailard, Giraud and Claude mounted their horses to escort Reeve, Aldcot and Elstan atop the empty wagon. Margaret asked them to repeat their shopping list before handing the coin purse and permission letter to Gailard. "We hope you are home by Wednesday dark. I want your gardens replanted before Second Sunday."

"As do we, my lady," replied Felamaere.

Margaret turned to Father Gregory. "Father, we have been together long and seen much. I shall miss your wise counsel and gentle ways. Oxfordshire is far. I fear I shall never again see you."

"As God wills it, my child." Father Gregory took her hands into his.

Why is it not an insult when you say it?

The priest walked her away from the crowd. "His Royal Highness has given you good men, Lady Margaret. Please heed their counsel. Even wearing that sword, you are still but a girl. You have winning ways. You did well with the milk and Erwina. Use those same ways on your knights and they will follow you."

"Yes, Father, I will remember." Margaret added, "I remember everything you have told me."

"One more thing, my dear. Father Manntun fears losing his place and being banished. Make peace with him—and soon." The priest leaned in close. "I know you can charm when you will. Priest or not, he is still a man and has his pride."

Margaret smiled. "Yes, Father. I shall do that. I ask a great favor of you, Father. I owe mine tithe from the king's gift to the Bishop of Reading." She pulled two large leather bags from her mantle inside pockets. "Eleven pounds, ten pence. I trust you to see he receives it. Shall you do that for me?"

"I shall. I am glad you handed it to me away from the others Too great a temptation."

"Please ask for a receipt from the bishop or his agent and give the receipt to Sir Gailard for mine records."

Father Gregory chuckled. "So the bishop cannot claim you never sent the tithe and ask for it again. You are a clever girl. I shall do as you ask."

Before you go, may I have your blessing? And a hug?" The old man gave them. As they embraced, Margaret whispered into Father Gregory's ear, "Please remember you are always welcome here. I can support two priests."

Father Gregory backed from her slowly.

"You are dear to me, Margaret. I pray for you every day."

"And I you."

Gray-haired and thin as he was, Father placed his foot on the wheel hub and easily hopped onto the seat.

Margaret stood apart. The wagon pulled away as her knights not on watch and the Saxons waved and said "fare thee well" and "safe journey."

They are so thin; their garments are too shabby to be warm. They need new boots, clothing. Margaret noted the men's tunics were both raveled at the sleeves and darkened with sweat circles under their arms. The bottom hems were torn and shredding. The women seemed to have taken better care of their tunics, but they were still thin from too much use. Margaret guessed they had not received their clothing allotment the previous Easter and were trying to stay modest with the worn garments their lord should have replaced. Most of the men and women scampered over the cold ground because they were bare-footed as were their children. *They will sicken and die without better clothing. Wait not for mid-lent to give them cloth. Do it today. With this cold weather, they need clothing and footwear now. I pray some women hid their bone needles; I have only mine iron needle.*

Margaret observed parents swinging little ones to their hips, taking the hands of their older children, and walking toward their homes. Jorgon led Night to Margaret and watched them greet each other. He lifted her to her woman's riding chair and held Night's head as she settled in and tied herself to the seat. Margaret took up the reins and followed the wagon party down the path. Behind her, Sirs Roussel, Claude and Sauville followed. Margaret smelled the heads before she saw them.

Rank. Foul. Putrid. Margaret wanted to look away. *You ordered this. Now*
harden yourself enough to look. She saw scavengers had already dug at the rock-lined graves. *The wagon's passing likely scattered animals into the brush.* Margaret looked up to see a row of poles on each side of the path where it met the king's road. She spotted the back of heads—one skull stove in, like a bloody roast half eaten; another, with curly auburn hair, untouched; still a third with blood clumped in the wispy blond hair but no pieces missing. There was dried blood down the poles, and fleshy tendrils of skin and flesh like dirty cloth waving in the wind; the sight nauseated her.

Look not away. They are watching me. Margaret followed Roussel left and down the king's road until Gailard, Claude and the wagon disappeared around a bend. When they turned back, Margaret joined Roussel. They rode two and two until they reached their road. Margaret stopped Night, who again snorted at the smells. With one hoof he pawed the ground.

Margaret looked at the visages of each of her attackers. Six to the left, five to the right. Some looked terror-stricken; some looked merely dead.

"A terrible sight," she said aloud.

"A fearful warning," responded Roussel.

Dry eyed, Margaret looked at the king's man.

When he saw she was moved, but not quaking, Roussel told her, "Please go first, my lady. You missed an important custom the first time you took this road. Now is a good time to name your estate. We will follow. Please stop when you see the stone which marks the start of your land."

When Margaret reached the large gray rock exposed about two feet above ground, she stopped Night.

"Lady Margaret, the custom is for a new owner to name his land before he first steps on it. As the king gave you this land, you may name it."

"Is that not the office of mine husband when he arrives?"

"Yes, but who knows how soon that will be. Mayhap you can consider the name you give to be temporary. What will you choose?"

A name. A name. What name? Think.

Margaret smiled to herself. She flicked a rein end on Night's flank. As he sprang forward and past the stone, Margaret whispered, "Mine!"

Roussel was so shocked at her boldness he looked away and dismissed his thought to chastise her. As he rode past the stone marker, he reminded himself she was but a girl and odd one at that.

9

Creating Order

Margaret waved Caitlin forward and gestured to the stool next to her. She placed her elbow on the dais table, her chin in her hand, and turned her head so no one could read her lips.

"How did you three precede me?"

"We hid at an inn on a back street until we learned your news. We set out and got rides when we could. I regret I only had time to clean the hall and create our bed."

"Jorgon and Dena are staying with a widow. Please remind me to tell Reeve to allot them a plot and garden and to include them when he assigns crop land."

"As they are free, I am surprised they are staying."

"He said for now, but for how long I know not. I pray they will stay, but Dena is unhappy. He will do what he must for her." Margaret stared at her former nurse. "Caitlin, I cannot be both lord and lady."

"Glad you admit it."

Margaret shook her head when Cormac motioned he wanted to leave. She smiled, pleased at Caitlin glancing his way.

"I am too old for a nurse. Are you willing to take mine place? Be the lady of hall and beyond, a chatelaine, while I act the lord?"

"Having a chatelaine who is not Norman is not usual," she retorted. "I doubt they will obey me. Even though I told them I preceded the new owner and had mine instructions, Bedwin first refused me entry. Then Cook balked at my orders. The threats I made in your name just to get this hall ready!"

"They will comply if I command it."

"In whose name?"

"The king's."

"Ha! This lot are tree branches. They blow whichever way then does the wind."

"Then I will be a big wind," affirmed Margaret. "I will command in the king's name and in mine unseen lord's. Were he actually gone serving the king, they would obey me." *Will that work? I dare not tell them my lord is on his way, for that would be a lie.*

"But you have not your lord nor is he away in service. They may not listen."

What can I do if they defy me? Father will not support me. If Roussel takes control, I will be reduced to deciding menus and mending clothes. I am done for.

"Do they need a gentle hand or a hard fist?"

"Good thinking. Be both, gentle as a lady but hard as a lord when need be." Caitlin finished with her best advice. "Switch from one to the other instantly if they balk or disobey. Keep them off balance so they never know before which they stand. Even the knights."

Margaret grinned at Caitlin's sage words.

"By the by. There is no 'they' in this hall. Only Cook and me."

"Please send her to me."

Margaret straightened and pushed back her shoulders. *Like a lord.* She watched a plain, gray-haired woman of middling girth enter through the kitchen door and shuffle toward her. The woman wiped her hands on a filthy apron and kept her eyes lowered. Margaret stared malevolently. In the silence, Cook looked up then gave a quick, shallow dip.

"Again!"

Margaret's tone threatened Cook's safety. The men in the hall stopped visiting to watch. Without looking up, the woman curtsied low.

As an afterthought, she muttered, "M'lady."

Margaret dropped her voice to a lower range to sound more authoritative, more manly.

"Never forget." Margaret glared at those in the hall. They looked away. Keeping her expression hard, she turned back to Cook. "How came you to this job?"

"I am a widow, my lady. Mine son works the land now. I dislike his wife. When the king's men arrived and asked for a cook, I came here."

Much to the relief of your son and his wife, I wager. "Are you an experienced cook?"

"No, my lady."

"If I permit you to stay, you shall meet mine conditions." When the cook did not respond, Margaret reminded herself, *Be more lord-like. Expect no answer. Assume obedience. Command.* "Caitlin shall train you. When mine lord arrives, you shall meet his food demands. Until told otherwise, you shall obey Caitlin in all matters related to hall, kitchen, gardens, bailey and land; she is mine chatelaine. Understood?"

"Yes, my lady."

"Do you wish to stay as mine cook?"

Cook answered with a proper, respectful curtsey and, "Yes, my lady."

Margaret hid her relief. *I need staff. That she stays may help me gain some.*

"What of your helpers? Do you work well with them? Do you want any replaced?" With each question Margaret softened her manner a bit more.

"I have no helpers, my lady," admitted Cook in a hurt tone.

"NO helpers!" Margaret acted shocked. "You do all this work alone? Were I you I would be tired and cross too." Margaret shifted on her stool, softened her back. She asked kindly, "Tell me, Cook, how many helpers want you?"

Cook lifted her eyes, glanced at her new lady and away before she ventured to look at Margaret's chin.

Well, she knows some etiquette. I have hope for her.

"Three, my lady. If you please. A scullery, a chopper, a baker, or a cook's helper if she is skilled. I enjoy making bread."

"Yes, your bread is good."

Even with this compliment Margaret kept her tone low, her manner formal.

"Thank you, my lady."

Ah, the crack of a smile. "Have you suggestions as to whom?"

"Mine nephew can be a good scullery. He is big and strong and can wrestle wood and cauldrons. He listens to me, follows mine orders." Cook paused and said cautiously, "He is … a bit … simple. But he is a good boy."

She expects me to reject him because of his defect. Surprise her. "As long as you can keep him in hand, Cook, you may send for him. Any others?"

"Not that I can think of, my lady."

As hard and dour as you are, I guess not. "I shall get you two workers. Please ask Caitlin to come to me at her convenience." Margaret again stiffened her spine and dropped her tone. "I dismiss you."

"Yes, my lady. Thank you, my lady." Cook curtsied.

After Cook left the hall, Margaret caught Cormac's eye and gestured him to join her.

"Thank you for waiting, Cormac. How are mine Saxons faring?"

"Starving but hopeful, my lady. Your sharing the milk has softened most. They are pleased you are spending your dowry for their new garden seeds and for food. They scrounge the forest daily…"

"And eat bark or acorn soup," Margaret finished for him.

"Or nothing at all. Many are starving. Expect a few to die."

"Not if I have the coin to stop it. We need them, Cormac. Every one of them. We also need a rich harvest if we are to last the winter. God willing, we will have it, but it will take the hard work of every man, woman, and child. At our next trip to Reading, we must purchase more boots, leather for boot making and servant cloth. The Saxons are practically naked so thin are their garments." Margaret remembered the cook's apron. "And soap. Add soap next time. She paused before she dared ask, "And their grievances?"

"They worried over being led by a woman. They thought you soft until you put heads on pikes. They admired that. And you defying Father Manntun. They shun him."

"I noted that at Mass. They speak not to him and walk away when they see him coming. Know you why?"

Cormac nodded. He glanced around and changed his position so no one else saw his lips.

"Father Manntun supported de Warenne in all matters. Even when de Warenne's acts were questionable or illegal."

"How so?"

"De Warenne took their seed grain for 'storage' over the winter and charged them for its safekeeping. No payment, no seed in the spring. Of course, they fell into debt. He also held for himself double what they owed for growing their own crops. That kept them on the edge of starvation. Forced to pay their rents and debts with livestock, the villeins further depleted their winter stores. They fear you will extract as much as he did—or more—just to prove you are 'man enough' to rule them, unmarried as you are."

"Father Manntun was expected to protect them, force de Warenne to follow the laws, report his actions to his bishop and to the king's reeve."

Cormac spoke slowly to emphasize his next words.

"Father Manntun enjoyed the largess de Warenne provide, including white bread."

"Like the royals!?" Aghast, Margaret looked both shocked and angry.

"Exactly. De Warenne ate and acted a royal. Belleme pledged to raise his rank after he disposed of Henry and became king himself. One, or the other, or both of them, promised Manntun a bishopric or greater. For the false deference they gave him, de Warenne expected a free hand to do whatever he liked. That is how the traitor raised some of the coin he needed to buy men when he and Belleme revolted."

"Father Manntun gave a traitor a free hand to abuse his people?"

Short of seduction, failure to protect his flock from their lord's immoral and unlawful actions is the most serious offense a priest can commit. What can I do to him? Dare I even try? He might have his bishop excommunicate me. Yet, I must do something. With coin and a traitor on the estate, Belleme's army could easily overrun us and take everything. We are in danger from within.

"Nothing, my lady. You cannot turn him out and send him back to his bishop as would a lord. You cannot ask the bishop for another priest. He will not listen to a female."

Margaret half lowered her lids and in a throaty voice averred, "I can threaten him. Make him think I will turn him out. Scare him enough to change."

"And if he does not?" From her expression, Cormac knew two points: she had a plan; she was not about to share it. When she spoke not, Cormac changed their talk. "My lady, the accounts book is a mess. Written over and hardly readable. How do you wish me to proceed?"

"Does it have any empty pages?"

"It does."

"I need an exact list of every family: husband, wife, children with names and ages. Record the status of the husband or widow: freeman, villein, sokeman, whatever, plus skills like carpenter or black smith. A complete accounting. The sizes of their gardens, the amount of crop land they are owed. Their debts to the estate. Boundaries of each house and garden. Everything."

"Like the King's Book? The one started in 1085 by William the Conqueror."

"Yes, exactly. I purchased a new accounts book for mine lord when he arrives, but we need it now. After you show me your findings and we are cert your information is accurate, you will transfer it to the new book so it will be ready for mine lord."

"I will begin anon."

"Please keep me informed of your progress." Margaret added, "I almost forgot. Please instruct Reeve to give Jorgon a plot for a hut and garden. Ask Reeve to also assign him crop land. Mayhap, if I set them up in the village, Dena will agree to live here."

"You want Jorgon to stay?"

Margaret nodded. "Please ask what they need to start their own household and add the items to the list the next time we send a wagon to Reading." She added, "Especially the metal items. He may not have the coin for such expensive items. Tell Jorgon and Dena they are a portion of Jorgon's pay, so they will think not I am trying to bribe them. Then record their expenses against his coming income."

To Father Manntun, Margaret sent an invitation to dine with her to show him she was still consuming only bread and water. *Act innocent. Learn what I can from his tone, his words. Let him be superior for now. See if he softens to me. Calm down. Breathe normally. Remember his power over all of us. Follow Father Gregory's advice.*

Margaret gave Father Manntun a small smile. "Father, what happens to the tithe we send to the Church?"

The priest retorted, "Why do you ask, my child?"

Endeavoring not to bristle, Margaret straightened as she thought: *Again 'my child'? I must tolerate it. Not for long!* In neutral tones Margaret replied, "I remember what was done on mine father's land, but I know not if it is the same for all estates. Please inform me what is done here." She regarded his eyes and saw him internally debating what to tell her.

Father Manntun admitted, "It should be the same, but each bishop may change the ratio if circumstances such as the weather or war create hardship or need."

I expect more specific information. Freeze and wait. Margaret did not blink, did not move.

"Well," Manntun began again, "of the ten percent to Holy Mother Church, I save a tenth and the rest is sent to the bishop. He holds two-tenths for the needs of the bishopric and sends the rest to the Archbishop of Canterbury." When Margaret nodded, Father continued, "The archbishop hold two-tenths for the good of the country. The remaining half is sent to Rome for the good of the whole church. The pope sends back aid for special circumstances or for projects the Church wants done."

"What becomes of the tenth you keep?"

"I hold it for the poor and needy—and for mine bread and needs as well. I also use it to pay villeins to repair the church or to do other needed tasks."

"Thank you, Father." Hiding her anger at his misuse of his office, Margaret kept her face and voice neutral. "I have another question. If a man strikes his wife, can anyone stop him?"

"No. She is his property. Not even her father can stop him. Though he can threaten. Why ask you that?"

"I am aware of a husband who strikes his wife." *Say no names, even if he asks.*

"I regret, Lady Margaret, you may do nothing. In fact, if you go to her aid, she is likely to suffer worse when they are private at home."

"Can you not attend to it?" Margaret asked hopefully.

"Only if I see it done." Manntun thought and added, "Because of the sanctity of Confession, I can say nothing of what I am told there nor can I do anything unless I have the man's permission." He paused again; then he finished with, "I dare not ask for permission. If she reports being hit, he will realize she has informed me."

"And you cannot tell me you recognize of whom I speak; you can tell me nothing." Father Manntun nodded as he kept his eyes on her face. *A strange system. Because Confession is secret, he can say or do nothing. So a priest has some limitations after all.* "Thank you, Father. Now I have a request of you. I have mine document from the king on the platform. May I please place it in the chest under the altar with the other estate documents?"

"Of course, my child. That is the safe place for it. Your copy stays with the land." He added, "I stayed in the church while the attackers were here. I threatened them with excommunication if they so much as stepped inside. No one was going to pillage my church or burn our documents!"

"How brave and wise of you, Father Manntun." *And how politic of me to say so.* She watched him puff his chest. "I used almost all the honey you sent. Thank you Father, for your help in healing the wounded. If any remains, I will return it to you. If you will excuse me, Father, I will fetch the parchment."

He seems reasonable enough when he thinks he is in charge. Cormac did report he was well-liked before he agreed to de Warenne's false promises. Mayhap I can appeal to his pride and his position. Remind him he can be loved again. When Margaret returned wearing her scarf and mantle, three knights stood and took up their cloaks. The group left the warmth of the hall and stepped into the remains of another gray day. Fortunately, the wind had diminished with the coming sunset. At the church, one man entered, drawn sword in hand. After he returned to the door and motioned them forward, the other two knights stayed outside and stood guard.

Father Manntun pulled the chest from under the altar from the front. He removed a key from a pocket and unlocked the chest.

"Father, I need to see the documents. Please tell me what each is."

"I keep each family's records on a separate parchment. Names, births, christenings, marriages, deaths. When a new couple is formed, I start a parchment for them."

He piled several of them on one side of the altar.

Margaret counted. "Twenty-five families."

"Including one widower and two widows. These are royal papers."

As he picked up each, Margaret saw the wax seals.

"The Crown keeps one document. The land gets the other." He named them: "the original land grant from King William the First to the first Baron de Warenne. At his death, William the Second transferred the grant to the second Baron de Warenne. On it I recorded his banishment and the return of the land to the Crown." He reached for Margaret's rolled and rib-tied parchment. "And now your document granting you this land." Father Manntun placed the parchment roll next to the other two at the bottom of the chest.

"Next will be my lord's copy of our marriage contract, transferring ownership to my lord, will it not?"

"It will," answered the priest as he set the other parchments atop the royal ones.

"Where do you keep the church record book, the one where you recorded Sir Walter's and Sir Richard's deaths and such?"

"In mine lean-to. I write in it daily, so I keep it to hand."

"Thank you, Father, for instructing me in the hall and here. If you will excuse me, I must see to other tasks."

"Go with God, my child."

Margaret bobbed a quick curtsey, turned and left. *That went better than I thought it would. Stop thinking ill of the man. Think he is trying to be nice to me. Remember what Mother said. "People become what you think of them. Think better of them. Expect better and well you may get it from them."*

Tuesday, Margaret inspected Hughes' arm. She wrapped herself in her mantle and scarf to complete her outside errands. She instructed the milkmaid on her duties to both the milking cow and the young one carrying her first calf; she looked in on the goats and chickens. After inspecting the kitchen and promising Cook fabric for a new apron, Margaret rode Night to inspect the planting, still guarded, of course. Later she held meeting after meeting about matters inside the bailey and out. Before Margaret began her bedtime prayers, she reviewed her day. *Each time someone accepts mine decision, I prove I am worthy of being followed. Ask only what is reasonable and necessary so they are willing to give it. Caitlin's advice is working. What I must do next will determine whether they will follow mine lead. Whether Father will stay or go. Dear God, please save us all from de Belleme and his army. From rebellion. I cannot have a traitor among us. I must do this. Oh God, guide mine words; let me succeed. I want us safe. Your will, Oh God, in all things.*

After finishing her regular prayers, Margaret silently plotted and practiced words a long time before she wearily fell into sleep.

10

Father Manntun

Wednesday morning began with Mass as did every day of their lives. After the service, Margaret waited outside. Expecting her to give orders, Margaret's villeins stopped and waited. She smiled at the children as they held their parents hands or hid behind them.

"I shall walk you into the village if you have clean hands." Margaret held out her arms and wiggled her fingers. "Does any child want to join me?"

Girls giggled and looked to their mothers. At her nod, they stepped forward. Margaret took their hands in hers and turned toward the huts."

"I like holding your hands. What are your names?"

The older one answered, "I'm eight. I am Alura. Hludaelf is six. How old are you?'

"I am pleased to meet you." Margaret turned her head and spoke to those following her. "When I am about, I am happy to walk with children who have washed their hands." Each girl walked her lady to her door. "Thank you for the lovely walk, Alura and Huldaelf. I hope I see you again soon." Margaret turned away and let her guards escort her down the lane, up the road, and through the palisade gate.

Those in the hall broke their fasts with a bowl of pottage so small they could have held the ball of grains in one palm.

"My lady, why put you a bucket and a rag outside the church? Hold hands with those girls?" asked Sir Roussel.

"Sirrah, from the Saxons on her estate, mine mother learned washing hands keeps people healthier. Though Mother knew not why. She made us children wash our hands before we ate. None of us has ever been sickly, so it must do something good. Then, she insisted we wash our hands before we touched a woman ready to deliver her babe so she would be less likely to sicken or die afterward. These children are weak with hunger and in danger. Mayhap washing their hands will help keep them alive."

"You do this even though you know not why it works? Think you this is God's will?"

Be careful not to be called a witch because I do something different. "Of course, it is God's will if we are well, sick, or dead. The bucket is outside the church, which teaches us God's rules our lives. I have prayed over this. I asked Our Lord what He wants me to do here. If the children stay well, I am doing His will. If they sicken, He is telling me to stop. I await Our Lord's judgement on mine deed." At Roussel's nod of acceptance at her reasoning, Margaret smiled back. *Please God, let that be enough to save me. I pray the Saxons like my practice. Mother used it so it must have some benefit, even if we have no soap. Soap. At the next trip, I must ask for some.*

After servants cleared the tables, Margaret ordered the hall emptied. She apologized to her knights that they must find warmth elsewhere for a time. No one was to re-enter until she opt the main door. Margaret wanted complete privacy—as complete as it could be in such a small community—to proceed with her problem. The five of them sat on a bench in the middle of the hall so they would not be heard should someone accidentally enter. The guards on the walls had been instructed to order everyone away from the building.

Sir Verel and Reeve sat opposite the priest. Father Manntun sat between Margaret and Roussel. Margaret smiled disingenuously at Father Manntun.

Wanting no one else to overhear them, Margaret spoke barely above a whisper. "What we say here is deep secret. You may never speak to anyone other than who is here about these matters. No one must ever overhear you should you speak to one of us outside our meeting. Do you understand?" At their nods and assents, she proceeded. "We are in grave danger. I have an idea what to do, but I also want to hear your thoughts."

"What danger?" asked Reeve.

"Lord Robert de Belleme is plotting against the king. He built an army and intends to take the crown for himself. Sir Roussel knows the traitor is hiding in the forests somewhere in the realm. With mine dowry chest, we are his perfect target. He can replenish his supplies and pay his men. Belleme knows this estate because de Warenne allied with him in this treachery against His Royal Highness. De Warenne left behind one who supported him. If Belleme is anywhere near, he will attack. We are neither ready nor have sufficient knights to stop his army."

109

Three looked to the one. Reeve glowered. Sir Verel looked confused.

"I am no supporter of Belleme," Father Manntun averred.

Margaret began her case against the priest. "Father Manntun, you sat with him at table in this hall, heard his treason, and did not report it to the king."

"That is a lie! I never heard Lord Belleme speak treason within mine hearing."

"Someone overheard de Warenne promise you a bishopric when Belleme was king. Deny you that?"

Manntun was silent for a moment. "That person lied."

"More than one individual heard him promise you more than once. Each is trustworthy."

Manntun accused Reeve, "You did this! Liar!"

"Reeve was not present when de Warenne promised the bishopric." *Thank you, God, for Cormac's skills in getting people to talk.*

"While you served de Warenne, you did not object when he took not twenty percent but forty percent of their harvest. You ordered the villeins to obey when he took their seed grain to store it. You said nothing to de Warenne when he took handfuls of grain from each bag as so-called 'rent' each spring before he handed back to the villeins' their own property. You served a traitor, not the people. You grieved when he left you behind. I challenge you to deny any of this!"

Manntun spoke not.

Sir Roussel attacked next. "Has Belleme or any of his men contacted you? Are any of them near? Speak up, man!"

"I am no 'man.' I am a priest and you will respect me!"

"You are a confirmed traitor we will turn over to King Henry if you are not immediately forthcoming," promised Roussel in icy tones.

Manntun flicked his robes nervously and dropped his eyes to his knees. "I have seen no one. No one has contacted me."

"Look into mine eyes when you repeat that," ordered Roussel. "I will see if you lie."

Manntun did so.

"You committed wrongs. You are untrustworthy. Now, you will rectify what you have done!" Roussel demanded.

Father Manntun looked across the table and asked, "Is that knight going to kill me?"

"No, Father," replied Margaret. "Sir Verel's office is otherwise." She continued more gently than she had begun. "I want my people to love God, love the Church, and respect their priest. At present they do only one of those. Cert you have felt their ire; it fills the church at every Mass and Vespers."

Manntun glanced toward Reeve then looked toward Margaret. "What do you demand?"

"I need you to change," answered Margaret. "Mine terms will seem harsh. If you are willing, then I will keep you in your office and let mine lord decide what to do with you. If you are not willing, Sir Verel will take you safely to your bishop. You will ask for a different position. When the bishop asks why, Sir Verel will speak the truth. He will also carry my request for a different priest."

Father Manntun crossed his arms over his chest. "What terms?"

"First, in church you will vow, on the Holy Cross and to God, you are no longer a supporter of de Warenne or Belleme. You will vow to report to Sir Roussel, to me, or to any of mine men any sighting or contact with Belleme, his messenger, or any of his men."

"Agreed," stated Manntun.

"You will change your behavior toward mine Saxons. You will no longer eat at their tables unless they freely invite you. After de Warenne was banished, you ate every meal at the expense of each household by turns. You took food from children's mouths even though de Warenne had already taken more than his legal share. No more."

"The king's men took mine food and grain," Manntun rationalized. "What else was I to do?"

"You should have suffered with your flock, not causing them to suffer even more," retorted Margaret. "That is but the first change. I will give you your own grain. No longer do you demand of the women in the village they winnow and grind your grain, knead and bake your bread. You will ask who is willing to do so, and you will give her double the amount needed for each loaf. Half the grain is payment for your baker's labor."

"Nonsense! As their priest, I am owed certain privileges."

Margaret leaned toward him. "They have already tithed the Church. Each demand is another tithe. You will no longer double and treble their obligation. You will now wait for them to offer you service."

"They will never do that!"

Margaret gentled her voice, "Of course they will, Father. First you change. Then they test you. When they see you are constant in your changed ways and remain kind and thoughtful, they will relent, only a little a first and then more. That is when you will know."

"Know what?" huffed Manntun.

"They have forgiven you your past deeds." Margaret's gentle voice softened her words. "It will happen thus, Father. You pay double the grain for a round of bread. Not all, but many women will bake for you at that payment. After you thank the baker for her labor every time she makes bread for you, one woman will take pity on you. She will say, 'Oh Father, grain that is but half again a loaf is plenty of payment.' The other women will be angry she has set a lower price and chide her. She will come to your defense, and continue to bake your bread at that cost. Then another will want your business, so she will take only a quarter extra to bake your loaves. They will only do this after they have gotten back the food you took from them. Because they now set the cost of baking your bread, they will consider it fair and right. You will have your bread, and they will be rewarded and feel appreciated. Problem solved," Margaret ended cheerfully.

"You truly believe they will do this?" asked Father Manntun with incredulity.

"Of course, Father," replied Margaret airily, "but you must be patient while they test you. Now to the other changes. You will continue to dine in the hall with us at midday, but you will cook your own first and last meals. In this you become closer to the people. I will supply you with salt, butter, milk, and a ration of ale when we have them. You may ask Cook to teach you how to break your fast and to make soups for supper."

"You are undermining mine station," charged Manntun angrily.

"No, Father. You are still our priest; you are still in charge of our immortal souls. But you can best be our consciences when you are also an example of charity, of modesty, of kindness, and of all the good things you know how to be."

And once were, so Cormac was told. I must gain his assent. Now what was I going to say to get him to agree? Oh yes.

113

"Father, I am guessing de Warenne first tricked you and then threatened you. Am I correct?"

"Yes," Manntun said in a rush. "Yes, he did."

Margaret ignored the men's display of disbelief. She held Manntun's eyes on her and continued with, "Unfortunate it may be, the traitor has left you to repair your own reputation with those whom you serve. I believe you can do it. Be the good priest and the good example you were and can be again." *Is mine appeal to his better self working?*

She started her final requirement for change as a story. She gazed at the rafters and began. "When I young, we had the most wonderful priest. After Mass, Father Albin blessed us in our work for the day, offered a prayer for our safety, and reminded us to be good to one another. We children followed him when we could because we loved him so. He patted us on the head and told us when we behaved well. When we asked for a special favor, Father pressed our hands between his, and we prayed together. I still recall a prayer mine brother Charles recited. 'Please, God, let me stay on mine pony so Father will be proud of me. If I fall, may I not be harmed. Amen.' After every prayer, Father placed his hand upon our heads and said Latin words. He became old with us. When he died, we were inconsolable for months." No one spoke. Margaret looked directly at Father Manntun. "Be good to the children. What parent can resist that?"

Manntun retorted, "Is that why you give each child milk after Mass each day?"

"Partly," admitted Margaret evenly. "I also feed them because their swollen bellies told me of their starvation and the danger they are in. Their skin was gray; now it is getting pinker, and their eyes are brighter too."

"I suppose you will also hand out meat on Second Sunday."

"That depends on Reeve's and Aldcot's success in Reading."

"Every morning, during the day, every night, I pray to God to give us good planting time, rain when we need it, and a rich harvest. These people need a good year." Margaret turned to Reeve, "Reeve, Father Manntun will plant the land you apportion to him by himself. He will weed it, grow his summer vegetables, harvest his own crops."

"This is too much! I will not bear it," raged Manntun. "You truly want me gone!"

"That I do," stated Sir Roussel forcefully. "I want not your blood on our hands." At the priest's questioning look, Roussel continued, "If Belleme attacks, the Saxons may blame you. I want them not to commit murder."

"They dare not! God would send them to Hell."

"Please remember, Father, our previous king got an arrow to his heart in a supposed 'accident' while he was hunting." Verel shifted on the bench and added, "Who failed to see the king before him? Very suspicious, I say, and bad precedent. One of Saxons might remember this and act the same."

"Father Manntun." Margaret called his attention to her. "I do want you to stay. Mine reasons are several." Margaret looked at the others before she continued. "You understand the strengths and needs of these people far better than I do. Mine sources say you were a good priest to them before de Warenne's treachery. The Saxons trusted you once and will again. For a Norman, you speak excellent Saxon, and both groups need you. Also, you can inform me of what has gone before, what has succeeded and what has not."

"I doubt your ability to change, Father," admitted Reeve. "You liked your privileges too much."

"Decide not at this moment," offered Margaret. "Think on it. Tell me your choice after we dine on the morrow. If you wish to leave, Sir Verel will escort you. If you stay, you can always decide otherwise if you think mine conditions are unbearable."

Please God, let him choose aright. Your will, Oh Lord, in all things.

Margaret switched to her next plan. "Now to the matter of Belleme and his army. Father, after Mass tomorrow, I need you to announce I will make an important announcement outside. I intend to issue a Seon ond Heour on Belleme, his men, and any who serve him."

"A what?'" asked Sir Verel.

Margaret explained, "It means 'see and call out' in Saxon. We Normans say Hure e Crie. Should any one of us see or have knowledge of Belleme or his men, that person must tell as many as possible at once. While I want not to frighten our people, the more eyes and ears we have searching, the better our chance to learn Belleme's location. We make such an order only under the most dangerous conditions. I will speak it in both Norman and Saxon so all of us will know what to do. We must protect ourselves, and Hure e Crie will help warn us. Father?"

"I will speak that announcement."

"Please remember, Father's decisions and actions may not be discussed. After I declare the warning, we will set out sentinels, both Saxon and Norman."

Sir Roussel ordered, "Please come with me and Verel, Father. We leave for church. Stay or go, you will swear your loyalty to our King and vow to protect Lady Margaret, her household and these people."

"If you leave by the main door and leave it open, the knights and servants will return," Margaret reminded the men. When Scandy entered through the servants' door, she asked him to find Caitlin.

I just behaved like a man, a lord. I may have succeeded it gaining what we need, but at what cost? Did they accept what I did out only out of fear of Belleme and attack? Will they accept the next time I order something done or will they call me a weak girl and deny me? What to do next? Stay acting like a lord? Switch back to behaving like a lady? Ah, Caitlin!

Margaret gestured Caitlin to take the place next to her. "I just ordered a priest, Caitlin. I commanded him, defied his wishes, and ordered him what to do. Have I gone mad?"

"Not yet, but trying to be a lord may make you so," warned Caitlin. "Putting on a man's airs does not make you one. Think on this. After you assume a man's ways, later it will be difficult to dispense with them when you have a lord and must let him rule. I understand you must do what is needed to set this estate aright, but you must also be careful, Margaret, to remain a woman."

"What else could I have done? His previous support of de Warenne puts all of us in danger."

"You should have kept Father Gregory."

"That was not possible."

"Then Father Manntun needed putting in his place. You should have seen him when I arrived. He strutted about, making demands beyond his station."

"Yet we must confess to a priest who was bought by a traitor. I fear him, and how he might utilize the Church to harm us." *I must be careful with him. Win his good graces. I pray he has some.* Margaret changed the topic with, "Cormac is here as mine seneschal. He said he asked for the position to be near you." When Margaret saw no change in Caitlin's expression, she added, "I told him he may stay only if his doing so upsets you not."

"It upsets me not," replied Caitlin with a neutral tone.

"I need him, Caitlin. I need friendly faces about me."

"Whose face is he?" asked Caitlin pointedly.

"I know not," revealed Margaret. "Elstan asked to come with me, and he is the queen's cousin, but Cormac served her and her family for a long time. One of them is a royal spy in our household. Does it matter which one?"

"Not really," lied Caitlin. She wanted Elstan to be the queen's spy even as she suspected otherwise.

"I will see how well he performs his duties, and then I will decide whether to keep him." Margaret knew not what else to say. She took Caitlin's hands in hers and pleaded, "Please pray for me, Caitlin. Pray a husband arrives soon. Pray I do well until he does so."

"Every day, mine pet. Every day." Caitlin leaned forward and touched her forehead to Margaret's, Caitlin's "I love you" signal.

Margaret reached for her friend; they hugged each other hard. When they released each other, Margaret's eyes were moist. "You are half mother and half sister to me."

"I am an Irish slave," countered Caitlin as she spoke her innermost feelings of inferiority.

"Not since mine first year! And not here!" Margaret touched her forehead to Caitlin's and whispered with hard resolve, "Here you are mine closest friend. You are mine ally. You are mine right hand. Your rank may not be that of a lady, but all had best treat you as one. They will answer to me should they not. Caitlin, please act the lady, so I can act the lord. I cannot command this of you, but I do respectfully ask it of you. Ple-ea-se."

"I can deny you nothing," Caitlin whispered back.

Margaret straightened and in full voice reacted. "Ha! You deny me all the time. You are a worse conscience than was Mother!"

"Good!" retorted Caitlin with a broad smile. She held Margaret's hands.

Sir Demetre entered the hall. Uncert how to address the pair whose familiarity with each other each was well known, he uttered, "Lady-ies?"

Margaret squeezed Caitlin's hand as a signal to respond. "Yes?" they replied in unison.

11

Fear and Fire

Despite the darkness, men came out of their houses to watch the wagon take the switch to the bailey gate. The gate opt, and the wagon and knights disappeared. From the palisade a guard yelled, "Reeve!" A shadow moved toward the path. He too disappeared through the gate. Soon the Reeve stood beside the guard.

He yelled into the dark, "One man or woman from each household come to the bailey."

In a dark pierced by few torches, Margaret enjoyed distributing food from the wagon. She handed over a pregnant ewe to the milkmaid and ordered her to tie it in the barn. In the wagon, she started on top with the crates of rabbit pairs.

To the first villein, she said, "Keep them warm or they will drop their kits. Eat these on the next two Sundays or wait for them to keep breeding. Your choice. I shall get you no more." When she ran out of rabbit cages, she asked Reeve what to do.

"I will attend to it in the morn."

She gestured over the sacks of seeds and the boxes of garden vegetables toward Reeve with a mind for him to distribute. Jorgon took all the oats for the horses, cows and donkeys, and Margaret sent what wheat she thought she needed to the kitchen. Bolts of common cloth, boots, and leather hides filled one corner. Three sacks remained at the bottom of the wagon. Those she had carried through the hall's main door to keep them dry and safe.

Give this much now. I can distribute more later if need be. Wish I could afford imported barley, but that needs wait until we have a good harvest. No, a great one. Must get the cloth and leathers to the Saxons on the morrow. They need spare clothes as well as new. Next, the knights must hunt game. They will revolt if they eat not meat. Tell Roussel they may cook half what they catch away from the estate and only bring in half to share. That will please them. The rest of us still get some meat to keep our strength. Bread is good, but meat is better. Get this done first, then see what needs be done next.

Several men carried sacks of wheat and rye to Gytha, the aleman's widow. She took them inside and promised them ale as soon as possible.

Margaret addressed the remaining men. "After Mass come to the bailey with containers or sacks. I shall distribute wheat, one portion for every person in your household save the nursed babes. Remember to thank Reeve and Aldcot for the fine job they did in getting our supplies. Elstan too."

Men slapped the men on their backs with words of congratulations, praise and appreciation. The villeins returned home, and Margaret headed for the hall. Before removing her mantle, she stood close to the fire pit to warm her hands.

"Well done, my lady," began Roussel. "Rabbits, I had not thought of that. Breed often, grow fast."

"If they have the sense to feed them instead of eating them."

"Some will; a few will not. Those who keep them will have the advantage."

"And I will learn who are the clever ones who think ahead," added Margaret.

The next morn the men lined up for wheat while the women and children went to Erwina.

Now an old widower and a babe gone. We need more supplies or more will die. I cannot help a poorer dowry. I need people to work the land.

Escorted, Margaret walked into the village to meet Gytha. At the door cloth, she coughed twice as was customary. Gytha came out, saw her mistress and curtsied. "May I enter your home?" *I can see why an attacker grabbed you. Nice figure, beautiful face. Soft hazel eyes, now saddened by grief.*

"My lady," replied Gytha as she held the door cloth for Margaret.

Not round. Deep with the barrels in back. Two huts combined. Smells of mash. Clean and neat. Why is there a door in the back hut as well?

The boys held their forelocks as they nodded; the girl curtsied and blushed. Margaret guessed the boys looked like their father. They were thick-necked, a bit round in the middle, and stood on thick, sturdy legs. Each bore gray eyes and shocks of hair the color of wheat. Their big feet portended they would be tall when full grown. The girl was the picture of her mother, only smaller, with wheat-colored, wavy hair. blue eyes, and a slim build. They looked not as starved as the rest of the children. *Mayhap they had the advantage of being richer and better fed than the field villeins.*

"These are mine children, my lady. Linton is twelve; we named him after his father. Lindene is ten. Mine Goscelyn is eight; I am named Gytha after mine mother. The boys are learning ale making."

"I am so sorry they killed your husband, Gytha. You lost a good man. I am sorry your children lost their father. I shall continue to pray for the repose of his soul til the year and a day have passed."

Gytha curtsied. "Thank you, my lady."

"May we speak of ale making?" At Gytha's nod, Margaret began, "Linton Elder was a skilled aleman. I understand you two worked together and made excellent ale. You now head this household. If you are agreeable, I shall employ you as our alewife at the same pay your husband earned."

"Agreed," replied Gytha quickly. She had not expected to be paid as much as a man.

"That you are training your sons is good. Please continue to do so. What may I do to aid you?"

"My lady, know that after the attackers drank all the ale, even the new, undeveloped barrels, they came to the bailey and asked for the aleman to come out to make more. When Lord Bedwin told them whom they had killed, they left. They pissed in two of the barrels. Your household is large enough to need those barrels, so I asked Reeve to purchase two barrels on this last trip. I hope I did not overstep mine place in doing so without asking you first."

"I appreciate your initiative in replacing the spoiled barrels as you knew we need them. However, the next time you have a need or an idea how to better our lives, I expect you to consult me first. While we needed to spend for new barrels, I must also husband mine dowry carefully."

Gytha curtsied. "Yes, my lady. I promise to do so." Gytha added a sop. "I had to burn the staves, but I saved the metal rings. May I ask Rammeg Elder to make new barrels after we finish the planting? I believe we will need them."

"Please ask Reeve to do so for you. I support his authority. We must maintain the proper line of command."

"Yes, my lady." Gytha curtsied again.

"God give you a good day, Gytha," said Margaret as she departed.

She left the village with a guard on each side. An arrow struck Sauville's helmet, pinged against the metal, and bounced away. The threesome jumped back. A moment later, a second arrow struck the ground at their feet.

"Attack!" roared Sauville and Roulin in unison. They grabbed Margaret between them, lifted her off the ground, and ran for the bailey. One sentinel yelled orders as the one on the other side of the gate pointed toward the trees from which the arrows flew. From inside the bailey a horn had sounded three short blasts. Margaret dropped her head to be shorter than the men. A third arrow skittered across the back of Roulin's leather jerkin and dropped to the ground. The men raced on. Villeins in the fields rushed for their homes; those in the village cried out in alarm or stood frozen with fear. Brandishing their swords, two mounted knights dashed out the gate and past the threesome. Roulin and Sauville deposited Margaret behind the still-opt gate. Sauville yelled, "Close the gate after we leave!" Roulin ordered Margaret, "Run for the keep! Secure it!" The men ran for the horses Jorgon and his helper held for them. They mounted and flew out the gate, as the two hostlers and three knights pushed shut the gate and dropped both bars into place. Only after Margaret saw the gate secured did she turn. "Everyone into the keep!" she yelled. Two pages held the ladder as first Margaret, then everyone else still within the bailey scampered toward the keep door. The pages pulled up the ladder after themselves before men shut and barred the door. Trying to count who was present and who was not, Margaret looked about.

"We are all here save Syghelm,"reported Cormac. "He went toward the gate."

"Have we water?"

"Yes, my lady, reported Nearra, the cook, as she pointed to a pulley set into the stone wall over a hole in the floor opposite the fire-place. A rope coiled on the floor went through the pulley, dropped down, and was tied to a bucket resting next to the hole.

"Good." Margaret strode to a window slit but could only see part of the palisade wall, half the gate, and tree tops. "The gate is secure. Do what we must. We may be here a long while." Margaret heard movement behind her, so she turned to put her ear to the window slit as she listened for the sounds of an army. *Oh God, thank you for saving mine life. I pray mine villeins live. I hear no battle horns, no clashing of blades. Is this Your warning I should step away from ruling and ordering to be more a lady? What should I do? Whom will I trust to lead well, to know how to manage an estate as I have done? Your will, Oh Lord, in all things. Please tell me what is best.* Margaret prayed for guidance and she waited at the slit.

What seemed hours later, everyone heard one, long horn blast.

"That means whatever happened is over and to our advantage," said Giraud. "We should wait until one of the king's men tells us what to do."

Whooshes of air being sighed out sounded in the room and several spoke in hushed tones as they crossed themselves. Margaret heard them guessing the outcome. She watched as half the gate opened, but she could not spot who had come through.

Sir Roussel rode to the bottom of the hill upon which the keep perched. "It is over. You may come out now," announced Roussel still ahorse. "The gate is shut and barred even though we are out of danger."

Hughes opt the keep door and peered out. "Only our men. We are safe."

The pages dropped the ladder and went down it first. Margaret led everyone out of the keep and into the hall. Roussel and Father Manntun were already there. Margaret took the dais steps and sat in her place. Everyone else arranged themselves against the walls.

"Sir Roussel."

"We still have men ranging afield to be cert the attacker was alone. We found him running away, bow and arrows still in hand. He was the leader who yelled the commands that day. He meant to kill you, my lady. In revenge for the death of his brother. The light-haired archer in one of the trees. When he returned to search for his brother, he found his head." At Margaret's nod, Roussel continued his report. "I think he went mad at the sight. He said he had been waiting in the trees for you to be a good target. I am so sorry, my lady. We missed spotting him. I swear we will be more vigilant. This will not happen again."

"Thank you for catching him. Our men were swift and did well." Margaret added her sop. "A lone attacker is harder to catch than spotting an army. Thank you for insisting I am guarded." She looked into the hall. "Sir Sauville. Sir Roulin, I count you men of great worth. Thank you for saving mine life." Margaret accepted their formal responses. She again looked to Roussel. "I would not be alive without you, Sir Roussel. I hope His Royal Highness knows how fortunate he is to have you in his service. I know mine good fortune and am more grateful than I can say. You will always be in mine prayers."

Roussel nodded his thanks.

"What became of the man?"

"He joins his brother. Please inform the Saxons a body needs burying and a head added to the last pole."

All looked to Father Manntun. He shrugged. "He tried to kill our lady. He deserved death."

At first everyone looked shocked at Father's words. Then they applauded the priest.

Well done, Father. You have won back some of their approval. Keep paying for your bread, tending your crops, and cooking your own meals, and they soon will come round.

"Cormac," called Margaret. At his response, she added, "Please inform mine Saxons they are safe. Ask them to see to the burial."

"Cook, we are in need of food. When may we eat?

Second Sunday of Advent was a happy day for the knights because the meal included the small game and birds they had caught. Rich with the meat the hunters had provided and fresh vegetables from Reading, the stew was flavored with the salt and herbs Margaret's coin had also purchased. The men frowned as Cormac and Reeve marched the Saxons into the hall. Margaret heard grumbling about sharing. Margaret pushed back her stool, stood, and waited for the hall to go silent.

"We are one estate, Norman, Dane and Saxon, including our Irish chatelaine and our Scots seneschal. As we have all hungered together and have lived with empty bellies, so shall we now all share in any bounty God gives us and we earned by our labors. I thank our Gracious God for His largess this day. I thank His Royal Highness, King Henry, for his generous dowry that allows me to provide for us all. I thank our knights, who guard us well." Margaret paused as she smiled at those before her, knights at tables and Saxons standing behind them. "As one estate, we will also thank each other for what we eat. Knights provided the meats." Margaret pointed to the knights and clapped her hands; the Saxons followed and loudly applauded Margaret's men. "The Saxons searched the forest floor and found the wild onions that flavor our stew." With both hands extended, Margaret pointed to those standing behind the two rows of knights. She glowered at the knights to follow as she clapped; their applause was light and short. "Cook and her new staff baked the bread." With a two-handed sweep of the hall, Margaret showed she expected them all to applaud, which all did. "Father, if you please, bless this meal and lead us in the Te Deum." After the blessing and song, Margaret announced, "Pages and serving girls, proceed."

Scandy and Hartun carried trays into the room and placed them on the platform floor. One contained rounds of bread; the other tiny pieces of meat. Margaret left her place and sat on the edge of the platform beside the food. She took up a small wooden spoon. "Reeve, please lead your family forward," she said to the man in front of the Saxons on the right side of the hall. "Please take one round for your family," Margaret instructed as she lifted the spoon with a tiny piece of meat on it. She held the spoon forward and dropped the morsel onto Felamaere's palm. She motioned Erwina forward and gave her a morsel of meat. Then she did so to their three children who had followed their mother. Reeve and his family departed through the servants' door. When the rest of the Saxons realized what to do, they formed a line with the head of each household first. Scirburne's family was next.

While Margaret worked, two serving girls brought a tray of bread and a platter of bowls to those on the dais. The other three served the knights. Each man received a full bowl and picked up a round of bread. They grumbled over the lack of butter. Margaret was too busy to note the looks of disgust from the knights at the paltry bits of meat in their bowls, which Cormac later reported to Margaret. Before taking food from Margaret, each male nodded and each female bobbed a short curtsey. In turn, Margaret smiled at each individual. The first child to speak to her was a little boy who bolted his meat and then pulled his forelock.

"Thank you, my lady."

"Your name and years?"

"Haelum. Four, my lady."

"Are you a brave boy?"

Haelum puffed his chest. "Very brave!"

Margaret pointed. "Those knights hunted the meat you just ate. A brave boy would thank one of them by saying 'Merciete pour moise' in their language. A brave boy would pull his forelock too."

"Normans eat little boys!"

"No, good knights feed them. They fed you. Can you say 'Merciete pour moise?' Are you brave enough to thank the men who guard you and feed you meat?"

"Just you watch me!" declared Haelum. He turned and marched to the first knight at the table. Haelum pulled Sauville's sleeve, pulled his forelock and yelled his thanks as if Sauville were deaf. He spun back toward Margaret and called out, "See!" in Saxon as he raced out the servants' door.

Margaret laughed. Sauville smiled at her, and she nodded to Sauville as she continued to chuckle. The pages presented her with another tray of bread rounds, so she could finish feeding her villeins before they departed to their homes. By the time Margaret reached her own bowl, her stew was cold, but she cared not. She ate while the others on the dais chatted. After she finished her last bite of bread, Margaret again stood before her men.

"Good knights, I thank you for your skilled hunting and generous hearts. Saxons may not be your favorite people, but please remember come harvest we will eat all winter foods they have grown. Let us keep good will among us. They need you to keep them safe. You need them to keep you fed." With that Margaret stepped off the dais and walked the left side of the fire pit to speaking to each knight about the days ahead, their needs, their suggestions. She did the same for those on the other side of the fire pit.

A good day after a bad one. Again, I thank you, God, for having the archer miss us. Such a fright! We need no others, Lord. I pray You keep us safe. I pray Lord Belleme is far away, and the king is right behind him with an army greater than his. Please, God, let our crops grow and yield us a good harvest. I will continue to pray each day, to thank You each day. I am grateful for all You have done to give me some success. The children are pinker, and everyone is eating regularly now. I feel pride in mine part in all this, but I also know it is Your doing, Your generosity that keeps us safe and fed. Margaret felt brave enough to stand tall as she admired her fields and the grassy meadows from her palisade wall. *William, are you with the king, or are you home in Avondale? Has the king's anger at me melted? Dare I pray for that too? Am I asking too much of You, Lord? Best I wait. If you are as clever as I think you, Lord William, you will wait until after Lent, after the king has enjoyed his Easter feast and some good hunting before asking for mine hand. I dream it William. Do you?*

Cormac kept Margaret posted on the doings in the village. Elstan lived in the hut in the village left empty by the widower's death. He reported to Cormac daily to be of service. Margaret approved his getting a strip of land for planting like the village Saxons. He was already making friends. One doe had dropped a litter of kits. Margaret inspected the hairless babes. She had left instructing how to keep the kits alive to Reeve, who knew about such things. Other does soon followed. The kits were nursing well and growing fast. Some of the rabbits might be ready to eat Palm Sunday, just about the time the next wagon load of grain might run out. She hoped everyone said the same prayers she did.

Please God, keep the weather warm, the rain gentle. Please God, keep the crops growing. Please God, let us starve not. Please take no more from us, especially the babes. Losing them is the hardest. Please God, keep Belleme far away.

Soon Margaret watched Reeve, Aldcot and Elstan again depart. She stayed on the palisade walkway until the party disappeared into the trees. From there she could see her crop land. Green things inched from the dirt. Even in the village, gardens displayed green stems yearning for the sun. Margaret descended the ladder and headed for the barn. She needed to spend time with Night. Petting her beloved gelding calmed her a bit, but she still would not sleep well until another full wagon rolled into the bailey.

Still praying, Margaret again thanked God for his goodness toward her. *The crops are already planted and growing. The farm animals are enjoying the meadow. The ewe had dropped her twins, and they thrive. The pigs are fattening on our swill, and the chickens are now regular with their eggs. The men follow Roussel, and he is polite when I ask questions. I am learning how men think, and I enjoy watching them practice. They appreciate when I mend their clothes and seem to accept mine authority. All is well. Thank you, God.*

The next day, Reeve reported, "Gytha's first batch of ale is ready. Would you like to taste it before she sends it up?"

"Indeed," replied Margaret as she stood from weeding her sprouting vegetables. She picked up the basket and dropped the greens into the pig pen on her way out the bailey.

Wide-eyed with concern, Gytha watched Margaret sip. Margaret looked up and smiled. Gytha sighed her relief. "It is young, my lady, and mine first batch without him."

Margaret finished the small mug. "I like it. Tart yet refreshing. May I ask what you put into the gruit to flavor it so?"

"So far all I have is bog myrtle, yarrow, and a few blossoms. With more blossoms and a bit of honey, when we can get it, fully-aged ale will be a bit sweeter."

"I look forward to tasting that brew too. For now, please send this to the hall. I am cert mine men will enjoy it. Even after boiling water, drinking it still frightens me. Thank you, Gytha. You did well. Have you enough grain?"

"I shall use all you can send, my lady. Saxons like ale even more than do Normans ."

"I would like to feed the spent wort to the pigs."

"I shall send it to the bailey after I extract the yeast for the next batch."

"Thank you, Gytha. Again, well done. Your Linton would have been proud of your product."

After Margaret left the hut, she greeted those she met. Halfway to the bailey and alone with Reeve, she frowned and admitted, "I should not have said that, Reeve. I did not mean to make her sad."

Silently, Reeve agreed, but he only responded, "You meant well, my lady. She loved him, and widows are often sad for a long time when they loved their husbands."

Thursday, 13 March, terrified everyone when a shadow began covering the full moon. The gate guards saw it first and called warning. People streamed out of buildings, screamed, cried out, and fled into their homes to pray the night. Such a fearful thing portended danger, death, crop failure. Friday Mass was delayed because so many had sought solace in Confession. Father Manntun preached a harsh sermon of evils that might befall even confessed believers; almost everyone wept in terror of what might occur. Normans and Saxons alike spent the next two days stepping lightly, being careful not to offend, and praying to live. The Fourth Sunday of Lent gave them little comfort Easter would soon be upon them. When no one attacked them, no one died and nothing bad happened to the crops by midweek, many took heart their prayers had been heard.

At the dais table, Cormac sat with Margaret. "I dislike sleeping in the seneschal's hut in the village because it is cold, damp and has no bed. Also, I have no one to keep a fire going all day."

Margaret remembered learning the people of Winchester doused their fires each night so as not to burn the town. *What if you do a reverse covrefeu? Have a fire all night and douse it in the morning?* "Is the roof sound?"

"I suppose so."

"Cormac, if the thatching needs repair, please order the work done. Have Rammeg Elder build you a stool and a single cot base; I will give you sailcloth for the top. Ask Rammeg to build whatever else you need. I suggest you then take a whole Sunday to keep a fire blazing to warm the building. Burn a fire at night and let the embers die in the morning."

"A single bed?"

Margaret smiled. "A single bed. You want not to give false hope to any village girls or widows, do you? If you marry, then you can order a proper double bed made."

"I enjoy sleeping in the hall," he admitted. "I feel not so alone at night."

"I understand, but the knights want you gone. They say they are not free to talk with you present. Cormac, to stay safe, I need all mine men. If you sleep in the hall, I may lose knights, even Verel and Syghelm, whom I value most highly. I want you sleeping in your own house before Easter Sunday. Tell the knights what you are doing, so they will consider staying." *I pray that is enough to keep each of them. I need them all. Belleme is still about, and we are still in danger.*

Cormac's shoulders drooped as he murmured, "Yes, my lady, I will begin anon."

The first day of spring, 20 March this year and seventeen days before Easter, broke sunny and warm. After Mass, everyone stepped lighter and with merrier talk as they headed home to break their fasts before work. Father Manntun entered the hall accompanied by Reeve. Long able to read people from how they carried themselves and from their expressions, Margaret knew they brought news so bad they needed each other report it. *Please God, no more deaths. They have food; we have planted crops. Please let mine people live. Your*

135

will, Oh God, in all things. She watched the pair climb the dais steps and stand directly before her.

"My lady, we have news from Winchester," began the priest.

Margaret held her breath. *A husband on his way?*

"A fire in the city," reported Reeve.

"How many died? What burned?"

Reeve saw tears welling in his lady's eyes. "The small castle. The courts building. Several shops on High Street. Almost a quarter of the town the night the moon disappeared."

"The queen! The princess," gasped Margaret. She grabbed Cormac's arm. He winced.

"Alive. Saved. Some said lightning. Most blame the moon," reported Reeve.

"The Devil using the dark to hide his evil deeds," averred Father Mannton. Margaret ignored his claim. "They are trying to kill her! They used the eclipse and started other fires to draw men away. Swear they are alive!" Margaret looked about wildly. "Where was the king! Oh God, they are trying to kill her! Why?"

Father Manntun stepped forward and took Margaret's free hand. "My lady, my lady, calm yourself. The queen and the princess are safe." The priest squeezed her hand so she would look at him. "The fire harmed no one; it just frightened people. Many raced to the keep and took the royals away." He released her hand and stepped back.

Reeve added, "Saxons and Normans alike threw water on the ground for a path out the barbican. Two knights escorted the queen. A knight carried the princess still in her cradle. Servants saved the crowns and even some of her furniture and clothes."

"And the king?"

"He was sieging Belleme at his Tickhill castle and raced home. The royal family now resides in the new castle, which is by the West Gate." Reeve reported to Margaret what even Father Manntun knew not. "Saxon servants called warning when the wood pile blazed. In the wind, either fiery arrows or fire sparks flew and started both the hall and keep roofs aflame. As they were oak and burned slowly, servants had time to save everyone. When the roofs caved, other things within the buildings burned. No one died, my lady. Not even in town."

Margaret looked skyward. "Thank you, God, for Saxons!" Margaret took in a big breath and looked at the men before her and exhaled. "Who guards them now?"

"Saxons." Reeve smiled. "The queen has her own wing in her new home. Norman knights guard the door to the wing, but the Saxons insisted they guard the hallway and her room. Each night Saxons stand in the hall to her room so no ladies leave their rooms or let anyone into the wing. They have chosen Saxons to taste her food and drink. She will never be alone again. His Royal Highness is so shaken he agreed to their demands. Worry not, my lady. We Saxons have our ways. If the fire was man-started, we will learn who did so. His Royal Highness will execute every one of them."

"Good! And I care not who thinks me unnatural to say so." Margaret narrowed her eyes at Reeve. "Promise me they will die."

Reeve's leaned over the table edge and spoke in a hush. "One way or another, they will."

Margaret gave Reeve a tiny nod. She turned. "Father. Vespers?"

"We will recite extra prayers of gratitude for their safe removal from danger and for no townspeople dying."

"Thank you, Father. If you will write it, I will send a letter to Her Royal Highness, telling her of mine great joy in her family's safe removal from danger and of our special prayers for her and the princess's continued wellbeing."

"I will return anon with parchment and ink."

"Thank you, Father Manntun. Thank you, Reeve."

After the pair left, Margaret turned to Cormac. "Please escort Caitlin here. I want her to hear the news from me."

Oh God, life is up, then it is down. I feel I am riding waves on a dangerous sea. If I do one small thing wrong, one deed amiss, mine little boat will capsize and I will fail. Or worse. Die. And whom will I take with me? Who will die if I make a misstep? Even one would be too many. Be mine guide, Oh Lord. I need your help. Margaret sighed and propped her head with her hand. *I need a partner. This is so much harder than I thought. Getting a dowry was good. Having enough coin is good. But I need help. I need a partner. Someone strong, capable, a leader men will follow. Please, God, send him soon. Suddenly, I am so tired. So very tired.*

12

Eastertide

Ten days after the first day of spring, Palm Sunday started Holy Week with each one on the estate holding a palm, said to have been imported from Rome or from the Holy Land. Father Manntun preached Jesus's actions. Thursday's Maundy Mass was held in the evening in commemoration of the Last Supper. The Church celebrated it as its second holiest day: the start of Holy Mother Church when the priesthood was created, first communion was served, and the sacrament of Baptism instituted because Jesus washed his disciples's feet. Afterward, the priest stripped the altar, left it bare, and said no Mass until Easter Sunday, the holiest day in the Church's calendar. All Christians spent Friday and Saturday fasting, in prayer, and in contemplation of Jesus's crucifixion.

While still drinking only ale, everyone prepared. Villeins cleaned their houses and cleared the lanes of all debris. In the hall, girls cleared away the cobwebs; they scrubbed tables, benches and everything they could reach with soap and boiling-hot water. They removed fire debris, cleaned the pit of all ashes and set new logs. Finally, they removed old rushes, swept debris from the dirt floor and put down new rushes. The fire would be restarted after Easter Mass. In homes and hall, those who believed in washing had done so—at least the parts that could be seen. Villeins and Normans alike set out clean or new garments for Easter morning. Cook and the kitchen helpers worked feverishly to prepare the Easter feast.

At dawn on 6 April, Easter Sunday began with High Mass that continued for three hours including an hour-long sermon. Everyone wore new clothes or newly washed ones to symbolize the start of the Church's New Year and of the renewal of their faith. The people left church greeting each other with, "The Christ has risen and we are saved. Thanks be to God." Margaret took a long time reaching her hall. She took a dozens steps, smiled and thanked her escorts before releasing them. Two more children from the troop behind her charged up and took a hand. The three of them said the Easter greeting together, and Margaret would take another set of steps. Margaret laughed often and said a kind thing to each child. Finally, the last pair stopped at the gate. Margaret thanked them and watched them dash back to the village and their own celebration before she turned to her own special meal.

The Easter feast varied by station. Villeins tasted birds or rabbit, enjoyed spring greens and filled their bellies with bread. Gytha and her sons had worked hard to produce ale for every household, though most of it went to the hall. The hall feasted first on bone broth, then roasted lamb, greens from the replanted bailey garden, bread and ale. Only those at the head table enjoyed butter. To Margaret's left sat Cachier, Gailard, and to her immediate left Roussel. To her right Father Manntun, Cormac and Caitlin. As Verel had been elected by Margaret's men to lead them, he was eligible to sit at the head table. When Lady Margaret invited him to do so, he asked he be permitted to sit with her knights. She had agreed. *Lead but not from above but from among. Good decision, Sir Verel.* As they dined, several volunteered songs and story telling. Cook and the staff ate in the kitchen while the ale continued to flow. Leftovers were popped into a pot for soup later.

Margaret left the hall and climbed to the palisade walkway. She looked over lush fields, a cleaned village, and green forest as the sun warmed her and a gentle breeze caressed her skin. When she inhaled deeply, she smelled the end of spring and the start of summer. She sighed happily. In the village several women walked with arms around each others' waists. Margaret faintly heard children laughing and saw a few dashing about playing tag. Men stood in clumps.

Please God, let the worst be over. They are good people. Please let them continue to get healthy, stay safe, and bring in a bountiful harvest. We will be grateful. Then she dreamed of Lord William of Avondale, her sworn champion from Forest Keep. *Three long months since I have seen you, William. Have you thought of me? Is the king calmer? Will I soon greet a suitor? Please, God, soften the king's heart and have him send me a good man.* A woman in the village waved at her; she waved back. *Forty-four days since I have gained this land. Lent is done. Now is the time to ask for mine hand, William. I would accept you. Do you want me?* Margaret blew her thoughts from her mind and prayed to the wind. *O wind from God, take mine thoughts and put them in William's head. I think him a good man. I want to be his wife. Your will, Oh God, in all things.* A small boy jumped up and down as he waved hard at his lady. Margaret waved back. She descended the ladder and returned to the hall.

On Easter Monday all was work again. Margaret declared Hughes healed. Even the stitch marks only dotted his skin.

"Now may I begin to strengthen mine arm? It has wasted with no use, and I must test it to see if I can hold a shield and still knight."

"I suggest you start slowly and work it a little at a time. Mayhap only two or three times a day and wait until your arm strengthens before you pick up a shield. You want not to tear apart the insides. If it troubles you, Caitlin is a skilled healer and may be of help."

"Thank you, my lady," replied Hughes as he slowly twisted his arm this way and that. "I shall do so." He bowed and left.

Reeve reported the work needed to be done, and Margaret approved his plans for the week. Cook discussed her kitchen needs and menus. Cormac waited to be last.

"Who is the girl I see walking with the carpenter's son? They walk far apart, but they are together to and from Mass. From the way they stand and gaze at each other, I think he is courting her."

"They are Leoma and Rammeg Younger, my lady. She helped Cook your first days here. She is a good worker, pretty, and kind-hearted to the little ones. He has already won her approval, but she has no dowry in these times. I think the families are waiting for a good harvest. Pretty as she is, I am cert he is sorely tempted at times to wed her Saxon style." At Margaret's frown, Cormac explained. "They meet in secret, bed each other, and reappear to announce they are married. I heard they stand so because he follows the Church's command that a bride be a virgin. I was told he is cert they are always in sight of an adult when they are together so there will be no question about her purity."

142

After Margaret conferred with her seneschal about his progress with the inventory of her people and property, he left to continue the project. *Leoma is fortunate. She comes from a good family, a good man wants her, and he treats her with respect. If I have the power, I will grant their union, but not until her father pays me the merchet. If I have a husband by then—God, are you listening?—he will decide and set the tax for them to marry. Ah well, I pray he arrives soon. Oh God, I do want a husband.*

Nine days after Easter, King Henry secretly rode to a hidden place in Lord Warwick's forest and dismounted. With a gesture, he instructed the five men from his corp d' elite to range around the wattle and daub hut. He coughed and asked, "Are you there?" At the affirmative answer, he said, "Stay. I am coming in." As a precaution, Henry drew his sword before he pulled back the cloth to peer inside.

"I am alone, Your Royal Highness."

Henry entered and saw a large wooden table littered with wood and metal items, the weapon he sought, a bed, and a tripod over a rock-lined fire pit. He glared at the tall Saxon. "Does it work?"

"Yes, Your Royal Highness. If you wish, we can go into the forest, and you can use it."

Henry popped his head out the doorway and called, "Ride a hundred yards in every direction and face outward. Let no one enter your circle." He led the pair into the forest and stopped in a copse. He pointed to the largest tree and ordered. "Retreat thirty yards and hit that tree." Henry stood in dappled sunlight and enjoyed the light breeze as he waited.

Alfred did as instructed. He cocked the woven guts string onto the latch, removed a small metal-tipped arrow shaft from his pocket, and inserted it into the track. He lifted the weapon, put the end against his shoulder, aimed, and pulled a trigger at the bottom of the device. The arrow disappeared.

King Henry spotted the flash before the arrow struck the tree and buried half of itself into the trunk. He watched the Saxon smile at him as he returned. "No chain mail can stand against that," he reported as he point to the arrow."

The Saxon handed over the weapon. "Your Royal Highness. I have seen it fly from even farther away and surprise the man it strikes."

"Why have you fastened a stirrup to the front?"

"The bow limbs are so strong, you needs point the front end down and hold it to the ground with your foot, so you can pull the string back into the latch with both hands. That is why it can fly so fast and so far. He handed a second arrow to the king. "Because it is shorter than a regular arrow and has only two feather fletchings instead of three, I call the arrow a bolt It strikes a man like a bolt of lightening."

Henry pointed the device to the ground and held it down with his foot in the stirrup. With both hands he pulled the drawstring over the latch. He accepted the arrow and lay it in the track. "Now what do I do?" Alfred pantomimed his placing the wooden stock against his shoulder and putting his pointing finger in front of the trigger. He contracted his finger. Henry walked away, turned, aimed, and released the arrow. His shot landed above the Saxon's and pierced the tree as far as its fletching because Henry had stood closer to the tree than had Alfred. He walked to the tree and failed to pull out the arrows so he broke off the arrow ends and pocketed them. Only a person knowing what to look for would find the evidence in the tree bark. Henry returned to the hut and stepped inside; Alfred followed. The Saxon watched the king position the bow upright like a traditional bow and then parallel to the earthen floor.

"No longer small and used for hunting. Now we make it a weapon and hunt men with them," smirked Henry."According to your account, the prince of Bavaria has one and I have the second. As he is not yet home from the Holy Land, mine is the only one in the west."

Alfred noted the king's possessive tone ant the glint in his eyes.

King Henry looked at the wood and metal on the table. "I want more of these. Are you making another?"

"Not yet, Your Royal Highness. If you are to keep this weapon secret, I made the parts, both metal and wooden, so you could take each part to a different place to be made by others. I instructed Lord Warwick's black smith how to make the metal parts, but he knows neither what they are nor how to assemble them or use them. The stirrups I just took from a saddle. This way no one man will know what his part is for or what it will do. I am willing to assemble each weapon. That way only you and I know what you are producing. I can wait here or return to mine lord until you summon me."

"I like your thinking."

"This crossed bow arrows are narrower than traditional ones. The man who forms the metal tips needs a shaft to be cert they will fit together. I made regular-lengthen shafts for the metal worker so he will think his tips will be on regular arrows, just thinner ones. Another can whittle the bolt shafts using my sample; I will carve the notches so he will not think that piece of wood is an arrow. I will also need feathers and the strongest horse-hoof glue you have to attach the tip and fletching to the bolt. Shall I assemble the weapons and the arrows?" At the king's nod, the man continued. "If you remember, Your Royal Highness, you agreed to pay me half once I made a working model."

"What will you do with mine coin?"

"My lord accepted me back. He has also agreed to sell me land for coin and services. I would like to purchase the land now. I know it is late to plant, but I want some vegetables of mine own. Also, I can be cutting trees for a house while others make each of the parts."

"I will send for you and you will return here." Henry smiled. "Have you chosen the girl?"

"Not yet, Your Royal Highness."

"If you marry a Norman, I will give you an extra two pounds and tell her father to accept you."

Alfred smiled and pulled his forelock. "Your Royal Highness, you make a generous offer. I will think on it."

"Good. The sooner English children are born the sooner this country will be one people. Stay inside. I want none of mine men ever to know who you are." The king pulled a bag from his hidden pocket and dropped it on the table. The coins clinked in their leather pouch as it hit the wood. Without speaking the king walked out of the hut, mounted and spurred his horse. "Knights! To me!" he roared as he rode away.

Inside the hut, Alfred held the bag. He heard pounding hooves approach then fade as the king's men followed Henry to Warwick's castle three miles away. He smiled as he muttered. "I am half way to winning you, my love. Soon you will be mine."

13

Visitors

Margaret sat with the hall to her back as she watched boys on tall ladders finishing re-chinking the keep's third-story stones. *Glad will I be this night. I will have mine bed and mine things moved from the first floor to the top one. Caitlin and I will sleep on our own floor. Oh, the privacy! The serving girls will be glad not to have to share the fireplace. I can order the horse trough I bought for bathing taken to the keep and leaned against the wall near the fireplace. I do want a bath, but only Caitlin. Shock not the servants. Drat! Then I needs confess and take whatever penance he assigns for caring for mine body instead of guarding mine soul.*

"My lady! My lady!

"Here!" Margaret yelled back.

She lowered her mending into the basket and straightened her stiff back. She leaned against the wall and lifted her face to the sun and squinted. The stable boy rounded the corner of the hall and reported between hard gasps, "A party... at the gate... looks to be a lord... says he is your brother."

Margaret stood. *Brother? Which one? News of Fa... Sir Charles?* She climbed the palisade ladder and peeked over the wall. "Charles! You are most welcome!" Margaret's voice was even warmer than her words. Then she grew cautious. "I recognize not your party."

"Lady Margaret, may I present Lord Thibaud de Reims, our father's eldest brother. Lord Thibaud's lands are east of Reuen near Beavais. These four are mine men."

Escort? Guard? Either way, we outnumber them. Two above them and four in the bailey.

Lord Thibaud sat stiff in his saddle. His demeanor disdainful, his frown deep and menacing.

"Lord Thibaud, I beg your forgiveness. These knights were most remiss in not admitting you at once." Margaret waved a command. As she scrambled down the ladder, knights removed the bars, opt wide the gates, and stood at attention two on a side. She barely had time to hand off her apron and scissors. She pulled her fingers through her hair to bring it to order. Margaret patted down her bliaut and realized Charles and Lord Thibaud had seen her do it. She blushed. Charles waited for their uncle to dismount before doing so. Thibaud's green eyes startled her.

Why is he angry? What have I done? Margaret curtsied deeply to Lord Thibaud and bobbed a half curtsy to her brother.

In a cold voice, Thibaud said, "Lord Charles of Royal Oaks deserves better."

Margaret's jaw dropped. She drew breath to speak and then clamped her mouth shut. She made proper obeisance. *Dead? How? When? Why?* Slowly Margaret righted herself and intoned stiffly, "Welcome, Lord Charles of Royal Oaks." She stared at him. *Do you relish your position as much as did he? Are you as hard as was he? Why have you come?*

"My lords, may I present Sir Verel, who leads mine knights and Sir Hughes, Sir Roulin, Sir Claude."

Left hands on their hilts, the men made the proper greetings.

Margaret offered, "Please dine with us and stay the night." At her uncle's nod, she continued, "If you will follow me, the coolness of the hall and our ale may refresh you. As we have no barracks, your men are welcome to sleep in the hall as well."

Lord Charles' men sat at the door end of the hall. Margaret walked her guests to the dais end, watched them sit at the end table, and ordered ale. She stood until her uncle and brother had been served. Then she made the point to sit as well. Because she chose to sit beside Charles, she missed seeing him crack a smile. Margaret answered her uncle's pointed questions about her land and property, but she was confused by the anger in his voice. He refused to look at her; his tone and manner announced his disapproval.

"You wear a sword."

He is causing me of being unnatural. "His Royal Highness, King Henry, bid me do so, Lord Thibaud."

"Is it true you ordered those heads on poles to be left as carrion?"

"Lord Bedwin did. He was the king's man here. I concurred."

"Damnable business for any landholder, much less a woman."

"I agree, Lord Thibaud, but I cannot have us attacked again and again because His Royal Highness has not yet sent me a husband."

At the second mention of the king, Thibaud stopped talking and frowned. Verel offered to show him the grounds. After they left, Margaret offered Charles a walk. They climbed a ladder and strode the walkway of the palisade wall.

"I am not allowed to leave the compound alone and may only walk the wall under the watchful eyes of the guards."

"So as not to tempt marauders or a man who would win you by ravishment."

"So it seems." Margaret sighed. She stopped and, with a wide gesture, displayed her land.

"The crops look lush and tall for the season," Charles began. "The village is neatly laid out and clean. "What is that?" he asked, pointing to a structure in the distance.

"A forge under a roof. I hope to attract a blacksmith, but I have not the coin to pay him."

"I heard you are wealthy almost beyond measure."

Margaret motioned and they both sat in the palisade's shade with their backs against the poles. Their feet extended into the air.

"I spent much of it getting here and feeding starving people until Easter. I must pay mine men every month. Then I pay mine household: Cormac mac Cennedig, mine seneschal; Caitlin, mine chatelaine; Jorgon, mine hostler; Elstan, mine translator and helper; Cook; three more in the kitchen; the alewife, serving maids; stable boys, and a milk maid." Margaret finished with, "At home I had no idea how much such a household cost. Mine wealth now is the land. And the crops—if God will let us have them all."

"We wondered where Caitlin and Jorgon had got."

"Dena too. She and Jorgon married." Margaret changed the subject. "At fourteen, you are now a half a head taller than I."

"And still growing fast." He added happily, "I wager I will be as tall as Father, mayhap taller with broader shoulders."

"How?" was all she dared ask.

"A wasting illness. Complained of stomach pains. The household was in ruins without you, Caitlin, and Cook. She disappeared when you left. By the time I had restored order, he was fading. Drank and drank to kill the pain. By spring he was gone. In truth, he died drunk."

"Gone a year, but no fault of mine." *You would not blame me, brother, if you knew. What I could tell you!*

Charles responded not. Instead he added, "Toward the end, Father sent for Lord Thibaud to be mine guardian. Father asked for Mother constantly. Kept looking far off and asking her forgiveness. Know you why?"

"No," Margaret lied. *Keep your good opinion of him. Not spoil that for you.* "Tell me of Lord Thibaud. Even though he appears fit and strong, he looks to be fifty years old."

"Fifty-two. He drinks sparingly and is very critical of Father drinking so much it killed him. But then, Uncle did not have to live with Mother."

Margaret let that jibe slide by. *I want not to fight over this matter.*

"Father had to send for him. By law, I am both a lord and a ward until I am eighteen. With his son commanding the land in Normandy, he had naught to do. When I sent word at Father's request, he was happy to come. He said he would teach me to be a proper knight, a proper lord. He is also very critical of Father for not sending me to be fostered with another family and for teaching me himself." Charles paused and then added, "But he never fought with King William like grandfather. Grandfather taught father and he taught me. Uncle has never been in a real war. Father taught me more fighting, hand to hand, with sword and lance, even ahorse, than Uncle thinks he knows. I showed him that."

"And you are on your way to Normandy?" *Would that I could travel. See more of the world.*

"Returning. We spend Eastertide visiting. Uncle introduced me to daughters of friends of his." Charles's screwed up his face. "He cannot compel me to marry."

"No, he cannot, but he can suggest. Tell me of them."

"I am only considering two. Both well bred." Charles stopped.

"But…" offered Margaret.

"But I want not a match like Father and Mother. I want not to be as unhappy as was he."

"He was unhappy?! She was miserable!"

"You always took her side. You never saw his side, Margaret."

"His side!"

"His side," repeated Charles. "How easy think you it was to live with a woman who constantly reminded him his rank was inferior to hers? They raised Father to serve Uncle and never to be a lord."

"What?" Margaret did not believe her ears.

"Yes, Mother. You believed her perfect. You never realized how she tortured him." Margaret was too stunned to respond. "How often I overheard her telling Father he owed his position to her family, to her. 'You were only a third son until I married you,' I oft heard her tell Father. She overrode his decisions she did not approve because the lands had been hers first. 'You had best make no decisions without mine approval.' I heard more than once."

"I saw him strike her."

"Only after she first struck him with words," Charles responded hotly. "She countermanded his orders, subverted his power. Finally, he gave up and let her run things. He turned to drink and other women." Charles gazed at his sister. "You think I knew not about that."

"I knew it not until well after Mother's death."

"Know you why Father claimed you had lain with Jorgon?" When Charles got no response, he continued. "Because Jorgon was born on the left side of the bed, and he asked Father if he was a Norman, if our father was his father too. Father tried to beat him to death, but you stopped it. In the middle of the bailey, you humiliated him for all to see. When he broke his promise to teach you to ride, you jumped on mine pony man-style. Later, you ran away into the forest twice. You were too strong-willed, Margaret. Too much like mother." Charles paused and whispered, "Did you ruin yourself when you rode astride?"

"Mother said not. I am still a good girl." *I pray she told truth, or I am ruined and un-marriageable. Please God, not that!*

Charles wondered if their mother had lied to protect her, but said nothing.

"He hated me."

"You made public what only our villeins knew, but not the Normans. Father accused you of being with Jorgon because he is our brother. His revenge was to make you his slave. If you had not relented and obeyed, I believe he would have thrown you away and declared you a ditch woman."

Margaret's eyes popped wide. "Jorgon is our brother?" Charles nodded. "Does Jorgon know?" Charles nodded again. Margaret put her hands over her reddened cheeks as she imagined her father with Jorgon's mother. After a time, Margaret uttered, "I pray you tell me he is the only one."

"He is not. After you, each time Mother got with child, he strayed. The boy born after Raymond died of fever when he was three. The girl the same age as Cecily lives. I watch over her. I will

153

see she marries a good Saxon and has a decent life. That is all I can do for her."

"All this time I believed we just liked each other. I have always felt an affinity toward him. Now I understand why."

"Jorgon is devoted to you because you saved his life, because you take care of him." When Margaret again looked at her brother, Charles added, "I am aware he saved Night for you and what else he did. I did not want our brother killed, so I kept silent."

Margaret knitted her fingers together on her lap and then undid them only to curl them together again. "Mother tortured Father because she knew of his faithlessness."

"I am sorry, Margaret. I should not have spoken. I should have let you believe her an angel still."

Margaret shook her head; she had no words, only confusion and shock. *How little I knew her—even with traveling with her to midwife Norman ladies! How little I really saw. Only what she wanted me to see, to know. I took her side against Father and did not recognize his pain, his sorrow. He lay with other women for comfort and to hurt her, so she hurt him back. A war I never saw. What a child I was!* To stop her thoughts, Margaret asked Charles whom he had met.

"The one Uncle wants me to marry comes with a rich dowry but has a haughty air that reminds me too much of Mother's. She is pretty enough, but the dowry is too much for a second daughter."

From Charles' tone, Margaret guessed, "You fear they are trying to marry her off to a stranger who will take her off their hands and far away."

"M-m-m. She is imperious with servants. She overacts the lady. When I asked her about her herb garden, her medicines, she reluctantly admitted another maintained them. She was proud to have never dirtied her hands. When I spoke to the servants about her, they were careful to speak only good, but their eyes, Sister dear. Their eyes warned me."

"Uncle sees only the dowry, not the girl," Margaret correctly guessed. "Tell me of the others."

"One other. Not as pretty, but she has warm eyes and a kind smile."

Margaret smiled at her smitten brother, but his gaze away from her saw someone far away.

"Her father is not ranked as high as the one Uncle prefers, but he rules a happy household. I felt it when I entered their hall. She has not so much dowry, but she is able. Sews, not just embroideries, but real sewing. Clothes and shirts and such. She can oversee a household and cook as well. She keeps a lovely garden and knows all manners of simples. Lady Cleanthe is eleven."

"Is she pleasant to talk with?"

"Very!" asserted Charles. "She is not so proud she does not laugh." Charles smiled to himself.

"You like her very much," *He gets to choose his wife. Will the king let me choose mine husband? I fear not.* Margaret quelled her jealousy.

"The best part is she wants to come to England. Her father is well pleased with her rise in rank if we marry. The other looks at me as if I were a bumpkin and England is nothing. Lady Cleanthe favors me. Of that I am cert."

Charles nervously picked at a sliver of wood on the plank to his right.

"Then choose the Lady Cleanthe and make the contract."

"Lord Thibaud will not permit me to marry until Cecily leaves the household."

Margaret furrowed her brow. "What has Cecily to do with this?"

"Margaret, she is even worse than when last you saw her. Not even Uncle can manage her. She is haughty, disobedient. Will not be taught. Refuses to do anything but preen. She is out of control, unruled by anyone. We return because we received word the convent to which we sent her wants her gone. They will even return her dowry to be rid of her."

"I will not have her!" Margaret stood and dusted off her backside.

"But Margaret, you are..."

"NO! Never! She hates me. She will disobey me. Ruin my life. I will not take her."

Margaret stomped her way back and scampered down the ladder. She started for the keep gate. Charles pulled his sister's sleeve to stop her.

"What are we to do with her? This is the second convent to return her."

"Marry her off to an old widower and let her warm his bed," countered Margaret. Remembering her pampered, spoiled sister, she smiled wickedly at how Cecily would hate any loss of rank.

"No one who has met her will have her!" yelled Charles in frustration.

Those in the bailey turned toward the noise and stopped to observe the pair. Margaret stopped walking and faced her brother. Behind him she saw both workers and knights watching them. As she looked away, an idea came to her.

"Is the Lady Cleanthe well bred? Is she well trained? Are her parents strict?"

"I have met her siblings. Each is well mannered and behaves properly."

"I have an idea. Please follow me to where no one will hear us."

Margaret led him through the gate and halfway up the steps to the keep. She turned to face the bailey and sat on the wooden plank that edged each grassy step. Charles sat beside her. Margaret waited until those in the bailey turned away and returned to their tasks.

"You are right, Charles; take the better woman despite her lower rank and having less dowry. You deserve happiness. Neither you nor I want a marriage like our parents had. Make a clause in the marriage contract that Lady Cleanthe's parents take up the training of Cecily. If her father is pleased to make this match, he will accept. If you must, offer to reduce the dowry. He will think it easy to take Cecily to foster in exchange for a decrease in land or coin."

"But that is less dowry."

"But you are rid of Cecily. If Uncle lives four more years, whom do you think he would rather have in your hall, Cecily or Cleanthe?"

Charles smiled and said, "Cleanthe. She is gentle and kind. She cooked for us to demonstrate her skills; he liked her cooking." Charles frowned and added, "Cecily will not agree."

"You spoke of Mother's faults. What of Father's? He spoiled Cecily so badly she is untrained and unfit to be a wife. No one wants her. Convents have returned her. He left her to you and you are stuck."

"How do I become unstuck?"

Margaret looked past the bailey and gate to the trees far beyond as she thought. Charles silently watched her and waited.

"First gain your lady. Get the marriage contract signed by Uncle and her father and approved by the king. Inform Cecily she is to accompany you to Normandy for the church ceremony. She will like that. Once there, tell her she will stay to be trained by Lady Cleanthe's parents."

"She will refuse to stay and have a tantrum. Of that I am cert."

"Then beat her if need be. Have her held down and beat her hard. That will shock her. If she will not listen, if she will not agree, strike her again and again until she is ready to listen to the rest."

"What 'rest'?"

"In order for Cecily to have a good life, a proper marriage, she must change her ways. Inform her she must become a good and obedient woman. She must become a model chatelaine. In front of Cecily, compliment Cleanthe's parents about how well they raised their daughter. Tell Cecily only they can teach her all she needs to know and what to do. Have them do as Mother did to me. I started with emptying chamber pots. When I did it perfectly and without complaint, I moved to the next task. Scrubbing pots in the scullery, for example, then making beds."

"That is very harsh."

"Mother required I learn that way; I learned the same way Mother did. No lady can command what she does not understand. Nor can she set the standard if she has not done the task herself. Look around you. Mine hall and hearth are clean and well maintained. So are mine kitchen and outbuildings. Mine garden is weedless. I sew both cloth and man, heal wounds, minister to the sick. I grow or find mine own herbs and healing plants and mix mine own simples. I can command because I have done each task I require others perform. You know I was as good a chatelaine at home as I am here. Cecily must become one too if she is to marry well."

"Even if she agrees, it will take months, a year or more."

"Give her foster parents permission to refuse her food if she will not learn and to beat her if she is sullen or disobedient. Say it with Cecily present. Tell Cecily should she fail to satisfy her foster parents

158

and you within a year and a day—or whatever time you set—you will marry her so far below her rank she will be emptying her own piss pots for the rest of her life. Tell her if she fails to become all she should be, you will marry her to an old merchant who will use her to warm his bed, cook his food and clean his house herself. Mean it and be ready to do it. She will test you! Whether Cecily succeeds or fails, you must marry her to one who will agree—in writing—to keep her in Normandy. If she gets to England, she will wreak revenge on both of us. She will try if she is able."

"Is this revenge for her ill treatment of you? For Father's cancelling your marriage and making you a slave? Are you trying to get back at Father through Cecily?"

"No, Charles, no." Margaret spoke with passion. "She has a CHANCE! She can go to Normandy and have a new life. Become a proper woman, raise her rank and gain a good position. If she behaves well and learns what she must, she will make a good match. She is comely and can charm when she wants to do so. Someone of rank will want her and treat her well. Tell her she can have a happy life; but, first, she must earn it."

Margaret turned from her brother and looked far away. After a time she spoke again. "She is only ten. You have two years. You can save her—even against her own will. Let her not ruin her life with headstrong behavior. Once, I thought having land and coins would be enough. They are not. No man wants a lady who refuses to work and has a haughty manner. You want the lady who is modest, kind, accomplished, and hard working. Any man would want a wife like Cleanthe. Cecily must become like Cleanthe if she wants to marry well. Tell her that too."

Charles put his hand upon his sister's arm.

159

"Prevent her from becoming like me," whispered Margaret. Her eyes suddenly misted over. "I wear a sword and command men who think me not a woman. Despite all mine land and wealth, I have no suitor. If she needs proof, tell her of mine life. Charles, please save her while you can."

"Margaret … I think …"

"Promise me one thing," Margaret said in a rush to stop Charles from speaking. "Never, never tell Cecily any of this was mine idea. In the end, she will accept this from you because she loves you. If she learns I gave you the idea, she will find a way to reach England and destroy me or mine children. Of that you may be cert." Margaret jumped up and dashed down the steps and beyond the keep gate.

Dinner was most formal. Rank forced Margaret to place Lord Thibaud to her right, the place that should have been her husband's. Thibaud enjoyed her wide-eyed admiration of the accomplishments he willingly enumerated. The old man's manner had softened toward Margaret by the time she ordered wine for the men and retreated to the kitchen to set the next day's menu.

Thibaud and Charles stayed to hunt with two of Margaret's men. Margaret envied their romp through the forest, but she also appreciated their contributions to table and larder.

Waiting until the page announced supper, Margaret walked Charles around the bailey.

"How fares Raymond?"

"He studies with the priest. Soon he will go to Cluny for further study if he is accepted. He still wants to be a priest."

"Now tell me the other reason for your visit." From her uncle's not-so-subtle earlier remarks, Margaret had guessed. Now she sought confirmation.

"There is none."

"Cecily was your reason. Lord Thibaud's is a higher placed one, is it not?"

For privacy, Charles walked them between the stockade wall and the lean-to of stacked wood. He looked hard at his elder sister and was as frank as he dared.

"If you are as 'well favored' as some gossip, Uncle wants me friendly enough with you to benefit by your association. If you lose your favored status, he had reason to visit, mine request about Cecily."

"Am I back in the royals' favor? They are a fickle pair."

"By leaving on the morrow, we will not have stayed long enough to look as though we curry favor. Or damage mine loyalty to the king."

Margaret looked toward the hall. "Our uncle is wiser than you credit him." Margaret took Charles's hands in hers and whispered what she knew. "I have lived close enough to the royals to know the truth of their lives. Fawning sycophants. Power seekers. Treachery behind smiles and pledges. They have not one friend in the lot. Even with a son next, King Henry is almost an old man, thirty-four. Already too old to get a son old enough to reign. Three factions want to dethrone him. His older brother Robert, who already has two sons, wants the crown. Some lords support Robert and want Henry dead. I heard talk the clergy also oppose Henry and want Robert, who is weaker and more easily led. Henry lost the battle to appoint bishops himself, but no one becomes a bishop without his approval, and he only approves those he can intimidate. Archbishop Anselm is again in self-imposed exile over their fight on the matter."

"Who is the third?"

"The most dangerous man of all, Lord Robert de Belleme, Earl of Shropshire. The king has compiled forty-five counts of his breaking the law. Talk is the king has already sieged and taken one of Belleme's estates. The man has an army somewhere in England. If the king catches him, King Henry will hold a trial and behead the traitor. One faction or the other—or two working together—had the king's first son poisoned."

"I thought that only a rumor."

Margaret shook her head. "If the king loses and you get too close, you will fall with him. Believe me, we will both live longer if we stay as far from the royals as possible."

"Just now you sounded like Mother. You are standing like her too."

Margaret ignored his jibe to make her point. "With all their faults I think Mother and Father knew to stay far from Court. Mother often said, 'The ranked can be difficult, but royals are impossible.' They never went near a royal unless summoned. Now I know why."

"What will you do, Sister?"

"Just now all I can do is pray. Whatever happens, stay away from me, Charles. You have Raymond and Cecily to protect. I want not what befalls me to harm mine family. Let Father's disowning me be your shield."

Charles nodded agreement. He hugged his sister, kissed her cheek and watched her blush. "Finally, we can talk to each other without fighting. Only now it may not be safe. What a pity."

Margaret hugged her brother in return. "We have this evening, Charles. Let us make it merry with singing and stories." They walked arm in arm to the hall.

The next morning, as the visitors broke their fasts, Margaret drew her sibling aside.

"Charles, I believe you will choose your bride well." She liked the smile in her brother's eyes. She took a deep breath and admitted her guilt. "When I left, I took things of Mother's that should belong to your lady. Her scissors…"

"I know."

Margaret took the item from her girdle and handed it to him.

"Please tell your lady only Mother's best qualities. I wish you both happy. Please. wish your lady well and tell her I wish you both happy."

"Thank you," said Charles as he lovingly held the treasure. "But I already have a scissors Uncle bought for the estate. Cecily took so much from you." Charles returned his mother's scissors. "As first-born daughter, this should have been yours anyway."

"I also took her thimble."

As she reached inside her sleeve, Charles stopped her. "Keep it in remembrance of her."

"Thank you. After Night is gone, these will be all I have that was hers."

Lord Thibaud's call interrupted them. Keen to depart, he strode out of the hall and mounted his horse, which sidestepped, was reined in, and sidestepped again.

"I know not when next I will see you."

Margaret nodded agreement.

Charles looked as though he might hug her, but he checked himself.

Margaret gave him a tiny nod of understanding. *Better politic not to show me too much favor.*

Charles took up his reins, stopped and reversed himself. He reached for Margaret, grabbed a bunch of her hair in each hand and gently tugged twice.

Remembering all the times he had pulled her hair in an effort to force her to obey him, Margaret grinned. Playfully, Margaret lifted her right foot and twice touched her toe to his shin. Charles released his hold; Margaret put down her foot. They beamed at each other and hugged hard.

"I love you," Margaret whispered.

"And I you."

"Stay away. Be safe." *I may never see you again, but you will always be in mine prayers, dear Charles. Raymond to. Even Cecily.*

Thibaud led the party out the gates. Margaret climbed the ladder and watched the group walk down the lane. Just before they rode out of view, Charles turned in his saddle and waved. Margaret waved back. She was glad the distance was too great for him to see her tears.

The rest of the morn was a rush of activity. Margaret charged to the practice field and worked so hard with a practice sword against Sauville and Claude that wet curls ringed her face. Her armpits soaked her gown. Claude insisted she practice her cross over steps back and forth across the practice field several times as she cooled from her exertions. She cared not because, after she dined, she rode northeast using deer paths through the forest.

She exclaimed, "A Giants road!" as they stepped into what appeared to be a long stretch of treeless meadow.

"We thought seeing this might please you," responded Roussel as he dismounted.

Margaret untied herself from her riding platform and accepted his aid. She stepped onto the stones and put her hand to her forehead to shadow her eyes from the western sun. "It goes a long way," she said to no one in particular. Margaret crouched down to lay her hand on a stone. "I am touching where giants walked. I see what you meant, Sir Roussel. Huge pieces fit together so tightly no weeds are growing." Margaret slanted her head and added, "It has a slight slant to the outside so rain runs off just as you described, Sir Roussel." Margaret stood and walked down the road with Sirs Hughes and Claude riding their horses on either side of the roadway as Roussel held Night's reins and looked about for intruders.

"Sir Hughes, you hold a shield again. Well done, Sir." Hughes smiled as he saluted her with his right hand. Margaret returned to Roussel, remounted, and the party headed home.

In her room, Margaret knelt beside the buckets she had ordered. She washed her upper body but lacked the time to wash her hair. She tied it at the nape with one of her plain cloth ribs, redressed, and had a servant girl tighten the laces down the back of her bliaut. She descended the keep ladder and strode to the hall to sup with her men. Clearly tired from her exertions, Margaret retired to the dreamless sleep she desired. The next day, she repeated her self-set schedule.

This time she ordered the keep emptied and, with Caitlin's help, washed her whole body. Bound in a linen cloth, Margaret knelt beside the wooden horse trough. Caitlin poured warm water over her head, soaped her hair, and twice rinsed it. She cloth-dried Margaret's hair and bound it a dry cloth. Margaret stood, doffed her binding and knelt in the shallow water inside the trough. Caitlin poured water over her shoulders. Margaret soaped her body before Caitlin rinsed her. She stood and bound her self again in the linen. Margaret sat fireside. Caitlin offered her a clean rag to wash and rinse her face. As Margaret dried, she again toweled her hair. Caitlin brushed out the tangles and helped Margaret into a clean chemise and bliaut. They left the bath things for the girls to remove and ordered the work done. Margaret and Caitlin strolled to the hall. Because sword practice and riding were forbidden on Sundays, Margaret spent the next day visiting in the village. The next week Margaret kept the same self set schedule and was much the happier for it.

Tales of past Midsummer's nighttime events had filled the hall the night before the event. Father Manntun related why signal fires have circled the island for centuries. Manned day and night, a watchman set his stack aflame the moment he spotted Northmen's ships, which oft slipped in under fog or through mists to attack. Because Northmen's shallow boats could also glide up most rivers, both banks of wide or major rivers had watchmen should an overland attack kill one of them. A watchman fired his signal, which other watchmen passed from hilltop to hilltop to warn all in the area. Midsummer night, being the shortest of the year, was the best time to build the new firewood stack and burn the old one. Everyone on the coasts and along the rivers stayed up all night to keep watch.

Father Manntun said the worst of the predations have stopped. Once in a while a lone ship or two may appear, so men still watch. Warned, the locals now summon knights to meet the boats. Being so far inland and so far from a major river, Mine is safe from attack. At home, Mother forbade me to take part. All I could do was listen to the singing and watch the dancing from our keep doorway. This year I am in mine home, and I may do as I wish. The villagers built a great pile of wood at the edge of the meadow far from the trees. Their buckets of water should douse any escaping spark that may burn the meadow, or worse.

The villeins' dancing, singing, and carousing all night were for enjoyment after the hard spring work. At dawn they trooped into church for Mass and to pray for a secure remainder of the summer and for a good harvest.

14

❧

Twin Troubles

Two days later, a visitor arrived accompanied by Sauville. The young man drove his cart into the bailey, hopped down, and stood beside his roundsey. Margaret's knight dismounted. With a word, he dropped his reins over his steed's head, and the horse froze. Sauville strode into the hall and approached Margaret and Cormac.

"My lady, someone arrived who says the king sent him for your approval. He stands waiting for you in the bailey."

Margaret looked up and stood. "Cormac, I leave you here to finish this. *I want to see him before you do.* "Thank you, Sir Sauville. Please escort me to him." At the main door, Margaret placed her hand upon her knight's left forearm and let him lead her outside. She squinted against the morning sunlight. Her page Scandy loitered nearby. "Stand here," she ordered as she squinted again and looked forward. *A pony and a cart? What manner of man did His*

Royal Highness send me? Judge not, but be wary. Sauville led his lady to her waiting guest.

Young. Golden hair. Comely. Well dressed. Blue eyes. An image flashed in her mind of seeing blue eyes through her drunken stupor the night before she became fifteen. Of being kissed by a man with blue eyes. *Not those blue eyes. Not tall enough.* She spied boxes in the cart. *Is he a peddler?*

"My lady, I present Sir Eustace, whom His Royal Highness sends to you. Sir Eustace, I present the Lady Margaret, holder of this estate."

Eustace bowed, "Lady Margaret, I am honored to meet you."

In return Margaret curtsied. "Welcome, Sir Eustace. Please join me in the hall for a libation. Your journey on these dry roads must have made you thirsty." Margaret released Sauville, but left her arm poised in the air. Taking the hint, Sauville stepped aside and Eustace gallantly took his place.

"How kind of you to think of mine need. I hope you will join me, my lady."

Margaret eyed him full in the face. "Of course, my lord." *Fuzzy beard hairs but no shaved beard. The king sent me a boy!* "I look forward to our conversations, if that will please you."

"It does, my lady. It does," replied Eustace as he walked her to the hall.

At the door, Margaret instructed Scandy, "I desire a pitcher of ale and mugs. Please tell Caitlin we are in the hall." The pair watched the boy scamper toward the kitchen. Eustace opt the door and moved his left arm forward so Margaret preceded him. Margaret walked the right side of the fire pit. With Eustace behind her, she could throw Cormac a warning glance even as she gestured for him to join them.

"Sir Eustace, please meet mine seneschal, Cormac mac Cennedig."

"You are far from home, sirrah."

"Indeed. I am honored to meet you, Sir Eustace."

Margaret's first guest frowned at Cormac and barely nodded. Margaret noted the interchange and was about to say something, but Caitlin entered through the servant's entrance and approached.

"Sir Eustace, please meet mine friend, Caitlin. She is also mine chaperone."

Eustace acknowledged Caitlin with a nod and no kind words. Margaret's eyes narrowed, but she said only, "Ah, here is our ale, sir. Please let me serve you." Margaret took the tray and set it at the end of the trestle table. *You have not yet deserved the dais. While courtesy requires I let you stay three nights, you will stay no longer. You are a beardless boy. You treat mine people ill as no true knight would. Those boxes had best not be your way of telling me you intend to stay.*

Had Eustace read her eyes instead of her half smile, he would have known he was already in trouble. He put first one foot over the bench, then the other and sat. As he did so, Margaret signaled with her head she wanted Cormac gone. He returned a small nod, stepped back and disappeared the way Caitlin had come. Margaret poured a full mug and set it before Eustace, who picked it up and only sipped.

The young man looked up and smiled, but he did not hide his surprise. "This is very good ale, well-flavored and refreshing."

"Thank you, my lord." Margaret poured herself half a mug and sat three feet down the fire pit on a bench of her own.

Eustace frowned, but said nothing. Caitlin shifted to the other side of the fire pit, leaned against the wall, and looked toward the dais. She pretended she was paying no attention to the pair and was far enough to hear not them.

Margaret took a sip. "Please tell me something of yourself, Sir Eustace, your family and such."

Eustace turned to face her. "Mine father's holding is far south of here, north of a village called Glastonbury. I am second born. I was studying in York when I met His Royal Highness."

A holding is on an estate, not an estate. "Your father is…"

"Sir Charles, knight to Lord Aluin who serves Lord William…" Margaret's heart fluttered. "…who is the Baron of Cornwall Downs from Glastonbury to the west coastline."

Margaret's heart settled as she felt a moment of loss. *Not mine Lord William.* "Then your father is a knight landed?"

"And well favored by Lord Aluin."

"You were in York studying to be a priest?" *You are no lord, nor lord's son. You have no rank. I will use "sir" only when I must. Sirrah will do between us, and even that is a kindness. What are you about, King Henry?*

"Oh no. I was only studying with the priests. I prefer the old books, church history and maps." Eustace puffed his chest. "I own books. I have worked as a scribe here and in Normandy, and I take mine pay in books when I can. When I cannot, I use the coins I earn to purchase parchment and copy books. I carry mine books wherever I go. They are as valuable as land, my lady. More valuable because of the knowledge they hold." Eustace looked at Margaret hopefully. "Have you a book?"

Margaret lowered her head and said sadly, "No, Sir Eustace. I have none." *You insult me, King Henry. You sent me a boy, not a man. I doubt he rides, much less fights. You are furious with me still. I will be a good host as required, but he is a weak fish, and I throw him back to you!* When Margaret looked up she saw serving girls stacking wooden soup bowls and dinner boards at the entrance end of the hall. Margaret pointed as she spoke, "Sirrah, I regret to inform you we have only the sleeping platform above those storage rooms for guests. After we dine, I will have the platform prepared for your stay."

"I must get mine books inside in case of rain and to guard them."

"I am cert you will want to oversee mine servants as they take the boxes to your sleeping area. As it is sunny and warm, may we wait until after we dine?"

"I suppose so."

Margaret stood. "Let us take a turn about the bailey while the girls prepare for our midday meal."

Margaret sat him on the dais as was proper, but placed him to her left. At his question, she informed him the empty place to her right was for her future husband, as yet unchosen. When she asked him to accompany her to the village after the meal, he reminded her of his books. A servant girl and a page moved them inside. Margaret walked Eustace about the village, pointing to well-kept gardens, clean lanes, newly white-washed huts. The old women watching the babes and toddlers stood as they approached and curtsied. Soon, Eustace appeared to have lost all interest in the village, the meadow, and all else Margaret showed him.

"Over there is the practice field. Will you join mine knights on the morrow? You may use our practice swords, and I shall watch."

"I think not, my lady. My father taught me sword play, but I am skilled not."

"Do you carry a sword when you journey, sirrah?"

"No. Carrying a sword challenges others. I prefer to talk about mine books."

I wager you bore them into leaving you. "We have fine woods, sirrah. Would you like to hunt on the morrow?" Margaret suspected he would decline. When he shook his head and did so, she made her last effort to engage him in an activity. "Then we will go riding after Mass and we break our fasts. Knights will escort us and we will be safe, I ascert you." At his nod, Margaret turned toward the bailey and announced, "July is hot in the afternoon. I prefer to be inside the hall. I must manage the estate's accounts. What will you do while I work?"

"I will lounge in the shade or in the hall's opened doorway and read, Lady Margaret." Margaret put her hand on his proffered arm and walked briskly up the lane.

"He is looking up from his book and at you, my lady."

"Keep your head down, Cormac," Margaret ordered as she pointed to a blank spot on the open page before them. "I intend to keep him at bay until we sup."

"I wonder what you have learned."

"He will not fit. Eustace is a scribe who collects books. He bears no sword, refused practice with our men, acted bored in the village, and will not hunt. I had to order him to ride out with me on the morrow. I am counting today as day one. The next two days are going to be very long and very dull."

"I have a suggestion what you can do with him. On the morrow and after your ride and dinner, sit with him and ask him to read to you from his favorite book. Play the willing student; ask many questions." Cormac chuckled when he saw Margaret roll her eyes. Fearful her guest would interrupt them, she dropped her chin, mumbled and picked up the quill beside the book."

"And the day after that?"

"Five months have passed since you mounted those heads by the road. No one has attacked us. We—you—have been talked about all over the countryside from York to Gloucester to London and beyond. The skulls are now sun-bleached and Father Manntun wants them down. Mayhap you could spend the whole day with church matters. Mass, break our fasts, removal and burial of the skulls, dinner, another Mass, this time for the dead. A quiet time of rest before we sup and have Vespers."

"I will learn if he has the stomach for ruling and facing death. I wager you coins he sickens at the poles."

"You know I will lose."

Margaret laughed. At once, she was sorry when she saw Eustace close his book and stand. *Be nice. The poor boy is just the king's plaything.* She sighed, stood, and moved around the table to meet him on the hall floor. *And I too am the king's plaything.*

That night Margaret faced her side of the bed and felt her sheathed blade on the floor. While Caitlin fell asleep facing the other side of the bed, Margaret considered her choices. *If I accept him, I will do all that I already do. Untrained as he is, I doubt mine knights will follow him. Perforce, he must ask one of them to lead, to schedule guarding , and to keep the men fit with training. Would they treat him with respect? I doubt it. I would be standing beside a weak man. Henry still chases Belleme. Where are they? If they war and Henry dies, Belleme will be king. Henry's protection will be gone, and Eustace could not protect me. How long before Belleme wars to take the estate, kill him, and forces me to wed someone else. If Henry loses his crown, that will happen. If I refuse him, the king may send me a better man. Or a worse one. I cannot accept him; I would not be safe in these troubled times. Send him on his*

way and pray for a better man. He is only a reader when I need a fighter,
a man able to keep me safe.

Margaret had been right; the next two days were long. As they
supped, Margaret spoke quietly with Eustace. "Sirrah, we both
know His Royal Highness thinks highly of you. Despite His Royal
Highness's wishes, we both are also well aware we are not suited for
each other. You want to read and discuss ideas, which are fine things
if all goes well, but life rarely goes well. I need a husband who can
fight, ride to battle if need be, lead men, and protect our lands, me,
his children." *I had best stop with that.*

"I knew the moment I refused to practice fight with your men
and told you I bore no sword. You were not even surprised; your face
revealed your thoughts. They were not kind ones." Eustace buttered
a bread chunk before he continued. "I thank you for your politeness.
And for your calling me "sir" before others when you knew I am not
even a knight errant."

"You can read, and you are a clever man. I learned from you
yester afternoon. You would make a very good teacher. You need a
man of high rank who wants his heir or other son to be well taught."

"I prefer the quiet of the scribing room. I will report to the king
or his official. Then I am for Normandy. I can find work there."

You believe us an ignorant lot who care more for land and crops
than ideas. We are not ignorant. We know weather patterns, growing
seasons, crop rotation, and how to plant and harvest our own food. We
defend ourselves, manage the forest, and so much more. Useless to point
out any of this. Let him be. Let him go. What he thinks of us matters not.

At the end of the meal, Margaret stood and announced Sir
Eustace was leaving in the morning for Normandy. She thanked him
for his visit, for reading to her and sharing his ideas. The men politely

pounded their mugs against the table boards. Margaret smiled at Eustace and at her men. As she sat and drank the last of her ale, she kept smiling, but her mind worried.

If this is the kind of man the king sends me again, what may I do? Will he send me more unsuitable men until I relent and beg him to double sign mine marriage contract? Might a letter to the king relenting and telling him to sign both parts win me a better suitor? Should I return to Winchester to face his wrath as he chastises me before the Court? Would it be better to wait for another suitor to test King Henry's mood? Do something. Do nothing. Which is better? How much longer must I wait? William where are you?

After attending Mass and breaking their fasts, Margaret accompanied Eustace to the bailey and waited with him while his boxes were returned to his cart. To pass the time, she asked him about his travels, which his eagerly enumerated a second time. Margaret waved to him as did he wave before his cart exited the bailey gate. She climbed the ladder and waited at the palisade wall to wave again should he look back before entering the trees. He did not. Margaret stared far ahead and sighed. *Please God, let the king's anger cool. Let a good family with a good son ask for me. I promise to be glad and accept whom You send. I will be obedient and a good wife. I will try hard to like him so our lives can be pleasant. A husband who is a good fighter and leader of knights would ease mine fears of attack. I like being in charge, but sometimes it is hard. I must care for the wellbeing of so many. So many decisions, the responsibilities of ... "*

"My lady, I have a question," called up Reeve.

Margaret looked skyward. *Please, God. Soon.* Margaret turned back to her duties.

She was so busy that, for a week, she went riding only twice.

The second week of July Margaret rode daily after breaking her fasts to avoid the summer's hottest month. After their ride, Margaret groomed Night as he stood in his stall, munching hay. Boar's hair brush in hand, she cleaned him of sweat and dirt from shoulder to withers in long gentle strokes.

"Ah Night, you are still mine best and most faithful friend. You gallup not so far as you used to, but your trotting is still good. At twenty-one, you are getting on in years, but so am I. Sixteen this Advent. I want to be married before then. I care not the queen married at twenty. She is royal and beyond the expectations of society. At sixteen, who will have me? Only a family who wants mine land and dower chest and must accept me to get them. Sixteen is old to start carrying babes. I need a husband now." Margaret frowned as she brushed Night's legs. "Is the king done being angry with me, Night? Has no other man or family has asked for me? Is that why he sent me Eustace? Is he drawing from the bottom of an almost empty barrel? Must I prepare to be single the rest of mine days? Rule here alone? If I must, will any of mine knights stay? How many need I to be safe? I am still in danger from the traitor Belleme. Should he come mine way his army will overrun us, kill and main, ravage and pillage. He will siege the keep for the coin. Even if I turn every pence over to him, he may still not be satisfied until he returns the land and us to waste in revenge for what the king did to de Warenne." Margaret continued to ruminate as she pushed Night to gain space to brush his other side. *All this uncertainty weighs mine mind and darkens mine spirit. No husband. If Belleme is still fighting the king, no safety. Should they war and Henry lose, mine protection is gone. If the king is still chasing Belleme, I am but an occasional afterthought. Where is Belleme? I must ask Reeve; the Saxons will know.*

15

An Addition

As the August sun beat upon her back and neck, Margaret was on her knees pulling up vegetables, brushing dirt from them and laying them in the basket beside her.

Hartun approached and said, "My lady, Sir Roulin is bringing a strange man up the lane."

Margaret stood and swept her apron clean. "Please take the basket to Cook. Inform me if she requires more. Send Scandy to me." Margaret walked toward the gate to meet the pair. Standing on the walkway, Claude announced, "My lady, Roulin and the stranger have stopped well before the gate. I suggest you climb here to inspect him."

Even from a distance, she saw the man was Saxon. *He has a thick neck and broad shoulders, well-muscled arms and big hands. Has he run away?* "Roulin, who goes there?" she shouted.

"He claims he is a black smith, my lady. He seeks work."

Someone below her coughed.

"Ah, Scandy. Where is Cormac?"

"In the village, my lady."

"Tell him I need him. Then go to Reeve and Father Manntun and ask them to meet me in the hall." To Roulin, she yelled, "Sir Roulin, please wait there with this fellow until I send for you." At Roulin's salute, Margaret turned. "Sir Claude, I want two knights to meet Roulin and the stranger at the gate. They will escort him and stay with him when he is in the hall with me. Send Roulin out again. We needs know if this man is scouting for a group hidden in the forest."

"Yes, my lady. May I suggest we send two men not on sentry duty with Roulin as a precaution?"

"Good thinking. Yes." Margaret looked to the village and spotted Cormac between huts. "Thank you, Sir Claude." She left the walkway and strode toward the hall.

Margaret smiled at the threesome walking toward her with the stranger wedged between Verel and Giraud. *Such a soothing sound. Creaking leather jerkins with clinking mail rings. Almost as comforting as hearing chain mail and seeing helmets. Glad they always wear their swords.* Her knights positioned the man and settled in front of him. They left him only the single foot of space between them from which to see the four sitting on the dais.

"Your name and from whence come you?"

"I am Garwig, my lady," he responded as he lowered his head and pulled his forelock. Garwig stood tall and continued with, "I am a smith trained in Gloucester; I have mine medal to prove it." He removed the double sided coin from a pocket and handed it to Giraud, who stepped forward and placed it on the table. Father picked it up, read both sides and nodded. "I wander seeking work. When I learned you had an anvil but no smith, I came hoping you can use me."

"Do you make chain mail, armor, helmets, and swords?"

"No, my lady, a white smith does that. I am a black smith and do common iron work, hinges, nails of all sizes, pivots for wagon tongues, axels, plow tips, common tools. I have forged locks, keys, pulleys, and other devices. I can form cups, plates, and candlesticks. I am skilled at making wheel rings. I have even repaired a few wheels, but I am no wheelwright who makes them from raw wood."

"Gloucester is famous for training iron mongers and their good work. Why did you leave?"

Garwig shifted his weight to his other foot. "Over a woman."

"Explain."

"After mine apprenticeship, I worked at a large ironworks. I became betrothed, and we were to wed as soon as I provided a house. While she waited, another man saw her, a rich merchant's heir. His father has several businesses and is very important. She would live in a great house on a hill overlooking the bay. She wanted servants, fine clothes and such. He courted her behind mine back and she chose him. I got drunk, sought the man, and beat him. He took me to court; they fined me thirty days hard labor and the loss of all mine possessions. I still have mine paper saying I am a free man. They wed while I was chained and making locks. After a month and a day, the guild turned me out of town and ordered me never to return. The bag I left outside the gate holds what little I have gained by working here and there. If you hire me, I shall show you mine worth. Then you can decide what to pay me. All I request is to be housed and fed while I labor."

"You have a temper. Whom else have you beaten? How often do you drink too much? Have you murdered anyone?" challenged Margaret.

"That was the first time I ever got drunk or beat a man. I have killed no one, I swear. I had a temper then. In mine wanderings, I learned to curb it."

Margaret turned to Father Manntun and placed her hand by her cheek so no one read her lips. After they conferred, she turned forward and waited.

"My son, escorted by these men, you shall follow me into the church. There I shall hear your confession. While I can never reveal what you say, I can tell Lady Margaret if we can trust you. Lie to me and you damn your immortal soul."

Garwig nodded. "In confession you shal know I have spoken truths."

"Follow me." Father Manntun left the hall with Garwig and his escorts.

"Cormac?"

"I believe him."

"Reeve?"

"It is an old story and not uncommon."

"Have we any work for him?"

"Oh yes," said the men in unison.

Cormac spoke first. "He could form the rods and make the hangers for inside wooden shutters to keep back the winter winds. If he makes locks and things, we can barter with them. If he forms nails, we can use them in rebuilding the barracks and building the grain bins you want. Reeve?"

"Both Rammeg Elder and Rammeg Younger are skilled carpenters who make wheels, but no wheel will survive without an iron ring holding it together. If this man forms and installs wheel rings, we can make the wagons we need. We will let it be known we have a smith and make money from his labor. With our mill and a smith, we might get the king's permission to hold a market. Some day our village might even grow to become a town."

"While we wait, I will send for a pitcher of ale." Margaret went to the servants' entrance and called out, "Page!" When Scandy skidded to her, she gave instructions and waited. She soon re-entered with a tray, climbed the dais stairs and placed it before the men. "Please leave a mug of ale in Father's place," she requested as she sat. Cormac passed her a half-filled mug. "Thank you." Margaret sipped as she waited.

After a time, the group returned and re-took their positions. Before anyone spoke to Garwig, Verel entered, stepped forward and whispered to Lady Margaret and Father Manntun that no one had been found in the forest, on the road, or within a mile of the bailey. Margaret nodded. Verel stepped back and placed his left hand over the pommel of his sword.

Father Manntun announced, "Lady Margaret, his name is Garwig and he spoke truths to you. I believe him, but I suggest he be watched until we are cert of him."

"Do you still want to work here, watched as you will be?"

"Yes, my lady."

"What tools have you brought with you?"

"None, my lady. As I said before, they took all my things, even the tools I had earned."

"Garwig, please go to the other end of the hall and wait." Margret motioned her knights forward. "Let us whisper. Where can he live?"

"I will let him sleep in mine house. He needs to cook for himself, for I am no cook."

"Thank you, Cormac. Reeve, can you be gone three days, mayhap four?"

"The harvesting waits not, my lady, and it must be supervised. If you want me to go to Gloucester, you could ask Scirburne to reeve while I am gone. He was reeve before me and knows what needs be done." He thought a moment before adding, "Or you might send Scirburne. He is older than I and may have better bargaining skills."

Cormac added, "I could go for you, but I think a Saxon would be a better choice. Someone might not like selling to a foreigner."

"I appreciate your wise counsel, Cormac. Felamaere, if Scirburne will reeve while you are gone, I prefer you go. As the current Reeve, they will think you important enough to represent me. Think you Scirburne will serve?"

"Yes, my lady."

Margaret asked the group, "Which is better, send Garwig, escorted of course, to Reading for tools and iron or leave him here and have Reeve and two knights take a list to Gloucester to get what we need?" She heard advantages and disadvantages as the men talked among themselves. Gloucester was disliked because the trip might be in vain if they learned who was their blacksmith, and they refused to sell Reeve any goods. Reading was not favored because a blacksmith's tools were so valuable they might cost double or even treble. *Gloucester will cost me less.* As she listened, Margaret envisioned her pile of coins shrinking even more. When she saw the men realized the choice was even for both cities, Margaret decided.

"I am for Gloucester. Tell them not who is our black smith, or even that we have one. Let them think we are setting up a smith in the hopes of attracting one. If they will not sell to us without hiring one of their smiths first, then we do so and send Garwig away. Either way we win. I will not promise him anything until we have tools." When even Father Manntun agreed hers was the good plan, Margaret asked Verel to call Garwig forward. Giraud followed and stood behind him.

"All we have is the anvil, Garwig. Reeve will show you the work we plan. Cormac will follow you and write a list of tools, goods, iron, and such you will need to complete those projects. On the morrow, Reeve will take a wagon to Gloucester to make the purchases. The tools and goods are mine. If all goes well, you and I will set your pay after we see the quality of your work. What say you?"

"I will help you by telling you which smiths sell the best goods. Also, I will pray for a successful trip so I may stay and work for you."

"As will I," offered Father Manntun.

That is as good a recommendation as you may have here. "Father, please write the letter giving Reeve permission to go to Gloucester for me. I leave the three of you to begin the tour and the list." After only Verel and Giraud remained did she say, "Sir Verel, I leave the choice of the men to accompany Reeve in your good hands."

The knights exited the hall. Elstan arrived and volunteered to accompany the party to translate, observe and report to which Margaret agreed. After Elstan left, Margaret put her elbows on the table and her head in her hands as she guessed how many coins this new endeavor might cost her.

Send a thousand pennies. Almost half what I have sent to Reading! Pray they return with some in hand. Send more than a thousand should they need it. A thousand pence is... more than seventy shillings. Dear God! Seventy shillings!

16

New Sister

Villeins were busy harvesting their third crop of hay. Scythes with tall wooden handles swished through the golden crop as three men cut stalks heavily laden with large grains. A row of uncut grain stood between each of them. The men wanted not to slash another worker's legs with the sharp blades. When they reached the end of the field, they turned and cut the rows they had left between them. Women behind the cutters scooped up the stalks, bunched them, and used a long stalk to bind them together. They left the bunches on the ground for the next group. Behind them the older girls gathered the stalks into piles of three to lean against each other. Workers on the wagons accepted the hay bundles men threw to them and stacked them for transport to the barns. Later, the widows and their children harvested the fallen grain for themselves, as was their right. Only stubble remained to hold the dirt against winter winds.

At the edge of the field., Margaret sat upon Night watching the Saxons work. Night had lowered his head to the meadow grass at his hooves. A sudden gust threatened to take Margaret's straw hat, so she grabbed the brim with her left hand. She looked up to study the sky. *No rain clouds, but the wind may blow them our way. Best they get this grain inside before dark.* Behind Margaret, Demetre and Hughes came alert and turned their horses toward the lane.

"Someone coming, my lady. Please stay behind us," instructed Hughes.

With a hand still on her brim, Margaret used her other hand to signal Night with two light jerks on the reins. Night lifted his head, felt Margaret's shift on her platform, and turned too. As Margaret saw who were walking their horses up the lane, she announced, "They are mine uncle, mine brother... and mine new sister." Margaret commented. "Let us meet them," she urged.

After Roulin, who had followed the group, signaled all was well, he returned to the forest and rode west through the trees. Margaret's escorts led the way.

"Welcome, Lord Thibaud. Welcome, Lord Charles. Brother dear, please wait not to be in the hall. Who travels with you?"

Charles removed his hat and waved it as he pointed toward Margaret. "My lady, this is mine sister, the Lady Margaret. Dear Sister, I present mine bride, the Lady Cleanthe."

Margaret drew Night beside Cleanthe's horse, forcing the young lady to twist to her right. "Welcome, my lady. I am most delighted to meet you. Hughes will lead us. May I be permitted to follow you?" *Married women before girls.*

"Of course, Lady Margaret."

Those niceties completed, Margaret followed Cleanthe. Inside the bailey Margaret watched Hughes dismount and hold a leather strap on Thibaud's horse's cheek as Lord Thibaud dismounted. Jorgon ran out of the stables and held Lord Charles's horse. After Charles dismounted, Jorgon turned his gelding over to a stable boy and reached for the next horse. He waited until Lord Charles had helped his wife dismount her palfrey before handing its reins to the second stable boy. When Lord Charles strode toward Night, Jorgon took long steps and reached for Night's halter.

With her hands on Charles's shoulders, Margaret dropped to the ground. She grabbed him into a quick hug and a peck on the cheek. "I am happy for you."

"Thank you."

"Lord Thibaud, please lead everyone into the hall. I will order refreshments and make arrangements." She walked ahead of her guests with Scandy and Hartun beside her. Hartun headed for the kitchen; Scandy left for the motte. Margaret arrived in the hall ahead of the rest. She served the ale as soon as Hartun delivered it. He stood at attention by the servants' entrance. Verel arrived to sit with the men. Margaret waited for a servant to step into the hall, nod at her, and leave.

"Lady Cleanthe, if you will accompany me to the keep, I will take you to your sleeping arrangements. You may wish to refresh yourself."

"Thank you, Lady Margaret. I shall."

The women excused themselves. Margaret pointed to the kitchen as they walked across the bailey toward the gardens. Cleanthe complimented Margaret on the neatness of the gardens and the variety of vegetables. Margaret bragged she had grubbed the land herself. Cleanthe admitted she liked to grub her own gardens as well. They giggled at each other's comments. The pair backtracked to the motte and stepped through the gate. Margaret led as they walked up the stairs and up the ladder to the first floor. Servant girls in a line curtsied as the women passed. They collapsed onto stools after the women started the stairs. The girls giggled with delight at their success.

"I have placed Lord Thibaud on the second floor and Lord Charles and you on the third floor."

Lady Cleanthe looked surprised to find her bags already in her room. The bedding looked fresh. She peeked behind the curtain in the corner and wondered why the chamber pot smelled of lavender. She used the pot.

She is eleven and married. Just right. Charles should have waited until he was eighteen, but he needs a wife now and three years older is far enough. Good on him. I too should have been wed four years ago, but here I am, waiting for the king to send me a husband. Dear God, soften King Henry's heart and have him send me a husband before we are attacked again or worse. Margaret frowned at the worry of what might be worse.

Lady Cleanthe caught Margaret's expression as she stepped from behind the sailcloth curtain. "Lady Margaret, do you resent mine husband's position?"

Margaret was aghast. *Who told you that?* "Of course not! I love Charles. He is my brother. Did you not see me hug him and kiss his cheek in greeting?"

"Then why do you address him as Lord Charles?"

"Lord Thibaud insisted upon it when last we met. I want not to anger the man who will be mine brother's guardian for the next four years."

"I call him Uncle Thibaud, and he tolerates it. Why not call him uncle as well?"

"You match his rank, not I."

"Uncle is too stiff; we are not. You are family. If Charles calls you Margaret, will you call him Charles and me Cleanthe?"

"As you wish."

"I will tell him to do so."

"May I suggest?" At Cleanthe's nod, Margaret advised. "I have learned men like neither to be ordered nor to be corrected. I suggest you ask him privately. If he agrees you and I may call each other by our Christian names and omit the titles, then ask him how he wants me to address him. Only in family settings, though. We must still maintain propriety in public."

"You give good advice." Cleanthe unpacked a beautiful green linen bliaut banded at the neck, wrists, and hem. As she smoothed her wedding garment against the bedding, she commented, "You have not asked after Cecily." Cleanthe doffed her travel clothes as Margaret assisted her.

"I thought it better if I did so when Charles and I were in private. If you know how she fares, I am happy to learn it."

"She is being fostered by mine parents."

Cleanthe's even gaze at Margaret unsettled her. She smiled her gladness. "Cecily will enjoy being in Normandy. New sites, new people. Fostered, you say?"

"For a year or more, depending how long it takes her to complete her training as a chatelaine. Then Uncle and Charles will decide her future."

"Cecily is fortunate be in your family's company. Charles spoke highly of them when he visited in June, but he talked most often about you." *I hope it pleases you to hear that. Nice blush. How to change the conversation?* "He told me so little of your family. Will you tell me about them as I assist you?" They finished unpacking and setting things about the room. They were sitting on the side of the bed when Charles arrived.

"Margaret, please stop that 'lord' business when we are with family. It is enough we must do it in public." Cleanthe and Margaret looked at each other and giggled. Cleanthe put her arm about Margaret's shoulder; Margaret put hers around Cleanthe's waist. "That is much better. Now you look like sisters."

"Where is Uncle?" asked Margaret.

"Downstairs inspecting the bed."

"You two rest until we sup. I will visit Uncle," offered Margaret as she bounced from the bed. She hugged Cleanthe. She hugged Charles again. "Thank you for stopping on your way home." She whispered in his ear, "I like mine new sister," before she left and closed the door for them.

Charles is fortunate to make the match he wanted. It is true; men do the choosing. I pray someone chooses me. Please, God. Soon. Margaret reached the second landing and knocked on the door. "It is I, Lord Thibaud. How may I serve you?"

Margaret seated Sir Verel next to Lord Thibaud, then Cleanthe, Charles, herself, the empty seat, Caitlin and Cormac. They dined on broth, roasted chickens, boiled vegetables, bread, butter and ale. Uncle complained the food was too rich for an evening meal.

"I have provided you with choices so you might eat what best suits you, Uncle. I want not that you say I set a poor table for mine family."

Charles offered, "The chicken is delicious, Margaret. You know how hungry I get when I travel." He winked at her.

"And I, dear Sister," added Cleanthe, who leaned back and also winked at Margaret behind Thibaud's back.

Lord Thibaud scowled. Hartun replaced the platter of meat and vegetables he had placed before the lord with a bowl of broth and another round of bread. At bedtime, Margaret and Caitlin slept fireside on pallets set beside each other. The servants slept across the room on blankets over straw.

I see how they look at each other. Would that a man looked upon me with such favor.

"Caitlin," Margaret whispered, "I want to give them a wedding gift, but I know not what?"

'Your mother's scissors or thimble."

"Charles already told me I may keep them."

"Then one of them truly would be a gift."

"The old Lord Charles hated goats and would not have them. Might they like one of our already-bred does?"

"Stop avoiding what you already know you must do." Caitlin rolled away and refused to speak again when Margaret tried to engage her.

The thimble? No, it is too precious to me. He replaced the scissors. Having two scissors is better than having one. Oh, but the cost of replacing it. Stop your thinking! This gift is more important than cost. Ask mine heart. Which one do I want more, heart? No answer? Tell me in the morning.

After Mass and their first meal and before Margaret's family left the hall, Margaret took Cleanthe aside. With an honest smile, she offered her gift with both hands. "Please accept mine wedding gift to you. Mother treasured the scissors her father gave to her at her wedding. It was her mother's. I want you to have it. I hope you pass it to a daughter some day."

"Oh, Margaret, I cannot take something of your mother's from you."

"Cleanthe, dear sister, I have Mother's thimble. That is enough for me. Please take it." Margaret extended her arms further and waited. Cleanthe accepted Margaret's offering.

"Sister, dear, you are kind, thoughtful and generous to give us what I know is precious to you. I will continue to believe what mine husband says about you and not what Cecily claimed."

What might Cecily have said? I know. She repeats what old Lord Charles said of me, disobedient, willful, defiant, too proud. Stop. Stop. Enough. She will never think well of me. Mayhap, nor I of her. I will never go to Normandy, never again see her. Long ago, I forgave your hurts to me. Go your own way, Cecily. I wish you well… and happy. I wish the same for me, Oh Lord, I know. Your will in all things. Please count not what she did to me and be good to Cecily despite it.

Cleanthe carefully placed the scissors in the satchel by the main door.

When she returned, she whispered, "We have already agreed. Our heir will be Charles Younger and our first daughter will be Rosamonde, after your mother. Do you object?"

Margaret hugged Cleanthe hard and whispered back, "Not at all. Mother would love that. I am so pleased you thought of it. Thank you for remembering her." Margaret embraced Cleanthe and pecked her on her cheek. "I hope we will see much of each other in future years."

"I pray we will watch our children grow and play together," add Cleanthe. She put her arm around Margaret's waist or held her hand and refused to part with her until they were in the bailey. Farewells were long and loving. Margaret and Night escorted her family as far as the road. Margaret waved until they rounded the bend toward Gloucester and north. She spoke with the sentries; all was quiet.

She informed them she was returning to her duties and turned Night up the lane. *Dear God, I want what she has, a good man who cares for her. I am wrong to be jealous, and it is a sin. But jealous I am. I stupidly thought being in charge, making decisions, having mine own property was going to be pleasurable, what I desired. The cost is great: worry, fears, no lord's protection, the weight of all this responsibility. Mother was wrong; it is better to share the burdens. Take mine part as his lady, and let mine lord have his part.* Margaret stopped at the lane's end and watched her people working in the fields. *She is a good person. You chose well, Charles. At least men get to choose. I want to choose as well, but I fear the king has other ideas. William, have you already chosen another? Why do I hear nothing of it? Put that aside now and tend to this day. See the Saxons have enough water. Donkeys too. Be cert none are getting too hot. The Saxons have been harvesting since shortly after Mass and will be very hungry by midday. Ask Reeve if I need do anything. If not, I will help in the kitchen. Making bread will be fun. Three weeks to Michaelmas, and we still have so much to do.*

A week later Margaret was in the kitchen helping prepare vegetables. Wearing a dirty apron with sweat trickling down her back, damp armpits and wet tendrils curling around her face, Margaret looked more like a serving wench than the lady of the estate. She stepped outside to meet her visitor. He stood inside the bailey between two knights as they waited for her arrival. Behind them, stable boys held their horses' reins.

"My lady," began Sauville, "this knight claims he is from King Henry and has a message for you."

"I am the Lady Margaret, good sir. Please state your message."

The man bowed low. His smile revealed three missing lower teeth.

"I am Sir Cavel. This letter is His Royal Highness's first message. He told me to tell you he gives his permission for your request, with conditions." The knight handed over the roll of parchment tied with a bare cloth rib.

"Thank you, Sir Cavel. I suspect you have carried this a long way. May I offer you the coolness of the hall, a mug of ale, and a plate of cheese and bread to enjoy?" Margaret held the parchment at her side and called out, "Page." Scandy quickly arrived. "Page, please take this document to Father." After Scandy left, Margaret turned to the king's messenger. "Sir Cavel, I await His Royal Highness's second message."

Sir Cavel bowed. "Lady Margaret, meet Sir Cavel, knight of the realm, who pleads for the honor of your hand in marriage. Treat him well, for he is a favorite of mine."

This time, Margaret remembered to ask, "Have you the password?"

"Second boon, my lady."

Margaret curtsied and replied, "Welcome, Sir Cavel, who comes at the king's command." Margaret raised her right arm and moved to Sir Cavel's left side. "It would honor me, Sir, if you will escort me to the hall, for I would like to sit with you while you partake of your repast."

Sir Cavel accepted Margaret's arm on his with, "No, my lady, the honor is mine."

As before, Caitlin was in the hall to chaperone; Margaret introduced her and explained her presence. As before, a servant appeared and left the tray on the side tables. This time Margaret's decision regarding this suitor was immediate. She waited to share it until the knight had eaten and was sipping his second mug of ale.

"Sir Cavel, I am sorry to report I believe His Royal Highness has forgot a condition of our agreement. Sir Cavel, any man who asks for mine hand must be sixteen to twenty-five years old. Sir, you are older than that, are you not?"

"I am forty-one, my lady."

Margaret wanted to gasp, but, smiling not, she only nodded. *Old enough to be mine grandfather! You are playing with me, Henry. I will not have it.* "I am cert you are a knight of worth and breeding, Sir Cavel. From the state of your clothes, I surmise you have travelled long and hard to meet me. Unfortunate for you, I must refuse your suit because of your age, but you are welcome to stay the customary three days. Mine knights will see to your needs. I will be busy elsewhere. We are but a fortnight before we pay our tithe and taxes, and we must finish the harvest and inventory the animals. Sirs Sauville and Masselin will keep you company while I work elsewhere." Margaret looked behind her and saw Hartun. "Fetch a pitcher of ale and mugs for this good knight and mine men and serve them here." Margaret looked back to the men. "Knights, I must return to mine duties." With that, she turned on her right heel as she spun away, exited, and strode across the bailey with the church, Father, and the king's letter as her goals.

"Her manner is brusk, not lady-like at all," said Sir Cavel in an angry tone. "I saw the whole roast pig on that spit outside the village. She is very wealthy to order one roasted daily."

Masselin explained, "Sir Cavel, the villeins work from Mass to almost sunset and hunger. During harvest we eat meat twice a day. As it takes all day to roast a whole pig, we sup on half tonight and dine on half on the morrow. We are a long time until we sup. so I can order another board of bread and cheese, if you like."

"I would like that." Sir Cavel complained again, "She is curt and not given to the niceties of a well-bred girl."

Sauville defended his lady with, "She is busy, Sir Cavel. When she is at her leicert, the Lady Margaret is a well-bred young woman who treats everyone well."

In bed on the top floor of the keep, Caitlin first asked about the king's letter.

"King Henry has given me permission to use the stone blocks de Warenne had intended for a barbican. Reeve will assign four men to begin on the morrow with the base of the first grain bin. As the trees are already cut and sawed in half, putting up the building should take but a fortnight. God grant it not rain before the crop is stored inside."

Caitlin then reminded Margaret of her duties to a guest. "While you introduced Sir Cavel as your guest, you placed him on the other side of Father instead of beside you as you should have."

"He had not washed. He smelled of horse, his breath was bad, and his clothes bore the filth of travel."

"And you came from the kitchen and smelled of sweat and bread. This will not do, Margaret. You washed before bed. I requested Verel ask Sir Cavel to do the same. If he meets you at the gate, you will place your hand on his arm and permit him to escort you. You may avoid him during the day if you like, but you will seat him next to you at every meal, be polite, and act interested in the topics he chooses. I will not have him report you lack manners and courtesy."

"Yes, Caitlin. Now may I sleep? I am very tired."

"God give you a good rest, child of mine heart."

"God give you a good rest, Caitlin."

Another reject. Why are you deliberatley sending men I cannot accept? How long must I wait while I pretend I am ruling in an unknown man's name? *Why are you still angry with me after seven long months? Well you know I need a husband's protection, his strength. Every day I am in danger of being attacked and ravaged for mine land and property. Is that how you expect to punish me? Wait for an attacker to take me unwilling? And then gloat at your success? I will not have it!* Margaret pounded her pillow and shifted in her bed. *What are you plotting, Henry? I will thwart you. I will thwart you. If I must, I will rule this place alone.* Margaret slept not until the exhaustion of worrying overtook her.

In Winchester, another woman took to her bed, but she too slept not. She turned to face the wall and then turned back toward the room in the discomfort of being in her courses. She wished she could cry, but she was not alone. Slivers of silvery moonlight beaming onto the floor from the upper windows gave her no comfort. She pulled the tapestry closed to be in the dark and shut her eyes. From the shadows, a woman stepped forward,

"Your Royal Highness, I have a message for you," she whispered, "from the one who returned from the Grand Crusade and handed His Royal Highness a letter from the pope." From behind the bed curtain she heard one word.

"Speak."

"Your Royal Highness, I have accomplished almost all you asked of me. I have a lord, land, and coin. Mine garden is ripening; the house is built and soon will be thatched. I respectfully ask you to remember mine request."

The woman waited. She faintly heard a long, slow sigh.

"Sent this," began Queen Matilda. "I will reconsider your request when I have what I need. Until then, you must wait."

The woman receded to the wall and disappeared into the dark. From within the curtains Matilda again turned to the wall. This time she shed silent tears of sorrow at another month gone and no heir in her belly.

17

※

Tithe and Tax

"We are done. Tomorrow truly will be a day of rest. Monday is Michaelmas." Margaret nudged Cormac with her shoulder. "Cormac, smile. We are done!"

"Not quite, my lady. We still have the matter of your knights to discuss."

Margaret frowned. "Who has decided to leave me?"

"None. I asked each separately, and they all have chosen to stay." Cormac closed the accounts book and turned on his stool to face her. "You needs pay them so they can pay their tithes and taxes."

Still frowning, Margaret averred, "I have been paying them. Sixty pence until Easter is five shillings. Three shillings a month for five months is…"

Cormac looked not in the accounts book and reported, "Fifteen more shillings for a total of twenty shillings. So says the accounts book. Since all you have is pennies, your debt to them is two hundred and forty pence each for your nine men."

Margaret tapped the thin wooden slat that topped the pages of the estate's records. "Less what I have already paid them."

"My lady, none of them have taken their wages. Where have they gone? Nowhere. What have they done? Only serve you. No one has gone to a market. Their wages are still in your hands."

"Oh drat! More deductions from mine money chest. When will it end?"

"Never. You have debts, my lady. The Church, the crown, all your knights, Garwig, Gytha, Jorgon, Caitlin, even me. None of us has taken our wages, yet we must also pay what we owe."

Margaret dropped her head into her hands. "I know you, Cormac. You have a plan. What is it?"

"Meet with your knights on Monday. Pile coins on this table and ask each what he wishes to do with his wages. You can pay them part or all. Or you can give them only what they will owe on Michaelmas, so they may pay their tithes and taxes. I deduct from the accounts book what they take. Offer to continue to guard their remaining coins until they ask for them. Let each man decide what he wishes to do."

Margaret looked up and dropped her hands. "Agreed, but I want to speak first with mine knights as a group. I have something to tell them; then I will call up each man. Afterward, I will see the others. Do you mind being last, Cormac?"

"No, my lady. As the morrow is Sunday, I suggest you create two large bags of coins now and store them in the chest. That will be faster than your making your men wait as you make bags Monday morn."

"I can meet with mine men at the end of breaking our fasts." Margaret thought a moment and asked, "Whom shall I trust to carry such a heavy load for me? Will you?"

I suggest you ask Syghelm; you have been ignoring him and he admires you so."

"Syghelm! I have forgot him! I never see him at Mass. Not during the day." Margaret furrowed her brow. "I only see him... evening? Why is he at table only when we sup? And far down the line at that."

"Syghelm chooses to guard you at night. At night others take turns watching at the gate, but Syghelm guards all the rest all night, axe in hand. He strolls the walkway, checks the gate to the motte that it stays locked, and more. He breaks his fast in the kitchen and is abed for the day before the end of Mass."

"Another knight could take his place. He should attend Mass."

"Men have offered. He says he is not Christian, follows his people's ancient ways, refuses to attend Mass. At first Father tried hard to convert him and failed. Now Father tries only now and then. Whom do yo wish to carry the bags?"

"Syghelm. I will stay up past dark. If I walk to the gate, think you he will meet me so I may ask him?"

"He will."

"Good. He said he will stay?"

"Yes, he did."

Margaret sighed. "Best we make bags now. Soon we will sup." Margaret rose. Book in hand, Cormac followed Margaret as she left the hall, turned left and walked toward the motte. Heavy in thought, Margaret chose silence.

"The waning moon is too faint. Here, take this candlestick so you stumble not and fall. I will stand in the doorway and call out if something untoward happens."

Already on the rungs, Margaret reached up and took the light. 'Thank you, Caitlin." Her mantle billowed as she climbed down the ladder with one hand and with the other balanced the candlestick so wax would not burn her. Soon she called up cheerfully, "On the ground." Margaret picked her way to the stairs. She planted her feet solidly on each step before she descended to the next one. Halfway, she spotted a dark figure walking toward the gate, a figure carrying a long stick with its head behind the man's shoulder. Margaret smiled to herself; she stopped at the gate opposite the Dane on the other side.

Syghelm shifted his axe off his shoulder and leaned it against the high stone wall surrounding the motte. "My lady."

"Hello, Syghelm. Do you hide from me?"

"No, my lady, I prefer to work at night."

"Why?"

"It is easier for me and for everyone else. I sleep while the knights guard and practice. No chance for fighting. I guard while they sleep. I depart before everyone leaves Mass so I vex not Father Manntun. Besides, mine hearing is very good. At night I hear well for a distance. At this moment I hear three boar walking and snorting. Sneaking up on me is hard, my lady."

Margaret looked passed his head and saw a guard near the gate stop walking. She asked, "What is the gate guard doing?"

Syghelm listened a moment and smiled. "Farting, my lady."

Margaret covered her mouth. After she stopped laughing, she turned serious and asked, "You spend so much time away from everyone. I am curious as to why you chose to stay."

"I am tired of fighting. I am already thirty-nine years, my lady. Guarding is easier than fighting. After you put those heads on pikes, I was cert being attacked again was unlikely. Especially after you left the poles standing."

"Do you miss your family, Syghelm, your home country?"

"Mine parents died long ago. I have cousins northeast in the Danelaw area. One day I may visit them, but not yet."

"I have two requests of you, Syghelm." When Margaret heard, "Done, my lady," she added, "But you know not what they are."

"No matter, my lady, I trust you."

"On Monday morn, I need you to stay awake. After I break mine fast, I want you to accompany me to the top of the Keep. There I have two heavy bags of coins for paying people; they needs be carried into the hall. You are free to leave after I pay you." When Margaret received only a nod, she added, "As to how others treat you, I want you to continue to sup with us, but I want you to change where you sit. Almost everyone sits in the same place, but I am asking you to move closer and closer to the front of the hall. Talk to the men to become friends. By Christmastide, I wish you to sit as near to me as you can."

"Why, my lady?"

"Because I need the others to know you. Because I trust you. God give you a good night, Syghelm."

"God give you a good night, my lady."

When Margaret was again in the keep's doorway, she saw the shadow that was Syghelm pick up his axe, walk eastward, and disappear.

Margaret closed the door, and she and Caitlin dropped the bars into place. She picked up the candlestick and led Caitlin. As she climbed the stairs, Margaret commented, "We pray our guardian angels watch over us and protect us. I just learned a guardian angel can also be one who carries an axe."

On Monday, Margaret ate quickly and left the hall after asking her men to wait. At her return, she sat in her usual place to the left of the empty chair. Syghelm followed and placed the bags to her right before he joined the knights. Cormac moved from his usual place to sit to Margaret's left. Father Manntun stayed on his stool to the right of the empty one. After Scandy refilled each man's mug, Margaret asked him to leave.

"Today is Michaelmas. I declare the morrow to be a holiday with no unnecessary work or patrolling. Father will say a special Mass of thanksgiving. Cook and I planned a special midday meal for Norman and Saxon alike. The Saxons will squeeze us in this hall; but, as we have worked together so well, we will celebrate our rich harvest together. You will pay your taxes to me on Wednesday."

After the "Huzzahs!' died, Margaret began the important work of the day, paying her debts. "Father Manntun will witness. Cormac will record. Michaelmas is when all tithes and taxes are due. I know not when the Church's and the crown's reeves will arrive, but I want our transactions completed before they do. Announcements first. His Royal Highness sent two suitors, both most unsuitable." Margaret smiled at her own pun as did her men. "Each day I pray the next man he sends will prove to be mine future lord. I know not how long that may be. Next, knights, I thank you most heartedly for choosing to stay past Michaelmas. Because you work so hard and to thank you for your loyalty, I increase your pay one shilling a month." Margaret had to stop until the pounding of mugs on table tops stopped. She enjoyed hearing the thanks and compliments.

She raised her hand for silence and continued. "I would pay it to you today, but then you would owe tithe and tax on it. I will continue to record your pay the middle of each month so you will owe not more until a year from now. Does that suit you, or do you want the additional pence now?"

After the men conferred, Sir Verel stood and spoke for them when he said, "Thank you, my lady, starting next month suits us."

"Now to the next matter. The coins I owe you are in these bags. The record is in the accounts book Cormac keeps for me. Each may do as he wishes. You may take all or a portion of what I owe you at this time You may take only what you owe. Your tithe is two shillings as is the tax you owe. Please remember, be it Church or Crown, if you give more than the exact amount, they keep it and count it a donation." Margaret heard Manntun harrumph, but she ignored him.

"Cormac and I will see you one at a time. I ask those going on guard duty to come after Syghelm, who has already patrolled all night." Margaret reached over, loosened the ties, dipped into the first bag and brought forth a handful of coins. She liked hearing them clink together as they hit the table. So did her men. At the far end of the group, Syghelm rose and walked forward. He requested four shillings. After asking Margaret to keep his wage safe in her money chest, each knight took only what he owed God and realm.

After the last knight left, Cormac fetched a page. "Hartun, please send for Garwig, Gytha, Jorgon, Reeve, and Caitlin. Ask them to wait outside the main door until I summon them. Then return with ale and mugs for us."

After the boy left, Margaret turned to her priest. "Father, what did the traitor pay Reeve each year?"

"Six shillings a year."

"Is that enough?" Margaret was incredulous de Warenne had paid a reeve so little for so much work.

"Wait. I think he reduced his debt to ten percent as well." Manntun looked away and thought before he said, "Yes, he did. Ten percent."

"Without your remembering, I might have insulted Reeve. Thank you, Father."

Hartung arrived and exited the main door; Cormac poured the ale. The three chatted about Tuesday's holiday as they drank. Hartun returned and announced everyone was at the main door.

"Do you both agree we should start with Reeve?" When Cormac and Father did so, Margaret told Hartun, "Please ask Reeve to meet with us. We need you not after that." The boy pulled his forelock and exited the main door. Reeve closed the door behind himself and walked to the dais.

"God give you a good day, Reeve."

Reeve pulled his forelock and replied, "May God give you a good day, my lady."

"On this estate, a man who is the reeve all year owes only ten percent of his wealth of crops and animals to me. He is also paid six shillings at Michaelmas. Is that correct?"

"It is correct, my lady."

"I will keep the debt owed at ten percent, but I raise the shillings to seven to thank you for your hard work. Does that meet with your approval?"

"It does, my lady," said the smiling man.

As Cormac wrote, Margaret stacked the coins and passed them to Reeve. "Please take up the quill and make your mark here," asked Cormac, "as proof she paid you."

Margaret thanked Reeve for his good service and asked him to send in Gytha, who took half what she was owed and asked the rest be kept safe in the chest. The pair repeated the process with Jorgon and Garwig. Jorgon was paid in coin as his work was service only. Garwig asked Margaret to pay his tithe and tax for him; she agreed to do so. Caitlin gave them much trouble because she did not want a wage. Margaret insisted and promised she would keep Caitlin's coins in the chest until Caitlin asked for them. She finally persuaded Caitlin to accept the tithe and tax she owed. Margaret finished with, "Caitlin, when the knights and villeins learn I pay you, they will hold you in greater respect. They will know you are here by your own free will; they will also see I value your many contributions to our lives."

After Caitlin departed to delay dinner, Margaret addressed her seneschal. "I know not what a seneschal earns; I want to pay you as much as I did Caitlin. That way you are equal in wage and in how much I value your work. What say you to the same pay as I gave Caitlin?"

"I will agree if you will provide mine clothes as you do Caitlin."

"Only if you purchase or make your own boots."

"Agreed."

"Done. Now, how much do you want today?" Margaret counted out the tithe and tax as she had for Caitlin. She watched Cormac deduct from his own account and sign his name under it. "I am glad we have been paying Cook, her three helpers, and Duone each month. As we gave them September pay the middle of the month, we need not pay them until middle October."

With all debts paid, Margaret asked Cormac to carry the remaining coins back to the chest. As they walked toward the motte, the hall filled. Cormac placed the bags beside the chest and waited on the main floor while Margaret removed the key from her pocket and emptied the bags into the chest.

On their walk back to the hall, Margaret said, "Cormac, after we dine, we must total the coins I need for mine tax owed the crown. I already paid the tithe on mine gift. Father Gregory carried it to the bishop in Reading after we arrived. As I have no new coins, I owe the Church naught."

"Before we count it, we will remove the coins you owe your knights and the others. Those coins are not gain, they are debt. I will bring the book with us to count out your debt first." After they had dined, Cormac opt the back door for Margaret, and she strode through it to the keep.

Tuesday started with a Mass of gratitude for a successful harvest. Father's sermon spoke of God's graces upon them; no one would starve this winter. Father named each group from highest to lowest rank and detailed all they had gained because of the goodness of their Lord God.

After Mass Margaret made an announcement outside the church. "Our animals prosper and have increased. We are well and strong. I am sending you a goat carcass to share. I appreciate all you have done to give us a successful season, including full grain bins and grain sacks stacked almost to the roof of the hall. Yesterday, I wiped out all debts you owed the traitor. Cormac struck through them all and marked them paid. We start afresh, each of us."

Shocked, the men bowed from their waists and said, "Thank you, my lady!" The women curtsied. The Saxons looked at each other and shouted "Huzzah!" several times. In their happiness, men slapped each other's backs and women hugged. Children danced. Several children rushed Margaret and hugged her knees, hips and

waist. Margaret laughed and hugged them back. From the back of
the group, Elstan grinned his eagerness to report her generosity. She
accepted the villeins' good wishes. Several children reached for her
hands. Margaret chose one boy and one girl, each from a different
family, grasped their hands, and walked with them to the bailey.

In the hall, they dined on broth, roast pig and boiled vegetables.
Each adult received a mug of wine as if it were Christmas Day. After
the main part of the meal ended, the Saxons left to continue celebrating in the village. As Margaret lingered with those on the dais;
her men tarried over their dessert of cheese, apples and more wine.
Even Syghelm had stayed awake for the feast and was conversing
easily with knights.

For the estate, October first was tax day. Cormac sat beside
Margaret at the table in the middle of the bailey. Everyone entered
with animals, goods or coin. Cormac counted and weighed. Villeins,
who owned not land, their homes nor the land they were allotted
each year to grow crops, owed twenty percent of their wealth in crops
and animals or coin of equal value. While not her villein, Elstan too
owed tithe and tax on his crops and garden harvest. Sokemen, who
owned their land and homes and could buy and sell property, owed
service or rents. If at tax time, a sokeman had no coin for what he
owed his lord for tithe and royal tax, he still owed those debts. His
lord paid the tithe and tax for him; the sokeman then owed his lord
that amount in service. As Scirburne was Margaret's only sokeman,
his service as reeve while Felamaere traveled to Reading paid part
of what he owed her. Scirburne paid her the rest and still owed his
tithe and royal tax. The freemen Jorgon, Caitlin, and Cormac paid
Margaret the twenty percent they owed her. Margaret paid herself
Garwig's tax for the labor he had already given her.

At a table next to Margaret's sat Father Manntun. While Cormac recorded the ten percent tithe paid to Holy Mother Church from each person or family, the priest portioned the tithe into two sacks, a tenth for his use and their church building and the rest to be sent to the bishop. The church preferred coin, but accepted crops and animals from those who had no coins, which Father Manntun exchanged for coin from Margaret.

Two mornings later, a convoy of priests, warrior priests and wagons arrived. The head priest was angry Lady Margaret had both a receipt for the tithe she had sent the Bishop of Reading and for reporting no new revenue. He insisted on seeing the accounts book and poured over its contents until meal time. As required, Margaret fed the group. Afterward, the head priest used the accounts book to verify the coins and goods Father Manntun had collected. Choosing coin first, then grain, he returned the tenth to Father Manntun as required. At the end of the process, Margaret paid Garwig's tithe. She thanked the priests for their visit and stood as if expecting them to leave; her men followed her lead and too looked as if they wanted the party to depart. With no excuse to stay to force Margaret to feed them supper on Friday, house them for the night, and to let them break their fasts before they travelled to the next estate, the head priest was short and curt with his thanks for the midday meal. From the walkway, Margaret watched them disappear toward the main road.

Glad I am to see your backs. May mine new lord deal with you next year. Twice disappointed in suitors. Oh William, I fear mine wish for you is false hope. If you have not come by now, you never will. Why? Why? Is it because I carry a sword? Because you taught me how to use it when I should not have tricked you into doing so? Oh God, please have the king send me a good man next. All this is so hard. I need a lord.

To cool her mind, Margaret walked to the area of the barracks to watch Saxons lay the foundation stones, a single layer for the floor and a second layer around the edges to hold in the roof poles. Then she stopped near the grain bins and inhaled the sweet smell of harvested grain. *We are saved. Thank you, God, for your goodness to us.*

On Monday, the sixth day of October, the king's reeve arrived with assistants, an armed escort and even more wagons than the priests had brought. As they had arrived before sunset, Margaret supped with Lord Saloman to her left and all his men crowding hers. She was glad to leave for the quiet the keep afforded.

I envy not that mine men must share their space. The barracks is only fit if it does not rain. How long will the villeins take to thatch that roof now the harvest is done? Find wandering pigs? We must butcher and smoke meat as soon as these men leave. Soap making. Herbs gathered. Simples formulated. Acorns and firewood gathered. So much to do before winter arrives.

After Mass and breaking their fasts, Sir Saloman ordered the dais tables and stools taken into the bailey. Cormac had them placed as they had been for Lady Margaret. While everyone else paid their taxes in coin, animals or grain, Margaret walked to the keep to fetch the bag of coins she owed, including Garwig's tax.

Ten percent of all I have and all the taxes mine people just paid me. How can I increase mine wealth and replace some of mine spent coins if I prosper not more than the twenty percent I pay Church and Crown each year? I must think what to do. Margaret shook her head as she locked the chest, restrung its key on her necklace and dropped it beneath her bliaut.

"Margaret, why are you sitting in the corner hugging your chest?"

"All I spent establishing this estate, feeding the people, adding livestock, paying wages. Gone! Now I owe ten percent of all I have left plus all I just gained. How shall I regain enough lost wealth to make the dowry worth marrying me? Tithe and Tax. Twenty percent a year, every year, can destroy an estate's prosperity. Especially if a crop fails or illness befalls the villeins so they cannot work. Now I understand why mine parents worried over costs, crops, and increasing their wealth. While he resented Mother's bringing coins from midwifery, she did help keep their estate prosperous. Might I be forced to do be gone from husband and children to keep this estate?"

Caitlin extended her hand to Margaret, who grasped it and rose. "Worry not. Think of your poor villeins. They have only sixty percent of their wealth and no coin chest to smooth the road should hard times befall them. Be thankful for what you do have. Who knows? Your future lord may be wealthy. Think on that and smile."

Still full of worry, Margaret shook her down-turned head. She picked up the heavy bag of coins and preceded Caitlin down the stairs.

18

An Attack

Another rich harvest. Two more grain bins added to the compound. The roof of the grain bin and the barracks housing the knights thatched. The hall scrubbed clean, given new rushes, aired, and again smelling of food and ale. Another harvest feast done. October was the month for finding wandering pigs. As workers searched the forest, they gathered acorns to feed livestock over the winter.

Leoma, Willa, and Scirwode were with the party. The boys and men carried ropes with which to lead pigs. The girls and women wore aprons; some carried sacks. The siblings slowly separated as they drifted from tree to tree. The deeper into the forest they walked, the farther away they were from the sounds of others. Leoma stopped to smile at her apron full of acorns. She thought of her family's full grain sacks, of her father's comment that now he had the means to pay Lady Margaret the merchet, so she and Rammeg Younger could marry, and how the gift of a pig or two would be more than enough dowry. She looked for her sister and brother. In the shadows between the trees she spotted someone walking toward her, someone taller than her father and unfamiliar.

With both hands holding her apron, Leoma called out, "I am here. I have a full apron. Have you a sack I may put these in?"

The stranger was dressed in common Saxon garb, but his tunic and leggings were clean instead of work-stained. His boots were well worn and scuffed. His sandy hair hung as long as the law allowed and was damp as if it had just been washed. It swayed gently against his cheeks as he walked. Leoma noted his warm brown eyes, his friendly smile and the empty sack he carried over his shoulder. He approached.

"Gathering acorns for the pigs, I see," he started. "I did that in mine youth as well. Where is everyone?"

"They are near," answered Leoma. "Who are you?"

Without answering, the man strode forward and dropped his sack. In one gesture, he clapped his hand over Leoma's mouth as he grabbed her hair and pulled her to him. Acorns flew. Terrified, Leoma pushed at his chest to escape, but he was too strong. He slid his arm from her head to her shoulders and held her tight. Before Leoma could scream, he pulled a rag from his pocket and crammed it into her mouth. Leoma loosened one arm and scratched the corner of his eye and down his face while she kicked at him. In her mind, she screamed for her father then for Rammeg. The man was prepared. He reached into his tunic and pulled out a length of rope. Winding the rope around her wrists, with a secure knot he tied her hands in front of her. Leoma clenched her jaws and pushed her bound hands against his chest and kicked to no avail. With the sweep of a foot,

214

he unbalanced Leoma and pushed her to the ground. She fell onto scattered acorns, hurting her back and hips. Leoma's fall knocked the wind out of her. She froze as she watched him lift his tunic and untie his waist band. Leoma dug her heels into the ground and pushed herself backward. The stranger dropped his leggings below his knees, stepped forward, and knelt. For the first time, Leoma saw a manhood; it was huge and menacing. Leoma again dug her heels into the ground. He grabbed her feet and pulled her legs apart. The man's former smile grew into a cruel grimace as he rolled her gunna to her waist.

"If you fight me it shall hurt," he warned in a cold, harsh voice "You girls know what is coming. And you like it, yes you do," he added with a smirk.

As Leoma tried to scurry backward, the man clutched her hips and pulled her tighter to his thighs. He glanced around to be cert they were alone. Then he lay upon her. He pierced her maidenhead. Leoma screamed through the rag and tried to push him away, but he had pinned her hands between them. Leoma tightly clenched her eyes together as tears rolled into her hair. His movements jolted her. He used her body; he pierced her soul.

In her pain and panic the only thought Leoma registered was *Rammeg. What will Rammeg say? What will he do?* Leoma heard a cry. Suddenly her attacker rolled away. She felt a foot scrape across her breasts.

"I shall kill you! I shall kill you! She is mine sister!" Scirwode clung to the attacker's back even as the man rolled to shake him. Scirwode screamed. "To me--to me! Attacker! Ravager! Death!"

Leoma heard not the voices or the footfalls of those racing to their rescue. She felt pain, stickiness between her legs, and shame.

She rolled away from the scuffle and tried to push down her dress with her tied hands. "Oh God!" she heard from a voice above her. Unknown hands gently pulling her gunna to her ankles. Someone dropped to her knees, gently lifted Leoma's head, and cradled it in her soft lap. Willa untied the rope that bound her sister's hands, threw it aside, pulled the rag from her mouth and tossed that too. Leoma's crying became sobs. The woman holding Leoma's head in her lap whispered, "You are safe now," Leoma felt her cheek being stroked as she cried out her grief. She knew what she had lost and what it might cost her.

The boys and men dragged the ravager away from the women. A large man sat on his back. One villager grabbed the discarded rope to tie the stranger's hands. Another villager used his own rope to hobble the man's feet, and a third made a noose. He pulled it tight enough to force the man to stop struggling.

Scirwode kicked the attacker and ordered, "Hang him! Strangle him. Right now!" When one man and then another refused, Scirwode demanded, "Well then, cut off his balls! Who has a knife?"

Again, the men refused Leoma's brother. They informed the Scirwode only the Hundreds Court could decide what to do with the man.

"You shall be all right. They captured him. You shall be all right," Willa murmured as she knelt beside her sister. A little later, again Willa spoke. "Uncle Scelfdune shall pick you up. He hall carry you home. Please stop crying, dear sister. Mother shall take good care of you. Father shall avenge you. You shall be all right."

Leoma knew better.

Scirwode ran ahead. At the edge of the southeast meadow, stood Leoma's parents. Scirburne was scowling with his shoulders hunched forward and anger in his eyes. Ifig stood first on one foot and then the other with her arms crossed before her chest; her pale face contrasted with her brown eyes, wide and worried. Scirburne had led the procession and the crowd that followed. They stopped. When the villagers behind the couple saw Leoma, they became silent. Scirburne's expression of anger fell and turned soft with love and concern as he took his daughter from his brother, cradled her in his arms, nodded thanks, and turned away. Leoma buried her face in his shoulder. Scirburne's stare at the crowd warned them to remain silent. Ifig held her daughter's hand as they walked; she repeated, "Mine poor girl." Scirburne whispered "No," and Ifig went silent.

Daeltun ran into the hall to the head table. Lady Margaret and Cormac, who had their heads together over the accounts book, looked up. "Trouble in the village, my lady. A girl. Carried to her home. A crowd. Men leading a hobbled stranger with a rope around his neck," reported the stable boy. "What shall I do?"

"Nothing," replied Lady Margaret. "Return to your duties. We will see to it."

Cormac remained silent until they were outside. "My lady, perhaps you had best let the villagers handle village matters," he advised.

Margaret stopped and faced her seneschal. "Let us take the walkway." From that vantage, Margaret and Cormac saw villagers milling before Scirburne's home. A party of men led a bound man by a rope around his neck. Margaret noted his disheveled, dirty garments and his light hair bouncing about as he fought those pulling and pushing him forward. They watched as the bound man struggled hard against being taken among the huts. Garwig strode to the man and gave him a great blow to the jaw. As the man collapsed, Garwig grabbed him, flung him over his shoulder, said something to the men, and turned away. Garwig headed for his forge with men trailing him. Margaret and Cormac watched Garwig dump the man next to the forge and reach for the heavy rope one of his followers handed him. Margaret signaled Cormac to follow, climbed down the ladder, and strode into the hall. Cormac waited at the doorway. He led Reeve and two other men toward the head table where Margaret sat with her accounts book. She glanced up as if they had interrupted her.

"My lady, these men have a grievous deed to report."

Cormac stepped aside so the men could stand in a line before their mistress. Lady Margaret closed and set aside her book and placed the quill next to the ink pot. With her hands clasped and on the table, she nodded at Reeve.

"My lady, Leoma has been attacked and ravaged by an intruder. The smith tied him to his anvil and is guarding him. Scirwode stopped the attack. He is her only witness. These two men are among those who were in the forest and can be further witnesses."

At Lady Margaret's request, the men reported what they experienced.

God, how could you have let this happen to such a good girl? She is ruined, and we all know it. Poor girl. She did fight, so will Rammeg still have her? Margaret tried hard to concentrate on the men's words, but a fear jumped into her mind and took hard hold. *Without mine guards, that could have been me. He could have pulled me off Night, ruined me, and then taken this land. Saxon or not, he would have forced me to marry him. If we release him, he will ravage again, and another innocent will be ruined. I want him dead. Now.*

"Reeve, what can we do to him?"

"We cannot kill him. That is against the law." He saw Margaret's scowl of disapproval and watched the anger in her eyes rise. He tried to placate her. "The men have already beaten him. Were you a lord,

218

you could determine his fate: payment, punishment, even death. As it is, your only recourse is to take him to the nearest Hundreds Court. There, twelve Saxon men will hear the evidence. If they find him guilty, they set his punishment."

"Why did you say Scirwode was her only witness? These men and others saw the results of what was done. They can testify to the attack."

The Reeve explained, "Under Saxon law only a person – a male – who has actually witnessed what he was doing can testify to it."

Margaret's eyes narrowed and her voice turned both disbelieving and hard at the same time. "Are you telling me a woman who is ravaged cannot testify against the man who stole her honor?"

The Reeve shook his head. "No woman may testify in court. No woman may be a juror. Saxon law. In fact, it is also Norman law. Because they are both Saxons you can send the attacker to the Saxon Hundreds Court in Suindune."

"Outrageous!" exclaimed Margaret. "When is a man convicted of debasement?!"

"My lady, the law is strict to protect a man from a woman who falsely accuses him. Such an accusation already damages his reputation; it could be his ruination. She must have a witness, a male witness."

Lady Margaret leaned forward. "What of a woman's ruination? Are you telling me a man can ravage a woman with impunity if he can do it unseen?" She asked in a voice rising in anger

"It is the law, my lady," was all Reeve could think to say. He hid well from his lady his own distaste over what she could not do. Had he been alone when he found the crime, he knew he would have strangled the man and claimed self defense. He believed in justice more than man-made laws. He would rather confess his sin and answer to God.

"Then a woman has no protection for her honor. None. If that man had fled, Leoma would have had no recourse; no law would have protected her." *I thank God I carry a sword. Is this why the king let me keep it? Would it have done any good against such an attack. I pray, God, that it would. It would, would it not, God? Please answer me. Deal with Leoma's pain. Worry about myself later.* Lady Margaret stiffened. In her most formal, official voice she asked, "Do we have a cause? Will the Hundreds Court listen? Whom do we take with us to further support Scirwode's testimony?"

"As these two men reported, they were the first to arrive. They saw Scirwode fighting the man. I'm sorry to report, my lady, they also saw the position of Leoma's clothing. They saw blood between her legs. They stopped the stranger from running off. When they picked up the man, they saw scratches on his face." Unwilling to repeat what the men had already reported, Reeve paused and added in a softer voice, "They saw blood on his manhood. They can testify to that."

"That had best be ample proof," warned Margaret with a cocked head and a deeper voice.

Reeve stayed silent.

When Margaret received no reply, she started her orders. She looked first to Cormac. "Keep his hands bound; when he eats, free only one. Tie him securely. Not a stake. To a building far from the rest of us. Give him a slop bucket. When he is released to eat, one of mine knights, sword in hand, will watch him. Tell mine men, if he tries to escape, they are to kill him."

She looked to Reeve. "You will remain behind. Scirwode will testify; Scirburne will speak to his son's honesty and his daughter's honor, and you two will report as well. Leoma, mine knights and I will accompany them."

"Bringing Leoma is to no avail; she cannot testify."

Margaret glared at Reeve. "I need a lady's maid," said Margaret with false sweetness. "I simply cannot do without one. In a firm voice, she added, "I choose Leoma. Tell her and the others to prepare. We leave at dawn Thursday." With a wave of her hand, she dismissed them.

"Cormac, please report to Sirs Roussel, Gaylord and Cachier. Please ask them to assign four knights to escort us. Please send for Caitlin. Thank you."

Later Elstan stopped by to report. "The villagers decided they will take turns guarding the ravager. They agreed not to harm him as you had ordered. Still, they are hoping he will try to escape, so they can kill him."

"I will have Cormac remind them not to kill him. I want him tried under Saxon law." *Not mine choice. Taken from me. Prefer to hang him, but I dare not. I defied custom, mayhap law, with those heads. I have been told the law, so I am forced to follow it. Drat!*

"Why?"

"A good lord obeys the laws of the land, Saxon, Norman, Church. I want good said of me." *That might satisfy any who criticize mine rule. I hope it will.*

In bed that night, Margaret and Caitlin whispered as usual.

"Ifig said first she was hysterical with sobbing then she curled into a ball and went silent. When I arrived, Leoma was facing the wall. I let her hear mine voice so she knew I was not a man. Ifig and I whispered together and she agreed."

"She fully understood what was in the potion? She will never tell?"

"Of course not. Ifig knows what will happen if a priest or some other man finds out. She said she appreciated I had thought of it. I said nothing about you."

"Thank you."

"I mixed the potion and included the sleeping draught. I knelt beside the bed and explained the drink would help her sleep. I promised Leoma her father and brother were at the door guarding her. No one but her mother and sister would be in the house this night."

"I am surprised she agreed to anything in her state."

"I warned her," Caitlin reported. "I said, 'If you refuse to drink this, I will call your father, your brother, and anyone else I need to hold you while I pour it down your gullet.'"

"Hearing that tone of voice, I would have done everything you ordered."

"I told her the drink would also relieve some of her pain." Caitlin paused for effect and continued, "'You can sit up yourself or your mother will help you.' I told her. She sat up. She stayed facing the wall, took the mug and sniffed it. In one gulp, she downed it all. I told her I was proud of her. I told her I was covering her before I did."

"I assume you put in double the honey to mask the bitterness."

"Yes," Caitlin responded with annoyance.

"When will it start?"

"By the morrow midday. Her courses will come in a rush and be done. Either it will work or it will not."

"Has it ever failed?"

"Only twice. Your mother said each time, the woman had waited too long for the potion to save her. Each had the child."

"I will pray the potion works."

"As will I." Caitlin rolled from the middle toward the other side of the bed, her usual place; she closed her eyes.

19

Court

The party had taken the road toward Gloucester to Suindune, nineteen miles west of Mine. Because Norman law forbade Saxons to own or ride horses, the group traveled with a wagon and stopped one night at an inn. Near dusk the second day, Margaret's party entered the largest town in the Wiltshire district. Suindune covered one hundred twenty-seven acres and held seventy-six houses, two churches, three inns, four alehouses and a square that hosted two market days a week. Suindune was old, large and rich. The major part was called both Old Suindune and High Suindune and had been a hilltop Saxon settlement before King William I's invasion. The market square was in high town with the main road, Nyweport Street, running through it from high town to low town.

As agreed, Margaret's party met Hughes in the market square. He informed them he had secured a place that would provide for both

Normans and Saxons. However, the cost would be more than she had expected. Margaret replied she had enough coin. Hughes led them from Nyweport Street and turned right on a lane to a cul-de-sac. Margaret saw a large two-story building with stables and a barn in the back.

"It is an inn, my lady, all ours," said her retainer. "I could find no private home that would take both our groups. The cost includes both our first meal and supper. The Church of the Blessed Mary is down the lane to the right as we leave this place."

Lady Margaret asked, "Did you locate the priest Father Manntun recommended?"

"He is present, but I thought you should be one to contact him, not I."

"Thank you, Hughes. You did well." Margaret asked one more question before she dismounted. "How far are we from the Hundreds Court?"

"About five minutes walk, my lady. I suggest you ride to clear a path in these busy streets; we will follow you. One of us can guard Night, or we will find a boy to guard him. At the prices I have seen, a horse guard will cost you tuppence a day."

Roulin assisted Margaret's dismount. She was glad to be on her feet again and looked back with interest at the bustling town as the innkeeper's boy directed the Saxons where to put the wagon and animals. The prisoner stayed tied inside the wagon. Margaret spared him no thought. She met the innkeeper's wife and daughter, both homely, with long faces and rounded shoulders, alike as two women could be. *Too much bread making a too low a table, a ewe and her aging lamb.* While others carried baggage to the rooms, Lady Margaret and her retainers sat in the great room with its pleasant scents of ale and herbs as the fire smoked a bit. Only after serving girls set food trays and beverage jugs before them were the Saxons on the other side of the room fed.

After the meal, the innkeeper approached. "My lady, your knight has asked for you to stay a week. That you will pay me for the whole week whether you stay or go. Did he speak aright?"

"Have I a private room? Does it include a cot for mine maid? Will both our bed linens be changed every second day as I asked?"

"I have prepared everything as you requested. Even the linen changes."

"Mine retainers will sleep in the great room; one will guard mine door. Mine Saxons will sleep here as well."

The innkeeper furrowed his forehead and grimaced at the same time. "There is a room beside the stable."

Dare not you hold your nose. Mine Saxons are clean. "That may do for other people's Saxons. Not for mine. They have important work at the Hundreds Court. I want them protected, so they will stay within sight of mine knights. You may choose which side of the great room they sleep on, but they stay in the same building." Margaret added, "We tied our prisoner to a stable stall and we will guard him." Before the innkeeper could object, Margaret added, "At these prices and with mine guarantee of at least a week's income, I expect you to accommodate what I want. You do agree, do you not?"

Refusing to meet her gaze, the innkeeper looked at his shoes and muttered, "As you wish, my lady" in a tone that proved he wished he could mean it not.

Ignore his distaste at treating Saxons like people instead of livestock. He agreed to mine conditions for the coins he wants, so give them to him. Then ignore him until I need him again.

Margaret pulled her coin pouch from inside her left sleeve and counted out the man's pay. He swept the coins off the table and into his large, meaty hand. That done, he shuffled toward the kitchen. The party attended Sunday Mass at dawn. Lady Margaret left word with an acolyte she needed to meet Father Simeon.

On Monday gaining justice for Leoma began. After the party ate, several prepared to leave. Hughes guarded the prisoner; Leoma locked herself in Margaret's room. Sauville walked Lady Margaret's horse. Roulin preceded the Saxons, and Claude followed. That early in the morning, few workmen and shopkeepers were in the streets. Those about stepped back as the group passed. Lady Margaret smiled to herself at the number of windows thrown open and heads poked out. She stopped her party at the lane's entry to a huge square. Across and to her left, the largest building overshadowed the others and took up half one side of the square. The greenness of the wooden outer layer announced either the building or the siding was new. The half logs had been fastened horizontally. Halfway to the wood-shingled roof, the logs switched from horizontal to vertical. The windows on either side of the wide entry door were small and narrow. Neither man nor boy could climb in or out of them. The four windows on the second floor were taller and wider. Margaret urged Night forward and dismounted on the steps of the building. As the group had gained a following, Sauville had several boys from which to choose.

He informed the urchins, "The boy I choose must be responsible and trustworthy. I will not have this horse disturbed or harmed. You must stay with him until I return. He does not like men, so you will keep both men and boys away from him. You will see he drinks when he likes; you will whisper to him. If you do as I ask, I will pay you a penny to start. If we stay all day, if you do a good job, if my lady's horse is calm and happy when I return, I will pay you a second penny. Do well this day, and you will have a job as long as we are here." Sauville suggested to Margaret, "Please enter the building. I have selected three who will approach Night. If he likes one, I will use him. If not, I will guard him."

Escorted by Roulin and Claude, Margaret approached the door with he Saxons following. They entered the building and walked to the last window on the right. Margaret glared at the closed shutters. She walked toward the entry door, turned and strode to the back wall. Each time she did so, she frowned at the shutters as if she could will them to open and reveal a man behind the hole they covered. She continued to pace back and forth. Practiced at waiting, the Saxons patiently leaned against a wall. Roulin and Claude chose the wall opposite. The moment someone else was in the hallway, the knights stood between Margaret and whoever had arrived. Margaret was glad they were first in line. By the time the clerk opened the window shutters, the hall was full. The clerk was a beardless Saxon no older than twenty. His shock of almost-white straight hair stood out from his head in all directions. Pale blue eyes perched above fat cheeks, fat lips and a chinless jaw. His shoulders were so high he looked to have almost no neck at all. "My lady, how may I serve you?"

"A Saxon wanderer ravaged a Saxon girl. I want him tried," commanded Margaret in her most imperious voice.

The clerk began so politely because he had never addressed a Norman lady of rank, "My lady, this is a matter for Saxons. Is her father present? Are the witnesses Saxon? Are they available? I am sorry, my lady," the clerk continued, "only her father can ask for redress for damaged property; the only witnesses allowed are Saxon men. All this is Saxon law, my lady, and His Royal Highness, the king, has decreed it shall remain so."

"I understand that," Margaret was impatient for the process to begin, "but I expect to be seated in the room. I want to view the proceedings."

"As long as you are silent, that is permissible. If the girl's father is here, I needs speak with him."

Margaret stepped aside and motioned for Scirburne. She listened as the clerk took the information he needed. Once he had everyone's names recorded, he looked at his schedule book. The clerk informed Scirburne, "As you are the first this day I schedule you to be heard first. Court convenes only on market days, so you must wait until the morrow. If you are not here on time, I shall drop you to the end of the schedule. That may mean they shall not hear your case until Saturday, which is the next market day. Have you questions?" At Scirburne's "No," the clerk thanked and dismissed him.

The party stopped on the courthouse steps, so Margaret could confer with her retainers. Afterward, she told the Saxons they needed to stay together and that they might examine the town. They were to be back at the inn to sup. Scirburne indicated he wanted to explore, so the Saxons followed him. At Margaret's request, Claude guarded them to see they were undisturbed. Margaret asked Roulin to follow her because she would explore the town as well. She took the direction opposite her Saxons. Twice a local woman approached Margaret. Each spoke briefly, but each conversation startled her. She looked thoughtful, worried. Roulin knew to keep his distance from these meetings because Margaret had signaled him with a hand wave.

As the noon bell chimed, Margaret stood at the lone food stall in the square. They ate heartily of sticks of cooked meat, torn wedges of bread, and fresh apple cider. Roulin offered to fetch Sauville and Night. Once they were again together, Margaret and her retainers walked back to the inn. On the way another woman stopped Margaret. She again motioned her retainers to stop while she visited with her. When a girl approached Margaret, the men knew to hang back. As they waited, they saw Margaret shake her head.

After reaching the inn door, Margaret asked, "Who guards the prisoner this night?" When Sauville offered, Margaret thanked him and entered the inn. After explaining to Leoma she had an errand, Margaret left and asked Hughes to escort her. They returned to the square and made inquiries. Margaret asked Hughes to take some of the items she had purchased to the stable and to place them where they were both hidden from the prisoner and unlikely to be seen by anyone else. In a corner of the courtyard, Margaret whispered to Hughes what she needed, when, and what he was to do. Then she swore him to secrecy. Hughes' solemn nod did not reveal how pleased he was with her plan.

A good man I can trust to do all I asked and never to speak of it. In her room, Margaret laid out her own scissors, thimble, and her needle. She showed Leoma bolts of cloth she had purchased. Margaret wove her needle into a bolt of undyed wool, which she handed to Leoma.

"A new gunna for you," Margaret offered. She picked up a half-bolt of similar fabric and showed the girl. "I thought you might like to make a shirt for Scirwode. Please accept it. You may use mine needle."

"Oh my lady, this is so much!" Leoma's eyes filled. She took the materials and hugged them to her breast. "You are too kind."

Margaret took the fabrics out of Leoma's hands and set them aside. She held Leoma's hands in hers and guided her to the bed.

They sat. "Leoma, I hope you take into your heart what I say." She did not wait for the girl to answer. "You are a good girl. No matter what happened to you, you are still a good girl." Leoma shook her head. Margaret ordered, "Lift your chin. Please, Leoma, look at me." Margaret waited until the girl reluctantly complied. Still holding her hands, Margaret continued, "I want you to keep your face up. I want you to look every person in his eyes and to smile. At first, that shall be hard, but you may practice on me. Wear your honor with pride and others shall accept it. Come now, look at me."

Leoma saw only the sheets as she choked on, "I have no honor. I am damaged goods. He doesn't want me anymore." Her tears spilled.

"Rammeg told you that?"

"Father told Rammeg what happened. Scirwode even told him I had fought mine attacker and scratched his face. Rammeg sat there, said nothing. His father spoke for him."

"What said Rammeg Elder?"

"Father did not tell me everything. Rammeg had wanted a virgin. He still does. That is why he and I have been so careful. We touched not. From the time he first looked at me, he made it very plain we were to stay pure until our wedding night. From the very first he told me he wanted a virgin, just as the Church demands of every girl."

"I am so sorry, Leoma."

Margaret gathered the girl into her arms and let her cry. *Mayhap the law is right. Mayhap it is better Leoma not testify. She can barely face me. This is so unfair. Leoma is the one harmed. A man destroyed her future. Other men will judge her attacker. Will men condemn one of their own? I think not! They will accuse poor Leoma of luring him. They will blame her and find a way to excuse his despicable act. They will find him not guilty on one pretext or another. How can I stop them? Are the women who spoke to me strong enough to help me see justice is done? I will tell them we women must help each other in this world of men. Yes, that may work. If I convince them, mine plan may succeed.*

Margaret spoke softly. "He is a fool, you know. Rammeg Younger does not deserve you. You are still a virgin in your heart, where it matters most. You believe not anything I have said, but I am cert a much better match is in your future. Some day a good man shall see you as the good woman you are; he shall ask you to be his wife. And you shall be happy with him because he sees the real you, not what has happened to you."

"How may it be?" Leoma asked through her tears.

Margaret's voice was strong as she answered, "I know not, but I am cert. I believe God is both just and kind. He knows your heart is good. He shall find a man for you and send him. Ask me how I know this; mine heart tells me it is so. Believe God loves you. Believe He wants you happy. Pray for love and happiness, and, in time, both shall come to you. I cannot promise it, but I do believe it."

"Why?" Leoma asked with disbelief.

"Because I had a father who was unkind to me. Cruel really. I asked God to free me from the servitude he forced on me. While mine father tried to crush mine spirit, I prayed for release. God sent the king, who took me away to serve the queen. Now I am a landed girl of rank with property and more coin than mine father has seen in his lifetime. All I lack is a noble husband. I pray for a husband every night and, through the king, I am cert God shall provide me with a good one."

"Father Manntun told me God will see justice done. He said nothing about someone wanting me."

"He is a priest. What knows he of love and marriage? He means well, but your parents know more what makes a good match, a happy marriage, than Father Manntun." Margaret let Leoma ponder her words. "For you, tomorrow is a day of waiting. Let us cut a gunna for you and a shirt for Scirwode. Caitlin packed work for me. Think on the morrow and decide what you want to do after we break our fasts." Margaret hugged Leona and told her it was time to sup. "Go sit with your father and brother. The villagers worry about you and want to see you. Greet them with a smile. Pretend if you must. Let us go down."

Leoma decided they should cut the fabric at a table in the great room. That done, she gathered scraps and put them in the basket the innkeeper's wife had lent them. Margaret and Leoma sat beside the fireplace. With each decision Leoma made, Margaret hoped more of her spirit would soon return. Leoma's head jerked from her work every time someone opt the main door. She sat with her back to the fireplace, yet she startled at every noise. Margaret let her be. Together they sewed on their pieces, stopping only to sip at the cider the innkeeper's wife had offered. At bedtime Leoma gathered all the sewing into the basket, picked it up and announced, "With your permission, I am going to our room, my lady."

"I will fetch mine mantel."

Margaret stood outside the room and heard the bolt sound. The men stood when they saw her. Claude volunteered to accompany her, and they left for the church to attend Vespers.

Before going to bed, Lady Margaret informed her men, "Father Simeon has agreed to be our priest while we are in town."

"For a fee," sneered Claude.

"For a donation," Margaret countered. "Sauville, please advise the Saxons Father Simeon is available to them whenever they like. Who will relieve Hughes and stand the next watch?"

In the middle of the night, the sounds of crying roused Margaret. She did not stir, did not shift her head, did not speak. She prayed. She was a long time waiting for silence, for falling back to sleep. *Let her cry away her pain and sorrow. I have a plan, a plan that will shock the men of this town. Yes it will.* Hours later, Margaret raised her eyes to the window slit to see the sky lightening. After dawn Mass and a quick meal, the group left for the square. She had expected the streets would be busy, but they were alone on their path. When she reached the market square, she observed people milling about, doing nothing. *So this is where they are! They had best leave space for us!*

Margaret entered the building hallway half-filled with people; the clerk was reminding a man to wait until someone called him to court. When the clerk summoned Scirburne, Margaret followed the Saxons. She turned right and took stairs to the second level. Margaret and her retainers walked the short, narrow hall and through opened double doors. The large room was lit by opt windows and fat candles perched on wooden pillars. Opposite the doors were twelve stools in two rows, staggered so each juror could see everything. The men looked more alike than not. They appeared to be laborers with their wide shoulders and strong arms. They varied in height and coloring, but none were fat. All were dressed in tunics; the few prosperous ones wore leggings, but most of them had wound a long strip of cloth from boot to above the knees to keep their legs warm. All wore brown leather boots to the ankles. A few feet in front of them benches held the principals. On one bench the accused sat alone, and Roulin stood behind him. To the right on another bench sat Scirburne, Scirwode, and their witnesses. A railing with an opening in the middle separated the spectators from the court. Every bench was full. Sauville looked left. The Saxons pretended to ignore him.

At his "Move!" several men pushed together. Margaret sat; Sauville stood behind her. From her place, Margaret noted her Saxons sat in profile to her, but she saw only the accused's hair. One juror walked to the doors and closed them.

A priest stood to the right of the jury and began the proceedings with a long prayer that God is the only true judge, and of their need to temper justice with mercy. The priest instructed the jurors to look into their own hearts before judging another. Margaret had clasped her hands and lowered her head, but she heard not the priest. She was plotting.

A man of average height rose from his stool, but he appeared to be taller because of how proudly he stood. The grey strands at his temples and his receding hairline indicated he was the eldest juror. A small, red cut mark near the top of his right cheek proved he had shaved that morning. The clean clothes, pared nails, and combed-back hair proved he cared about his appearance. That the other jurors behind him smiled at him as he stood hinted he was well-liked, even respected by the others. With gray eyes he gazed somberly at the crowd. He coughed lightly, and the whisperers stopped.

"I am Saebroc. The jury has chosen me to be their speaker." The trial began with Saebroc reminding spectators to be silent. He then asked Roulin to step back. Roulin walked past the railing and stood behind the last row of benches across the aisle from Sauville.

"The aggrieved one will please stand."

"I am the aggrieved one. I am Scirburne, father of Leoma, whom he ravaged." Scirburne pointed at the accused.

"That is a lie!"

"Silence!" ordered Saebroc. "You will have your turn."

Scirburne presented his facts in an orderly, clear manner. He began with a description of the day and the people involved. "Mine daughter is a good girl. She was doing what a good daughter does. Following mine request to find winter food for our pigs. She was with her sister, brother, father, and uncle. She wandered not; she obeyed me. The Sunday before the attack and after Mass, our priest made the first announcement of mine daughter Leoma's coming wedding to her betrothed. Rammeg Younger is his father's heir, a skilled carpenter, and a fine young man. Rammeg and Leoma kept themselves pure for each other, just as our Church teaches. We know they stayed pure because they were always under the supervision of either their parents or of other married adults in the village. "When he", Scirburne pointed to the defendant, "stole mine daughter's honor, he also stole her wedding from her. Rammeg shall now have her not. No man shall have her to wife after what this ravager did. Her life is destroyed, and we all know it." Scirburne looked at each individual juror. "If you have daughters, beware. Your child may be next." He repeated his beginning as his summary. "Mine daughter was an honorable girl about to be wed. He attacked and stole her honor. She fought him, but he was too strong for her." Scirburne pulled at his chin and swore his oath. "By mine beard, I swear I have spoken true. Mine son Scirwode shall speak next to what he saw and what he did." Scirburne pointed to the boy and sat. Scirwode stood.

Leoma's brother told the court what he had seen and what he had done. Each of the others testified to the aftermath. Then the men and Scirwode stood as one. In unison they pulled on their chins as if they had beards and swore, "By mine beard I swear I have spoken true." They sat.

No juror asked questions.

At Saebroc's nod, the accused stood. Shaven and in clean clothes, the defendant looked like every other man in the room. He appeared to be an upright person, just more handsome than most with his regular features, bright eyes, winning smile, easy manner, and a pleasant voice. He looked at each juror then he turned to the crowd. Palms upward he extended his arms wide and began in a smooth voice.

"You know me. For five years every summer, I have come to Suindune and worked on your farms and in the city. We have drunk and joked together. You know me. I am not the man who did what they say. I am innocent. I was strolling through the forest on a known path to the next town to help with the pig slaughter as I do every year." The man turned and took a small, friendly step toward the jury. "I am innocent. She is not. She invited me. I knew not she was a virgin. Mayhap she wanted an encounter, a pleasurable time before she had to wed the man her father chose. She was fine until she spotted her brother. Only then did she start to struggle. Only when she worried about her lost reputation did she fuss."

By shifting her position, Margaret watched Scirburne grimace and his neck muscles flex and flex. She saw his shoulder move as he grabbed his son to prevent him from jumping up.

The accused continued to state his case. "I know not these people. I know not how trustworthy they are. You know not these people either. Can a stranger never seen before pull on his chin and swear he is telling the truth? Of course. His daughter lied to him. The poor man believes her. Now that she has no betrothed, I suspect all he wants is for you is to find me guilty so he can get geld. You know me. I would not hurt a woman. I have never ravaged a woman in mine life!"

"Liar!" Margaret jumped up. "You have ruined women in this town and I have proof!"

"Silence, woman! This is a court of men! This is a Saxon court!"

It happened of a moment. Margaret pulled her sword out and marched to the railing. Those on the aisle seats shrunk away. Roulin and Sauville, right hands on their sword hilts, stepped behind her. The accused jumped back between the jurors. The jurors stood as if to stop her approach. Fearful of what an unpredictable woman might do with a sword, Saebroc glared with wary eyes. Margaret stopped at the railing. She lifted her sword and took one long step into the court. She said her next words with great emphasis.

"I got this sword at King Henry's command. I wear this sword with King Henry's permission. I hold land. A landed, sword-bearing Norman is a lord. I am no lady. I am Lord Margaret, and you shall address me as such." Before any man could speak, she continued, "Each year the accused has been among you, he ravaged at least one of your women."

With each accusation Margaret pointed her sword at a different man. She started with two jurors and then turned from side to side and picked three more men from among the spectators. Each cowered as she pointed. "Was she your daughter? Was she your wife? Was she your niece? Was she your sister? Was she your mother? Your women cannot tell you of the ravager's deeds. Your law requires a male witness." With that she pointed her sword at the accused. "This man uses your law against your women." Then she lowered the blade to her hip. She could raise it in a flash. The jurors sat, but the accused backed to the wall behind them. Those on the benches sat still, but their eyes darted about seeking the reaction of the men near them. When Margaret stomped one foot, the sound reverberated in the wood and all looked her way. She had everyone's attention.

"Since I arrived, four women have approached me. I will tell you one of their stories. She is a wife and mother. On a fine summer day she was hanging her wash on bushes. Her children played a short distance away." Margaret pointed at the accused. "That man grabbed her and pulled her behind a bush. He threatened her children's lives. If she made even one tiny sound, he would drown them. He pushed her to the ground, lifted his tunic, and smiled. He untied the drawstring and dropped his leggings. She was crying before he even touched her. He ravaged her. Then he used the bottom of her gunna to wipe his manhood. He threatened her again before he walked away with a cheery wave. She walked into the stream to clean herself and her gown of him. One of you is fortunate," Margaret paused. "that the woman returned to the land rather than drown herself. She finished hanging the clothes, took her children in hand, and returned home. The ravager's victim told no one, not even her priest. She prayed for days. When her courses came, she wept."

No one moved; no one spoke. Saebroc frowned and looked among the spectators in hopes of finding one who reacted, so he might ask that man to corroborate the woman's claim. He found no one.

Margaret continued. "Three of the women who spoke to me are so brave they are ready to appear before you as proof he ravaged them."

Margaret spoke Sauville's name, and he turned for the entry. Both doors swung open; every man turned. Beyond the doorway stood three figures. Each wore a dark brown mantle with a matching scarf pulled so far forward it hid her face. No hands showed outside the mantles. They touched the top of their boots, which matched.

"These are your women who came to me unbidden. Now do you believe me?" At Margaret's call, Sauville closed the doors. Over her shoulder, Margaret gave a backward push of her thumb; Roulin walked to the doors and stood guard too. Margaret did not move. Several jurors stood and tried to get past Margaret, but she brandished her sword, and they stepped back. She heard, "How dare you! Who are they? We must speak to them." One man threatened to throttle Margaret, but no one believed he would try.

"Wait!" called out one man. Several in the crowd stood.

"No one leaves until they are gone!" Margaret ordered. "If you are unwilling to protect your women, why should they reveal themselves?"

Stand tall. Act brave. Reach for your sword even though I dare not use it. Convince them I will, or they will overrun me and I will have failed.

When the men realized Lord Margaret had locked them inside the room, they settled. Margaret watched how the jurors looked at each other. She prayed for the right vote.

The accused clapped three times. "Nice job! Good mummery!" He stepped forward and faced the jurors. "Those figures could have been anyone. She paid them. Ask her."

They did not have to, for Margaret shook her head before she spoke. "With God as mine witness, I swear on mine mother's grave I speak true. They came to me unbidden and told the same story. May I be condemned to Hell for all eternity if I speak not the truth." Several jurors looked shocked at her oath. "If Leoma was so willing, why did you stuff a rag into her mouth? Why did she scratch you? Why do women I have never met tell the same story as Leoma?"

The accused pointed at Margaret. "If you are real men, you will rid yourself of this bleeding, posturing fluff."

All heard Roulin. "Mine lord practices with us daily. Mine lord is as swift and as deadly with his dagger as he is with his sword. Anyone who attacks mine lord meets God. You anger him at your peril."

"Enough," ordered Saebroc. He pointed at the accused. "You. Sit." He looked at Margaret. "I suppose you are not going anywhere."

Margaret's silence was her answer.

At Saebroc's gesture, the jurors stood and headed for a corner. They stood in a tight pack; the room saw only backs. Margaret turned on her heel and glared at the accused with a baleful stare. *Move toward me so I can kill you.* Her face revealed her thought. From the corner she heard soft voices; the only word she understood was 'witness.' She was patient. She had already decided his fate.

The jury reconvened. Saebroc gestured, and the accused stood. "Jury, what say you?"

Each man glared at Margaret as if to announce they feared her not before he spoke. Their anger at her was visible in their stances and their faces. Each wanted to believe his decision was based on evidence and not because he had been cowed by a girl into stating his judgement. The accused heard 'guilty' eleven times. Saebroc spoke the twelfth. The guilty man sat hard. Several spectators spoke against Margret's interference in their courtroom. Half the jury nodded agreement at what they heard. Still holding her hilt in her right hand, Margaret ignored them. *This next part must go well. If it be Your will, Oh God, let it go well.*

At Saebroc's second gesture Scirburne stood.

"You can make him wed her."

Scirburne shook his head.

"What amount of geld shall quit this man of his guilt and his obligation?"

Scirburne again shook his head. Scirburne looked only at the jurors. "I prefer our old ways. When someone attacks, you disarm him. Take his weapon from him and send him on his way. Ravager uses his manhood as a sword. I say disarm him. Take his balls. He shall need both hands to hold up his pintel to piss. He shall ravage no more."

The ravager jumped up. "NO-O-O! I would rather die than be unmanned!" he roared.

Margaret raised her blade to stop him running toward her.

As the ravager looked her way, Scirburne slammed his hand on the wooden bench upon which he had sat. "DONE!" he shouted. "I accept his offer for punishment. Death he wants! Death I accept!"

We have him! He walked right into it.

"You cannot do that!" Ravager looked about wildly for help. He got none.

Saebroc said, "Oh…yes…he…can. Saxon law. You stated the punishment you would accept. He pounded wood and accepted your offer. Now he gets to decide how."

Margaret's sword tip was still to the guilty man. Her eyes warned him to sit, and he saw the blade tip dip. He sat.

"Hang him from a gallows in the square next market day," decreed Scirburne.

No one stood to the accused's defense, neither his employers nor his drinking pals. Three swords kept them quiet, prevented them from saying what they really thought, *Women are never to be believed when they accuse a man of anything.* The room was quiet. Ravager looked at the floor, his hands covering his face, but he was not defeated. Suddenly, Ravager grabbed for Margaret's blade to pull it into himself. Scirburne looped his arm around the man's neck and pulled him backward. Scirburne choked his daughter's attacker as the man cut his hands on the blade tip and bled. Jurors jumped into the melee to separate the men, but Scirburne held fast. Margaret lifted her blade to prevent any more damage. Shocked she had drawing blood, she stared at the droplets as they dribbled down the blade.

Blood! I drew blood. I want him dead, but I want not to do it. Thank you, God, for Scirburne and the other men. Hanging is bloodless; hanging is what I want.

A juror leapt to the wall and grabbed different lengths of rope.

Oh, that is why loops of rope hang on pegs! Margaret watched men wrestle the ravager to the floor, tie his hands behind him, hobble his feet, and fasten a long rope around his neck.

"How shall we keep him until then?" asked a juror.

"We have a stocks at the edge of town," offered a second juror.

"He might escape," said a third.

Margaret's words were not an offer. "Mine men shall guard him all day, all night. No one shall harm him. No one shall touch him. No one shall throw anything at him. Not even a rotten apple. In Christian charity someone may bring him food and drink. Only that."

"You shall kill him in the night," charged someone from the crowd.

Margaret did not look his way. "We shall harm him not." She stared at the ravager. "I want to see him hanged. When he is dead I want to see his body piss and shit itself. Have you not heard of the poles on either side of mine lane? They held severed heads. No man harms one of mine own and lives."

Ravager looked up and then straightened his back. He challenged Margaret. "You have not the stomach for it. You are a soft, weak, useless woman. All you women are for is bedding, and you are likely poor at that."

Margaret's smile was dangerous. Loud enough for all to hear, she responded, "When you stand on the gallows, look to the back of the crowd. You shall find me upon Mine horse so I am tall enough. I shall be looking at you. If you have stomach enough, look back. Let mine face be the last you see. I shall not shrink. I shall sit ahorse and watch you die. When your body pisses and shits itself, I shall smile. Only then shall I leave the square." Margaret shifted her sword to her left hand and placed her right across the sword hilt. "I so swear. You have mine word on it. The word of a sword-carrying, landed, Norman lord." She looked to the jury. "Shall you guard him and guarantee him? Do you want mine men to guard him? Visit him as often as you desire. You have mine word: we shall not harm him. Anyone who harms him answers to mine sword. He shal be present on hanging day."

Saebroc ordered, "Spectators, leave this hall. Only those in front of the rail may stay. He turned to his fellows, "Empty this hall."

The jurors did so over the crowd's objections. For the men to walk through the opened doors, they had to pass Sauville and Roulin. The spectators quickly turned left and exited the floor. The priest stayed. So had one tall, lean man with a haggard face and sad demeanor. His slumped shoulders made him look old and tired.

"I have a right to be here," he said without explanation.

Margaret read his face; she nodded assent to him.

Saebroc roared. "You are not a true woman. You are an abomination! You charged into OUR court. You bypassed our ways. You insult us! You think you own the world and use your swords to make it so! You tread on our laws and deny us any honor or respectability. You think we know not what is right. You think you are the only ones who can judge aright. You think we are lost sheep without you and must be ruled at every turn."

Margaret shrugged indifferently. "I am Norman."

Saebroc softened his approach. "We need their names. Please tell us their names."

Margaret looked into his eyes and saw no guile. "I tell you truly. They did not say. I was so shocked at what they reported I did not ask. If you paraded every woman and girl in town past me, I could not identify them." She gazed at each juror before she admitted, "You are good men. You want to do what is right," she said to the jurymen.

Saebroc retorted, "Glad you finally noticed."

"I can only tell you what mine mother told me." When they did not interrupt her, she continued. "A woman's heart is a well so deep no one knows its end. At its bottom she drowns her deepest secrets. Mayhap, after the women see the ravager hung and buried, finally they will feel safer. Mayhap, after you have been good to your women and guard them well for a long time, one of them will pull that secret from the bottom of her heart and reveal it. If the first man responds with love and understanding, another may tell. But I warn you. You must be patient. Women smile and act pleasant enough, but they trust not with ease."

"You want to guard a man when we jurors should."

"Then you guard him." She shrugged as if she were indifferent.

"I suppose your knights will guard us," he fumed.

"Mine knights are free to walk when and where they wish. I command not their every moment."

Saebroc snorted in derision. "Leave!" he commanded.

I cannot," Margaret said evenly. "This man wants to tell us something. Let us move away from the one on the floor and speak softly."

Those standing moved to a far corner and stood in a tight circle. The stranger said, "I shall not speak before a priest." He crossed his arms over his chest.

"You have mine silence, my son," answered Father Simeon.

"I heard what you priests do. When you gather, you swear each other to secrecy and then you talk. I shall not be talked about."

"We never do that."

"Those who know you say you do. I believe them."

The priest's face colored. With each word he got redder. "You shall confess your insolence to me. I shall set your penance."

The man did not back down. "I spoke truth so I shall confess only to God."

Saebroc mediated. "Father, if you shall leave us, I shall talk with you later."

Father Simeon harrumphed his displeasure and left in a huff. He slammed shut the door. The group waited.

"Three years ago, mine daughter Gleda." He took a deep breath. "He ravaged her when she was ten. She was playing hide and find with the little ones. He grabbed her and told her he would kill us all if she told. She was not yet a woman." He choked out that last bit. Every one looked away. They gave him time and respect by not looking at him.

"She had a vision in church, a calling from God to serve Him. I was there."

The man looked at the juror and shook his head. "When Gleda's first courses came, she thought he had killed her, that she was bleeding to death. When she wept for dying, we made her tell us why she cried so. She begged to be put far away; she knew she could never wed. That scene in the church was our way to explain why she went to the convent." He took another deep breath. "Without having to tell why." His eyes filled. "She won't see us. She told the abbess to tell us she is dead to the world. Dead to us. We shall never see her again."

The man wiped at his eyes with the back of his hand and looked straight at Margaret. "Lord Margaret." Margaret looked up. She saw his pain with so much sympathy she clenched her teeth to stop tears forming. "You were right to do what you did. He is a monster. He killed mine little girl's life. I shall watch him die."

Margaret guessed what he meant. "This man and his family have suffered enough. He does not need gossip." She looked kindly at each man in the room. "What say we swear to silence? What was said in this room never leaves it. Ever. Not for any reason nor to any person, not even to a priest." She nodded kindly at each man. When she had seen them all nod back, she added, "Who shall be the first to pull his chin and swear to perpetual silence on this matter?"

In disbelief at her boldness, Saebroc shook his head at her. "I shall," he said with resignation. *This woman will not be contained. God help the man who weds her. I pity the man even if he is a Norman*, he thought. After the Saxons finished their oaths, the Normans lifted their swords. With their right hands they grasped their hilts at the cross section and swore the same. They sheathed their blades.

Margaret turned to the stranger. "Now you swear. Swear you shall do nothing to the ravager. You shall go nowhere near him. Swear you shall let this jury do their jobs. Swear you shall let him hang."

"He deserves to die."

"That he does. He is base and a criminal, but I shall not let you slit his throat."

The jurors looked shocked.

Margaret stepped toward him and put her hand upon his arm. She reasoned softly, "Your wife and children need you. If you kill him, I must kill you. I swore in court to keep him alive for the hanging. Your family has suffered enough. Please live. Swear and I shall get you what you want."

He looked at her hard and she nodded. He pulled his chin and swore.

"Jurors, who sees to the hanging?"

"We must."

Who takes the body? Who wraps it in the shroud?

"We do."

"Would it be a desecration to let this man slit its throat before you wrap the neck and head? If someone digs up the body, he shall know the man was a criminal. All this man would do is to mark the body as such before the burial."

The men looked at each other. Saebroc answered for them all with, "Agreed."

The stranger pulled his chin and swore not to touch the criminal, first to Margaret and then to the jury.

"Now to the final matter."

Saebroc swore base words and ended with, "Good God! When shall you be done!"

"Anon," answered Margaret in a honeyed voice.

"We must protect this man," said Margaret quietly. She looked at Gleda's father and asked his name. Still out of hearing of the ravager bound on the floor and with great warmth Margaret whispered what she wanted the jurors to overhear. "Heardwine, you knew me as a child. You stayed behind to speak with me. I was glad to see you. We stood in the hall and visited while you shared your memories of me.

We forgot the time. When the jury left the court, we followed them down the stairs. Smiling at each other, I took your arm going outside. When we part, I will kiss you on the cheek as a child would, and we will wave at each other. If others ask you about me, you will tell them you knew me long ago. If they ask, 'Was she always so froward?' you will shake your head and answer, "Every day."

Margaret smiled at the jurors. "Will you support that?"

"We shall not lie."

Margaret whispered, "You need not; we shall be in the hall." In full voice, Margaret began the charade. "Heardwine, how kind of you stop to greet me." She gestured to him. "Let us go into the hall to visit. We will disturb not the jurymen. Please tell me about your life now." Margaret linked arms with him as they walked the aisle. The knights followed. They shut the door on the jury.

When the jury left the room with the ravager in tow, they heard Margaret say, "Oh dear, where has the time gone? We must away. Your family awaits you."

The midday bells chimed. Downstairs, the jury informed the waiting people court would reconvene after they had they had bound the guilty man and had dined.

After Heardwine waved farewell and she waved back, Margaret returned to the inn. Two knights walked their horses before her, two behind. No one dared accost her.

20

An Execution

Two days later the town's carpenters completed the gallows. The lumber had been stored on the beams of a stable, and some pieces had rotted from rain dripping through the thatched roof. Rotten boards had been replaced with new, green ones. The old gray structure look pock-marked. The men had cut four new foot treads as well as the cross beam that held the noose. The platform also looked mottled, but not the trap door.

Wednesday, after Leoma had been called on by the head priest of Church of the Blessed Mary, Margaret and Leoma had used their time sewing. Thursday afternoon the women were sitting before the fireplace in the inn's great room with their work in their laps. Father Simeon arrived for the second time that day. He stood before the pair.

"Leoma, I would speak with you."

Leoma dropped her chin and shook her head. She hugged her brother's shirt to her chest.

"I want you to change your mind, child. I ask this for your own good."

Again, Leoma shook her head.

"Father, may I help you?"

Father Simeon frowned at Margaret's interference, then shrugged his approval. "Convince her to marry the man before they hang him. She can be a wife and a widow the same day. If she is with child, the babe will not be a bastard."

"Father Simeon, please join us, I want you to hear what I tell her." After Father dragged a stool to the fireplace and sat so he could see both girls in profile, Margaret began with a question. "Leoma, why is Gytha the richest woman in our village?

After a long silence, Leoma whispered, "Because she makes ale."

"True, but that is only part of the reason. She is rich because she is a widow." When Leoma did not speak, Margaret continued. "Think on this, Leoma. When you are a daughter, you are your father's property. He decides whom you will wed, hands you to your husband, and you are then his property. The children you birth are his; you have no rights, no wealth. Even your dowry is his. When he dies…"

"Go no further!"

"Father, when she arrives at home, one of the other women will tell her why saying no to you was unwise. If you permit me to finish, I believe she will recognize the right in what you propose." Both discomfited and unhappy, Father Simeon gestured Margaret to continue. "Leoma, when a husband dies, all he possesses becomes his widows's property, land, house, coin, children. She is then free to live her life as she desires, even live where she wishes. When you are a widow, no one can gainsay you. You make all decisions, rule your children, and do all a man may do. Widows may even go to court to sue for redress. When her eldest son reaches eighteen, he receives two-thirds of what was his father's wealth. His mother gets one-third plus all the wealth she has made since her husband's death. If a widow weds again, all she has still remains hers, hers for life. Her new husband cannot take anything from her nor order her what to do with her own property. This is the old Saxon law. All this and more is written in the Charter of Liberties to which King Henry agreed before he became king. He follows his father's laws and the old Saxon laws."

"I am free? From mine family? From ever having to wed again if I choose?"

"You are. You are a widow for as long as you wish."

"Does mine father know any of this? Does he agree?"

"Your father knows all. I have spoken with him, and he said these matters are yours to decide," reported the priest.

Leoma looked at Margaret. "I shall not bed him."

You just agreed! I spoke well. Be strong, Leoma. What may I say to support Father?

Father Simeon stated, "But child, you have already lain with him. The marriage contract and the Church's blessing acknowledge this and make you a widow legally. You shall then have all the rights and privileges Lady Margaret..."

"Lord Margaret!" she corrected the priest in a stern voice, but he ignored her.

"Privileges mentioned, " he said with an effort. "We have the ceremony at the gallows. You leave. After they hang him, I write

251

his death on the marriage document, and you are a widow. All he possessed is then yours."

Agree, Leoma. For your own benefit.

"I want none of it," retorted Leoma. "No kiss of peace," demanded Leoma, suddenly sitting tall and looking directly at Father Simeon. "No kiss. I shall not let him. I am saving mine lips for a real husband if I ever have one."

"The kiss of peace is the required seal of your words. We must include it."

Think of something quick or we lose her.

After Margaret watched Leoma look away, she turned to Father Simeon. "May the kiss of peace be on her forehead? If he kisses her forehead only, may that be sufficient?"

Father put his hand to his chin in thought. After a time, he said. "One kiss of peace from him on your forehead only. I shall agree to that."

Leoma threatened, "I shall put mine hand over mine mouth so he cannot defile mine lips. If he tries, I shall strike him."

"Agreed."

Margaret breathed a sigh of relief. "Leoma?"

"Agreed."

"Done!" Father Simeon's expression showed pleasure at his success.

"Leoma, I needs speak to Father Simeon on a personal matter. We shall sit at the table over there. I shall keep you in sight. Is that suitable?" At Leoma's nod, Margaret led Father across the room. She sat where she could see both Leoma and the main door. Father took a seat. Margaret leaned her chin again her hand to hide her lips.

"Father, I have been considering what you said. I must do the Christian thing. Please tell him I am having a Mass said for him on his death date for a decade. Will you say them?" Father Simeon nodded. "I want to donate to your church in thanks for your saying the Masses." When Father said nothing, Margaret continued, "Further, I promise to pray for the repose of his soul every morn and night for a year and a day after he dies, as is Norman custom. I doubt he will care; he hates women. He may even mock me from the gallows." *I did nothing wrong. I only caught him in a trap of his own making. Lower your head or he will see your thoughts.* "Thank you, Father, for helping me in this matter." When the priest still spoke not, Margaret reached into her sleeve and withdrew the small fabric pouch into which she had sewn thirty pence. She watched Father Simeon roll the bag in his right hand as he counted how much she had given him. When he nodded his acceptance of her donation, Margaret finished with, "Thank you for your help during our visit here. I look forward to attending Sunday Mass. We will return home Monday."

Saturday morning broke with a cloudless sky and a bitterly cold wind. The group huddled together as they walked to and from Mass. The wind whipped at them both ways. Margaret took Roulin's advice and broke her fast with only sips of ale and no food. In scarf and mantle, Margaret stood before Leoma still sitting on the edge of the bed wearing no mantle or scarf. "It is time, Leoma." At the girl's shake of her head, Margaret said, "Your father shall stand beside you. You need only say 'yes' once. Immediately afterward, he shall take you back to the inn, so you need observe nothing of what will follow. You shall be a wife and widow before midday. Then you are free to live as you wish."

"Could I stay in this town, find work, and live here?"

"A widow may do whatever she wishes within the law. Rise and gain your freedom."

Leoma nodded and stood.

Escorted by knights front and behind, the group left. Margaret clenched her mantle between her knees to keep the cold from freezing her legs. A throng filled the square with more people continuing to arrive and crowding together. Those on the west and north edges bore the brunt of the gusts. People huddled together or in doorways; every shutter facing the square was cracked open and filled with faces.

Hughes skirted the crowd until his steed was opposite the gallows. He dismounted, reached left and held Night's halter, so he controlled both horses. To the left of Night, Roulin did the same. Now Margaret's horse was less likely to rear, sidle into a horse beside him or to bolt. Night snorted, stamped his forefeet and then settled. A wave of words passed from the back to the front of the crowd announcing "she" had arrived. Most looked Margaret's way and noted her straight mouth and impassive expression; Margaret ignored them and studied the gallows. Anyone entering the square from the street behind her scurried around the threesome and pressed forward for a view.

Set mine face. Shift not or I will appear anxious. Or worse, fearful. Roulin prepared me for what I will see. Think heads on poles. I looked on them and cried not. I can well do that here.

People turned as the court building doors opened. The crowd had become a living thing that moved as one; it turned, surged a step and stopped. With his sword in his right hand, Sauville led the group. The priest and then the hooded hangman followed. Saebroc led half the jurymen. When the ravisher stood in the doorway, the crowd gasped. Wearing no mantle, he stepped outside, and the remaining jurymen followed him. With arms linked to her father and brother, Leoma exited the building; Claude followed them and stopped at the foot of the stairs.

One by one, the group climbed the gallows steps. Two jurors took the ravager's arms and positioned him over the trap door. They turned him to face Leoma and her father. They kept their hold on him during the brief ceremony.

Father Simeon started with a comment to the condemned man. "Remember you do this in hope of God's mercy upon you. For the salvation of your soul." The pair answered "yes" to Father Simeon's questions, though neither spoke loudly enough for anyone below to hear them. Margaret watched Leoma and Scirburne take one step forward. Leoma put her hand over her mouth; the ravager leaned over and kissed her forehead. Leoma cringed and her knees gave way. Scirburne helped Leoma stay upright. while the priest blessed the union in Latin and Saxon. Leoma and her father turned away and took the gallows steps. Scirwode, who had stayed below, took Leoma's other side. The trio disappeared below the line of heads and emerged at the left side of the crowd. With Claude in front and Sauville behind, the group had carved a path through the spectators to the nearest street. They disappeared.

Once her people were out of sight, Margaret became the focus of the mob. *Now smile at the ravager and freeze your face again.* Margaret did not blink, did not waver. She cared not if he looked her way or not. She was ready to watch him die. No. Eager.

On the gallows, a juror held the prisoner's tied hands while the hangman removed the neck rope and replaced it with the noose above his head. The hangman grasped the man's shoulders and positioned him facing the crowd and in the center of the drop. Careful to be standing only beside the trap door, Father Simeon stood near the condemned man and continued his quiet words and prayers. He turned and spoke to the crowd of justice and mercy, God's grace, and His forgiveness of all sins.

Too many words. Just do it.

The crowd leaned forward as they thought, "Would he take the hood? Might he refuse?" The throng roared its approval when he shook his head. Then he looked over their heads and sneered at the woman who had plotted his demise.

Margaret's small smile broadened. She blinked once. *No stare of yours will move me.*

The hangman jerked the lever and the trap door fell away. As one, the crowd gasped. The man fell into the hole to his waist. His mouth gaped open as his body jerked. Margaret could not see his legs kicking; she saw only his waist banging against the sides of the hole as he twisted and gasped for air. The hangman jumped off the gallows and disappeared.

He is still alive?! Margaret continued her stare, but her stomach roiled. *Roulin told me not this. So much worse! May I never again take part like this. Horrible. Horrible.*

Seen only by those in front, the hangman grabbed the ravager's ankles; he pulled hard and fast. Those in front heard the man's neck snap; the crowd watched his head loll to one side. The crowd moaned. The execution was over. But not for Margaret.

That is what you get for killing a girl's honor. Heardwine will see to you now. I am not sorry. I will not be sorry. Ever.

She continued to stare at the gallows, the stillness of the body, the head to one side, its face gone blank. Now the crowd turned as one and stared at her. Wind and cold had frozen Margaret's face, both her horror at such violent death, and her half smile. She did not move. The crowd waited. Margaret saw the hangman reappear on the platform and pull the hanging rope to raise the body. The priest took a small kit from beneath his cloak. The hangman lowered the body to the platform. He knelt to put his head to its chest; he stood and backed away. The still-hooded hangman took the steps, the closest lane, and disappeared. Father Simeon knelt beside the body and blocked everyone's view of its head. He administered the Church's last rites ceremony.

The crowd again became individuals, murmuring and becoming louder. If they were blaming Margaret for the man's execution, she cared not. Pride held her firmly in place. *I have done what I set out to do. Avenge Leoma's debasement. I will not weaken. They will know nothing of how I feel. What do they expect of me? Oh yes, a smile.*

Margaret smiled. She opt her lips only enough to say "now" without seeming to have spoken. Her knights released Night and mounted. Roulin led and Hughes followed Margaret as they walked their horses back to the inn.

21

Aftermath

The front door being taken by the wind and slammed shut behind her comforted Margaret. Warmth enveloped her. Still, Margaret dared not relax. Her every move and word this day would be passed to the town's people, commented upon and analyzed. *I am still on display. Only in mine room am I safe. Not even there. Leoma.*

The innkeeper rushed to Margaret and Roulin. "My lady, a Saxon is in your room with the girl. Is he her father? We forbid such a thing. After you depart, I must scrub the ceiling, the walls, the floor, everything before I may let it to a Norman lady."

Margret nodded and said, "Good." She walked to her accustomed table. She unclasped her mantle but left wearing it to warm herself. Margaret untied her scarf and draped it over her shoulders. "I desire something hot," she asked of the innkeeper.

"I have a meat stew, bread and butter."

"And a bottle of wine," she added. "The same for them," said Margaret as she pointed to Scirwode and the other Saxons on the other side of the room.

"Yes, my lady," he said with resignation.

Margaret remembered he had been a courtroom spectator. She narrowed her eyes, lowered her chin, and put her right hand upon her hilt.

"What called you me?"

"I mean yes, my lord," he blurted.

"Remember!" *It is stupid to insist on a fallacy. I am still a girl, but I must maintain this charade until we leave.*

The innkeeper nodded, stepped back and fled.

As Margaret approached, the Saxons stood. "How fare you?"

One reported, "Our knights saw us here. Scirburne is with Leoma. We are fine, my lord." He bobbed his head at his last two words.

"Your dinner is coming. I ordered a bottle of wine for you. After you finish that, you may have ale, but not too much. I want others to speak well of you. We are on display every moment until we leave, and we must behave. Think you the weather will hold so we can leave Monday?"

"I am uncert. That wind is blowing in something bad. If it arrives by nightfall or sooner, I pray it blows over by Sunday evening, but mayhap not. The weather could force us here several days."

"If we are, at least we are warm and fed. I prefer we appear not to be rushing out of town. Others might say it is with guilt in our hearts, but that is not so."

The innkeeper's wife and a servant carried trays and served the meal. At the bottom of the stairs Scirburne took Leoma's hand and led her to their table. Margaret noted her forehead was chaffed red.

Margaret nibbled a cube of turnip. When her stomach accepted it, she tried a portion of onion and then a chunk of carrot. She waited to be cert her stomach had settled before she chewed a piece of meat. She pulled a bite of bread from the round she shared with Roulin.

After they dined, Roulin stayed. "My lord, we want the wagon, our gear and our horses guarded until we leave. Angry citizens who liked the man may harm them. May we place a Saxon and a Norman in rotation until we depart?"

"You may. I am pleased you work with Saxons."

Margaret ordered a second bottle of wine. "I only sipped; this is to warm Sauville, Hughes and Claude as they dine." Roulin left and the other three knights joined Margaret and ate. Even though she hungered, she refused another bowl of stew because she trusted not her stomach. Margaret chose to stay and listen to her men talk of the weather and their horses. *I must appear calm and in control. At mine ease. Silence the gossip. When will mine heart settle and mine stomach too? Mine back is tense. Mine neck is tight. I need mine bed, silence, dark, and sleep to settle mine nerves. Hide behind a small smile, but go abed soon. Please God, keep bad dreams away. Help me unsee the horror I saw. I must pray for the repose of his soul, so forgetting must wait. A year and a day and then I will forget. I will forget.*

The storm struck with rain beating hard on the roof and the west wall. Shutters rattled. From somewhere cold drafts swirled just above the floor and chilled everyone's feet. At the end of the meal, Margaret stood. Her knights rose and waited to reseat themselves until after she had draped the scarf and her mantle over her arm and strolled to the stairs. *I am eager to repair to mine room, but I must keep a measured pace. No hurrying or looking worried.* As before, Margaret announced her plans to Leoma from across the room, so all heard her. Leoma offered to precede her and did so.

Once behind the bolted door, Margaret asked if Leoma wanted to share her bed to keep each other warm. Leoma demurred and added she would sleep alone. Margaret crawled into bed and gathered all her coverings around her curled body. She took deep breaths to relax the muscles she had held so tight all day, especially the small of her back. *Think being warm in mine own bed, hot buttered bread, flickering candles, any warm and comforting thought.* Margaret only thought her prayers and began with her request to God the roof not leak on her as she slept. After completing her series, Margaret sighed and started the new prayer. "Dear God, I pray for the repose of the soul of the ravager because…" *Even to You, Oh God, I refuse to think his name much less to speak it.*

Soaked, the party returned from Sunday Mass and stood before the fireplace as steam rose from their boots and cloaks. Taking pity on Margaret and Leoma, the innkeeper's wife handed them wool cloths to dry their hair. To Leoma, she nodded her approval at Leoma's wearing the double braids of a married woman now a widow. The innkeeper arrived next to ask for his pay for the extra day. As she dribbled the coins from the pouch around her neck, Roulin saw she was running out of coin. The men sat on their respective sides of the room. Margaret and Leoma sat face to face before the fire.

"May I leave and work on another estate?"

Margaret shook her head. "I am sorry, Leoma. While playing I was a lord, I forgot the law. Were I truly a lord, I would free you. I wish I were so I could. Even before you are a widow, you are a villein, bound to the land and responsible to its owner." When Margaret saw Leoma's shoulders slump, she added, "Even though I am but a girl,

I can help you gain your freedom. You owe set days of work each month. If you work more days, I pay you. Save your coin, and you could buy your freedom. Then you are a free woman and a widow, and you can do anything you like."

"How much need I to be free?" asked Leoma in a petulant tone. She had expected the ceremony to free her and was bitterly disappointed to learn she now had to work for her freedom.

"You are a valuable person, Leoma, young, strong, and fertile. Only a lord can set your worth and permit you to pay for your freedom. You can earn coin until I have one. I promise to speak for you and your freedom after I am wed to him."

"What work would I do for you to earn coin?" Leoma feared it was field work. She wanted something easier, something daily so earning coin would be quick.

"Caitlin is worn out with helping both me and Cook. If you apprentice yourself to me, she will teach you to bake. I only feed and clothe you during your training, but you are clever and will learn fast. In winter, when Saxons owe but two days each week, I will pay you for the other four. You double bake on Saturday and are free on Sunday."

"I like that. Might I live with mine parents?"

"If you live at home, someone needs escort you each morn; the gatekeeper would op the gates to let you enter. Not the best for your safety or ours. If you live with Cook in the kitchen annex during the week, you could sleep at home Saturday night, but you must return before dark Sunday eve."

'That sounds reasonable. What might be mine pay?"

Margaret set her stitchery on her lap and smiled at Leoma. *First you looked at mine knees and then mine chin and now in mine eyes. With each question, each decision, you get stronger. If you continue this as home, I have hope for you.* "Caitlin and Cook will know. Are you willing to wait until I confer with them before you start working for me?"

"Yes, my lady. While I wait, may I stay at home?"

"Of course, you may. As long as you stay on the estate, you free to live where you will."

That afternoon the rain dribbled to a stop, but the wind still blew.

May the blasts dry the roads so we may leave in the morn, prayed Margaret.

After supper and before leaving for bed, Leoma informed Margaret her father wanted to speak with her. They met before the fireplace, turned to gaze at the fire, and talked so low none heard them or read their lips.

"My la…I mean my lord."

"Here I am Lord Margaret. At home I will answer to either, but I prefer Lady Margaret." She smiled to ease his frown. "You have done well, Scirburne, in all you did. Mayhap in time she will recover. Leoma is stronger than she knows. I pray for her."

Scirburne pulled his forelock. "My lord, on behalf of mine family, I thank you for what you accomplished. You believed Leoma and championed her better than any lord would do. You treat mine son as a grown man, and he has become one. Your example taught him how to protect women and, even more important, to believe them. Now you offer Leoma work away from the village, giving her time to recover and to understand her new place in this world. Our debt to you is great."

"You are most welcome, Scirburne. I accept your family's debt. I know not when or how I will ask it repaid."

Scirburne lowered his chin and looked askance. "My lady, I will only do what is legal."

Margaret chuckled. "Of course. Of course."

"May I ask a hard question?" Margaret nodded. "What might you have done had they had acquitted the man?"

"The reasonable thing. We would have tarried two or three more days. The innkeepers and town folk could swear to our whereabouts, Norman and Saxon alike. When the man's body had been found, we would have been accounted for and declared innocent."

"But who…"

"After what we revealed, someone from town would have taken it upon himself to do the deed. 'Who' is not our concern, but justice would have been served."

Scirburne stared into the fire and pondered what Margaret had said and what she had not.

Margaret decided to speak her thought. "Scirburne, you are a good father. None of what happened is your fault. You love and protect your children. They are blessed to have you." Margaret's eyes filled. She stood on tiptoe and whispered in the Saxon's ear, "I wish I had a father such as you." Quickly, Margaret turned away to hide her tears and loudly announced, "I bid God give you good rest, Scirburne." Margaret climbed the stairs.

After Mass and a quick meal while standing, the group left Suindune. Claude rode ahead to check the softness of the road and for risks of attack. Those who attended or heard of the hanging knew she would not abandon her Saxons. Everyone stayed alert, scanning and listening for noises in the wooded areas. Margaret comforted herself by pressing her left elbow on the sword under her mantle. The party stopped when Claude returned.

"I see something strange ahead," the knight reported. "A few Saxons milling at the side of the road. Women and children too. They appear not to be armed. Please move to the other side, my lady."

Margaret frowned. *Are the Saxons angry because I dishonored their court? Are these a diversion to stop us so hidden men can attack?*

Scirburne stood in the wagon bed, "Nothing to worry over, my lord. They just desire to see you."

What do they seek? Margaret unsheathed her sword. "Un-sheathe your weapons, but brandish them not. Be ready."

As soon as the Saxons had sighted Margaret's group, they ran to the side of the road Margaret was on and again stood in a line. As Margaret passed, the women curtsied, and the men pulled their fore-locks. Not knowing how to respond, Margaret looked straight ahead and gave the silent group neither smile nor nod. Several miles down the road, the party observed another group was roadside, Margaret turned to the Saxons. "Why are they doing this?"

Scirburne responded, "They are giving a respect. I am cert they will welcome a smile or a nod to show you understand their appreciation for what you did for one of their own."

They like a Norman? No, they like what I did for Leoma. Margaret smiled as her heart warmed her whole body. *They like me! Saxons show not respect for Normans unless forced. Yet, they are showing me a respect. Respect. For a long time, I have had that not. It feels good. Do mine Saxons respect me? I must look into their eyes the next time they curtsey or pull their forelocks to see if it there.* After she passed the group giving smiles and nods left and right, she pondered. *How do these people so far from Suindune know I am passing? How can they pass the word when no Saxon may leave his lord's property without a Norman escort and written permission?* Margaret pondered for several miles more before she recalled the saying Reeve on Sir Charles' estate had taught her. *Saxon tongues are swifter than Norman hooves. How they do it we Normans may never know. Ah, I spot the inn ahead.*

The second day of travel passed has had the first. Three times Saxons lined the road and showed their respect to Margaret as she passed. Between times, she worried. *Leoma's fate could be mine. At any time, I could be ravaged and forced to marry the monster who took mine honor. How do I prevent it? First, pray daily and ask God to let it happen not. Second, be not alone with any man for any reason. Even in Confession with Father Manntun; have knights within shouting distance to come to my aid. Third, mine knights. Look into their eyes for clues they are thinking what I fear. Keep them in pairs or threes and vary them so no one man thinks he has my favor. One of my knights is more likely to attack me than any other kind of man. They have the most to gain so they are the greatest danger. Dear God, protect me. I want a contract and a proper marriage ceremony before I must submit to a man.* Well after midday, Margaret remembered a dip in the road and the next curve.

"Almost home!" she called.

At that wonderful word, everyone smiled. The horses lifted their heads higher as if they smelled something familiar. The roundseys picked up their feet and moved the wagon faster. Night began to prance. Margaret steadied him as she speculated. *In almost a fortnight what has been taking place? What if all is not well? Should not a sentry be greeting us?* Her stomach rumbled. *On what might we be supping?*

22

Home

Saxons lined the lane and waved as did the guards beside the gates. The wagon turned to deliver the Saxons to the village. Jorgon, Daelton, and the pages waited in the center of the bailey to take horses to the barn and gear to the barracks and the keep. Cormac helped Margaret dismount as Reeve walked the roundseys and empty wagon through the gate. Father waited at the hall door to bless Lady Margaret and her escort. Inside, Caitlin offered them mugs of hot herbed wine. As Margaret, Sauville, Roulin, Claude and Hughes walked to the front of the hall, knights not on duty stood before the dais and warmly welcomed them home to a hearty supper of stew and bread.

Margaret emptied her mug of wine and set it at her place. She smiled as she looked about. *Mine warm cozy hall. All mine knights here but sentries. The smells of meat and bread. Home! They stand and look at me expecting something. What? Of course, kind words.* I will speak after Father's prayer and our Te Deum.

"Your welcome warms our hearts. We thank you. In Suindune, we wandered among strangers and longed for our home. For our friends who are like family to us. Glad we are to return. Let us enjoy this wonderful-smelling meal. As for me, I plan to eat overfull of stew, bread, and ale, the best meal I will have had in a fortnight." Margaret grinned at her men through their huzzahs and cheers. The girls, Scandy, and Hartun served the hearty meal with good cheer and speed. They refilled ale pitchers and bowls quickly, and they passed many bread rounds down the tables. Two bowls of stew, one bread round, and three mugs of ale later Margaret stopped eating and looked around.

I have the best place in the world with good land and good people. Look at them, good men all. They may be at their ease and joke and laugh, but they will rush to protect us. We are safe because of them. Behind them stacked high are sacks of grain. Full bins. No one will starve this winter. Good Saxons too. Margaret smiled at Father Manntun. "Father, God has been so good to us, to me. I am so grateful. How shall I thank Him?"

"I will think on it, my lady."

Margaret ordered another round of full pitchers for her men, stood, and excused herself. She accepted Syghelm's offer to escort Caitlin and her to the keep.

Exhausted, Margaret slipped into her bed. The next day, Father postponed the service two hours to let the travelers rest further. After Mass, Saxons and Normans alike enjoyed a fine dinner. The hall was so crowded the Saxons had to eat standing behind the Normans at the trestle tables. Still tired from the journey, Margaret did not think to question how her household and Saxons knew when the group would arrive. She was just glad for her own bed, her own people, and the good bread she had missed.

I feed them well and make merry this day too. I like spoiling them even though I know they have earned every bit of good will I give them and every bite of good food I can provide. Waiting for a husband may be hard, but not so hard when I have such good people to live among and such good company in the hall and in the village. Margaret ordered more ale for everyone to the cheering of all. Soon the Saxons departed for their own homes, but the party in the hall lasted past time to sup.

A few days after the party had arrived home, all seemed normal. The Saxon men were hard at work butchering hogs, smoking meat, and giving buckets of fat to the women, who were rendering it. Caitlin took what rendered fat she needed to make salves. The Saxons made the remaining fat into balls of soap or lotions scented with crushed dried flowers.

Sauville, Claude, Roulin and Hughes returned to guard duty and practice. The other retainers teased them for having gone soft in their absence. Several took unfair swipes with the practice blades. Retaliation from each man was swift and hard. More than one sparing partner bore bruises proving his teasing had been a bad idea. Margaret watched the practice from the palisade walkway.

Such strength and agility. Even wearing helmets and leather jerkins covered with overlapped metal rings sewn on, they move with ease, even grace. Will mine husband be that strong, that skilled with blade and lance, ahorse and on foot? I pray so. If he is, they might stay. They will follow one of their own if he is as skilled as they. Strong? Skilled? Might I be in danger from one of them or a pair working together? Is there one among them who would do to me what was done to Leoma to gain mine land? How to prevent such a thing? More escorts? No. More escorts

271

about will be no help if they work together and have one attack me. He marries me and keeps them on. All will win at mine cost. Whom to trust? Syhelm for cert, but who else? Roussel, Gailard and Cachier might lose their heads to defy the king's command to protect me, or at least their positions. Mayhap not one of them. The other eight have no land, no home and much to gain married to me. Margaret saw Claude defeat Roulin and raise his practice sword; she heard his cheer. *Stay home. Be not alone with any man, Norman or Saxon. Keep pages and servants near should I need to scream. The keep and only the hall when I must.* Margaret turned away and left for the company of others.

One day after supper, and still at the dais table, Sir Roussel asked to speak to Margaret. Margaret noted her men glanced her way before they left.

"Why have you ordered the hall cleared?"

"Are you well rested, my lady?"

"I am, thank you."

"Of late, you are alone in the keep. You sew most of the day. Caitlin or Cormac escort you everywhere."

"It is November. Epiphany gifts. Advent begins in three weeks."

"Indeed, Christmastide will soon be upon us."

Margaret waited. The man always took the long way round his point. *Mayhap because he has spent so much time serving the king.*

"Think you everything is back to normal, my lady?"

"Yes."

"I disagree. The others are, but you are not. You clearly are not."

"Of course I am," Margaret replied with force.

"You rarely leave the bailey; you are hiding. You look around when you are in the bailey as if you expect strangers. I am pleased you had agreed for an additional escort when you are outside the walls, but now you only leave when you must. Jorgon exercises Night. You have stopped riding. Caitlin chaperones you when you are at sword practice, which is now more seldom. Even the men have noticed your demeanor toward them has changed. All this is since your return."

Margaret knew not how to answer. She could not tell him her fears; she dared not appear weak. Margaret stared at a wall. *After Leoma's attack, I was too busy. Preparations, travel, court, the man's hanging. Only on the road home did I have time to think. That could have been me. Is that why the king let me keep the sword? To defend mine own self? I am a target for any man who wants mine dowry. He ravages me; I am forced to marry him as Leoma was. Who? Anyone. A man with armed companions while I ride with only two escorting me? One of mine own men? The longer the king waits to get me married the greater the danger someone will try. How? When? How soon?* Margaret's thoughts went swirling again.

Roussel saw her frowning and waited. Then he brought her back with, "My lady?"

"Sir Roussel." Margaret smiled, a contrived one. "I have not been as cheerful of late. Shorter days have always affected me thus," she rationalized. "I promise to remember mine blessings and smile more. You are kind to be concerned. Thank you for bringing mine behavior to mine attention. I will change."

Margaret did not touch men unless ceremony required it, so what she did was extraordinary. Laying her hand upon his arm, Margaret gave him a genuine smile. "When I count mine blessings, you are among them, Sir Roussel. You have been very good to me. If I forgot to tell you, please forgive me." Roussel stood, bowed to Margaret and left. She emitted another deep sigh.

I love mine hall. Sturdy walls, a roof that keeps us dry. Heavy entry door, iron hinges, a good latch and lock. Fire pit down the center, topped by mine dais with the head table, and stools. The dais high enough for me to see all. Margaret looked at the benches and the long boards that made the tables on each side of the pit. *We can seat fifty Normans with space behind them for the Saxons to stand. Servants by the side door. Everyone but the sentries and guards fit in here at once. Time to leave. Be brave,* she ordered herself. *I am safe here. Be brave.*

Margaret smiled broadly at the servants who had come to the side door. She waved them in and walked down the hall. She grabbed her mantle from the peg near the front door. *Find two men; go for a walk. Talk to villagers. Smile at everyone. Be glad you are home. No one attacked us on the road. No more thoughts like that. Smile.* Margaret reached for the latch. *Smile. I am a good girl. God watches over me. The Saxons like me; mine men protect me. Take different ones each time I go out. Favor none so none will think what I fear. Note how each treats me. Be good to them, but not too trusting. Never too trusting.*

The next day Margaret looked up from her sewing to see Leoma walking through the side door. Margaret laid the shirt she was mending for Roulin in her lap.

"My lady," Leoma curtsied. "I have come to be an apprentice baker. I am ready to start today."

"Welcome. I am glad. Where will you live?"

Leoma's eyes narrowed. "I have chosen to live with the kitchen staff. Cook says I may have a cot in the annex."

"Why frown?"

"He sought mine father's permission to court Willa. I will not remain to watch it."

Margaret understood which "he" Leoma meant. "Please inform Cook of mine approval. She will provide you a work dress and an apron. Introduce yourself to Caitlin; be respectful and modest. Get your belongings and move in. You sup with mine staff tonight and begin work on the morrow."

"Thank you, my lady." Leoma curtsied and left. The next morning Leoma rose well before dawn to turn risen dough into bread rounds.

A week later and after they had supped, Father Manntun announced, "My lady, Caitlin, Cormac and I will withdraw. Leoma wishes to speak with you; she needs your men to stay. Meet this with your approval?"

At Margaret's nod, the others left. Leoma entered with Elstan behind her; She stopped before Margaret while Elstan closed the servant's door and leaned against it.

"My lady, the men wish to speak with you. If you sit on the benches with them, they will be more relaxed and all can speak more quietly. We are your chaperones."

They asked a married woman, a widow. How appropriate!

Margaret took the three steps to the dirt floor and sat opposite her men. Leoma stood behind her.

Later they will inform those on guard duty, Margaret surmised.

Verel began. "They have chosen me to speak first." He looked down the table. "But anyone may do so. We will take turns, my lady."

Margaret clasped her hands together and placed them on the table.

"My lady, you are safe with us. Please believe us. We will keep you safe from strangers."

"Why should I doubt it?"

Masselin spoke next. "We realize you do fear us, though we understand not why. Since you arrived home, you peer at us as if we are strangers."

"To be suspected," added Demetre. "We are not to be feared, my lady. We promise."

Dear God, they have discovered mine concerns. I am ashamed they have read me so easily. I must be more circumspect. Mine fears are like any woman in this world, Norman or Saxon. Their laws say they own us; their power is complete. Father could have killed me at any time for any reason. A wife is her husband's property with no rights, not even to the children she births. Men are like poisonous snakes; if they strike, we die. How do we women sort the few good men from the lot? Their words are oft empty promises. By their deeds. Whose words have I trusted? Whose deeds have matched his words and make him worthy? Charles is a better man than I gave him credit when we lived together at home. I see that now. Cormac is a good man. Elstan? Yes, Elstan. Syghelm too. Though I know not why, I do trust him. Instinct! It's a feeling. Trust in mine feelings! If he feels wrong, he is wrong. Who feels right among these? Take mine time to decide. Then act. I can dismiss anyone who does not feel right. Yes, I can do that! Until I am wed and lose all power again.

Margaret clenched her hands. When she noted the men had seen them tighten, she slowly unclenched them.

"You now skip sword exercise. When you do practice, your nerve is not in it. Your parry and strike lack drive. As if you are unwilling to hurt us," added Roulin. "Or to anger us."

I recognize which are missing. And why.

"You are correct. Mine heart has not been in it. She almost added, "I know not why," but she would have lied.

276

Giraud spoke next. "We prefer you to come at us full force. As if you crave to murder us." He continued, "Actually, it is safer for both of us. We know what to expect. The way you have been practicing makes us too cautious—and that can be dangerous."

"May we ask?" Claude requested. At her nod he continued. "Are you thinking what befell Leoma will happen to you? Is that why you are wary with us?"

Margaret needed to cry. She clenched her jaws to stop from tearing up. She stared at her hands and nodded.

Her retainers were so silent they heard her shallow breathing. "You are safe, " reiterated Verel. "Any one of us alone, any pair of us, the whole group. No one will hurt you. We swear."

In unison the men repeated, "We swear."

"We swore allegiance to you," Masselin reminded her. "And we like you."

Roulin added, "Most men are not ravagers, my lady. Not a one of us even thinks such an action."

From behind, Leoma said, "And those who are, die. A powerful warning."

"Should anyone even gaze at you askance, the rest of us will beat him bloody," added Demetre.

"He would meet mine axe," promised Syghelm.

"Or a troop of Saxons in the dark," We have already decided that," revealed Elstan.

"We guard you front and back, on the motte and in the village. Here, there and everywhere." Verel grinned at her. "Please smile at us, so we know you believe us."

Margaret smiled. "I believe you," she countered in a cert, steady voice. *I needed to hear this. Their words give me strength.*

The men pounded the table with enthusiasm and voiced encouragement: "Good!" and "Welcome back!" declared several.

Margaret blushed. "Be warned. At practice on the morrow I will come at you full force."

The men stood and bowed. "We are pleased, my lady. I want to be first," announced Giraud to the rest as they moved to leave.

Margaret stood. "I am grateful you are mine men," she called after them.

They turned and waved to her before they quit the hall.

Margaret turned to Leoma and hugged her. "Thank you, Leoma. I needed to learn this. Elstan?"

"You have mine silence."

Leoma smiled fiercely. "We won't let them make us afraid, my lady. Not without need." She walked to the side door and ordered in the servants. Leoma and Elstan left The girls and pages cleared the remains of the meal and the wooden boards. After Vespers, Margaret climbed the steps to the keep. Syghelm locked the gate. This night, her list of blessings was long, and she was keen to start her prayers.

23

Another Suitor

Margaret's third suitor arrived Wednesday in the second week of Advent. Demetre and Claude escorted the man into the hall while she and Cormac were discussing how she wanted to celebrate her birth date five days hence. *They disarmed him of both sword and dagger.*

"My lady, may I present Sir Andre of Normandy."

The knight bowed. "My lady, His Royal Highness, the king, sent me. He found me suitable to marry you. Mine dearest wish is you will find me sufficient as well."

"Welcome, Sir Andre," Margaret's manner was the warmer than she had used on her earlier two suitors. *Handsome. Well spoken.* "His Royal Highness gave me a password, so I know he sent you. Have you it?" At his nod, Margaret motioned him forward. Sir Andre looked askance at Cormac and then at Margaret. "He knows it."

Sir Andre leaned over the dais platform and placed his hands upon the edge of the table to be as close as he could to Margaret. While he did so, Margaret gently sniffed. *Soap. No heavy ale or wine breath. Washed his clothes recently. Rugged with a strong jaw Broad shoulders, thick arms, well-formed hands. A fighter accustomed to wearing chain mail and heavy gear, yet tanned from years in the field.*

"Third boon," he whispered.

"Will you agree to stay in barracks with mine retainers?"

"Yes. Who guards you?"

"I sleep in the keep behind a locked gate and barred door. May I present mine seneschal Cormac mac Cennedig. He will attend to whatever need you may have."

"Thank you, Cormac mac Cennedig."

Good manners so far. "Did he come to me without a libation to quench his thirst and food if he missed a midday meal?"

"He did," replied Claude.

Margaret nodded to Hartun who closed the servant's door behind himself. She stood and walked around the table. Sir Andre walked parallel to her and stood by the steps. He offered his hand. Margaret gave him a small head shake. "Thank you, Sir Andre, but I need not your hand at this time."

Roulin's quick smile told her he got her meaning.

Knows when not to react. Margaret reached the floor. "You are tall, Sir Andre."

He smiled at her surprise. "A head and half again." He perused her from head to foot and up again. "A good match."

Margaret could not help grinning at him. "Well done, Sir Andre. You jest well."

Sir Andre waved her forward and followed her to a trestle table. She signaled him to sit. After Margaret sat four feet down the same table, she tucked her feet under the bench. From behind her came Hartun, who set the serving tray between them. Sir Andre waited. She chose the smaller mug of ale. Then he picked up his mug. Margaret's new suitor pantomimed a clink of mugs; Margaret smiled but did not reciprocate. She drank at the same time as he. Margaret picked up the trencher and placed it before him. Then she put the pitcher of ale between them and set the tray aside. Such service was not only good manners; it was a subtle removing of a barrier between them.

"Thank you, my lady."

Margaret lowered her eyes at the two words he emphasized. She hoped she did not blush. She did. Margaret waited patiently while he ate bread and cheese.

Good table manners. Chews with his mouth closed. Does not slurp.

After Sir Andre put his board on the tray and poured his second ale, he said, "Ask what you will. I want you to know me well when you decide."

Margaret asked after his people. She learned their estate was halfway between Reuen and Dieppe and had been in their family for several generations. His mother was alive, but his father had died. His eldest brother, married with four children, now owned the estate. His second brother was in the Church. He was third son, and had two sisters, one married and the other younger than he.

Sir Andre ended with, "We are all tall and light-haired. We are a hearty bunch. All their children have lived."

"That is good." Margaret shared her family information. Well, most of it. She did not speak of her father's infidelities or of how he rid himself of her mother.

"Will you stay three days?"

"As long as you wish." His storm-blue eyes met hers with a hint of flirtation though his manner was correct.

"Cormac, please invite Father and Reeve to join us at the head table. Sir Andre, before we sup, permit me to give you a tour of the bailey. We will also go to the church annex. I will introduce you to Father Manntun."

"His age?"

"In his young fifties, I think."

At supper, Sir Andre sat between Father Manntun and Cailin. *I want to see you you treat a priest and an Irish free woman.* Margaret looked to her left and conversed with Sir Roussel.

"Well?" Roussel asked one-word questions whenever he could.

"Clean, well-mannered, polite, nice voice."

"Why do women always start with 'clean'?"

Margaret chuckled, "What woman wants to be in the arms of a dirty, smelly man whose breath makes her swoon? Make no mistake, sirrah, clean matters!"

"His voice?"

O-o-oh-h Two words! "If I must listen to him for the rest of mine life, I had best like the sound of his voice."

Roussel harrumphed.

"Sirrah, on the morrow I will take him on a tour of the village and mine land. May I have three escorts?"

"Why three?"

"Because he is tall, and big, and looks very strong."

"He is. Three."

"He gained back his dinner knife. I suppose we must return his blade so he thinks we trust him."

"Three men? He will know better."

"Trust must be earned. I still want three men."

Roussel nodded.

I wish Reeve could sit beside me. He converses better.

The morning was cold and windy, but Margaret wanted to prove she was hearty. They walked through the village. The head of each family stepped outside to meet the knight. Each bobbed his head as he pulled his forelock. Margaret spoke each man's name. She told one of his accomplishments or skills before she listed the rest of his family. Most often Sir Andre just nodded. The only comment he made was to Widow Gytha; he complimented her ale making. It was far too chilly for little ones to venture out to hold Lady Margaret's hand, but she told Sir Andre of the custom. When they were out of the village, Margaret pointed to the distant hearth and anvil under the roof.

"I hired a smith."

"Good. Armed men need someone to create chain mail, swords and helmets and do repairs."

"He is a black smith and produces only common ironwork, not a white smith."

"Get a different one—or a second one. Knights need armorers."

"Thank you for your good advice."

I will not tell him Garwig had been desperate for a place or that I pay him less than he might have earned in Gloucester. That is private information. She wondered how costly an armorer was and guessed it might be cheaper to hire him to make things rather than to retain him. *I must guard mine coins. By now I should have a good husband who worries about such things. Are you he? Mayhap.*

Sir Andre took her silence for agreement. "Bit chilly for a ride. Mayhap it will be warmer on the morrow."

"You are kind to think of mine welfare." Margaret meant her compliment. "Let us return to the hall and await dinner. We can talk more."

Friday morn was warmer and windless. Margaret kept her sword at her side; she sat upon a chunk of a tree stump and watched the men practice. Sir Andre stood beside her.

"With your permission, my lady, may I practice with your men as well?"

"Please hurt them not too badly," Margaret asked. She liked Sir Andre's laughing as he promised not to do so. He displayed the easy confidence of one to whom fighting is as much play as work.

Andre removed his sleeveless surcoat and searched for a peg. Margaret raised her hand and he gave it to her. She folded it and laid it across her lap. Margaret's men stopped practice to watch. Sir Andre reached down for the bottom of his tunic to pull it inside out over his head. Margaret reached up and held his shirt hem as he worked himself out of the long, flared sleeves. The men looked shocked. No wife ever undressed her husband in public, much less a hostess her guest. They wondered what kind of announcement her actions were.

Sir Andre's muscles bulged through his shirt, braies, and chausses. To keep modest, Margaret looked away, though the sight nestled warmly within her mind as her cheeks warmed. Sir Andre laughed, turned, and called for a short and a long practice sword. Men grunted, attacked, parried, sweat, and took few pauses. Margaret called Scandy to bring drink to the thirsty men. The ale disappeared. At first, Sir Andre acquitted himself well. After he knew each man's strengths and weaknesses, he attacked. Not ferociously or in anger, but to prove his prowess. He used several moves her men had not seen. They learned them and turned them on him. He knew other moves to thwart them. Their actions fascinated Margaret. Verel called a halt to practice. Sir Andre thanked the men for letting him participate. Then he asked where he might wash before dinner. Margaret stood and handed Sir Andre's garments to Scandy with instructions for the boy to follow and serve her guest. With a friendly wave to the men, Margaret departed the practice field and walked toward the hall. *Fights well. Gets along with mine men. I saw respect in their eyes, and they laughed with him. Young, Strong, Manly. He could protect me.*

At the head table, seating was the same as the previous day's. *Am I testing him again? Am I too formal? Am I afraid to have him close? I am uncert of him. Playing "wife" at the practice field was fun, but doing so was within the safety of mine men. Is he the man for me? Am I willing to lose all mine power to him after we are wed? Would I let him rule mine life and take charge of this estate and all in it? Follow his orders? Yield to his every whim? Am I so eager to be married I am ignoring something? No man is perfect, but he appears to be suitable. I must take more time to know him better. Lead him not! You still know too little of him.* Margaret smiled at Father and asked him a question to start a conversation. Pleading women's work, Margaret excused herself from the hall. Caitlin accompanied her to the keep. To sew all afternoon, they had to move from an arrow slit to the fireplace when the light faded

He is a handsome one. I suspect he knows that. His manners please me. I like the way he looks at me. I feel mine heart flutter. He gazes as me like I am a woman, not land and dowry. He flirts with his eyes and small head tilts; I like it. Feels good. Am I desiring him? Look down so Caitlin sees not me blush at mine thoughts.

Saturday Margaret excused herself after Mass. Sir Andre asked when he could see her. She responded she hoped they would ride out after they dined. She returned to the keep and ate pottage with Caitlin and her servant girls. Because she and Caitlin were in a rush to finish their Epiphany gifts, they worked until they heard the midday bell. Margaret took her mantle with her.

The weather was perfect, cool but sunny with a light breeze. The five of them rode behind the bailey and north. Then they changed direction and headed west and south. Sir Andre stopped them several times, ostensibly to rest their horses. He asked questions about the land, the crops, the harvest. His interest and good questions impressed Margaret and she told him so. Sir Andre revealed he had worked his father's estate in his youth. His father had expected him to aid his older brother. Sir Andre said he loved horses and arms too much to become a seneschal.

"Let us skirt behind the village and ride east and into the forest," Sir Andre suggested.

A perfect ambush if he has men waiting. Margaret responded, "There is not much to see that direction. Let us return to the hall and talk more. I know not how old you are and where you acquired your fighting skills. Did you go on the Grand Crusade?"

"Twenty-three, my lady," answered Sir Andre. With a gallant bow over his stead's neck, he said, "I will answer your questions. Mayhap you will then answer mine."

"Such as?" *Am I flirting with him? I am!*

"Why do you ride a gelding instead of a mare? And of your sword."

"We have much to discuss." *This is more enjoyable than I thought courting would be!*

286

They rode into the bailey, dismounted and handed their steeds' reins to Daeltun. In the hall Margaret asked for bowls of hot broth. They sat on one end of the head table and visited. Margaret learned Sir Andre had been fostered by a lord famous for his fighting skills. He did not go to the Grand Crusade in 1096 because his older brother had been seriously ill. His father had forbade Andre's going in case his older brother died. He did not. At her query, Sir Andre told Lady Margaret he had not fought with the king's brother, Sir Robert, against the king last year.

"He never would have sent me to you if I had," he reminded her.

"How thoughtless of me to ask. I should have realized it."

"No matter, my lady,"

Margaret told Sir Andre how Night had been her uncle's. After he died so young, her mother had made a pet of him. He refused to be trained to fight, so grandfather had him gelded. Margaret warned Andre that, because of her father's mistreatment, Night hated men. The Percheron allowed only her and her hostler Jorgon ride him. Margaret told him how the king had given her the short sword.

"What will you do with it after you are married?" Andre asked.

"I plan to make it a wedding gift. Mine lord may return it to the king or keep it."

"And you will never pick up a sword again," Andre ordered.

"Never is a long time, Sir Andre. What if mine lord is gone? What if we are attacked and our walls are breached? What if the enemy reaches the keep and I have children? I will pick up a blade to save mine children."

"Are you saying only under the most dire circumstances?"

"I am. I expect to put away mine blade and trust mine lord to protect me and our children."

Andre leaned toward her. "Glad I am to hear it."

He is more rugged, more direct than William was. He lacks William's courtly manner, but what care I for that? The men of the Court are not sincere, but he appears to be. Did the king send the first two so I would recognize a good man when I met him? He is manly; he will take charge. Am I willing to let him? I must let mine husband be in charge, but I must be cert I am willing to let it be Sir Andre. Be friendly and give him more time.

At dinner Margaret stood before the hall and announced, "I have asked Sir Andre to stay three more days." She sat.

Those at the trestle tables pounded their mugs on the boards politely, but not with enthusiasm.

Sauville opt the keep gate and waited for Sir Andre to leave. "My lady," he called softly. When she return to his side he said, "Still no men in the forest."

She smiled at Sauville and wished him, "God give you good rest."

At Sunday Mass Lady Margaret stood to the left, the women's and small children's side. To the right, Sir Roussel stood with Sirs Andre, Cachier and Gailard completing the first row. Retainers, Reeve, Saxon men and older boys stood behind. The space between the groups was called an "aisle" but it was only a space. At the appropriate times, the groups stood and knelt on the dirt floor. At Holy Communion time, the men walked the aisle to the priest to receive the body and blood of Jesus the Christ. The women's side was second. After Mass, Father Manntun proceeded everyone to the door to speak with the congregants as they left.

"I will think of your homily," said Sir Andre to Father Manntun. "I will consider the question you asked."

Father Manntun thanked him.

Diplomatic too.

No one spoke of it when Margaret placed her hand upon Sir Andre's arm as they strolled to the hall to await the first of the two meals served on Sundays. The Saxons looked at one another with surprised expressions; several raised their eyebrows. Sir Andre walked with his head canted to Margaret's and with a wide smile on his face as he spoke to her.

With Sunday Mass three hours later than the rest of the week, everyone broke his fast at noon, which was a sumptuous feast, two roasted mutton. Like Lent, Advent was meatless, so everybody was grateful for the Sabbath. Most lingered in the hall for talk, storytelling, and singing. Individuals left for their duties or rounds of guarding. Margaret and Caitlin left for a time to finish their Christmastide sewing early.

"Ten days until Midnight Mass and meal," Caitlin reminded Margaret. "Will he be staying until then?"

"If all goes well, Tuesday night I will ask him to stay for Christmas Day and the Twelve Days."

"So you do like him." Caitlin fished for information.

"I suppose so. He has some admirable qualities. I suspect he acts proud and speaks oft of his exploits because he wants to impress me. Or is he a braggart? What think you, mine friend?"

"I suspect he knows you have already dispatched two, though he may not know why. He is trying hard, but that will change."

"Why say you that?"

"Your mother once said, 'A woman had better like the man when he is courting her because that is the best behavior she will ever see. Once she marries him, he stops trying. He owns her and he can do what he likes.'"

"I remember not her ever saying that."

"I do. She delivered a truth."

"Is that why you keep putting off Cormac? At Caitlin's shrug, Margaret added, "Are you waiting until I am wed? If you are, please wait not. Cormac cares for you, and I want to see you happy." Margaret thought and spoke again. "If you wait until after I am married, mine lord will make the decision for you. I rather you choose."

Sunday supper was a soup that included the leftover meat, so it would not be thrown to the dogs. Monday, December 15, was Margaret's birth date. *Sixteen and still unmarried. I cannot become drunk and sleep through this day as I did last year.* Margaret crept out of bed and reached for her bliaut. *Is he the one? Did the king send me two who were wrong so I would accept the third?* She continued to dress. *Is he right for me or is there something wrong about him as well? He will be here another fortnight. I will decide by then. Mayhap I should ask Caitlin. She has a clear eye. But not until after Christmas dinner. If I have not decided by then, I will ask Caitlin.* With that, Margaret reached for her mantle and scarf. She plastered a smile on her face. *They expect me to be happy to be sixteen. Disappoint them not.* As it was Advent, Margaret had asked only for a blessing after Mass. *Why was I birthed during Advent? The only birth date I like is when it comes on a Sunday, and I can eat meat.*

The next two days Margaret tried to show Sir Andre what life together might be like. She attended to estate matters in the morning and left him to himself. Dinner was pleasant, and she stayed afterward to visit. Then she disappeared again until supper to prepare for Epiphany. The next evening Margaret sat Sir Gailard to the right of the empty seat at the head table; she invited Sir Andre to sit to her left.

Sir Andre looked down. "There is a sword between us, my lady." Uncert how to respond, Margaret smiled wanly. "Hopefully not for long." He gave her no chance to respond. "Codfish stew again? I am eager for meat on Sunday."

"Have you plans to return to your family for Christmastide?" Margaret tried to sound only mildly interested.

"Not at this time."

"You are welcome to stay with us for Christmas Day. Mayhap you would like to stay until Epiphany, sirrah."

"I would like that. I would like that very much, my lady." His tone at speaking those last two words told Margaret of his immediate possessiveness of her.

I like he takes charge of me. I think. Mayhap I have been too long in charge of myself and have forgot how nice it is to be taken care of, even coddled. What do I really want?

"On the morrow I am going into the village to see how they are faring in this cold, wet weather. Would you like to accompany me?"

"Yes. You will be escorted?"

"We will be escorted, Sir Andre."

"When you retire to the keep, I would like to continue to accompany you to the gate."

"You may," responded Margaret. She was grateful the meal arrived. *This careful dance of distance and closeness is wearing. Of trying to ascertain a man's character from his actions. Mayhap having a father searching and then just introducing you to your future husband is easier. Mayhap it is not such a bad practice after all.* Margaret reached for her spoon. *Would that he had been a good father. Then I would have none of these worries or misgivings, and I would already be married with children.* Margaret reached for her bread round.

Sir Andre kept a slow pace on their stroll to her gate. He held Margaret's arm in the crook of his and close to his body. *I feel the warmth of him even over his cloak. Blush not!* Sir Hughes lifted the torch high, so they would see their feet; Caitlin followed. When they reached the gate, Masselin was already there. Sir Andre very slowly took her right hand and raised it to his lips. Holding Margaret's eyes with his, he kissed the back of her gloved hand and was reluctant to release her.

"God give you good rest, Lady Margaret," Sir Andre murmured as he bowed.

"God give you good rest. I will see you at Mass, Sir Andre." As Margaret ascended to the keep, she did not have to look back; she knew he was watching her. *He does make mine heart flutter. Think or feel? Which is better? Epiphany, I will decide by Epiphany.*

Well before dawn two days later, someone stood at the base of the keep and yelled. Margaret and Caitlin slid the wooden shutter aside and responded through the open arrow slit.

"Trouble, my lady, we need you in the hall," called up Demetre.

"Anon," Margaret answered. The women dressed hurriedly. Margaret did not brush her hair; Caitlin just threw a scarf over hers. They grabbed their mantles and hugged the outside wall as they descended two flights of spiral stairs with only one candle between them. Both lifted the heavy bar. Caitlin pulled the rope that pivoted the bar to its resting place beside the door and tied it off. Margaret pushed the door out and looked down. She was grateful for the torch Demetre held high as they climbed to the ground. She waited to talk until they were at the gate. Axe on his shoulder, Syghelm was waiting.

"Did someone die?" At Demetre's "No," Margaret asked, "Is someone hurt?"

"Not too badly. Verel will tell you." Both he and Syghelm followed the women.

Margaret charged through the back door entry and slammed into Verel's chest. She heard Sir Andre roar her name.

"Please wait, my lady, you need to learn what happened before you see him."

Margaret tried to look around Verel, but he would not permit it.

"He got drunk last night. We let him slumber. Giraud was on patrol at the gate. When Andre…

Margaret noted the lack of "Sir." She tried to concentrate. "Please repeat that."

"When Andre woke, he stumbled out of the hall. He leaned against the wall and pissed at it. Then he lurched toward the kitchen. Sauville climbed down the walkway and followed him."

"Oh, no!" moaned Margaret. "Leoma was baking."

Caitlin spun away and left for the kitchen.

Verel nodded. "He pulled open the door and Leoma screamed. He tore her dress. Sauville and Giraud tackled him. Leoma kept screaming; men came running. Andre was drink strong. Took several of us to hold and tie him. Cook is with her now."

"Could this have been an accident? Something that will never occur again?"

"My lady, I fear not. A few of us have seen him eyeing women, even your young serving girls. We are so sorry; we recognize you like him."

"Did you make him drunk?" *Three suitors and not one suitable. What is wrong with me?*

"No, my lady. I assume he became comfortable, thought he had your approval. After your last invitation, he just … became who he actually is."

Margaret released a long slow sigh. "I must consider." She exited the hall to the roaring of her name by the man she had expected would become her husband.

Margaret rubbed her arms to warm them. She turned.

"Syghelm, Thank you. I feel so safe when you are near. Did they deliberately make him drunk? Do they dislike him that much?"

"They did nothing. They sipped their usual ration. When he called for more and more, they said nothing. They watched him order wine and drink himself into a stupor. They let him sleep when he dropped his head to the table."

Margaret closed her eyes. *I want not to do this. I have failed again.* Margaret steeled herself and re-entered the building. Verel let her pass. She walked down the fire pit to the three men who held Sir Andre and stopped. Andre's clothes were a jumble; he reeked of wine. He spoke her name and tried to rise. Roulin, Demetre, and Giroud pushed him down.

"Remove the rope around his neck. Sir Andre is no criminal."

"Thank you, my lady. These men have treated me abominably, and they need punishment."

He seemed clear headed, but she had seen that before. *Like Father. Shock, a fight, something brought him around to the appearance of soberness. Now Andre as well.* Not wanting to seem superior, she too sat on a bench, but she kept the tables and the fire pit between them.

"Please tell me what happened," Margaret asked in a neutral tone.

"They plied me with drink. Got me drunk and left me to sleep in the rushes. In the rushes, my lady! No doubt they intended to call you to see my embarrassment and insist I am unworthy of you. I swear one or more of them have their minds on you for themselves. They need me gone."

"And mine baker?"

"An accident. I was seeking a privy. I stumbled at the door and lurched forward. She started screaming."

"Her ripped dress?"

"That too was an accident. I was reaching to gain mine balance. I meant her no harm. I swear it, my lady. It was a mishap. Lady Margaret, please believe me."

Caitlin stepped around Verel to Margaret's other side. She whispered in her ear. Margaret kept her eyes on Sir Andre; they widened at what she heard. Sir Andre watched her react. *I see fear in your eyes. Why? Because I have caught you being who you really are?*

"No," Margaret whispered. "Take her home. You and two guards. Tell her to stay as long as she likes." Margaret listened again, then added, "Yes, tell Cook."

Caitlin left as quietly as she had come.

Even now, he is handsome and manly. His eyes, how they pierce mine heart, so blue. He looks hopeful, endearing, eager for forgiveness. I pray this truly is an accident and will not happen again. I fear it is a pattern, one I will be stuck with if I accept him. Oh Mother, is this how you felt about Father; you loved him, but did you also hate him when he drank and chased women?

Margaret exhaled a long, slow breath. She needed time to decide how to begin. Her men heard sadness in her voice.

"Sir Andre, mine father was a drunk. Oh, he went through periods of soberness, of kindness, of living a normal life. Then he would start drinking again. He begged mine mother's forgiveness and promised he would never again become drunk. But he did."

"I am not a drunk; they tricked me."

"So you said. What I remember was mine mother becoming a midwife to women of rank in order to escape him. She took me with her. I observed how sober men treated their wives, and I learned how a good man behaves toward women. Mine father took Saxon women into the forest. He even slept with girls. After mine mother died, he often drank before picking a Saxon and bedding her. He cared not we children heard them. He lived a drunk; he died a drunk."

"You know me!" Sir Andre snapped.

"Actually, no. You presented yourself well enough; you gave me reason to hope. But this…this." Margaret waved her hand. "Sir Andre, I want not mine mother's life." Margaret stood. "Sir Verel, please give him three days' food in a sack. Let him clean himself and get his horse. Have men escort him to the road."

"You need me!" Andre roared at her. "I am the third you have sent away. The king will send you no more. You need me!"

Margaret was unmovable.

"You have told me several lies. I want to marry, but I want an honest man. An honorable man does not blame others for his drinking. An honorable man does not accost an innocent woman. An honorable man tells the truth. If you return, you do so as an enemy; and we will deal with you most harshly."

Margaret walked toward the dais.

"You want not to marry! You want a dozen retainers to worship and obey you! You are no true woman! You are a sword-carrying thing. No one else even wants you! Unless you have one of these in mind. Which one beds you in your keep?"

Margaret heard his ranting and kept walking. She heard the blow and kept walking. She walked through the back door and slammed it shut.

At the keep gate, she turned to Syghelm. "I will not be at Mass this morning. Send no one for me; let no one in. Not even Caitlin."

Syghelm watched the servant girls leave the keep and saw keep door shut; he heard the bar slam home. Caitlin and Cook baked bread, and Caitlin slept in the kitchen annex. Margaret did not attend Mass, did not request meals. No one knew when next they would see her.

She paced. *Oh, God, I have prayed over mine lot. In this world where men rule, I need a husband. Not a drunk. Please, Oh Lord, not a drunk. If I do nothing, the king may continue to send me unsuitable men. Nine months is too long for him to be angry. Something is amiss. Mayhap he wants me to remain alone as an example to other women not to defy the ways of men. If I go to Court, do I submit to his will or do I challenge him? I will pray until You tell me what to do. Marry or remain single? Your will, Oh God, in all things. Especially this.*

The Fourth Sunday of Advent, she appeared at Mass, but she only arrived when everyone was in their accustomed places. She walked to the front as Father Manntun appeared from the church annex where he lived. After Mass, they let her leave first. At the door Father tried to speak to her, but she held up her hand and kept walking. Those in the hall broke their fasts in silence while avoiding looking at Margaret, seated alone on the dais. Everyone stayed the hall until she left through the back door.

Margaret stepped into the kitchen. "Nearra, thank you for all your extra work." Cook nodded.

"You were ill," said Nearra's nephew Duone as he repeated what someone had told him. "Are you better now?"

"I am better now, Duone. Thank you for your concern."

"Christmas Eve Day is but three days away." Margaret asked, "Nearra, what may I do to help you prepare?"

"You could visit Leoma; we lack our baker."

"I miss her. She is nice to me," added Duone.

"As you wish." Margaret returned to the hall. Caitlin and Cormac were conversing; they stopped. Margaret took Caitlin's hand in hers. "Thank you, Caitlin, for your work and preparation for Christmas while I was gone."

"Are you back?"

"I am." Margaret turned to Cormac. "Thank you, Cormac, for all you did in mine stead."

"I helped Caitlin when I could."

Margaret watched him leave; she turned to Caitlin, "You look glad to have had his company and help."

Caitlin tilted her head and shrugged. Margaret smiled at her friend, turned and asked two men to escort her to the village. She sat with Leoma a long while. She listened to Leoma's version of what had transpired; her story was the same as Verel's report. Margaret asked Leoma what she wished to do. Leoma looked away.

"Please remember how respectful and polite the knights are toward you. We all need you, especially Cook. Duone said he misses you. You are important to us, Leoma. Will you not return to the bailey to live and work with us again?"

"You are sad to see him go." Leoma was not asking.

Margaret nodded.

"And angry as well?"

"And angry as well." Margaret did not say with whom.

Leoma commented, "We don't always receive what we desire, do we?"

"Few people do, Leoma. We like your bread. We hope you return. If you do, you will continue to earn coins for your freedom. Please think on that."

Margaret left to knock on the chapel annex. Father had been kind; her penance for missing Mass twice was just a few prayers. She left to find Elstan.

24

— ❧ —

Departure

To complete her last Epiphany gift, Margaret returned to the keep . She sat fireside on the first floor with servant girls coming and going. Her room at the top of the stairs was too far away from everyone. *I feel alone and cold. I want noise and activity to distract me from worry.* Finally, she decided to turn her mind to pleasantries. *The Christ's birth date. How I love it. A full chapel. Incense, High Mass. Singing. Then meat-laced pottage, hot bread and butter, sweetbreads, and mince pies. Bed again for a few hours. A sumptuous feast at midday that lasts until after dark.* Her mouth watered as she imagined the smells and tastes.

After midnight Mass, she sat at table with a full hall, and the delicious smells, both sweet and savory, she had imagined. The first meal of the day filled the air. *Soon a full belly. Then back to bed.*

The feast began at midday. Much later, Margaret looked down the two lines of knights, staff and servants that comprised her household. Everyone was eating and drinking heartily. The noises were merry with punches of uproarious laughter. *Christmas feast last year was in Winchester Castle. King Henry had shut me behind locked doors with his queen. Court ladies disliked me and called me "that country girl." They mocked me for mine paltry wardrobe. This year I am in mine own home with mine own knights and staff, liked by mine Saxons, and richer from a bounteous harvest. Better, much better. Yet I still lack a husband. Where are you, William?*

She decided now was the perfect time to move. She stood and left the head table. Margaret spoke to each person, thanked each individual for what he or she had done during the year. Each bit of praise was specific to the one she addressed. When she reached Elstan, he whispered his resistance to her plan. "You are being rash, my lady," he warned so quietly only she heard him.

Margaret looked around the hall to be cert no one was paying attention. She smiled sweetly as if she were thanking him. "I am going with or without you. With or without an escort. Have you found me two?"

"Roulin and Masselin."

"Did they swear to silence?"

"They did, but like none of it."

"No matter. It is what I need do. We leave at midnight."

"Dawn will be better," reasoned Elstan.

"Too easy to be stopped."

Margaret strolled down the line, rounded the end and spoke to each on her return to the head table. Once there, she offered those on the dais a posset, a hot, herbed wine drunk on special occasions.

Roussel only said, "Yes."

Caitlin smiled and responded. "That would be nice."

"It will warm mine blood on this cold day," affirmed Cormac.

Margaret smiled at Cormac. *I think you are not too cold if your face is already flushed, and Roussel's nose has reddened.* Margaret set to work. From the dais floor she picked up two pokers and placed their ends into the fire pit embers. She removed a pouch from a small basket below the dais table and explained she had already mixed the herbs. Margaret reached for the honey pot on the table to sweeten the drink and to mask its slightly bitter taste. She took Sir Roussel's and Father Manntun's goblets first. After she poured fresh wine in each glass, she added the herbs and honey. She stirred them together well. Then she reached for the first poker and plunged it into the drink. The liquid hissed and steamed and released a heady fragrance. Margaret handed the drink to Father Manntun. She repeated the process and handed Sir Roussel his mug. Margaret returned the pokers to the fire and chatted with Caitlin and Cormac while the metal rods reheated. Soon they too had their possets and were happily sipping.

Sir Roussel downed his wine and offered his cup. "Another?"

"Of course!" replied Margaret as she heated another drink for him and the other three as well.

The party continued well after dark, which came early this time of year. Surfeited with food and drink, everyone started to drowse. Margaret announced, "Cleaning the hall may wait until the morrow if you servants store leftover foods before you take to your beds. Permit the retainers with their heads on the tables to continue to sleep."

Sir Roussel stood. "I am for bed. Father, will you accompany me as far as the barracks?" Father Manntun stood and joined Roussel as they walked the hall and left by the main door.

Margaret helped Caitlin into bed. She kept repeating, "I understand not why I am so tired."

Each time, Margaret responded, "Because you labored so hard these last days," and "Because you need rest."

Margaret crawled in beside her bedmate, but she slept not. She listened for the distant sounds from the hall to quiet. As Margaret anxiously waited, she thought too many hours had passed, but her mind had run ahead of itself. Margaret waited impatiently. From outside and below the keep, a man coughed twice. *I pray that is Elstan and not Syghelm. I saw him asleep in the hall. God, please keep him and his sharp ears asleep.* She slipped from under her coverings, dressed, and grabbed the sack she had hidden under the bed. With stealth, she crept down the black hole of the stair well. At the bottom, she added shoes, scarf, and mantle to her Christmas Day gunna. Caitlin noticed not Margaret had left the ladder un-raised. She descended it without disturbing the girls fast asleep before the fireplace. Elstan waited for her at the bottom. Margaret offered a quick prayer. *Syghelm, stay surfeited with drink and sleep on.* They took the steps with only starlight to guide them and slipped out the motte gate without being seen.

To be out of the midnight wind, the guards leaned against the palisade wall as they dozed. They spotted not Roulin and Masselin leading four horses to the gate. They saw not two people skirt the edges of buildings and walk in their direction. Three mounted and waited. Masselin opt one side the gate for them. Startled, the guards awoke and shouted, "Who goes there!" Three rushed out while Masselin mounted. Hooves pounded on the bridge, but the dark hid who or how many had left.

Angry, Sauville and Claude called, "Masselin, whence go you?"

"A vital message for the king. Seal the gate," he yelled as he urged his horse over the bridge to the night-blackened lane.

The weather held cold, windy, and dry. *I care not for ill weather. I am for Court. If the king is holding a true Christmas Court, he will hear me. He must.* Riding from inn to inn over roads roughened and pitted from wagons and horses took three days. *Have I enough coin to stay for as long as it takes to speak with the king? No matter. I will sleep standing against the castle wall if I must.* Because Margaret was cert owners had let every available sleeping place in Winchester, she stopped at the Half Moon, a rustic inn two hours from the city's northwestern gate. Margaret chose a straw-stuffed mattress on the floor for her bed. To be at hand, her sword lay between her and the other women. *I will stand alone when I am before him. No one of the Court will support me. Have I the courage to do what I must? How shall I begin? What will he do to me? Sleep if I can. I have practiced three different speeches. Decide which to say on the road.*

She slipped out well before dawn, and the group grabbed what they could eat while standing. Dawn of 29 December broke as Margaret and her men arrived at Winchester's walls. Four horses champed their bits, neighed and sidled as they felt their riders' impatience. The city guards opt the gates.

25

Christmas Court

Knowing the king's habits helped Margaret. *Mass is done; his fast will soon be over. He will sit the morning holding court, dine, and then hunt. I must arrive early if I am to see him this day. Forget food; this is more important.*

The king's seneschal remembered the Lady Margaret. He informed her the king was most particular not to see people by rank. "His Royal Highness holds a true Christmas Court. Open to anyone. You must wait your turn. This morn you are fourth." He instructed her to wait in the back of the Great Hall with the others. Margaret and her men waited in the corner to the right of the massive double doors. After one land dispute, a marriage request between noble families, and a disagreement regarding the health of cattle sold, Margaret knew the king pretended to be holding an informal court as if he were just another lord. *"Ha! Not just any lord."* Margaret straightened her garments and shook her hair. The seneschal called Margaret forth.

"Elstan, please stay here," she whispered.

"The Lady Margaret is present to report," announced the seneschal.

Be brave. Be brave. Start with thanking him. List each man's good qualities first, then why I had to refuse him. Remember to compliment the men of the Court, their brothers and sons. Remember "flower of England's manhood." They will like that.

Margaret walked the center aisle with Masselin and Roulin behind her. She curtsied low with her eyes modestly at the floor and waited.

"Rise and speak," ordered Henry, King of England..

"Your Royal Highness, thank you for sending me three suitors from which to choose." *Best make mine case quickly before he silences me.*

Both lords' and ladies' heads turned and their ears perked; they realized they had a scene coming. Many took a step forward to hear better. They knew this girl caused trouble just by being herself.

"The first man you sent confused me. He was learned and well spoken. He arrived by wagon with boxes he said contained books. Eustace looked upon mine knights at practice but chose not to join them. When I asked him to go riding with me, he admitted he did not sit a horse well enough to be comfortable. When I asked him how he expected to run the estate, he informed me I would be keeping accounts, ordering retainers, managing our villeins, and planning our crops. In short, Your Royal Highness, he expected me to do all I am doing now. He informed me he would read, and the dowry you gave me would be spent for books. Books, Your Royal Highness! I was to do the work of both a lord and a lady while he read books! A young man of twenty, handsome with light hair. His having no beard should have been warning enough. After three days I sent Eustace away. I wanted a man; he was a boy."

The king harrumphed and Margaret quickly continued to forestall Henry stopping her.

"The second man you sent me was a man, a real man. Sir Cavel was experienced in battle and practiced with mine men. We rode over the estate, and he impressed me with his horsemanship. He was moderate in his drink. Sir Cavel spoke only when he had something to say, and I listened to him carefully. He related stories of his younger days in battles well fought and of his loyal support of you. Your Royal Highness if I recall correctly, you agreed to send me a candidate of twenty-six years or younger. Sir Cavel is old, four decades or more. What remained of his hair had gone white, his beard gray and scraggly. He wanted a home for his declining years and someone to warm his bed." Margaret heard titterers. *Ignore them.* She gazed at her king. *What are you thinking?* "Your Royal Highness, I am willing to warm mine husband's bed and more." A few titters became guffaws. The king smiled. Margaret smiled back. *A good reaction.* "But how am I to deliver healthy children from seed that is two score old or older? I sent him away. Now the third man you sent me I thought a paragon!"

King Henry frowned.

He suspects me and well he should if he knows Andre's true character.

"He is tall and young, handsome, well spoken, strong and manly. He practiced with mine retainers, fought them off, and even taught them new attack moves. He sat his horse as if he had been born on it. After three days, I invited him to stay three more. We traveled over the land; he asked piercing questions, which demonstrated his intelligence and his knowledge of farming. I walked with him in the village. He tolerated mine villeins, and even expressed a compliment. In short, I thought you had sent me the best candidate for mine hand."

Dear God, please stay him until I get to say it all.

"Six days before Christmas I asked him to stay until Epiphany. I thought mine early Epiphany gift to him would be mine consent to marry. I thought he would be in court today asking for mine hand, not me reporting what he did." Margaret took a loud, deep breath for dramatic effect. "What did he do that forced me to send him away?"

King Henry shifted in his throne. The lords and ladies were frozen in rapt attention.

"He believed he already had mine consent. He relaxed, Your Royal Highness. He became his true self. He became falling-down drunk and attacked one of mine servant women. He terrified her; mine men stopped him. He looked straight into mine eyes and lied about what he almost did. I was so sad. He told lies regarding mine retainers. An untruthful man. If he would attack a servant before I said 'Yes,' what would he do when he had power over me and the dowry you have given me? How oft might he drink and attack? What kind of life will I have with a drunkard and a liar? I regret to tell you I had to send him away." Margaret looked to the floor and loosed a deep sigh. "I am still sad."

"Mayhap your standards are too high," offered the king.

"I look around your Court and see fine men from good families. They are the flower of England's manhood. Your Royal Highness, I am cert someone here has an honorable brother or son I may marry."

Success! I got it out. They know. Mayhap now one of their families will ask for me.

The king spotted several men standing taller, straightening their shoulders, and preening. Henry frowned at her ploy.

"How dare you! A woman with a sword! Unheard of!"

Margaret quickly unbuckled her sword belt. She knelt and placed the sheathed blade in both her hands, lowered her head and raised her arms high.

"Your Royal Highness, I present your sword, given to me at your command. I wear it to protect Queen Matilda when she goes where men may not. It is still your sword, Your Royal Highness. Command me what to do with it, and I shall do it."

"Set it down. Look at me!" The King's voice did not soften. "I heard you practice daily. Tell me, Lady Margaret, who taught you how to use that blade?"

"Honorable men and true to you, Your Royal Highness."

"Their names."

"Your Royal Highness, after you gave me permission to wear this sword, I gave men loyal to you the impression you had also given them permission to train me. They only did what they believed you wanted done. If there is fault, it is mine. Not theirs."

The whole court leaned forward. They knew this bold girl would soon receive her due, and they were eager to see it.

"Their names. Now!" The king slid to the edge of his throne, ready to pounce.

"Your Royal Highness, they are men as loyal to you as am I. The fault is mine. The punishment should be mine."

"You dare defy me!"

"Not at all, Your Royal Highness," Margaret averred. "I told you I would protect Queen Matilda's life with mine own. Your order put this weapon into mine hands. I live to protect our queen." Margaret dared smile. "You really thought not that all I was going to do was to poke and hope, now did you?"

The courtiers had never seen such a thing—a mere girl on her knees before the king still refusing his command. She was doing what a lord would have done. Not relenting. Protecting the innocent. Accepting responsibility for her actions. Some courtiers were impressed at her daring; most were cert she was about to lose her head.

"So you think you can do more than poke and hope. We shall see." Henry looked about; he called for Sir Burgaud and ordered a page to fetch the man's sword.

"Woman, ready to defend yourself." Henry slid to the back of his throne, leaned easy on his elbow, crossed his legs and looked as if he were at his leicert. He expression said, "I will will teach you a hard lesson."

I will show you what I can do. Her Royal Highness was safe with me. She will always be safe with me as long as I have a blade. I can also defend myself. You will see.

Margaret heard the rushes rustle behind her. She felt their presence; Roulin to her left and Masselin to her right. Margaret stood and bowed her head to King Henry. He gave one nod of permission. Margaret picked up the weapon and handed it to Roulin. From the belt, she untied a leather thong. She put it behind her neck and drew it upward to tie her hair at her nape. As Margaret fastened a bow, a woman snickered. Margaret lifted her bliaut and shift over her girdle, first in front and then in back. She repeated the process until the hems of her gowns were at her knees. She patted the fold down firmly. *I must move fast and want not to be encumbered.* King Henry hid his lust by shifting in his seat so no one saw it.

Margaret looked to Roulin, who raised her weapon to her. Margaret grasped the hilt with her right hand and quietly pulled the short sword from its sheath. She laid the flat of the blade in her left hand and motioned with her head. Each retainer stepped back into the crowd. Standing before the throne and her imposing monarch, Margaret felt alone. She saw King Henry's chosen lord step beside the throne. *He is so tall, looks so strong. Can I defend myself? I must try. If he strikes to kill, I will die. What have I done! Mine pride has run away with mine mouth, and now I must face the consequences. Oh God, please protect me.*

At the right side of the dais, Sir Burgaud waited. A page stepped forward and delivered the knight's sheathed blade. Sir Burgaud extracted a long sword. He smiled at the king.

Oh no! I have only practiced against another short sword. His is a third longer than mine. Margaret watched Burgaud stretch his sword arm. *Longer reach too. I am about to die. God save me from mine own foolishness.*

"Stand so I can see you both." King Henry called, "Give way!" After the crowd cleared to the walls, he added, "Burgaud. Kill her not."

The king's man stepped off the dais and stood to the king's right; Margaret sidestepped until she was at the king's left. As if in a dance, they both sidestepped several times until they were in the middle of the hall. Margaret softened her knees and raised her blade. Burgaud smiled. He lifted his eyebrows as if to say, "You know the stance." Burgaud raised his blade and nicked his sword's tip at the middle of hers.

As Margaret caught the knight's thrust with her blade and held it still, she thought, *He holds his blade with one hand, and I must use both against his strength. I am done for!*

Burgaud cross-stepped to his right; Margaret did the same. He did so until their positions had switched. "You know to cross. But can you do it while fighting?"

Margaret waited. He thrust lightly; she parried and held his blade. They parted and took a pair of steps in opposite directions. At Margaret's honest thrust, Burgaud turned away her blade with ease and a smirk. He did not attack but gave Margaret a moment to choose her next move. Burgaud was playing with her and everyone knew it. Without warning, Margaret lunged and swung her sword to her left and blades clashed. She lifted Burgaud's blade as high as she could, as high as he permitted. Margaret disengaged and slashed to her right. Burgaud caught and held her blade and stepped back once. The king sat up.

This girl knows fight moves! Burgaud thought. He changed from amused tolerance to a determination to show her what she could not do. The knight closed in with a slashing blow as Margaret held her sword high. The swords rang. Half his blade was poised above her sword and her head. The shock reverberated from Margaret's sword to her hands, up her arms, and into her shoulders. Margaret knew one more hard blow and her sword would fly from her hand.

What if he forgets the king's command? Fearing death, Margaret dropped to her right knee and yelled, "I yield! I yield!" She dropped her sword tip to the rushes.

Burgaud kept his blade above her head. "I accept your yield; but if it is false, I will sever your arm."

"To yield falsely is dishonorable, my lord. Mine yield is true." Margaret waited for several moments before she asked, "May I stand?"

"You may." But Burgaud did not step back.

If I move wrong, I shall bleed to death right here.

She rose as she left her sword to hang at her side, tip to the floor. Margaret looked into the knight's eyes. "Thank you, Sir Burgaud, for not killing me." At his slight side shift of his head, Margaret addressed him again. "Lord Burgaud, may I ask you a question?"

"You may."

"If I were with the queen and she was attacked, could I slow a man until the king's men came to save her?"

Amazed, everyone in the hall stared at the girl.

"He would kill you."

"Yes, I know. But might I slow him while I raised the alarm? Mayhap our queen could hide or escape."

Burgaud's eyes narrowed. *Have I underestimated you?* he wondered. Burgaud answered, "In your fear you would flee."

"No, my lord, I have sworn to protect Her Royal Highness. Gladly I would die doing so."

The courtiers showed surprised expressions as they looked at each other. Because they had heard rumors to the opposite, they had believed the Lady Margaret refused suitors because she hoped to replace their beloved queen.

"Would I slow her attackers?"

Burgaud looked kindly upon Lady Margaret. "You would slow them, my lady. I swear, you would scare them half to death!"

Margaret's eyes crinkled with pleacert. "You are kind to say so, my lord. All I ask is our beloved Queen Matilda live."

Noises from the crowd startled Margaret. She had forgot they were not alone.

Do what is right. Be a girl a noble man would ask to be his lady. Margaret curtsied to Burgaud, who bowed to her. She turned and walked back to the foot of the king's dais. Again, she knelt in the rushes and lifted her sword above her head.

"Do you desire to keep it?"

"With your permission, Your Royal Highness."

"Why?"

Margaret looked up at her liege lord. "It scares away weak men, and I want a strong one." At the king's grin, Margaret continued. "I may still wear it in the queen's presence because I can still go where men may not." Margaret shrugged. "And I need it."

The king raised his eyebrows. "Need it?"

"To protect myself. I need a lord; I want to marry but…"

"Enough! I am done with you. I dismiss you. And for the sake of decency correct your attire. Begone!"

Margaret stood and looked toward the rushes. *Bare legs! What else did I display with mine moves? Too late. I leave without a lord. Or even hope of one.*

Margaret thrust her sword down left across her body. Roulin stepped forward, took it, and backed into the crowd. With both hands free, Lady Margaret pulled up her girdle so her bliaut and shift fell into place. Margaret saw the king eyeing her every move. Staring right back at him, Margaret pulled the thong away and loosed her hair. Margaret wound the thong around her left wrist. Then she fluffed her curls. *That is as bold a defiance as I dare. See, I am still a girl. Might not someone here want me?* Margaret curtsied as deeply as she had the first time. She took six steps backward; the crowd stepped in front of her. No one looked her way. She was invisible.

Margaret turned. With head held high, she slowly walked between the courtiers toward the back of the hall. On her way, she overheard two shocking things. "So she is the king's spare queen." and "Look away. Remember what happened to Avondale." Keeping her expression blank, Margaret pretended she heard not.

At the double doors, Lady Claire lay in wait for her target. She pounced. "Attempt not to see the queen. She refuses to see you. Her Royal Highness is ashamed of you. She wants nothing to do with you." With her chin high, the woman marched away.

Margaret's heart felt the blow and her stomach fell. *I have embarrassed her. I am abandoned still.* Roulin handed Lady Margaret her sword. She tied the thong to the belt and thank him in a soft voice. She buckled her weapon around her waist and looked at the three who stood before her. "I am hungry." Elstan handed Margaret her mantle. After she settled it on her shoulders and fixed the brooch, he handed Margaret her the scarf and gloves. Looking at the floor as she donned them, Margaret uttered, "We have the king's permission to leave. I say we eat."

26

Return

A throng packed High Street. Between Christmas and Epiphany every day was market day. Margaret loosed long, deep sighs and her shoulders drooped. The men saw their lady's spirit had been beaten down. She was not tired; she was defeated.

"My lady, I see a brazier of cooked meats with an ale stand next to it. Shall I lead?" Margaret mumbled something, which Masselin took to be approval. He shouldered his way through the crowd. Margaret followed while Roulin extended his arms behind his lady to keep the space around her clear. Elstan trailed. Margaret was generous with her coins, so the men ate heartily. She nibbled at one stick of meat and drank only half her ale before she offered the rest to Elstan, who downed it.

If what I heard is true, I must learn what befell Avondale. Not here. We may be overheard.

"I need fresh air. Let us ride. Which way is the stable?"

Margaret led them out the gate through which they had come. They rode single file: Masselin, Margaret, Roulin, Elstan. They met several men traveling toward Winchester, but they were the only ones leaving.

"Stop for a moment," Margaret ordered. "I need rest."

After Roulin assisted her to dismount, Margaret asked Elstan to follow her. She walked off the path, up a small knoll, and sat upon the rock she had spotted from the road. Margaret folded her hands in her lap, looked hard at Elstan, and cocked her head.

"What befell Lord Avondale? I know you know. Tell me," she ordered. Elstan shuffled his weight from foot to foot as he toed dead leaves. "Look at me please. What happened to Lord William of Avondale?"

"After you gained your boons, Lord Avondale asked the king for your hand. The king told Lord William to wait. The king wished to see who else might ask after you." Elstan stopped.

"And?" Margaret was impatient for more.

"And … several more asked for you. Each time King Henry put the man or his family off with 'I will consider your request.' They got the hint and asked not again. Sir William must have been unfazed by the king's words. After three months, Sir William asked again. At that time, King Henry was chasing Belleme with over a hundred men, including Sir William. The king said nothing, but, at the next town, he issued commands. Before the king stood every eligible girl and every widow with her children beside her. The king chose a young widow with two daughters. He said to Sir William, 'You want a wife and I give you one.' The king ordered the priest to marry them immediately. Then he gave Sir William permission to take his Saxon bride home until the king requested his service. No one has seen

Sir William since; he resides at his estates. No one dares visit him."

"Why did the king do that to a man who serves him so well?"

"My lady, I was told His Royal Highness was angry. Sir William already has two estates and two sons. The king has no son, no heir. If Sir William wed you, he would gain another estate and probably more sons."

"Oh-h-h." Margaret covered her mouth. *William, you is lost to me. And I am lost to everyone who asked. Please God, I pray what I heard is untrue. If she does not give him a son, what will he do? The king must be thirty-four or five. Old. Not much time to get a son and raise him old enough to be king. Damn his plotting! I want no part of it. She is under his control, but not me. I want not to be queen. I will not let him force me. God, please save her. Oh God, stop his evil plan. Think not on it. Think not at all. Reach home. Do not let him capture and trap me in a place like Forest Keep. Please God, give her a son and save us both. Flee! Flee now!*

"Elstan, I must post a message to the king. Which of them is the better to take it?"

"Roulin, my lady. Masselin is a man of action, but Roulin tells good stories. He will be more convincing."

"Please send Roulin to me. Keep Night company." *I want not you hear me.* After two suggestions of wording from Roulin and several practices, Margaret was ready to hear the full message.

"Your Royal Highness, the Lady Margaret asked me to deliver this message. 'Your Royal Highness, I have taken ill. I dare not risk your wellbeing, the health of Queen Matilda or the safety of your princess. Please forgive me for leaving in haste. I want not to sicken anyone at Court or in Winchester. I shall beg residence at an inn. If they will not take me, I shall seek help from the nearest abbey.

319

I desire you and your family to be well and safe. I send you mine wishes for a happy First Day and a joyous Epiphany. Please forgive mine leaving without your permission. Despite mine untimely departure, I remain your loyal subject and at your command.'"

"Remember Roulin, walk your horse. Arrive just before they close the city gates. Find a place to stay until morning. Wait to be last at the king's court. If mayhap the king is too busy to see you, continue to wait patiently. Another day or two will be fine. Whatever your reply, offend to the king. Offer mine abject apologies as often as you must. If His Royal Highness asks, tell him this: 'My lady was flushed of face. She shivered. A strange illness has stricken her. She looked weak and shook with both hot and cold.' After you present the message, return home. But risk not your health in bad weather nor risk your horse. Please take care. Sir Roulin, I want you home, well and safe."

"I will be very careful," promised Roulin.

"You have your coins. Go now. Mine prayers for your safety are continuous until next I see you." Margaret stayed at the rock until after Roulin had disappeared around the curve in the road. She returned to Night and whispered to him before re-mounting. Margaret announced, "We are for the Half Moon Inn where we slept last night.

Masselin frowned, "My lady, we will arrive well after dark."

"Then we had best move quickly. We stop not until we reach it. We must make that far immediately. We ride as hard as we can; then we walk to rest the horses. Ride and walk. Ride and walk until we are safe for the night." Masselin led, but not fast enough for Margaret. "More haste! More haste," yelled Margaret. "I must be catch not!"

A sprinkle became a downpour, but Margaret insisted on pressing onward. The party arrived at the Half Moon soaked. Their satchels and the clothes in them were as wet as were they. Maids helped Margaret out of her sopping garments and wrapped her in several blankets. They promised to return everything dry in the morning, but they knew not when the rain might stop.

Margaret stayed in the women's room and downed a hot meal. She shivered in the cold and damp. The braziers only took the edge off the chill and gave almost no warmth. Margaret chose the floor and lay on a straw mattress with an interior wall at her back. She had seen women of higher rank than she and had assumed they would claim the two beds. *I am not sick, just sick at heart. Oh, William, William. Should we ever meet, we must speak not. Gossip would ruin us both. She is young and can give him more children, the heirs he needs. How could he be so cold hearted? She will not see me. He plots her downfall. I hate royals! They plot and have no hearts. Keep mine eyes closed so none will speak to me. Dear God, please let me sleep. I am so tired.* Women filled the room and avoided the pile of blankets with a sword beside it. They whispered as each pointed to her chosen sleeping place.

As promised, Margaret's clothes were ready. She donned both chemises, a bliaut, and her mantle. When she entered the main hall to break her fast, she sniffed a delicious hot meal. Silently fretting, Margaret thought, *This pottage tastes like flour paste. It drops into mine stomach as if each bite is a stone. I am done with it.* She looked for a servant and requested a bowl of broth.

"My lady, the roads are unfit. No steed could remain standing in the muck," reported Masselin. "I advise we delay a day."

Before Margaret could respond, Elstan dropped his head close to hers and whispered. "No one is on the road searching for us. No one was asked if we had passed."

"How know you this?" she whispered back.

"I sought information when we arrived. I received the news this morning."

Once again, Margaret was stunned. *Saxons and their secret system of relaying information!* Margaret decided and told both men, "Thank you. I am returning to bed."

At supper Masselin and Margaret sat in the main room; Elstan had been relegated to the stables. She liked it not, but she had no power to change it. *At least he is guarding the horses,* reasoned Margaret as she dipped her bread into the soup. Margaret prayed as she ate, prayed her shivering only meant she was cold, not sickening. *I must gain home before his men catch me! Close the bailey. Stock the keep. At home I can withstand a siege. Home is preferable to the king's prison. He would hide me where mine people could not find me. Well, mayhap the Saxons could.* Though Margaret's thoughts bounced around inside her head, to others she appeared calm.

The rain stopped the next morning, but the roads were still impassable. Another day's delay made Margaret frantic. *I must reach home. If he can find me, he will trap me.* At supper she informed Masselin, "We leave on the morrow. No matter how slow our progress, we must leave. I am almost out of coin."

They left at dawn. Afraid their steeds might slip in the mud, they walked their horses all that gray, gloomy day. No one else was on the road. Near dusk, Elstan spotted a dwelling. The hut slanted toward a lean-to of wooden slats buried in the dirt with wattle and daub holding them together. The hut's thatched roof was blackened with age and looked thin. A stiff wind could blow the whole structure over. Elstan suggested they inquire if they might stay the night with that family.

Masselin objected. "How shall we protect her? No walls. No watchmen. Marauders will kill us for our horses."

Margaret agreed. "If we inquire how far we are from an inn, will they tell us true?"

"They will tell me," promised Elstan. Then he urged his horse as it clopped across the field of stubble and mud.

"The inn is ahead three miles. They said this road is better between here and there. They reported bandits have left this area for better pickings."

"I would rather arrive in the night and have walls around us and hay for our horses." Masselin added, "If we are set upon, you must leave us and ride hard, my lady. Do you promise?"

Upon Margaret's word, they urged their horses to trot. Precious daylight was receding fast. That night, Margaret prayed hard the weather would improve. *One more day's hard ride and we are home.* She prayed for the ravager last. Just before Margaret fell asleep, she remembered Roulin and prayed for him as well.

Dusk was upon the land. Day time was longer than the day before, but the few extra moments were unnoticeable. "Welcome home, my lady!" sang Giraud and Demetre as they rode toward the returning party. Giraud said, "We should escort you, but we are on guard duty."

"Sir Roussel is frantic—and furious," warned Demetre. "No one knew where you had gone."

"To the king," revealed Margaret. "Why are you two together?"

"We heard you coming. We go to our posts anon."

"See you on the morrow," she called as she turned from the road to the path.

Margaret let Night have his head. The gelding galloped down the lane; he sprinted over the bridge and through the bailey gate.

The clatter of his hooves on the bridge thrilled Margaret. *Home!* She pulled him to a stop.

"Verel, Sauville, close the gate! Keep it barred at all times!" ordered Margaret. "No one but our own enters. Not messengers, not soldiers, not even the king! No one until I order otherwise!" *Please God, let that command be enough.*

Margaret did not dismount until they had followed her orders. She eagerly watched the gates swing shut. From the corner of her eye, she spotted movement. Daelton ran from the stables. Cook opt the top half of the kitchen door and peered out. Men streamed from the hall. Cormac followed them. Jorgon's helper held Night's bridle. The excited horse almost lifted the boy off the ground when he shook his head and whinnied. Daelton stroked the gelding's neck while Masselin helped Margaret dismount.

"Welcome home, my lady," Margaret heard again and again.

Gailard stepped to her and confided, "Sir Roussel awaits your appearance, Lady Margaret."

"Have you supped?"

"We just finished," he reported.

"Cormac, please tell Cook we are hungry."

"I am glad to be among you again," Margaret told her men.

Margaret strode through the main door. She stopped at the bottom of the fire pit to warm her hands. The men walked around her and sat in their customary places. No one wanted to miss her meeting with Roussel. Margaret read the knight's body language. *He is very angry. How may I placate him?* As Margaret trudged to the dais, she looked toward Caitlin. *She looks worried but not angry. Why that tiny shake of her head? Why did she cock her head? Oh! A warning. That frown I know. Behave.* She climbed the stairs, sat in her usual place and turned to her guardian.

"Good eventide, Sir Roussel," said Margaret in a light airy voice, as if she had just arrived from the keep.

"Speak not 'good eventide' me, young lady. Where have you been?" demanded Roussel as if he were commanding an underling.

The hall was so quiet even Margaret's soft answer was heard throughout the building.

"To the king. I reported why I refused the three suitors he had sent me." *Let Masselin and Elstan reveal the details.* "Rain detained our return, sir. We came home as soon as the roads were passable."

"Did the king inquire why I had given you permission to leave without me?"

"No, sir. He did not."

"Did he ask after me?"

So that is why you are angry. You worry over what the king may think. "I am sorry, Sir Roussel, he did not."

Margaret saw the man's shoulders relax. Then she noticed him looking for someone. She watched Masselin and Elstan enter.

"Where is Roulin?" demanded Sir Roussel.

"I sent him on an errand." At the knight's baleful stare, she added, "He took a message to the king. He will be home anon."

At his query, Margaret summarized the message. She almost apologized for missing the First Day feast, but she stopped herself. *I will not be sorry for what I had to do.* Roussel lectured her on several matters: the impropriety of her leaving without him or his permission, her failure to take more men with her, her good fortune at not having been attacked by bandits, and more. He continued his lecture while she ate. She waited until Roussel stopped his rant and was calmer. Margaret gave him the promises he demanded. She would not leave the bailey without his advance knowledge and consent; she would accept the number of escorts he gave her without complaint. Finally, she was to go only where she said she was going, no getting permission for one place and then setting forth elsewhere. Margaret agreed to his demands—on one condition.

"I have sealed the bailey gate. No one enters but our own. No one else may enter—not messengers, not priests, not soldiers, not even the king." When Roussel began to object, Margaret held up her hand to stop him. "Sir Roussel, I do this to protect us. Ask not why. I have mine reasons." Then she added, "If the queen sends someone, that person may enter." She paused, "No others! Are we agreed?" Sir Rousel said nothing. "If you agree not, I will not be bound by your conditions."

Sir Roussel grumbled. "I agree."

I am cert he will demand details from Masselin. Let him, but I will tell him no more. Margaret sneezed.

"Enough, Sir Roussel," Caitlin declared. "Can you not see she is exhausted? Her eyes are bright with a coming fever. I must attend her now."

Sir Roussel left.

Margaret watched her former nurse dash a hot poker into the mixture she had prepared. Suspicious of what Caitlin had included in the drink, Margaret asked, "What is in it?"

"I should do what you did to me. I woke with such a head. I knew immediately what you had done." Caitlin handed her the mug. "Mulled wine and honey for your throat. Why did you trust me not!"

"By excluding you, I kept you innocent, mine friend. Also, you would have sounded the alarm." Margaret sipped the hot drink. "I had to, Caitlin. I had to."

"It is likely to cost you a stuffed head for a week or more. To bed now," Caitlin cooed. "To bed and slumber for as long as you like. You look exhausted."

"I am weary, most weary."

Caitlin helped Margaret out the hall, into the keep and to bed. Caitlin removed her girl's mantle, slid off her bliaut, slipped heavy stockings on her charge's feet, and tucked the covers around Margaret's body as she had when she was a child. With a silent prayer, Cailtin asked God to give her girl a good rest.

"Caitlin, that was not mine first sneeze."

"I know."

Caitlin waited for Margaret to fall asleep. Then she readied herself for bed and crawled in beside her. Caitlin was cert something was very wrong; she prayed again for her girl.

"Lady Margaret, rise at once. Awake! Awake!"

Margaret sat up. She thought she heard her father's voice ordering her. When she realized where she was, she became angry at being disturbed.

"Who goes there?" she demanded of the voice below.

"Father Manntun. You have missed too many Masses, girl! You will miss no more. Arise and dress. I will ring the first bell. I expect you at Mass. If I ring the second bell and you are not present, I will pull you out of bed myself!"

Margaret sneezed. "I am ill, Father, and beg to be excused."

"You are not! I will not have you turning godless. Get up!" the angry priest ordered.

Margaret sighed. She sneezed again.

"No help for it," Caitlin's voice was muffled by the bedding over her head. "We shall dress very warmly."

The frost had hardened the ground, so it crackled at every step. Sir Hughes offered Margaret his arm so she would not slip. Cormac offered Caitlin his and she took it. After Mass, Margaret thanked Father Manntun for his summons. She admitted she felt better for having attended Mass.

He harrumphed, "I knew you would."

I need to placate him. "Please join me to break your fast, Father," she asked. Even inside the warm hall Margaret shivered. She was loath to undress. Reluctantly, she unwound the wool scarf from her head and removed her mantle to hang them on her peg. After hot pottage and a hot mug of a bones and vegetables broth, Margaret felt more herself.

"Father, I have lost track of the days."

"Epiphany is on the morrow. High Mass. You did not take Communion this day. You need to confess."

"Yes, Father. May I do that now?" Margaret turned her face to Father Manntun's ear and whispered.

After Father departed, Margaret inquired of Caitlin the details of the Epiphany feast. Margaret told Caitlin her plans for gift giving. "I am so grateful you are mine chatelaine." Margaret added, "Would that you could rest, sew, and enjoy your days."

"Nonsense," retorted Caitlin. "That is not enough to keep me happy."

"Well, I am tired of doing a lord's job. So many decisions each day. So many people to care for," admitted Margaret. "I am so tired, Caitlin. I will 'lord' it on the morrow, but then I am taking to mine bed and sleeping for a week."

Cook, who desired a decision about the feast, interrupted them. Margaret made her choice and Cook disappeared. Villagers arrived and needed her advice as well. Margaret stayed at her place and let everyone come to her. By dinner, her energy was flagging, but she valiantly smiled, ate as much as she could given how ill she felt, and engaged Sir Roussel in conversation about the weather.

After the servant girls removed the meal, Margaret told Caitlin, "If I must make another decision this day, I shall weep. I am returning to bed."

At eventide Caitlin brought Margaret soup. "I am too cold to leave our bed, Caitlin. I cannot sit on the edge to sup; the bed is too soft. The ropes need tightening; someone needs to tighten the ropes."

Caitlin set the tray on the small table and fetched a stool. "Sit up," she ordered. "Wrap your blankets about you."

Margaret did as she was bid. "How can I eat and stay warm and eat?" she whined as if she were again five. Caitlin remembered that voice. She picked up the bowl and spoon-fed Margaret as the child she had become of a sudden. She even dropped chunks of bread into the broth and spooned each one into Margaret. The meal over, Caitlin tucked Margaret back into the bed. "Sleep now. You will feel better in the morning."

Margaret mumbled something unintelligible and rolled over.

In the night, the wind increased, howled around the buildings and attacked. The wind found the keep's stone chimney and dropped to the fire, trying to extinguish it. On the top floor, Margaret shivered and cried out. She stammered, "No. No. I shall not!" She rolled away from Caitlin and clung to the bed's side board. Finally, she released her hold and pulled covers over her head.

27

·❧·

January 1103 A.D.

Epiphany was on Tuesday, but everyone treated the holy day as if it were Sunday. Incense filled the church as Father Manntun swung the censer back and forth. Every adult took a cube of bread and a sip of wine transformed into the body and blood of Jesus the Christ. Only those deemed the faithful and who had confessed their sins received Holy Communion. Through it, they proved they belonged to the Holy Catholic Church, the one true religion, which bound them together and was their bulwark against paganism and chaos.

The villagers feasted among themselves, and Margaret's household in their way. The hall was decorated with new evergreen and holly boughs. Margaret stood and motioned for silence. All stood for Father Manntun's invocation. They sang the Te Deum. Margaret spoke next. "To God we give all praise for our bounteous harvest and the food we eat. To Cook we give our thanks for a rich feast;

she worked so hard." Hoots, hollers and words of praise interrupted Margaret, so she waited. "We thank Leoma for her fine bread." Another eruption in the hall. "We thank Duone, Hugiet, Beornia, and Cadda for their hard work. " More applause and foot stomping. "This year our toast goes to…" Margaret paused for dramatic effect. "Nearra, our beloved cook. Because of her skills, we eat well today and every day." Everyone watched Nearra, blushing furiously. "Nearra, you labor long, hard hours, and we deeply appreciate everything you do for us." Margaret raised her drink. "To Nearra!"

Everyone echoed Margaret's toast. More applause and foot stomping ensued. The fire pit flames rose as if in thanks. Everyone salivated in anticipation and sat. Into the two barrels of ale in the stall closest to the kitchen entrance, servants dipped pitchers and served round after round with each course. After the soup and the fish courses, everyone sat back and waited for the meat. Hughes and Roulin carried in the roast pig on a long board and set it on trestles in front of the head table. The smell of roast pig assailed the crowd. Everyone stood and sang the Boar Song. Nearra led the servants, who carried in bowls of boiled vegetables and honey-simmered fruit. Duone proudly carried the great tray of bread rounds. Hoots, hollers, foot stomping and applause greeted Cook and her troop. Leoma walked the bread platter down the aisle. The servants followed with the boiled root vegetables and stewed dried fruits. Nearra proudly carved the pig. The skin crackled as she cut it. Duone presented the first tray to the head table. Margaret waved her hand toward Father Manntun, who selected choice pieces of skin and meat. The strong kitchen boy lifted the tray high and served Sir Roussel, then Margaret. He served Caitlin and Cormac last. Meanwhile, Nearra carved tray after tray of meat to be carried to the tables. Hughes stood and offered to carve while Nearra sat and ate. Margaret called her to sit to Sir Roussel's left. Nearra shook her head.

"Nearra, you are the honored guest. Please sit with us." When Nearra did not move, Margaret called out, "Who wants Nearra to sit with us at the head table?"

The hall erupted with happy noises and "Nea—rra! Nea—rra!" and "Sit! Sit!"

Nearra shrugged and climbed the stairs. She curtsied to Sir Roussel, who gallantly stood, took her hand and bowed as she sat. *A good man to treat her like a Norman lady of rank.* More applause and praise followed. Everyone settled and quieted. Happy sounds of eating and visiting rose and fell. Several times a knight stood and grabbed a pair of pitchers. He dipped the pitchers in an ale barrel and walked his side of the room, pouring the drink for anyone who held up his mug. The servants were told to sit, eat, relax. If a tray was empty, someone cut meat and filled the tray to be passed. The lack of ceremony, the dismissal of rank pleased Margaret. *We have grown into a family. Each has his part; each helps the other.* Margaret glanced right and saw Cormac talking with Caitlin, and she was smiling. Father looked forlorn, so Margaret leaned over the empty place saved for her lord to visit with him.

When everyone looked surfeited with food and drink, Margaret stood and turned her back to the hall. She leaned over for the basket on the ground behind the head table. When Roussel saw how heavy it was, he stood and picked it up for her. Margaret motioned him to place it on the stool where her lord should have been sitting. She waited for everyone to look her way.

"Time for gift giving!" Margaret merrily called. "This year Caitlin and I have been sewing for months. We have divided the gifts between us and Caitlin has graciously said I may go first." Several laughed. Margaret stepped to her right. "Father Manntun, a wool cassock can be a scratchy thing. Here is a long linen garment to wear under it. I have embroidered a cross on each sleeve." She handed Roussel a shirt with a sword on his cuff. Margaret added, "So the laundress knows which shirt is yours."

To her retainers, Margaret revealed, "I put an emblem on each of your shirts, but I placed them on your left cuffs." She grinned at them. "You might soil your right one when you reach for sauces." The men roared at her joke. Margaret called each man in alphabetical order so as not to create a rank among them. As they came forward Margaret told why she had given that emblem: Claude, a lance; Demetre, a glove; Giraud, an arrow; Hughes, a horse; Masselin, a jerkin; Roulin, a bow; Sauville, a helmet, Verel, a mace; Syghelm, an axe. The men nodded agreement at some of her reasons; other times they laughed at her references to incidents from the previous year.

To Caitlin, Margaret presented a beautiful soft-yellow gunna. She had sewn a sturdy padded vest for Cormac. Margaret had made Elstan a Sunday shirt. "His emblem is smiling lips because he is such a cheerful fellow!" The men laughed and pounded the tables tops in agreement.

The villagers arrived and filled the hall. Reeve received a linen shirt with a sheaf of wheat on his sleeve. Margaret also gifted him one bolt of cloth for Erwina and a second one for clothes for their children. Scelfdune addressed the hall with news. The Saxons had voted Felamaere reeve for the third and final year. Felamaere stood and expressed his gratitude for being elected again and thanked the Saxons for their confidence in him. Everyone applauded.

334

"We have gifts for you, my lady," announced Felamaere. From the kitchen door—the only place anyone could have entered the crowded hall—Garwig rolled in an iron-clad wheel.

"My lady, this represents the two new wagons we made. Rammeg Elder and Rammeg Younger formed the wheels and led the Saxons as they sawed the boards and built the wagons. I provided the nails and clad each wheel."

"Thank you, Saxons, Garwig. We will put our new wagons to good use to ease our planting and to speed our harvest." Margaret sensed the excitement. *Something special is about to transpire.* As requested, Margaret closed her eyes. She heard the rustling of movement and a few "Oohs" and "Aahs."

"My lady, please op not your eyes just yet," requested Verel. "This gift is from all of us, Saxons and Normans alike. Please op your eyes now."

"Open your eyes," Normans and Saxons said in their own languages.

Margaret's jaw dropped. Verel and Felamaere held a beautiful, young dog. Its ears stood erect with tips that drooped. Its coat was a shaggy brown brindle with a swath of cream from his chin to his chest. His eyes were bright, and he looked intelligent.

"He is handsome!" exclaimed Margaret. "I have never seen the like. What is he?"

"Said Verel, "A Picardy shepherd from across the Narrow Sea. He guards stock. Now that you have him, you may purchase the sheep you want."

Margaret looked up from the dog and addressed her people, who were grinning at their lady. "I am overwhelmed and overjoyed at your generous gift. Thank you ever so much." She applauded her people; they clapped back. "Has he a name?" Margaret asked.

"Ferrant. His name is burned on his leather collar. We have not fed him for a day, my lady. If you are the only one to feed him and you tie his leash around your bed post at night, he will learn he is yours." Verel added, "Once he knows you, he will also escort you. Feed him and take him with you when you go about."

Cormac approached with a trencher of roasted pig, which he handed to Margaret. "Put your hands all over the meat, let him see you take bites first. Show him you are the lead dog." Cormac chuckled. "The lead dog in our pack of Normans, Saxons and others.

Take his leash and set the trencher before him. After he eats, pet him. Keep him with you at all times. He is clever; he will learn fast."

Ferrant squirmed and yipped. Margaret left the dais. Everyone watched her take charge. Margaret sat on the dais edge and petted Ferrant for a long time. He licked her moist fingers, and stood on his hind legs against her thigh. At almost two stone, he was too big to be a lap dog.

Caitlin gave her gifts. Gailard's shirt cuff bore a shield and Cachier's a stirrup. She presented Lady Margaret two chemises of softest linen; to Cook, the kitchen staff, the servants, and Cormac a gunna or a shirt.

The festivities wound down, but not Margaret's excitement at owning a dog. *Only the ranked can afford dogs. Only with royal permission may a lord own even one hunting dog and only a lord can afford a good one. The wealthy or the loved.* Margaret called for her mantle and took Ferrant outside. Cormac followed and showed her where the dog could relieve himself.

"We want not to have him messing the bailey," he told her. "This way, our boots stay clean, and we can harvest his dung for the gardens."

"Thank you, Cormac, for bringing him home."

"With the instructions from your men and Reeve."

"I cannot believe how much I have." Margaret wanted to tell someone. "I am so grateful. Eighteen months ago I had no future, no hope, and no prospects for either. Now I have a place, property, people who care about me, Caitlin, whom I love dearly, and now you."

"Fourteen months ago, I had no prospects either. I hoped I might serve the queen, but I am glad she said no. Being at Court got me thrown out of Scotland. Stay out of Court, my lady; the intrigue can undo you." Cormac added, "Now I have a place, and a woman to court. Not you!" he added.

Margaret chuckled. "You have a friend in me. I speak well of you to her."

"I have hope. She no longer scowls when she sees me. Today she talked with me nicely."

Ferrant started sniffing about, so Margaret pulled him back to her. Together Margaret and Cormac returned to the hall. Margaret took Cormac behind the dais; Ferrant smelled something inside Margaret's gift basket and backed away with a whine. "I have a special gift for you, mine seneschal." Margaret reached into the basket for the last item, a small leather pouch with a cork stopper.

Cormac sniffed at the leather; his eyes popped wide. He needed not to uncork the contents to know a drink from home. "Uisgebah! My lady, how found you this?"

"Sir Claude searched the markets for me," she grinned as she enjoyed seeing his surprise. "I remember you saying you missed it. What is it?"

"A strong Scots drink. The 'water of life' in your tongue. A few tiny sips will warm you to your bones against our cold, wet weather.

Drink too much, and you will lose your good sense, start a stupid fight and die." He uncorked the pouch and gave his lady a sniff.

Margaret grimaced, "Smells foul. I want none of it!"

"Good. All for me." Cormac took a sip and rolled it around in his mouth before he swallowed the brew. He re-corked the pouch and tucked it into the pocket inside he jerkin. "I am most grateful to you, my lady, for this taste from home. I have longed for it this cold. wet winter."

"Time for evening prayers, Cormac. Please escort me to church and tie Ferrant outside for me."

After Mass the next day, Margaret retrieved Ferrant, who pulled at his tied leash and barked for his mistress.. She waited for Garwig to thank him for the iron half-loop he had buried in the ground outside the chapel. The smith explained her men had thought of it, had dug the holes, and had hidden the half-loop's presence. Garwig also revealed Scirburne's family had hidden and fed her dog. Margaret smiled. *They are good people. All of them. I am blessed.* Then she asked the smith to come to the hall after she broke her fast. She hid her occasional sniffle behinds smiles and talk. At the meal Margaret inquired of Roussel if he had any knowledge of good smithing to evaluate Garwig's work. Roussel demurred he knew nothing. Margaret asked her retainers.

"I have seen good smith work, my lady. May I be of help?" asked Giraud.

"Please join me after you eat, Giraud. The smith is coming to show me his work."

Garwig explained how he made locks, formed keys, created hinges and fashioned many other pieces. Margaret praised his work and asked him to consider a trip to Reading for more iron. Margaret offered him half the profits from the sale of his goods, less the cost of the iron, of course.

She asked, "Garwig, I have seen leather boots tied to a horse's hooves. The king's horse wore shiny, scalloped metal on its hooves? What is that?"

"It is brass, a sort of shoe nailed to the animal's hooves to protect them from splitting or breaking because the horse is carrying a heavy weight or going over rough, stony ground." He added, "Night needs them not because you are slight and ride him mostly on dirt, not stone roads."

"Can you make them for the horses the knights ride?"

"I have seen them, but white smiths work in that metal because it is so costly. If I have the metal, I think I can."

"I will speak to mine knights on the matter before we do more." With that settled, Margaret took Ferrant for a walk. He sniffed everywhere in the bailey. Margaret shivered in the cold and wind, but she let him take his time. She tied him to the post of the lean-to over the wood pile. In the village, Margaret coughed at Scirburne's door.

Scirburne poked his head from the door curtain. "Come in, my lady. Come out of the cold."

"God give you a good day, Scirburne." She turned to greet his family. "Ifig, Scirwode, Willa. Thank you for your part in caring for Ferrant. A puppy with that much energy must have been hard to hide and difficult to keep quiet."

"I took him on long walks in the woods twice each day," offered Scirwode. Willa revealed, "He stayed quiet when I pet him, and I did for hours at a time. I hope he still likes me."

"I am cert he does," replied Margaret. "Mine guards must be getting cold, so I shall return home. Again, I thank you. You have been most kind to me.

The next day Ferrant ran loose in the bailey, but he still wore his rope so he would be easier to catch should he disobey Margaret. Ferrant was particularly interested in the animals in the barn and stable. He returned to her when she called his name. Margaret rewarded Ferrant with bites of raw meat Duone had brought to her.

"Good dog," offered Duone.

"Indeed, he is. But you are not to feed him, Duone. Not ever." Margaret could tell the young man wanted to do so. Margaret added, "Promise, Duone. Say 'I promise never to feed the dog.'" Reluctantly, Duone promised. Margaret sent him back to the kitchen.

Caitlin had ordered the simmering of a broth pot of bones and root vegetables at the end of the fire pit. No part of the pig was wasted. Margaret insisted she not be the only one to drink from the pot. Feeling chilled again, Margaret sought the warmth of the hall and broth. She spent the afternoon with Cormac and Reeve, adding to her accounts book. Cormac recorded which family was assigned which strips of farm land.

After three days of rain, the sun shone through the last whiffs of clouds. After the midday meal, Roulin arrived home and reported to Margaret. "The king accepted your message. He asked how sick you might be. I told him I knew not." Roulin paused. At Margaret's insistence he finished, "The king said, 'If she dies, notify me. I want the chest returned, and I will re-assign the land and property.' He dismissed me with a wave of his hand, my lady. As if you mattered not at all." Margaret's face fell at learning of the king's callousness. *Cormac is right; stay away.* She thanked Roulin and asked for his discretion. She sent him to the kitchen for food and to the barracks to rest. Roulin refused to speak of where he had been and what he had done. Not even Cormac's persuasive abilities opt his mouth.

Because Margaret was still sniffling after her journey, her retainers refused to permit her to walk Ferrant. "Any fool can take a dog to piss," Giraud told her. Grateful, Margaret stayed inside. She offered to mend the men's clothes and soon saw a pile in her basket. Margaret did not hum as usual as she worked. Both retainers and servants recognized something was wrong and wondered what news Roulin had delivered.

Sunday dawn broke grey and cold. From rain the night before, the ground was a soggy mess. Everyone stepped carefully and prayed to stay upright. They wrapped themselves in whatever coverings they owned and kept them on during the service. Sauville and Claude took Margaret by her elbows to steady her. When they returned to break their fasts, the dog's paws were muddy to his hocks.

Cormac teased his lady that Ferrant cleaned himself with ease. "Because of Ferrant's wiry hair, all he need do is wait until the mud dries and shake hard."

The next day the Saxons began planting while Roussel, Lady Margaret, and four retainers took Ferrant hunting. Everyone had a merry time, Margaret was pleased to watch Ferrant chase and catch a rabbit. Ferrant tore apart and devoured all but skin and fur. She was half fascinated and half horrified at what she saw. On the way home, a sudden icy shower slashed at and soaked the party. Sweeping into the hall, Margaret called for cloths to dry Ferrant. With no care for herself or her wet garments, Margaret toweled her beloved dog herself before removing her sodden mantle.

Caitlin arrived from the kitchen at the end of Margaret's efforts and issued a good scolding. "Margaret! Did you not care for herself first? Have you no regard for your health?" That Margaret started sneezing angered Caitlin even more. "March! I will see to you if you

341

will not. I am taking you to the keep. No arguments, girl. You will go abed anon and stay there. I will make you a potion to ward off illness. You are weakened from your journey, your labors, and your lack of sleep." Margaret started to object, but Caitlin cut her short with, "I have chaperoned your bed for sixteen years. I know when you sleep not." Abed at Caitlins' command, Margaret drank what Caitlin handed her. She crawled under her blankets and closed her eyes. *I am so tired. Ferrant distracted me, but now I want to sleep.*

28

Fever

A week later Margaret was still abed. Breathing had grown so difficult she slept sitting up. Her head felt stuffed with wool, and her chest was congested. Margaret's fever was dangerously high. Caitlin's simples, chest plasters, and hot drinks helped very little.

"I understand not why you continue to worsen," admitted Caitlin.

Margaret coughed and wheezed. She looked away. "I am tired. No more than that."

Caitlin sat on the edge of the bed and stroked Margaret's tangled hair. "This is more than tired. I have never seen you give up before, but you are giving up now. Why?"

Margaret shook her head and sank under her covers. The tightness in her chest was fear; she knew not how to stop it paralyzing her. Her every breath was hard won. "Please let me sleep."

Late than night, Margaret coughed herself awake. She listened and waited. Caitlin had taken one of the servant's pads and slept on the other side of the room so as not to disturb Margaret or to become sick herself. When Margaret was cert Caitlin slept, she slipped from under her covers to the chamber pot. To hold up her head, Margaret placed her elbows on her knees and her hands on her cheeks. She felt a chill upon her shoulders. *Has the latest wind loosened chinks in the stones?* At first the coolness felt good. Then cold crept through her chemise; Margaret shivered. *Mayhap this is the way.* She wriggled off the seat and crawled to the oak chairs in the corner. Margaret crept under the sailcloth cover and curled herself into the armed chair she had chosen for her future husband. She lay her head against its back and draped her legs over an arm. *Never have a lord. Never sit in mine. Hide. Can die here. Feels good.* Margaret closed her eyes.

At dawn, Caitlin awoke and approached the bed. Wild with dread, she took the stairs as she called out. When the girls reported the door still bolted and no sign of their lady, Caitlin dashed back to the top room and soon spotted the lump under the sailcloth. She whipped off the cover and grasped Margaret, who did not respond. Caitlin felt her arm; it was icy and her shift was wet. She cried an alarm to the servant at the door. Soon strong arms lifted Margaret and held her close.

Margaret faintly heard Caitlin's voice, strident and worried. "Let me die," Margaret muttered.

A deep voice answered, "No my lady. Never." Unconscious again, Margaret felt not Masselin kiss the top of her head.

Hours later, Margaret regained consciousness long enough to repeat her request. Caitlin begged her to live. She tried to tell her former babe, then charge, now friend how much she had to live for, but Margaret had slipped back into unconsciousness.

"We are losing her," Caitlin told Cormac as she broke down and cried.

"We will lose you too if you rest not. Take to that sleeping pad. I will sit with her this night." Cormac stopped Caitlin's refusal with, "I promise to wake you if she worsens." He hugged Caitlin around her shoulders and ordered, "Now off with you. Sleep." Cormac lifted Caitlin from the stool next to Margaret's bed, pushed her to take a step, and took her place. "Unless you want to sit upon mine lap all night."

Hours later Margaret stirred. She refused the water Cormac tried to give her.

"She would not see me. She wants me dead."

"No, she does not," countered Cormac.

"She believes I want her place. I want not to be queen."

At first, Cormac surmised she was out of her head with fever. Then he realized why Margaret would improve not. He looked over to Caitlin, who was sound asleep, and decided to wait until daylight to tell her.

Midmorning Roulin sounded the call and Demetre raced from his position to his partner. On the road, a party had stopped at the lane. The retainers blocked their path.

"Is this the way into the estate of the Lady Margaret?"

"Who wants entrance?" Roulin asked a stupid question given the knight was followed by a page who carried the king's banner.

Thinking Roulin meant them, one man behind the page explained, "We are court physicians sent by His Royal Highness to see to the Lady Margaret's health."

Roulin shocked the party with his response. "No one from the Court may enter. She locked the bailey to all but Her Royal Highness, Queen Matilda, or to her emissaries. Begone. Get the queen's permission to see the Lady Margaret, and we will permit you to pass."

"No one refuses the king's command!" the knight angrily reminded the pair.

"Here we obey the Lady Margaret's command," retorted Demetre. He gave them a clue in a persuasive tone. "If you will leave our sight and return with the right words, you may pass."

The knight reached for his sword hilt. The man stared at the pair blocking his way. Then he thought better of starting a fight. "Let us return to the Court and ask the queen to send us." With that, the party turned and walked their horses until they disappeared around a bend.

Demetre looked at Roulin, "A bit thick, is he not? Glad they did not attack. Saw you the three knights in back?"

"Of course. I prayed they would stay there."

Minutes later the party reappeared. Once again the knight addressed the men. "Her Royal Highness, Queen Matilda, has sent us to inquire of the Lady Margaret's health. These are court physicians. May we pass?"

Roulin bowed. "We are most glad to greet Her Royal Highness's envoys. If you say these same words at the bailey gate, they will bid you enter, and welcome you."

Roulin and Demetre rode off the path and watched the party take the road to the bailey. From opposite sides of the lane, they gave each other knowing looks. They silently agreed never to reveal who had sent the physicians.

"Margaret! Margaret! The queen!" announced Caitlin. "She sent physicians to heal you. Please hear me. The queen still loves you."

Margaret roused and opt her eyes to slits. "The queen?"

"Yes, dear. She ordered these physicians to heal you."

Three men stood on the other side of Margaret's bed. Each was dressed in a black tunic, black hose, and a black coat with brown fur around the collar. Each wore a different kind of black cap. They kept on their gloves as if they feared touching an ailing lady. Caitlin's comments had shocked the men, who looked at each other in amazement., then dropped their expressions into masks of indifference. Each man had his specialty. The slim, gray-haired man with high cheek bones and long fingers knew fevers; he addressed Caitlin. After learning how long Margaret had been ill, he made "tsk, tsk" sounds and the third man fetched implements. The physician explained to Caitlin the fever showed Margaret's blood was boiling. "By letting out some blood, it will no longer boil and the lady's fever will drop."

Caitlin had heard of the practice, but she trusted it not. Still, she said, "You are physicians; you must know best."

Almost a cup of blood filled the bottom of the pan. The physician pushed a rag into Margaret's elbow and bent her arm to stop the bleeding. As instructed, Caitlin held Margaret's arm at that angle. When the bleeding stopped, she took a fresh strip of cloth, wrapped it round Margaret's elbow and tied it. Margaret lay quiet and slept. The second physician, shorter and stouter than the first, removed the pan and handed it to the third man, who was the youngest of the three and appeared to be an apprentice.

The next morning Margaret took broth and a bit of ale. Her hacking cough still alarmed Caitlin, so she consulted the second physician. He reported that, while he knew coughs and illnesses of the bile, he could do no good until the Lady Margaret's fever fell. That afternoon, the first physician bled Margaret again. Her fever still raged. Weakened as she was, Margaret valiantly tried to drink the broth Cailtlin had offered. She failed to swallow anything and fell back into the pillows. Caitlin stopped forcing her girl and covered her well.

The next morning the head physician expected to bleed Margaret a third time. Now Cormac stood with Caitlin. "I refuse to permit you to bleed my lady again. I have seen strong men die from the practice," reported the Scot.

The physician pulled himself straighter. "And I have seen men healed."

Without opening her eyes, Margaret spoke very slowly. "Bleed me again ... let me die." With a final strength of will, Margaret added, "Tell mine queen I love her." Her head dropped to the right. Shock registered on five faces. Margaret roused and took as deep a breath as she could. "Caitlin?" she murmured. She paused. "Remember... Mother... opposites."

"That is why you were out of bed! You were trying to cure by opposites!" exclaimed Caitlin. "Kill the fever with cold! Cormac, remove these men." Caitlin walked to the doorway and called down to the anxiously awaiting knights. "Bring me cold water; use every bucket we have. I need Leoma and our servant girls. HURRY!"

Caitlin pulled Margaret into a seated position, and her helpers held their lady upright. At first, having her feet and hands in cold water felt good. Margaret sighed. Quickly, she changed her mind and struggled to escape. With a woman at each limb holding her firmly, she was too weak to succeed. From behind, Leoma slapped a wet cloth across Margaret's shoulders. At Margaret's yelp of protest,

Leoma said, "Sorry, my lady." She removed the cloth and replaced it with a second one. Then Leoma added one in front. Yelping, objecting, and struggling did no good. Soon Margaret's shift was wet, and she was shivering. Caitlin saw her dear girl's lips were turning blue.

"That will do for now," said Caitlin. The women removed the buckets and cloths. Now Margaret crossed her arms over her breasts and shivered. "Lay back into your bed, my girl," Caitlin ordered. "In your cold, wet shift and under this pile of blankets." She helped Margaret sip a potion. "Drink this and sleep. I will watch."

In the night Caitlin felt Margaret's hand and her forehead. She quietly wept with relief. The girl at the door silently crept away. Afraid of what he would find, Cormac dashed up the stairs. When he saw Margaret's head move, he too felt the girl's forehead. He took the stairs until he saw girls waiting below. Cormac raised his hand thumb pointing up. Even in the shadows of the banked fireplace, Cormac smiled at their happy reactions. Cormac returned to his love, swept her into his arms and held her as she cried.

Dawn arrived and Margaret stirred. "I hunger," she announced. "Mine head seems clearer. May I get out of this wetness, please?"

By the time they put Margaret into a clean shift and changed the bed linens, she had lost any energy she had. Leoma volunteered to feed her broth while Cormac attended Caitlin. He insisted she wash, change her clothes, and go to the fireplace to eat a hot meal. Cormac sat beside her and supervised every bite. After Cormac approved the quantity of food Caitlin had eaten, he escorted her to the pallet in the top room and ordered her to sleep away the day. Before Cormac left, he noted Margaret had curled into a ball and slept as well. On a stool by a brazier, Cleva kept watch.

Three days later, Sunday was a happy day. Margaret announced her chest did not feel so tight. She was still sneezing, but now she was using rags to empty her nose. The rags bucket was filling fast. Margaret asked to see her men. Grateful their lady was no longer dying, the knights took turns by rank. Margaret left one arm out of her covers. Caitlin watched her smile and squeeze Roussel's hand, then Gailard's and Cachier's. After Verel's visit, Caitlin stopped the line because she knew Margaret was fading again. The men reported to the others, and the volume in the hall returned to normal. Margaret continued to sleep most of each day and night. She swallowed every spoon of bone broth and every bite of bread they offered her. She continued to blow her nose repeatedly before she settled back and slept again.

29

·❧·

Lent

Three weeks later, Margaret was sitting up in bed and eating food. Ash Wednesday was 18 February, and Father Manntun brought the ashes to her. With them, he made a cross on her forehead and spoke the same words as he had for all the others. "From ashes you came; to ashes you will go. Only the sacrifice Jesus made for you will save your soul. Remember, He spent forty days and forty nights in the wilderness and died on the cross so you may have eternal life. Spend your forty days contemplating His life and death. Repent your sins and He will save you."

"Father, I seek your advice. I know not whether just to talk or to speak in Confession."

"Speak in Confession, so I may never reveal it should I be asked."

Margaret began with the required phrase. "Father, I confess mine sins. Through you, I beg God's forgiveness." Margaret inhaled a deep breath and began. "Oh God, I am an ungrateful child. Many times, I thought I was praying, but most of the time I was asking You for this or that. I would start 'Please God' but I never asked for help to be more Christian or a better person. I wanted or needed something. If You gave me what I asked for, I would thank You, God, but mine thanks was no more than if someone had handed me a mug of ale. I want to be more grateful. First to you, Oh God. Then to others. God in heaven, mine second sin is pride, the worst one. I am proud of mine bargain with the king, proud I knew a way for Dena and Jorgon to gain their freedom, proud of winning land and coin, and proud of all I have accomplished here. I forgot, all I did was to perform as You willed. Your will, Oh Lord, in all things. I said it. Now I want to mean it." She stopped and spoke what ended every confession. "I seek your forgiveness, Oh Lord of Hosts, and I accept whatever penance this good Father gives me, so that I may once again be one with You and Your Church." *What might he order? If it must be public, so be it.*

"My child, God forgives your sins of pride, greediness and ingratitude. Your penance is thus: each morning before you rise, you will thank God for giving you six things, conditions, or persons and include your reasons you are grateful. After your prayers each night, you will thank God again six times in this way. Do this for fourteen days and your penance is complete. You may then take Holy Communion and again be one with His Church."

"I shall do it faithfully starting this evening. Thank you Father."

"Know this. After you have completed your penance, I shall recommend you make saying gratitudes a lifelong habit."

A week later, Margaret, double-wrapped in both hers and Caitlin's mantles, stood at the keep doorway and waved to her men below. Then she waved at the Saxons beyond the gate. Ferrant stayed with her. Others brought him food, but this day Margaret put it down before her pet. That night her "gratitudes" as she called her penance included Father Manntun for his easy penance, Scandy for bringing Ferrant's food, Scirburne for caring for her pet before she had been given him, Sir Verel for leading her knights in daily practices, King Henry for sending her three such stalwart men, and Caitlin, always Caitlin, for whatever she did that day to make life easier and more pleasant.

Each day she conferenced with someone who came to her room and took a stool next to her bed as she lay in it. One day Reeve reported, "Ferrant does well guarding the goats and cows. The goats often try to enter the forest and give him trouble, but Ferrant always keeps them in the meadow. Two weeks ago, Cormac instructed me to buy sheep. In Reading, I got one ram, five ewes ready to lamb, and three lambs to fatten for Easter Sunday. After the ewes drop their lambs, I am cert it is safe to release them into the meadow. I believe Ferrant will do well with them. But I still think we should keep including the older boys as protectors. Lambs will draw wolves."

"Thank you, Reeve. I am glad for the sheep and for your thinking ahead to the Easter feast. Please thank Cormac for me."

Well done, Cormac. You knew mine mind before I did.

On a day, when no came to report, Margaret said, "Caitlin, I have been thinking."

Caitlin stopped her tidying and stood on Margaret's side of the bed as she asked, "Thinking about what?"

"Some of the things I have done. I ordered water and a clean rag at the church door. I wanted to teach people to have clean hands. Who sees to it?"

"The village women, who do it in gratitude for the milk you provide. Those first rags were filthy. so they rinsed them. Now even the adults use them. I gave them fabric, and they hemmed fourteen cloths. Once a week, by turns, a woman washes the last week's cloths. Their husbands provide the water. This winter, they even warm the water before they bring it to church."

"Do I still provide milk? I remember it not."

"Once the children were eating regularly and regained their health, you reduced the milk to Mondays and Thursdays. I think you have forgot. One of the first things Garwig formed was a cup with a long handle, so Erwina could dip it into the milk and the receiver could drink from it. Do you wish to stop the practice? If you do, we can use the milk to make cheese."

Margaret's voice faded as she replied, "Not yet. Ask me again after the weather warms." She closed her eyes.

Another time, Reeve asked to see Lady Margaret despite it was not his turn. "I have the news you have long sought."

Margaret adjusted her blankets and lay back against her pillows. "Belleme?"

At Reeve's nod, she asked, "How close? Are we in danger?"

"Far. No," he responded. "After the king took Belleme's castle at Tickhill, Belleme had no base in the south. He returned to Shropshire and stripped his lands of coin and food before he disappeared into the forest. Left his people to starve. King Henry was clever; he sent food and animals to the region on condition they notify him should Belleme return. They pledged their loyalty to the king. Belleme has been hiding in the northern woods, raiding when he could, and running from the king's army. Belleme's army has been shrinking as the men leave when they are not paid. He ordered coin and supplies from Ponthieu, but it has not arrived. The king has spies on the east coast. If anything arrives from Normandy, the king will get it. The man is on the run. I doubt we will see him."

"A desperate man may attempt desperate acts, even dangerous ones. If he stays in the forest, he can reach even here. Keep our guard up, Reeve, until he is caught or dead."

Before dawn on 5 March, Margaret completed her penance and asked to attend Mass. While she dressed, the knights drew lots. Two escorted her from the ladder to the gate. Two walked her to the chapel where Father Manntun had placed a stool from his own home. for her to sit upon. Two walked her to the hall and to her seat. Margaret ate her pottage and excused herself; two escorted her to the keep. She slept hard. She preferred to beg off supping, but she recognized she needed the food. She sat on a stool beside her bed and ate at a small table the Rammegs had built for her.

Two days later Margaret again attended Mass. The next day was the fourth Sunday of Lent. After that Mass she stayed seated on the stool and accepted the good wishes of everyone in the village. Haelum, impetuous boy that he was, politely pulled his forelock and then rushed into Margaret's arms. "I love you, my lady!" he said so loudly even those outside the church door heard him. Margaret laughed and hugged him back before his embarrassed parents pulled him off her. As Aldcot and Beornia made abject apologies for his boldness, Margaret just smiled at them. As was both the custom and the law, Margaret stood at the chapel door and handed out bolts of common cloth for new garments for each of her villeins and retainers. Halfway through the main meal of the day, Margaret excused herself and went to bed.

"Each day I feel stronger," Margaret told Caitlin. "Two weeks to Palm Sunday. I want to be well and awake the whole of Easter." Margaret set a two-day pattern. Sleep late and dine in the hall. Meet with someone, Sir Roussel, Reeve, Cormac or Garwig, to learn of events and to make decisions. Supper and to bed. Next day go to Mass and stay awake through dinner. Nap until supper and stay awake until bedtime. Sunday was Mass day.

Longer, warmer days helped her mood. Each day she tried to quicken her pace, stay alert longer, and sleep less. Father Manntun often visited her. He encouraged her efforts to improve. He shared his observations of the doings of both the Normans and the Saxons, told her village news, and prayed with her.

He has changed. Softened. Is more cheerful and encouraging. Cormac reported the Saxons say he is more himself now. More like the priest he used to be before de Warenne chose treason. I like him now; I hope he sees that.

One week after the first day of spring, Margaret and Father Manntun were walking about the bailey together. Margaret told him, "Father, if you desire it, I will speak for you to mine lord when he arrives. I will ask him to keep you."

"I would like that," he replied.

"Is it permissible for me to tell you I was right?"

"Right about what?" he asked in a cautious tone.

"They love you again. They smile at you and stop to visit with you. The children take your hands now and walk with you. Church is a happy place again. I have noticed."

Margaret saw Father Manntun frown.

"Am I too froward to mention it?"

"Yes. But that is you." The priest paused and added, "I am happy about it."

"As am I."

Father turned and placed his right palm on her forehead. His fingers splayed over the top of her head. Each day his blessing was similar. "Blessed Father in heaven, continue to give Margaret good health. Jesus, watch over her; she needs supervision. Holy Spirit continue to show her Your grace. Holy Mother Mary, remind her how to be a proper woman. May God grant she soon will marry and become one." Father removed his hand and made the Sign of the Cross before her.

Margaret smiled. *Your words are part invocation, part remonstration, part warning.* Impetuously, Margaret stood on tiptoe, leaned forward and kissed the priest on the cheek. "Thank you, Father." They smiled at each other. *I am glad we have made peace. I will save that for one of mine gratitudes. Thank you, God.* Margaret returned to the keep to nap.

Palm Sunday was an important religious holiday with High Mass, the handing out of palm fronds from the Holy Land, and a hearty meal. After they dined, Sir Roussel excused himself to dictate a letter to the king. Father Manntun went with him to write it.

Cormac slipped into Roussel's place and whispered, "Want happy news?" Margaret kept her face forward and nodded once. "The king's babe has come alive in the queen's belly." She faced Cormac with a dropped jaw. Cormac added, "She was two months with child at Epiphany. No one spoke of it for fear. Everyone wants this one to be the heir."

"As do I!" Margaret affirmed. "I will pray every day God grants them a healthy son. When is he due to arrive?"

"The first fortnight of August," replied Cormac.

Margaret smiled. *I have plenty of time to prepare.*

Holy Week followed the life and death of Jesus the Christ until his resurrection on Easter Sunday. Each day at Mass Father Manntun spoke of the tenets of their faith. All fasted daily, no luxuries like butter or wine, and still no meat during the week.

30

❧

April

The fifth day began with chill and fog. Margaret awakened happy. She had regained her strength and looked forward to another successful season and harvest, and she had a plan for her future. By the time the dawn High Mass ended, most of the fog had burned off and the sun shone. The most important day in the religious calendar, Easter celebrated both the resurrection of Jesus the Christ and the anticipated start of the Holy Roman Catholic Church fifty days later on Pentecost. Not just a religious season, these seven weeks marked the completion of planting and most livestock's births. Easter was for celebrating and resting. Each person wore a new garment or the best he owned, newly washed, to symbolize the rebirth of Jesus the Christ and of nature. Regardless of rank, the greeting was the same for all. One said, "Jesus the Christ has risen and we are saved." The other replied, "Thanks be to God for the life, death, and resurrection of his only son."

Lady Margaret stood a distance from the church door, so everyone greeted Father Manntun first. They came by rank: Sirs Roussel, Gailard, Cachier, the knights, Caitlin followed by Cormac. Also lined up by rank, the villagers followed suit: Garwig, Reeve and his family, then families, who arrived together to pay their respects to Margaret and to wish her well this Easter morn.

The villeins set three long tables in the meadow beyond the village and left to break their fasts in their own homes. The sun warmed the air and a gentle breeze made pleasant the spring day. Before noon one table was ladened with the meats, vegetables, and breads the women had prepared. Sitting in family groups, with the smallest children on their parents' laps, villeins dined and chatted for over an hour. Then they dismantled the banquet and took home their share of the leavings.

The feast in the hall was more formal and more sumptuous. Margaret had ordered a sun-bleached linen placed over the head table. Beornia had set a lit candle before each place except for the absent lord's spot. With mugs of ale in hand, Margaret's knights waited in the hall. Father Manntun entered with Lady Margaret behind him and Sir Roussel escorting her. The men cleared a path. Those at the head table stood behind their stools while the rest found their places, knights behind their benches, servants to the sides of the head table. The hall quieted. At Lady Margaret's nod, all except the priest bowed their heads and clasped their hands together for prayer.

"Jesus sacrificed his life that we may live eternally. We celebrate his resurrection with joy and with humble thanks for His great sacrifice. We will honor His name and our salvation by remembering Jesus died for our sins. We are reborn in the Church because of Him.

Blessed Father, we praise you for the gift of Your Son, an early spring and good planting time. The food we eat this day is a gift from You to remind us of Your love and care for us. Dear Jesus, we promise to remain faithful to your church. Let us eat these first fruits of spring and rejoice. We pray good weather will continue so we may have a successful harvest." Father Manntun raised his arms and palms toward the roof and ended with, "May God bless all our endeavors. May Jesus continue to guide us and save us from evil. May the Holy Spirit guide our hearts and hands. May our blessed Mother Mary continue to smile on our efforts." Father Manntun lowered his hands. The hall resounded with "Amen."

Margaret thanked Father for his prayer. Those at the head table sat; the rest followed. Hugiet poured wine for the head table as the serving girls walked the trestle tables and filled the mugs with new ale. Doune carried in the soup pot and set it on the side table. Nearra had cooked mushrooms in butter and added them to a creamed broth, which was served in new, small wooden bowls. Margaret tasted the soup and declared it delicious. Midryth and Haesel added bread and butter to the tables. The girls cleared the bowls and refilled goblets and mugs. Cleva carried in a large wooden bowl of a salad with three kinds of lettuce leaves. Cyne carried in a second bowl.

With great ceremony, Doune carried in the first platter of roast lamb, followed by Nearra, who carried a bowl of spring peas. They stopped before the head table, but faced the hall. Everyone cheered and clapped. Duone and Nearra turned and served the head table while the girls ran to the kitchen for the rest of the meal. They set the main course on the serving table. Nearra filled plates with meat and vegetables; Duone carried the platter of filled plates so the girls could hand them to the men. The feasting continued for two hours. Margaret requested a song or recitation. Every knight offered a poem, song, or story. The servants ate their own meals as they perched on stools behind the head table. They could hear the entertainment and still were nearby to be summoned. By late afternoon most were sleepy with meat-filled bellies and too much drink. Margaret wished to nap, but leaving would have been unseemly. She chatted with Sir Roussel and Father Manntun. She had petted and spoiled Ferrant with bits of lamb. Margaret left the dais to visit each retainer; she was pleased to note each had worn the shirt she had sewn for him. Hughes held up his right arm to show her there was no sauce on his cuff; everyone laughed. Then she left for a walk; Roussel offered to escort her and Ferrant. Margaret strolled in sunshine, enjoying the balmy spring weather and inspecting the bailey with a mind to improvements and additions.

People had congregated before each other's homes. From the palisade walkway, Margaret saw Hugiet, Gytha, and Ifig standing together as they chatted and watched Lindene, Hartun, Haeldun, and Rammethan playing tag in the lanes. Near the women, Felamaere, Haraleah, and Aldcot sat on stools and talked. Those in the hall who wished to eat supped on lamb-bone soup laced with leftover vegetables and served with leftover bread. After Vespers and evensong, the villeins left for their homes and everyone else walked toward the bailey and their beds. Another good day. *Tonight I shall say as many gratitudes as I can think, for six is not enough.*

Easter Monday Margaret's first conference was with Father Manntun, who shocked her with his request.

"My lady, I seek your permission to marry Gytha."

"May a priest marry?" asked Margaret. "I vaguely recall hearing a sermon how priests marry not because they serve God and have no time for a family."

"Twenty-five years ago Pope Gregory the Seventh recommended priests marry not to better serve the church, but he made it not law. Priests have been married for a thousand years. Why should it change? Marrying among the lower ranks is still common this far from Rome."

Margaret frowned. "Please explain."

"Pope Gregory declared any married priest who wished to be advanced should set aside his wife. She was sent to a convent for life. He could still care for his children. Now no priest, no matter his rank, may endow them with church lands, property or coin." Father Manntun revealed, "My bishop married after he became one and has three children so how can he refuse me? I am too old for a bishopric. No. The truth is neither King Henry nor Archbishop Anselm will ever permit me to be more than I am because I previously served a traitor. I might as well be happy. Gytha makes me happy; she is always merry. I can be a father to her children. I will eat well, live well and get to raise children." Father smiled and added, "And I will always have an unlimited supply of ale."

First smiles, then softer penances, and now a joke. She has changed you for the better. Margaret smiled back. "You have changed, Father. You are milder, kinder, and you laugh more. Tell me, is any of it Gytha's doing?"

Manntun shrugged. His smile widened.

"Who will perform the rite?" Margaret asked. "I expect you may marry not yourself to another."

"No, I cannot," Mannton replied, "but mine bishop can. I hope he will accept mine reasons for marrying. He married after the decree, still lives with his wife, and gave church lands and coin to his children; he even has a grandchild. I pray he will refuse me not. May I write a letter today to ask him if I may marry?"

While I still have the power, I will approve every match. Even this one. Let his bishop say aye or nay, not me.

"I want you and Gytha happy, so I approve. I pray your bishop gives his consent and will send a priest to marry you. I suggest you, being a person of importance, be the first one to marry this season. I know not what mine future lord may say of mine decision, but I want you to wait not. Happiness should never be delayed, you do agree?"

"My lady, we thank you for allowing us to marry. I might take the letter to mine bishop myself and leave in the early morning. I may be gone several days."

"I will send a knight with you for protection. If you will ride a roundsey instead of take a wagon, you will arrive much sooner. After you have finished your letter, please come to me with parchment and ink, so I may dictate a letter informing the bishop of mine support. Use it or not. Whichever will advance your cause." Then Margaret requested, "Please send Cormac to me if you see him." *Why not him and Caitlin as well. But only if he truly cares for her.*

Father smiled and nodded. He strode out of the hall with his head high.

Margaret took her basket to sew in sunlight as it streamed into the side doorway. She had not even finished mending one shirt before Cormac was beside her. Margaret stood and placed her basket inside the hall. "I will watch the villeins. Please join me on the walkway." Cormac followed. Margaret appeared as if she were on a casual inspection of the work below, but Cormac knew better. Once they were out of hearing of the watchmen, Margaret stopped and faced him. "Cormac, you love Caitlin. She knows it. In fact everyone does. It is time you ask her to marry."

"My lady, I hesitate to ask. If I do nothing, we can be as we have been. If I ask, and she declines, I am lost, for all will change. She insults me no more; she smiles at me." Cormac paused for a moment to reflect. "She has been smiling at me much more of late. She talks to me now when we dine and sup. Still, I am uncert what she will answer."

Margaret responded, "I should not act the matchmaker, but I will visit with Caitlin. If I learn something positive, I will smile at you and wink. If I look at you and frown or give a small shake of mine head, then propose not yet. She may not be ready. Caitlin likes to ponder before she decides things," Margaret added.

Margaret waited to speak to Caitlin until they were abed. "Cormac loves you," Margaret whispered, "and you love him. Oh not at first, but you have softened to his compliments. He cares for you. Remember how closely he attended you when I was ill. I have seen you follow him with your eyes and then look away when you think someone is watching you."

"If he wants something, he should ask for himself."

"Because you have been unkind to him, he hesitates."

"Of late I have been kinder."

"Well, that is encouraging. Caitlin, mine friend, now is the time to have your own life. I want you wed before me so mine future lord cannot hinder your happiness. If you wed Cormac now, I can give you a home and garden in the village. No matter what mine future lord decides, you will have a place. Cormac is both diplomatic and skilled enough to find some way for a lord to need him."

"What does he want you to do?"

"Cormac wants me to give him a sign of hope or despair before he acts." In the dark, Margaret could not see Caitlin's smile but she heard it.

"I will consider what you said." Caitlin rolled away and faced the curtain.

The next morning Father Manntun said Mass, broke his fast, and left before the villagers reached the fields. Margaret had barely finished her meal before Garwig arrived.

The villagers have guessed about Father. Others get to marry. Mine future happiness grows in the queen's belly. Please God, let it be a healthy boy. I know, say it and mean it. Your will, Oh God, in all things. Margaret stopped a sigh and waited.

Garwig lowered his chin and tugged his forehead hair in respect. "My lady, I have come with a petition." Margaret nodded. "I am tired of living with Cormac; he snores. I want mine own home. I want to build a house and have a garden on the empty lot at the edge of the village."

"Tell me the history of the place," Margaret asked. *The evil done may linger still.*

"Over a decade ago, a man went mad. He killed his wife and babe and burned the house with three of them in it. The villeins say the plot is cursed, but Father blesses it every First Day just as he does everything else."

"I can give you another plot," offered Margaret.

"I like that plot because I can see the forge from it. And I have plans," he admitted.

"Plans?"

"I will build on the garden side and plant over the ashes. The land is rested and rich; I shall get bounty from it. I have started over; this plot should start over as well."

I wonder who the girl is. Be polite. Inquire not. "You have mine permission." Margaret teased him with, "Given your height and muscles, I expect you to build a large wattle and daub house—large enough for you and a future family."

"Thank you, my lady. I am planning for a large family," replied Garwig, who smiled as he pulled his forelock, backed away and left.

I wish you happy, Garwig. Whomever you choose will be fortunate. Because of your trade, your rank in the village is even higher than whoever is the current reeve. With your skills, your hard work, and your wealth, even if she is a villein, you will soon purchase her freedom and your children can be born free.

Later Margaret remembered what the villagers sometimes did with their old garments after she had given them cloth for new ones. She sought Scirburne and asked him to get her a used set of women's clothes from those discarded into the rags bin. She wanted a shift and a gunna or two gunnas. "I need at least a gunna, a mantle, and boots," she informed him. "I want them neither washed nor cleaned in any way. Put them in a basket. Bring them to me only, no one else, and when Caitlin is absent," instructed Margaret. "I have need of them." Scirburne looked at her askance, so she added, "Something honorable for cert."

"Yes, my lady." He pulled his forelock.

Margaret sat in the sun with her basket beside her; as she mended, her thoughts ran elsewhere. *About four months. One hundred twenty days? Among us, only Father can read and write. Does he keep a calendar? I cannot ask; he will know. I learned to make mine name, but no more. Unseemly for a woman to do what men cannot. Men who fear a woman call her a witch and get her burned. Why must it be like that? I am as clever as any of the men here. God forgive me, but why did You make women with brains if not to have us use them? How to keep track? Sundays. Only four days a month to remember. Easter Sunday was April the fifth day. The remainder of April. She finger-counted on her knee. Twelve, nineteen, twenty-six. Yes, one month at a time. May Day, start again. I can do this. Be happy for one hundred twenty days of freedom. More, if Scirburne gets what I need.* Margaret smiled to herself.

The next day Garwig marked the dimensions of his house with thick stakes and planted his garden. Scirburne arrived with a basket. Margaret transferred the vegetables to a platter on the serving table in the hall. She strode to the keep and hid the basket under her side of the bed. *Now I have mine chance at freedom if need be. First coins sewn into hems. Then I must find a way to hide these clothes in the forest. I have time.* For the rest of the day, she smiled at everyone. Two days later, a couple stood before Margaret and Cormac as they finished the accounts book for the day. Cormac departed.

Good choice, Garwig! Leoma, I was right. God sent you a much better man.

"My lady, I seek your permission to wed. I love Leoma and she loves me. I have the house started, the garden planted and the coins for your merchet. With your permission, Leoma will continue to be your baker after we are wed. With your approval, Leoma will also prepare another so you will have an experienced baker when she gets with child and stops work."

Margaret turned to the girl. "You have someone in mind?" Leoma nodded. "Garwig, I am pleased for both of you. You may not marry yet, but I will have your banns read as soon as possible. For now, you have mine permission to announce your betrothal. However, Leoma still lives and sleeps here. You will lie not together until you are lawfully wed. You may hold hands in public; you may take her arm when you are walking, but no more. I will have modesty and discretion at all times." Margaret looked to Leoma, "No kissing. Leoma, remember your vow."

Leoma blushed, "Yes, my lady."

"With Father Manntun gone, I will make the announcement at midday before we sing grace. Leoma, please ask your parents to join Garwig in the back of the hall. I will have you two hold hands and state mine approval."

"Thank you, my lady; you are most gracious to grant our request."

Margaret noticed how they had gazed at each other with so much love and longing. *Will I ever feel that way? I long to know what that is like. Would that the king had behaved nobly and let me marry the man I wanted, who wanted me. God forgive me for mine thoughts, but I am wroth with him. I did not deserve such treatment. Nor did William.*

On Saturday, Father Manntun returned with his bishop's permission to marry. He had not needed Lady Margaret's letter, but said he would keep it with the other estate documents in the trunk under the altar.

At the end of Mass on the third Sunday Father Manntun announced his own marriage banns. Two more Sundays of announcements and, on the second May Sunday, he would marry Gytha.

On the last Sunday of the month, Margaret retired to the keep after they had eaten, but she did not nap. Margaret folded up the hem of the smaller of the two gunnas. Into the space, she sewed pennies and hapennies, dividing each with a seam so they would sound not when she walked. *Only Cormac knows how I altered the accounts book by over-counting our expenses and hiding the coins. He will never tell. I need a knife for protection and to cut out one coin at a time should I need them. Visit the kitchen on some errand or another and steal an old one.*

The woods cover the realm with only pockets of estates. Stay out of villages and cities. Hide far from here, I can find a stream, fashion a lean-to, live off the land. I pray I have enough coins to flee. Where? Wales is not safe; Scotland is too wild. Mayhap Caitlin's old home. West and a boat trip, and I will be safe. The king will expect me to head for Normandy. Hah! He will not find me. She continued to sew until supper.

Soon Garwig slept on the floor of his new home under a starry sky. Thatching a roof was next. The last day of April, the single girls were aflutter. They cooked savories and packed a picnic basket in hopes someone tricked them for May Day. Single men scoured the ditches and forest meadows for grasses to weave into baskets and for flowers to fill them. Married women attached ribs of dyed fabric to the May Pole cap. Married men lifted the May pole into the hole they had dug. They filled the hole with rocks and mud to hold it in place.

That night Margaret sat on a stool at the keep door to prevent any man from winning time with her on the morrow. She was not about to picnic with an eligible male because he had left a basket for her. She told a firm "NO!" to three retainers who tried to creep up the steps. *I will not cause jealousy or trouble among mine men by spending time with one.* In the middle of the night Cormac rose, snuck through the unlocked keep gate, climbed the ladder, and whispered to Margaret, "Please place this on her side of the bed."

Margaret nodded and took the basket. She waited until she was cert all the men below her slept. She crept away from the doorway while keeping watch out the opening. When no man moved toward the keep, she tiptoed to her bed and left the basket for Caitlin. The rushes stirred not with her cautious steps. Margaret returned to the keep doorway. *No basket on the doorway's edge and no man approaching.* She sat on her stool, but she leaned not on the door frame for fear she might fall asleep.

3 1

※

May

Father made his usual May Day sermon denouncing celebrating a pagan holiday. He warned them the pagan way was to get a girl with child and then wed her. The Christian practice was better; keep the girl a virgin until her wedding night. Then he shifted to crops. "Let this day be a celebration; the planting is growing well. Let us pray for good weather and fine crops," he said. Father returned to lecturing of behaving with decency, propriety, and with regard for women. He ran himself out of reprimands, finished Mass and sent them on their way. All broke their fasts. Bailey and village gathered at the meadow's edge.

Mother never let me take part. Said it was unseemly for a lady. Last year I was uncert of mine power and too formal. This is my only chance. Margaret's chest swelled with happiness. *I get a May Day!*

In the group of married folk and children, Margaret spotted Leoma looking happy even though she could no longer participate in the dance. One of the older village girls began the maypole song, and the other unmarried girls joined in.

What fun this is! How can this be wrong? All we are doing is singing and weaving the ribs in a many-colored pattern around a pole. Who dyed all these ribs and when? Stop thinking. Sing and enjoy this!

Forward and back they wove as they sang and stepped around the pole, decorating it into a colorful weave of strips. They looped and secured the ribs and left the bottoms to waft in a breeze.

Single men organized a circle outside the girls. They teased them about having left a basket and demanded the girls guess who had left them. Margaret stepped away and watched the fun begin. The girls who knew their suitors called their partners' names, picked up their food baskets, and departed. Caitlin called Cormac's name, and everyone laughed because they were cert of that pairing. Caitlin walked out of the circle on Cormac's arm; she pointed to her basket. Cormac picked it up and led her toward the trees. He did look back to Margaret and wink at her. Margaret chuckled.

Rammeg stepped up next and called for Willa. Margaret saw Leoma's face sour for a second and then become flat. Other pairs met; laughter and happiness filled the square. After the pairs had left, the remaining single girls were required to kiss each eligible male left behind—even the boys. Margaret knew she must also kiss every unwed male, Saxon or Norman. She also must choose her picnic partner from among them.

Leoma turned to leave, but someone called her name. She halted mid-step, put down her right foot and turned. Garwig picked up his basket and walked to her. Everyone stopped to watch. Leoma's eyes were large and bright at being treated like a girl. The villeins' looks one to another warned each other; no one gainsaid her right to act as if she had never married. Garwig bowed and made his request. Leoma nodded. Garwig offered his arm, and she took it. Leoma smiled. Widow or not, she was being courted. No one moved or spoke until they disappeared. The adults buzzed over what they had seen. *Oh Leoma, I could cry mine happiness for you. No tears now or others might feel sorry for me. Not today. Be happy. This May Day is mine to enjoy.*

The men called the remaining girls' attention back to them to demand their kisses. The inner circle passed inside the outer one. The men grabbed for shoulders to hold the girls, who often wiggled and sidled out of intended embraces. Young boys grabbed waists with more success. With much teasing and giggling, pairs kissed on the lips. Even the youngest eligible boy, four-year-old Haelum, got smacked. Margaret insisted she would only kiss foreheads or not at all. As Margaret walked the inner circle, each man dipped his head. Margaret kissed each forehead and quit the group.

Once the couples departed, the married folk looked to their lady. Lady Margaret picked up the basket Cook had prepared for her, and which Margaret had marked with a blue rib in a bow. She glanced about. The men of the village knew she would not name them, but they wondered which knight she would choose. *I could select Syghelm because he is oldest and least likely to expect I mean him to court me.* As she studied their faces, Margaret realized choosing one of them for any reason might produce discord. Margaret made another choice. She held out her hand.

Haelum squealed with happiness. "Me! She chose me!" Haelum turned serious and bowed. "I am honored to picnic with you, my lady." Then he offered his arm as if he were a man grown. When

Margaret bent to take it, many laughed, but not Haelum. He was "cock of the walk" as he stepped out with his partner.

The married folk gathered their children for their picnics. Father Manntun joined Gytha and her children. They walked into the meadow with the other families. Rammeg Younger and Willa had waited in the meadow. They sat a distance from the families but well within sight of Scirburne and Ifig. Rammeg wanted no talk about his intended wife's honor.

Margaret sat in the shade of an oak tree and within sight of the villagers as well. *Sword or no sword, I am not about to venture any farther away. Haelum will eat and then run off. Duty done, I can go home. This part is not fun. Sixteen and unwed. Sixteen and un-courted. Sixteen and an uncert future.* She released an unintended sigh. *Smile. Look happy. The poor boy is so eager.* The village women had prepared baskets of food for the loners. They may have been forlorn, but they were not forgotten. Cook had prepared food for Margaret's men. Duone had lead a wagon which carried their meals to the meadow; the bailey servants followed. Four knights ate and left to relieve the four on guard, who tied up their horses to the wagon and sat to enjoy the rest of the afternoon. This day everyone picnicked.

At first Haelum tried to engage in adult-like conversation. With a few questions, Margaret soon had him chattering about his favorite pig, the animal births he had seen, doings in the village, who was sweet on whom, and more. Margaret ate two meat pies, a honey-sweetened roll and a half-moon-shaped apple tart. Finally talked out, Haelum bit into his first meat pie. Margaret leaned against the tree and grinned as he devoured it. She handed him a second pie. While the boy ate, Margaret observed those in the meadow. She felt sleepy, but she dared not close her eyes. *I might offend Haelum, and I might not be safe.* When Haelum asked for ale, she poured a bit into a second mug and handed it to him. He asked for more. *Perhaps a sleepy boy with a full stomach is just what I need.* Margaret poured him a full mug.

Like everyone else, Margaret and Haelum lazed away the afternoon. The children ran and played games while the adults visited or napped in the sun. After Haelum reclined and lay his head on his arm, he dozed. Margaret rose and wandered among her people to visit. Near supper-time, couples returned from the forest. They, too, joined the groups in the meadow. When Haelum awoke, he ran over to Lady Margaret and took her hand. She held it for a while and then excused him to play. Soon Haelum tussled with an older boy so his father intervened. Aldcot returned to report his son was bragging at Lady Margaret's choosing him; the older boy put him in his place. "No harm done," reported the farmer. When the sun dropped behind the trees, the air cooled. Everyone picked up blankets and baskets, and headed home. Servants packed the wagon, and Duone led the donkeys to the bailey.

Margaret walked with her knights. *How to placate their feelings?* They started in silence; Margaret waited and soon one, two and then another made a comment. *We are back together after a good day of fun and rest. I am content.* Before Margaret slept, she counted out the May Sundays—three, ten, seventeen, twenty-four, thirty-one. *Which of the last two is Pentecost?* She closed her eyes.

The next day Margaret strolled, escorted, of course, to the forge. She gestured her guards to step away while she spoke with Garwig. Margaret asked him to show her the forge, the tools, his latest project and his completed items. Her interest was genuine. That over, she asked, "Did your enjoy May Day?"

"Yes, my lady, very much."

"How did you court her? I saw it not."

"My lady, thank you for permitting me to eat from your kitchen. That is when I saw her. She is a beautiful woman; I could not help but notice her. She is shy. At first,

Cook kept stopping mine efforts to speak with her. I won over Nearra first. That took some doing. I spoke only once in a while to Leoma. We often sat in silence enjoying each other's company under Cook's watchful eyes. I did not touch her," he added. "After a time, we spent afternoons telling each other of our lives. I revealed I hoped we soon would be more than acquaintances. She blushed and said nothing." Garwig smiled at his next thought, which he spoke. "She did not run off, so I took that as a good sign."

"Hurt her not. Lead her not to a betrothal and then back away. If you do, you will answer to me." warned Margaret.

"My lady. I shall wed her and see she feels safe the rest of her days. I swear."

Margaret nodded and turned away toward the bailey. *Father loves Gytha. Garwin loves Leoma. Cormac loves Caitlin. Who loves me? No one.* Margaret's eyes filled. She quickly wiped them with her sleeve. *Cry not. Smile. They expect me to be happy. Hide mine feelings.*

On 3 May, the Sunday rain was most welcome. The crops' well-being was more important than any inconvenience of weather. At the end of Mass, Father talked of the bishop's arrival and explained the proper manners toward a bishop. Finally, he reported the bishop would announce if the service next Sunday would be a High Mass because a priest was marrying.

On the way to their homes, the villagers talked of seeing a bishop for the first time. They wondered how such an important man traveled, when he might arrive, and how he would be dressed.

How might the Bishop of Reading treat me, a girl. Would he speak only to the king's men and ignore me? Would he respect mine position as holder of this estate? Father says I must get on one knee and kiss his ring of authority. I must remember not speak until he speaks to me. Behave so well, he will have no cause to speak ill of me. If I do well, he might recommend me to a good family, and I will get a husband. Embarrass not Father nor myself. Remember Mother's saying. "Quiet, calm, dignified, pure keeps a lady steadfast and cert." Practice now, so I live it while the bishop visits.

The week before the ceremony the villeins cleaned the village areas. Several whitewashed their homes. Both men and women prepared the keep. Men inspected and repaired the interior wall chinks. Women washed every surface they could. Men wove water-soaked withies into screens for the second-floor bedchamber for the bishop. Men cut reeds, and the women scattered them on the floors. Scirburne and Scelfdune carved and nailed wooden mounting brackets to walls for shutters. Garwig fixed them to the walls and installed rods on the mounting brackets. The men hung shutters from them so a sleeper might push them closed over the arrow slits during bad weather. Caitlin supervised the work. Margaret and Cormac worked in the hall, updating the accounts book should the bishop asked to see it. Wednesday, Margaret helped the servants appoint the second floor with everything the prelate might need and prepared the bed. Thursday, they cleaned the hall, and replaced the rushes on the sleeping platform should the bishop's people want it. The laundress had washed Margaret's proper attire. Reeve informed Margaret the bishop was expected Saturday to dine midday or whenever he arrived. By Friday afternoon the estate was ready, and the villagers went home to sup. Everyone in the hall ate soup and bread; Cook was busy preparing food for the bishop's stay.

The bishop's train was sighted shortly before noon. Eight men-at-arms, all priests, escorted him. Bishop Gabriel de Chanoise rode a war horse as would a knight. *He looks young! Thirty at most? No, wait. He has a grandchild.* He was followed by three wagons hauled by pairs of oxen. From the bailey walkway, Margaret watched with awe at the party and mentally estimated how much food and fodder this group was going to cost her. She dashed to the stairs and descended. She joined Father Manntun, Sir Roussel, Reeve, Cormac and Caitlin at the hall entrance.

He must be accustomed to travel. Look how his men arrange things. Was he here before so he knows where to place the wagons?

From his horse, Bishop de Chanoise looked around the bailey before he glanced at the people waiting for him to dismount. A priest stepped forward and held the bishop's horse's halter while de Chanoise dismounted. He pulled up his white leather gloves from the ends of the five-inch cuffs embroidered in blue and gold. Richly attired with a golden fur around the neck of his blue surcoat, matching chausses, and black leather boots to his knees, the bishop looked like a royal in formal dress. His easy gait as he approached the group indicated he might be friendly.

"Sir Rousssel, I am pleased to meet you. When next you see His Royal Highness, please extend to him mine warmest greetings."

How does he know Roussel's name and rank? Of course, he would have questioned Father when he petitioned the bishop.

"I am honored to carry your message to His Royal Highness when next I see him, Your Grace. Welcome to this estate."

The bishop looked to Father Manntun, who went down on one knee and kissed the ring on the bishop's right hand.

"Manntun, I expect to interview your intended wife before the ceremony. Please send her to the church to await me."

Margaret cocked her head to the right. Ten feet away, Scandy, nodded and walked out the bailey gate to tell Gytha.

Roussel looked toward Margaret. "Your Grace, may I introduce the Lady Margaret, holder of this estate in King Henry's name."

Margaret gave obeisance and dropped to one knee; she stayed down until she saw the gloved hand before her face. She kissed the ring and rose. When the bishop did not speak, Margaret knew her place was indeed low. *I had best try not to introduce Reeve, Cormac, or Caitlin. Rather he ignore them than to have them insulted as well. Sigh not; hide my feelings.*

Bishop de Chanoise clapped a hand on Roussel's shoulder and said, "Come, sir, let us enjoy the cool of the hall. I look forward to a hearty meal, if this estate as the means to provide it."

The estate? Whom does he think plants and harvests the crops, cooks and serves the food, guards and commands this place? Are we nothing to him? Then why did he agree to come, to perform the ceremony? Best I have Cyne reset the head table and omit both mine and mine future lord's places. I'm staying in the kitchen unless called for. Margaret missed seeing the bishop's men carrying beds, chests, and other goods into the keep.

Dinner was vegetable broth, fish drizzled with a butter and white wine sauce, roasted lamb in a red wine and onions sauce, and boiled vegetables. From the servant's doorway, Margaret heard the bishop, who sat in Margaret's place for her absent lord, compliment the bread and the spicing. *So he does have some manners toward those with less rank than he.* Margaret told Cook and Leoma what Bishop de Chanoise had said. They blushed, curtsied to her before they worked to bring the final course, dried apples simmered in honey and herbs until they were soft and golden. When Bishop de Chanoise called for Margaret and informed her he and his men had taken the second floor of the keep, Margaret offered to vacate the building. The bishop assured her she would be safe.

Will a barred door be enough? Should I sleep on the guest platform in the hall with mine knights guarding me? Might one of the bishop's men not be a priest and want me and this place? Not a priest, cert not a priest. Wondering if any of her retainers had heard the bishop, she looked toward them. Syghelm met her eyes and gave her the tiniest of nods. Margaret felt better. That night and the next, Syghelm sat on the top step to the third level of the keep with his ax across his lap.

"I will see your intended wife alone, Manntun," said the bishop as he stood.

All in the hall rose and waited for Bishop de Chanoise to depart.

Sunday, 10 May, Bishop de Chanoise held the marriage ceremony outside the church door. No one married inside God's house, not even a priest. He led everyone into the building and conducted a simple Mass. The head tables had been carried to the meadow, and the villeins had formed another table at its end for Gytha, Linton, Lindene, and Goscelyn. Other trestle tables festooned the meadow. Into the shade, Duone drove a wagon that hauled four barrels of ale. The villeins removed the donkeys to graze in the second meadow. Feasting, toasting, drinking and singing, everyone enjoyed the day. Babes sat or napped in a parent's lap. Children ran and played. Bishop de Chanoise spoke to Sir Roussel or Father Manntun. His guards, all priests, sat apart at their own table.

In the morning, the bishop again said Mass and announced his departure. That he wanted to be gone from her humble estate bothered Margaret not at all. Seated at the end of the dais table, she was gracious to the priest beside her as they broke their fasts. By the time the bishop had finished eating, his men had his wagons prepared. The party departed. Margaret breathed a sigh of relief and returned to the hall with Cormac to count her expenses of food, drink, and fodder.

Father now ate with his new family, so Margaret's table was one fewer; she stayed long after they supped because she wanted to be with her men. Eventually, she stood and accompanied whichever three men Roussel had scheduled her escort. Two to see the keep was empty of men and then to leave, and one to guard the locked gate until Syghelm relieved him at midnight.

At the end of Mass the following Sunday, Father announced the first banns for the marriage of Cormac mac Cennedig and Caitlin. Margaret reached under her left arm and pinched her friend. Caitlin flinched but kept her smile. After Father passed, Margaret whispered, "You might have told me first."

"Surprise!"

Margaret stood apart and watched the villagers congratulate the couple. She was happy for them, but sad for herself. *Soon Caitlin will be gone to a new life. Our friendship will not be the same, even if I invite you to join me. I will miss you, mine dearest friend.*

After they had dined and the hall emptied, Cormac asked Margaret to tarry. "Caitlin wanted everyone to be surprised after the talk about us," he began. At Margaret's smile, he continued, "We shared the sadness in each of our lives, and we decided to let our pasts fade away. We decided we want our futures to be together. I have a plot in mind for a house and garden. May I show you?"

After Margaret approved the site, she surprised Cormac. "A wattle and daub house is not good enough for mine seneschal and his family. Your home will be of wood. Use the leftover logs the villeins cut last winter."

"Thank you, my lady. Caitlin will be so pleased to have such a fine house."

"Because the villeins have little to do but weeding, I will have them pay their work due by building the house. You should have it in a fortnight. Design it as you will. Cormac, please call for sellers of goods to come here at mine expense. I want Caitlin to choose whatever she needs to establish your household." At his shocked look, Margaret explained, "She has always done so much for me. This is but a little I can do for her in return. I do wish you both happy."

"We are overwhelmed with your generosity. We are more than happy you are our lady!"

Would you said that to your lord and lady. Think no more of William. He is gone forever.

Later that week, Rammeg, his father, Scirburne and Willa asked to speak with Margaret. She put down her sewing, stood, and entered the hall. Only when she was in her place at the head table was she ready. She knew both what was coming and her answer. Rammeg Elder, Rammeg Younger's father, sought permission for his son to wed Willa, daughter of Scirburne. The fathers described the terms of the contract and stated they approved the match. "Willa and her dowry shall move to mine home, which Rammeg Younger shall inherit, as he is mine eldest son."

Margaret nodded recognition. "I shall consider your request and tell you mine decision soon, Rammeg."

Willa spoke up. "My lady, Leoma need not dance barefoot at our wedding feast; she is a widow now."

Margaret took a breath to calm herself. "Well I know that." Margaret tightened her clasped hands and then loosed them. "Rammeg, while you wait, you shall behave with perfect decorum. You shall not touch Willa, not even to keep her from falling. When you stand or sit near each other, keep two arms lengths between you. Always be within sight and sound of a wedded adult. If I see or know of any infractions from mine rules, you two shall wait longer or I might refuse to give permission. I want to see you are serious in your desire for Willa as a person, not just because of her purity. Honor her with your respect at all times; I shall be watching."

Scirburne interposed, "We deeply appreciate your considering our request, my lady." He gave his daughter a warning glance. "We await your decision." They left quickly.

Four marriages this summer. All good ones, but where is mine? Will I ever have one? If they have a son, the king needs me no more. What kind of man will he reward with mine hand and mine land? If she knows he thinks to replace her with me, what might she do? Should she birth a daughter, I am for the forest. No path is a good one. Come August I am out of choices, mine freedoms gone, mine power over, mine future decided. I will let God decide what becomes of me. Your will, Oh God, in all things, even this. Margaret sat alone for a time before she forced herself to return to her stool and sew in the warm sunlight.

Pentecost Sunday began with High Mass. Father wore a red woolen scarf around his neck to symbolize the fire the Holy Spirit had lit within the apostles. Father's homily told the story from the Bible. He reminded everyone this day was the Church's birth date. He reminded them for over a thousand years the Church had stood against the dark and had saved all who believed in the Trinity and followed the Roman Catholic way. The service lasted over two hours.

The final day of the month, Reeve met with Margaret as she enjoyed her Sunday rest. "My lady, I have good news. Belleme is routed and has fled to Normandy. All his lands and wealth are forfeit to the Crown so decreed King Henry's Royal Court."

"Royal Court?"

"Two years ago the king established his own court and denied the Church control over matters related to the realm. He started it to charge Belleme with forty-five counts of breaking the law, including treason. The Archbishop of Canterbury is angry at losing so much power over the king and the realm; he again left England in self-imposed exile. King Henry cares not; the Archbishop of York supports him. His royal Highness is elated Belleme is gone,

The Church's leaders should know by now they cannot control Henry. No one can. "So for now we have three courts in the land? Saxon, Church, and Royal?"

"It appears so. The Church court may now only deal with matters related to clergy and the Church. Nothing else. The Saxons have also lost power. No longer is murder a personal matter to be settled by the families in one of their courts. King Henry decreed that, as everyone in his realm are his subjects, anyone who kills one of his people must answer for his crime in the Royal Court. Each shire's royal reeve investigates crimes and then send them for judgement to King Henry's first justiciar, Sir Roger of Salisbury.

So many changes. Saxon and Church courts diminished. A Royal Court ruling the land. With Belleme gone and the king paying off his brother to stay away, Henry is preparing England for his heir. Oh Lord, please give him one.

"Thank you for your news, Reeve. On the morrow, I will have Father announce the end of the Hure e Crie after Mass."

32

June

Margaret awoke with mixed feelings. She listened to Caitlin washing her face and hands and humming. *I am glad for you, mine friend, but also sad. Today I lose you. You have found your good match, even at twenty-two. Norman custom is not so kind. Mine chance for a good match will be gone at mine next birth date. At least I can watch you happy with your new life. Quiet mine thoughts; banish them this day. Help Caitlin prepare. This is her day. Not time for mine concerns.* Margaret rose and quickly dressed. Having washed her body and hair the previous evening, Caitlin donned the soft yellow garment Margaret had given her for Epiphany. With a serene expression and bright, happy eyes, Caitlin sat on a stool and Margaret fetched her bone comb and boar-hair brush. Their roles switched, Margaret was now maid to her friend. She commented, "Your hair is softer than I remember and sun lightened. Your red color has now sun glints in it."

Caitlin frowned. "Please say not red. We Irish are accused of having bad tempers because many of us have red hair. We are just strong willed, that is all."

Margaret parted Caitlin's hair from forehead to nape and started the first braid. "You hair will look darker in your braids." At Caitlin's "Good" and return to a happy look, Margaret asked, "What are the blossoms and greenery on your wedding rib?"

I was taken from home so young I remember not its name. I chose it because it is white and looks so nice against the greenery, which is called clover. I was taught the three leaves are for God, Jesus the Christ, and the Holy Spirit."

"I remember not you stitching it. When did you that?"

"I began mine stitchery after Cormac asked. I had sewed not a rib because I believed I would need it never." Caitlin caressed her sleeve where the thin strip of cream linen contrasted well with her gunna. She spoke almost in a whisper. "I sewed it sitting in Cormac's old house because I wanted not to distress you by having you watch me sew a rib when yours is unused." *I am glad you did. I cannot dissemble, and you know me too well, but you might have mistaken mine sadness at losing you to sadness over mine lack of a match.* Caitlin commented almost to herself. "I am a strange combination. Because I am not Norman, I cannot wear a bliaut, yet I may have long hair and wear braids as if I were a married one. I remember mine mother's clothes being plain, fitted and belted, but not decorated."

"You look lovely," declared Margaret as she finished Caitlin's second braid and tied it with a second strip length of Caitlin's sewn rib. "You lack but one item." With her back to Caitlin, Margaret lifted the lid on her marriage chest and hid her gifts behind her back as she returned. "Please stand, dear Caitlin." Margaret brought round a plain leather girdle with two leather loops from which Caitlin might hang keys, a scissors, and anything else she desired." This girdle is for every day," she said as she displayed it and then draped it over her left shoulder. She revealed the second one as she said, "This one is for today and whenever you wish to wear it." Sewn to a leather backing was a cream-colored linen strip with the similar stitchery as Caitlin's marriage rib.

"How knew you mine pattern?"

"When I told Cormac what I wanted to gift you, he let me peak at your stitchery."

"That sneak!"

"Who loves you. Note his expression as you walk toward him waiting at the church door. You will see how beautiful you are in his eyes." Margaret wrapped the girdle around Caitlin's waist and tied it loosely so it dropped to her hip bones. "Now you are the perfect bride for your Scotsman." Margaret hugged her former companion. "Dear Caitlin, doubt not mine joy for you this day. Believe I desire you and Cormac happy together for many years." Margaret touched her forehead to Caitlin's and added, "I promise to be with you as you deliver every child you birth. May each be healthy, brave, and strong. Happy marriage day!"

Caitlin hugged Margaret hard. "Thank you. Thank you for our home and everything in it. You are too good to us."

"I am only trying to match the goodness you have always shown me." Margaret kissed Caitlin's cheek and asked, "Are you ready? Shall we go now?"

The seventh day was the first Sunday of June, and the weather was fine. Outside the church door, Father conducted the service of questions, answers, and a blessing given in Latin, Saxon and Norman for all to understand. He entered before the bridal couple, who were followed by Margaret and everyone else. Mass was the same as every Sunday, but the joy and warmth in the room was infectious. After Mass, they feasted in the meadow. Caitlin asked Margaret to accompany her to be the first to enter her new home. They walked around the outside so Margaret could admire how well the logs fit together and the quality of the white chinking. Inside, Caitlin pointed to the door's iron hinges and the metal latches of the shutters. Everything was new, the wooden bed frame, the stone fireplace, the iron swings set in the stones, the pots, pans and dishes on shelves, and the other household goods. Margaret's official gift had been two goose-down, stuffed pillows. In her happiness, arms extended, Caitlin twirled and laughed and laughed. She thanked Margaret for her generosity; Margaret hugged her.

"Shall I sent Cormac to you?"

"Oh no. Not yet. The village women wish to prepare me and put me to bed. The men need to push Cormac into the house. They will stand outside, drink and make noise for hours. Cormac must throw coins at them to send them away. This is a custom I have hoped for all mine life."

"I am very happy for you, Caitlin. Thank you for letting me be the first to see your home. It feels cozy and looks complete. I will have Cleva or Alura deliver your things from the keep. They will be here when you return. Back to the meadow we go." From the edge of the village, Margaret looked toward the meadow. She tried hard not to cry. *Caitlin is gone.* Margaret blinked hard twice to stop her tearing. She watched Caitlin's returned to sit beside Cormac. He took her hand and gazed at her with loving eyes and a broad smile. At the edge of the meadow, Leoma walked about holding hands with Garwig and was laughing about something. *They are next. Be happy. This is what you wanted. Every building done, every crop and animal well tended, every couple wed. Come August, no matter what happens to me, this place is well set. The people in it are healthy, happy and looking toward a good future. I have seen to it. Now smile at everyone and be glad at what we have accomplished. How many Sundays left this month? If this is seven, then fourteen, twenty-one, and twenty-eight. I can count inside mine head now.* Margaret stepped into the meadow and watched three little girls holding hands and singing as they danced in a circle. *God, men want sons because they need heirs, but please grant me daughters as well. August is soon upon us; Your future for me will be set. Your will, Oh God, in all things. You know this time I mean it; I submit to Your will, Oh God. On the morrow, I am chatelaine and lord until mine future is set.*

At the next Sunday Mass, Father announced the marriage banns for Garwig and Leoma. *True, everything I have prayed for has happened, but now it is not enough. I want more; I want a husband and that life. Or I want mine freedom. This life in the middle is no longer enough.* Tapping her fingers against her hip, Margaret counted the Sundays while Father preached. *Six, mayhap seven Sundays of freedom left. Enjoy the day; enjoy each morrow. I have not many more days to be here.* After Mass, the couple held hands and beamed at the congratulations they received, first from Margaret and then from the whole estate.

Since her arrival home after Christmas court, Margaret had not ventured farther than the village. Jorgon had not only groomed Night; he was the only one to exercise and ride him. Margaret headed for the kitchen. *Since the king already knows where I am, he did not have to confine me to a secret place. I am a fool! I confined myself. I am going riding on the morrow and every day. I will invite Caitlin to a forest picnic. First, I must regain Night's affection. He will be vexed at mine neglect. Apples. He will like apples. No apples? Then carrots needs do.*

Six days later, four knights escorted Margaret and Caitlin to the stream for their midday picnic. Margaret insisted on carrying the food basket. She laid out the meal on a blanket: bread and butter, cold smoked pork, fresh vegetables, strawberries, a wine bottle filled with ale and mugs. The knights rode in four directions and faced outward to give them privacy. As they munched, they talked.

"Being alone with you is precious to me," began Margaret. "We may never have this time again."

"Nonsense, you are welcome to visit whenever you like. We will send Cormac away for a while."

"Are you glad you wed Cormac?"

"Yes. At first, I believed him puffed up on himself. The more he chased me the more I rebuffed him. When you were ill, he watched over me, made me eat and sleep. I realized he cares for me. Those blowhard things he had said and done were to impress me. What impressed me was the care he took of me; the attention he pays me."

"He is so charming. He likely expected to charm you. When you did not succumb, you became a challenge. By the time you changed your heart, you had captured his. Very smart of you, mine friend."

"I did not plan it. We just came to understand one another. I never thought I would wed. Now I am a bride—and at mine age." Caitlin quickly added, "Sorry."

Margaret shook her head. "Mine life is not what it was supposed to be. Four years ago I was betrothed with the marriage contract signed. Then Mother died, and everything changed." Margaret paused. "No help for it." She reminded herself aloud, "In some ways mine lot is even better. Now I have land, coin, people I care for and people who care for me. I make mine own decisions. I have much for which to be grateful. I remind myself daily." *Yet I know something is wrong with me. With Eustace, I could have still run the estate as I wished. With Cavel, I would have had a man to rule knights and fight to keep me safe, but having healthy children was questionable. Andre, not Andre. Never a man like him. I will have no choice if the king chooses. I must be practical; I must be obedient and subservient every moment and work for friendliness. With William I might have had love. Hope no more; love is gone. When I served the queen in Forest Keep, she said that marriage is about alliances and wealth. Think only I will get respectability, and he will get wealth.* Margaret sighed. *Hope for that and pray it is enough.*

Caitlin watched Margaret looking at the ground and thinking sad thoughts. She called her back. "With Garwig and Leoma, we will have three weddings in three months."

Margaret finished a strawberry before she answered. "Mayhap four. Rammeg Younger wants Willa. I am making them wait."

"Why?"

"Leoma did not have a true wedding, just a gallows ceremony. I want her to have hers before her younger sister. Scirburne understands. I care not if Rammeg and Willa do."

"They understand. I heard talk."

"What are they saying?" Margaret need not add "in the village." She knew Caitlin understood.

"Some say you favor Leoma too much." Caitlin waited for a denial, which did not come. "Most think you are doing the right thing. Willa has always had eyes for Rammeg. The moment he abandoned Leoma, Willa stood before him so he noticed her. She knew what he wanted. She thinks him very handsome and well set with

Rammeg Elder's property."

I had Mother so Cecily took Father. Has competition between sisters always been thus? Could I have been such a younger sister? "Such a match," sighed Margaret. "He gets a pretty virgin; she gets good looks and a house. Seems rather superficial to me. Where are the matched hearts, the minds that meet each other?"

"You still dream of such things? Most people wed for practical reasons."

Margaret probe in turn. "Did you wed Cormac just because he asked? Do you care for him?

"I did not foresee how much he cares for me. I have learned I care for him too. Ask not how much; that I keep to myself."

Margaret rose and picked up the basket.

Caitlin's concern was audible. "What are you about? Where are you going?"

"I brought supplies in case mine courses came. I am bringing them with me into the wood. I will stay within shouting distance and return anon."

Good story. I know mine courses are not yet due. She located the lightning-blasted tree stump with its hollow core she remembered seeing before. From the bottom of the basket, she lifted the garments she had prepared, added the kitchen knife she had snatched, the fish hook and line she had requested from Scirburne, and two flint rocks. She stuffed the items into an old pair of boots; she pushed her escape items deep into the hole. *The dark, dirty clothes look part of the tree. No casual observer or traveler will spot what I hide. Now I am ready to disappear into the forest and live among Saxons should she birth another daughter.* Margaret looked into the trees ahead and imagined a three-sided hut leaning against a tall, sheltering oak. She imagined a nearby stream large enough to supply eels and fish. She saw herself cooking them on sticks over a small fire. Margaret returned with a smile and reported she had been wrong.

Margaret and Caitlin returned late afternoon to discover the villeins had set a feast in the meadow. The village women had brought dishes to share; Cook had outdone herself with the number she had brought. Duone proudly announced to anyone who came near he had dug the pit for the roast pig. Aldcot kept a firm grasp on Haelum so other children could take turns holding Lady Margaret's hands as she walked around the food table, marveling at everything. Each time she leaned over and sniffed a dish and grinned, its maker beamed with pride. Margaret conferred with her knights; they nodded agreement. *Norman and Saxon mixed is what I want. No rank, no ceremony.* Margaret sat at a table with villein families. The knights separated and sat with the Saxons. Several surprised themselves at their enjoyment at sitting with others of another peoples, a different rank.

After the meal, they gathered up the leavings for snacking later. Midsummer night was fast arriving. Saxons went for their musical instruments, drums, horns, and other noise-making devices. Children marched about banging together spoons or wooden sticks and laughing at each other. Everyone waited for dark so they could light the fire.

All day Margaret had been in the company of others. Yet, she felt acutely alone. Shadows whispered inside her. *No matter how many people I keep around me, I am still alone. This night I have company as we await the sun, but on the morrow night I will sleep alone. I always will. Face it: I am going to die alone.* Margaret climbed the ladder to the palisade walkway as if it were a gallows. She watched Saxons and Normans alike celebrate into the night. Before she rejoined her people, she visited Night. *Shortest night of the year this may be, but it is too long for me. Would that I could sleep through it, sleep until the future is decided for me. Which path? Forest or church? Whichever it is, I will leave behind this happy place and mine own happiness with it. Night, you are fortunate to be a horse and not a woman.* Even though Margaret pet and spoke soft words, Night was as restive as her mood was dark.

Sunday was first day after midsummer night, and all rested. Others assumed her behavior was a normal reaction, a letdown after the celebration. The second day they tolerated her mood. The third they started to worry. No food Nearra presented to the dais table enticed Margaret to eat more than a taste. Margaret met offers of sword practice with a shrug of denial. Not even offers to go riding elicited more than a head shake. Everyone decided; something was wrong with their lady.

That evening Roussel attempted conversation with Margaret. She turned the talk toward him. "I am truly sorry you have been forced to stay here so long," Margaret began. Roussel just smiled. She continued, "By mine count, sirrah, sixteen months is a long time to be gone from your position in the king's corps d' elite." Margaret used the familiar address very quietly so as not to embarrass the knight, "Will the king have forgot your good service with such a long absence?"

"I send him occasional reports to remind His Royal Highness we three still serve him. Father Manntun writes them and our sentries send them to the king with passersby on the main road. From the King's Inn, His Royal Highness's own messengers deliver them."

"Sirrah, when you next write to His Royal Highness, you must inform him that here you serve hard duty. Write to him going to war would have been easier than living with me." Margaret nodded her head through her last statement. "He will believe you."

Surprised, Roussel roared with laughter. The hall was shocked into silence; he had not laughed since his arrival. "I dare say he will!" retorted the knight after he had composed himself. She gave him a wan smile. Margaret looked at the man kindly and asked him about his day. She retired to the keep well before dark.

The next evening Roussel was called away immediately after the meal had been cleared. Cachier and Gailard were on guard duty in the forest, and Syghelm had declined to join the men. Before Margaret could inquire of her knights what had been so urgent, they stood. One sealed the main entrance, another the kitchen door after Leoma slipped inside.

"I am your chaperone, my lady, and I will never reveal what I hear."

Eight men stood before the dais. Verel began. "My lady, they have chosen me to speak for all."

Margaret set her clasped hands upon the table and prayed she did not have a revolt. She was glad there was a table between them and her sword at her side. She looked for anger in each man's face but saw none.

"We know why you are unhappy. You are well past the age of marriage with no candidate in sight. Claude and Masselin heard the rumors running through Court. You are thinking of August and what might happen if the queen births a girl. You are afraid."

They know too much! How did they guess I want not to be queen?

"We have the solution. You have eight choices. Marry one of us. We care for you. It would honor any one of us to be chosen. We have sworn to support and defend the one you select. We make Father write the contract and speak the ceremony. No banns. We just do it."

Margaret eyes filled fast. *Have you any idea what we will suffer if we do this? You are so brave.* Only Margaret's clenched hands revealed her feelings. She smiled at each man. Margaret's knights errant thought she was making her choice. *No matter mine choice, we both die. Mayhap all of them. How should I begin? With the truth.* "That you would save me from a fate I want not tells me you are even more honorable than I thought you to be. Think most well of each one of you I do." She spoke each of their names. "What you are offering me is more than I deserve, but to accept would mean horrible deaths for the both of us. Mayhap beheading for the rest of you."

Masselin spoke up, "We will risk it."

"Were I to choose and marry without King Henry's permission, he will have that man hung, drawn, and quartered. And he will make me watch every moment of it."

Margaret imagined Verel hanging with his toes barely touching the ground until he was near dead. After they cut him down, she saw him laid on the ground and his limbs tied to four steeds. A butcher cut open his belly and pulled out his stomach and innards. She imagined his offending manhood cut from his body. And then, at the moment before death, they struck the horses so they bolted. She saw Veres's limbs ripped from his body. She heard his screams. Margaret shuddered at such cruelty.

She said, "After the king would force me to watch that deadly punishment, he would make me watch each of you beheaded. Mine punishment would be last." *Thrown to a troop of men and used until I died bleeding from mine womanhood.* Tears spilled down her cheeks. "Each of you is precious to me. I will not have you killed. I cannot. I would rather suffer whatever is to be than to see you harmed."

Margaret shook her head. "We cannot defy him in any way. I beg you. Do nothing to draw his ire, for it is great. He can do whatever he wills; he is the king."

"It breaks our hearts to see you sad and fearful," revealed Claude. "If not this, what may we do to help you?"

Margaret wiped her cheeks with her sleeves. She took a deep breath and tried to sigh away her fears. She took another. "Let us enjoy each day. On the morrow I will return to sword practice. I do like it. And I want to ride every afternoon. I am tired of sewing, the accounts book, and mine duties. I have been sitting too much, thinking too much. When the weather is fine, we will go outside. Every morrow, I will ask, 'When is sword practice?' and 'Who rides with me?'" Margaret smiled at the thought of play and no work. To her requests she added, "Please?"

The men looked at each other and in silent agreement bowed to her and said as one, "As you wish, my lady."

"Each day you play," said Hughes.

"We will escort you," promised Sauville.

"Be forewarned. At sword practice, expect me to come at you full force."

"Good!" said several. Demetre added, "We are safer if you do. Half measures are more likely to hurt or cut both you and us. Full force from us as well."

"I am happier already," said Margaret as she beamed at her men. *I do so love you.*

I dare not tell you, for you will misconstrue mine meaning. Instead, I will give you a merry face. She did so.

Leoma slipped out of the hall unnoticed.

33

July

Thursday was a rush of activities. After a quick morning meal, Margaret charged to the practice field and worked so hard wet curls ringed her face; her armpits soaked her gown. She cared not because, after she dined, she rode all afternoon. Margaret retired to the bath she had ordered. Because she lacked time to wash her hair, she tied it at her nape with one of her rib gifts. Tired from her exertions, Margaret fell into a happy, dreamless sleep. The next day she repeated her self-set schedule, but took the time to bathe and wash her hair. *Third wedding coming. Such a match! She was ravaged and made a widow. His love abandoned him for wealth and position. He wooed her slowly while Nearra guarded her. They are so brave to choose love and to marry. He is protective, and she has a warm heart. They are well matched in dispositions. The way they gaze at each other makes one think they have never had a sorrow in their lives. I wish them happy.* Margaret chuckled to herself. *I wager they have a child before a year passes.* She bounced down the keep stairs, called her girls to follow, and left to sup in the hall.

On Sunday, 5 July, Garwig and Leoma's wedding followed the same pattern as the first two. Leoma had expressed a desire for a more restrained celebration like Father's and Gytha's. "After all, I am a widow," she had said to several women. Everyone followed her desires with one exception. That evening the villagers just happened to be milling about near Garwig's home. They laughed and talked but did not sing. Soon they left, and the village became quiet. Garwig need toss no coins, and Leoma was pleased at the compromise the villagers had made for them. Early the next morning Garwig walked his bride to the bailey gate. As agreed, Leoma continued to bake bread while she trained Carlia or until she was with child.

Margaret had planned a surprise for the second July Sunday. After Mass, Father announced the first banns for Rammeg Younger and Willa. Anticipating the couple, Margaret waited in the church yard. Silently Rammeg pulled his forelock; Willa curtsied deeply. When Margaret reminded them her rules still applied, they nodded. She walked away but turned back to watch as they accepted the villeins' congratulations.

I have done all I could to see everyone well and happy. Dear God, I pray you do the same for me. Your will, Oh God, in all things. Goselyn and Denemaere approached; they were too old to hold their lady's hands, but they walked and visited with Margaret as they escorted her to the bailey gate.

"Thank you," Margaret told the pair, "I hope we do this again." She watched them curtsey and pull a forelock before they left. *Children. They feel things adults miss. Bless you for distracting me from a sad thought. Smile and be glad for Nearra's fine cooking.* She waved at the guards as she passed through the gate.

The third crop of alfalfa had been as lush and heavy with grain as had been the first. They had piled both barn lofts high with winter fodder. Cormac suggested before they cut the final crop they spend the workers' July hours cutting trees into wooden slabs and building another grain bin. Margaret agreed and left for sword practice. Cormac ordered rushes cut for the barrack's thatched roof. Because this July was so hot, the villeins harvested the rushes early in the day or before Vespers. After Margaret dined, she passed on riding to inspect her crops. As she walked, she stroked the tops of the wheat heads and watched the stalks spring upright even as the tops bent over because they were so full.

In this heat they will soon ripen. Despite all the ale we are consuming and all the feasts we have shared, I still have grain from last year. Before I add the new crops, I will have the old grain swept out of the bins and stored in sacks to be used first. Mayhap that will forestall rot.

Margaret stopped at the edge of the knights' practice field. *They have long killed the grasses. How the horses kick up dirt!* Margaret turn her face as a gust carried dust her way. She watched the men dash at the pel stake in the center. *I suppose they must work their horses in the heat as well as in fair weather, so they remain strong and are ready to fight in any conditions.* A knight slashed at the pole, causing it to vibrate and wave. *The pel is nicked and weakened after over a year of attacks; they should replace it. I will suggest it to Verel when next I see him. The other practice devices still look sturdy.* Margaret smiled as Hughes, Sauville and Demetre waved their blades at her. She waved back before she turned toward the bailey. Behind her she heard the pounding of hooves and the clashing of wooden swords.

Midweek, Roulin called into the hall and interrupted Margaret's meal, "My lady, a Jew with two wagons is at our lane entrance. Says his name is Samuel."

"Please have Night saddled. I will see him."

Margaret rode out of the trees between Roulin and Hughes toward Giraud, who was guarding the lane. She noted the wagons were the same ones she had seen on Market Day two years ago when King Henry had hidden her and the queen in Forest Keep. The same young man in black was holding the harnesses on the second wagon's donkeys. Samuel stood before the side of his wagon.

"God give you a good day, Samuel, the jeweler."

"And to you, my lady." He bowed and rose.

"You have stopped at the entrance to mine estate."

"The donkeys are parched in this heat and can go no further. I am hoping you know a stream where they may drink and we may tarry."

Margaret smiled to herself at Samuel's cleverness. *Their claiming need requires I do the Christian thing and aid them.* Giraud, Roulin and Hughes looked dismayed but Margaret ignored them. "Have you goods to sell?"

"We have, my lady." Samuel bowed, and Margaret spotted the small, black round cap fastened to his crown of thick black hair salted with gray strands.

"Then you may tarry downstream from the village to water your animals and stay the night. Trade and sell you may this day, but you will leave before dawn."

"My lady, we thank you for your kindness."

Margaret turned Night and followed Hughes to the meadow's edge. There she pointed where Samuel's party could camp and left for the bailey. Roulin rode to Samuel's wagon and gave him further instructions. Villeins stopped work and stared at the strangers. Margaret sent for Reeve to speak to the travelers. From the palisade walkway, she watched Felamaere approach Samuel and speak to him before returning to the villeins, who were still staring at Samuel and his family. Margaret looked beyond the meadow to the stream's edge. The two men were bargaining with a few villeins when Father Manntun stomped up the ladder and to her side.

"That lot murdered our Jesus! How dare you let them on your land! They defile us with their presence and pollute our water."

"They are drinking and eating downstream of us," retorted Margaret. Then she softened her tone. "Father Manntun, Her Royal Highness Queen Matilda instructed me to be good to Jews. She said by being kind to Jews, we Christians show them our beliefs are better than theirs. Our kindness and charity will convince them to leave their hated ways and join us in following God's true church. Would you have me defy the queen, undo her good works toward Jews, and be the one who fails to get them to convert to our beliefs?" Father Manntun harrumphed as he thought how best to respond. "Father, I do not want to answer to Her Royal Highness should she learn I have disobeyed her. Would you?"

"I will not sleep this night for guarding us."

"For that I am most grateful, Father. I ordered them to leave before dawn, so they will not disturb your saying Mass. I wish you to leave them strictly alone; let another in some other place who more familiar with Jews speak to them about converting. Thank you for protecting us."

Margaret turned and descended the ladder. *I am getting coins and seeing what they have. Mayhap I can purchase Epiphany gifts and reduce mine stitchery. While I bargain, I can learn how Samuel and his family are faring and if they need help. I dare not reveal I believe Samuel is a good man. Father would never forgive me, and he would give me terrible penances to punish me for thinking well of a Jew.*

From Samuel and his family, Margaret acquired four bolts of common cloth, the hides of two cows for shoes and boots, and four spools of thread for sewing and mending. Samuel claimed the three kitchen knives he offered had been forged by skilled workers in a place on the Iberian peninsula called Toledo, which is why they were triple the price of Gloucester blades. He promised they would hold their sharpness better than any other blade. Margaret considered her dowery chest and bought only one. She politely refused the silver rings and gold bracelets he offered. Verel stood beside her the whole time, so she could not ask Samuel anything personal.

"Thank you for stopping, Samuel. We needed these things. Should you pass this way again a year from now, I hope you will have more that we require." *I am warning you not to stop more often than that. I know not how you will be received after I am gone. Do you get mine meaning?*

Samuel's silent nod told her he did. Margret took Verel's arm and turned toward the bailey. Hartun and Scandy carried her purchases and followed. On the way to Mass the next morning, Margaret glanced toward the spot where Samuel's wagons had been. It was empty.

The third Sunday was the nineteenth day, and Margaret enjoyed walking into the village with a boy and girl in hand. She chatted with Raedaelf, Ifig, and Cadda before she turned to leave.

Three days later, Margaret was on the practice field with Sirs Sauville and Claude, when Claude stopped to look over her head. "Hughes is escorting a priest, my lady. You may want to halt practice."

Margaret lowered her practice sword and turned. She squinted against the sunlight and used her hand to make a shade over her eyes. *Not Father Gregory. Somebody new.* The priest waved, dismounted, and led his horse as he walked toward her.

"Raymond!" screeched Margaret as she dropped the blade and ran. She jumped into her brother's arms and hugged him hard. "Oh Raymond, I was bereft thinking I might never see you again!" She kissed his cheek. At his hearty laugh and hard hug, she hugged and kissed him again before he set her down. Margaret grabbed his free hand. "Stay a week. Stay a month! Oh, Raymond, stay forever. I have missed you so."

"I thought you had forgot me in all your adventures."

"No," she averred. "I have just been busy, very busy." She tugged his hand and walked him toward the bailey as she asked, "Whence come you? Why are you in priest garb? Are you really a priest? How long can you stay? Where are you bound? Have you news of Charles and Cleanthe? How fares their estate? Is Uncle Theobaud well? What of Cecily?"

"Whoa! Halt! One at a time and after a mug of ale. I thirst."

"Forgive me Raymond." She turned and called to the approaching Hartun, "Ale in the hall for both of us." Margaret swung their clasped hands as she grinned and begged, "Like when we were young? Just a few steps. Please Raymond."

Her brother laughed at Margaret before he complied. Together they swung their hands to the rhythm of their skipping. The gate sentries looked down in astonishment at their lady acting like a child. The pair stopped under the gate and walked the rest of the way to the hall. Daelton intercepted the pair and took the palfrey to the barn.

"You did remember what I taught you."

"Indeed, I did, though I have not skipped in years."

"And now you cannot because you are a priest and must be serious?"

"Just so."

"Sit upon the dais with me as mine honored guest, Father Raymond." Margaret indicated the place she had been saving for her lord. She poured full mugs and placed his before him. Raymond gulped his, so Margaret poured him a second mug before she drank from hers. She turned her head, placed her left hand at her ear and explained, " I talk this way when I want not others to hear or to read mine lips. Some family matters should remain private. Have you good news?"

Raymond mirrored her and answered, "All mine news is good." At Margret's request, he began with himself. "While Father declined, I decided to take up the Church and began studying in earnest with Father. I knew Charles would inherit and have no place for me. I was ordained in Gloucester after the new year. The bishop wrote to Cluny for me. I have been accepted! I am on mine way there now."

"Raymond, I am so proud for you. Cluny, the most famous abbey on the continent. You will go far."

Raymond chuckled. "The bishop studied at Cluny. He warned of their tradition. Any priest who wants to study there must start with labor; most likely I will be told to scrub floors and empty piss pots for a year before they assign me a mentor."

"Start at the bottom. Like me learning to be a chatelaine." At hearing Raymond's chuckle, Margaret commented, "Hearing you laugh again cheers me so. Those last few years at home you barely smiled, never laughed, and seemed but a shadow of your true self."

"You know how hard were those last years, especially after Mother died. In those days, no one laughed or sang or told stories." At Margaret's "true" he continued, "Home is much more pleasant now; Cleanthe makes it so. Home is again clean, well managed, and a warm place. She has softened Uncle Theobaud, and he is much kinder. She ordered a rocking chair and placed it near the keep fireplace; he naps there almost every day."

"And Charles?"

"He is besotted. She is the perfect wife; she never raises her voice, never corrects or naysays him, always looks at him as adoringly as he does her."

Good advice, dear brother, I shall remember it and do it should I have the chance.

Raymond paused to give her the next good news. "Charles has freed me. he no longer needs me to be his heir now that Cleanthe has given him a son."

"A son!"

"Last month. He looks like his father but has his mother's hair color."

"Charles Younger."

"What else would he name his heir?"

"Healthy?" asked Margaret with worry in her voice. At Raymond's assurances, Margaret said, "I am so glad. I must sew something for him. Mayhap have Rammeg Elder carve toys for him." She spotted Hartun at the servants' door. "Please find Father Manntun; invite him to join us to dine and to meet mine brother, Father Raymond. Or he may like to wait until after he dines with his family." As she watched Midryth and Cyne bringing in the trays of clean bowls and dinner boards, Margaret again turned to Raymond. She whispered, "What know you of Cecily?"

Raymond answered without whispering, "Charles said his last letter reported her good progress. Several suitors have already asked after her, so she works harder now to improve. Charles thinks she might be ready for marriage by Christmastide and for cert by spring."

"Good. I hope she marries well and is happy in it."

If she marries before me, as her unmarried older sister, I needs dance barefoot at her marriage dinner. Oh how that would please her! But I care not as long as I do get a husband. When, Henry, when? Or is it if I marry? God, only you know the answer to that.

Margret proudly introduced Father Raymond to her knights and ordered an extra ration of ale in honor of his visit. She listened and spoke not when the two priests met and conversed about Raymond's training, the Bishop of Gloucester, what Raymond knew of Cluny, and more. She walked her brother about the bailey to introduce her staff, to show him her gardens and buildings, and to brag—just a little—of her accomplishments. As Raymond was family, he slept on the second floor of the keep. The next morning, the pair observed the villeins harvesting oats from the palisade walkway. After they dined, they walked the village and Margaret pointed to her animals in the southeast meadow. Raymond asked to spend the rest of the afternoon with Father Manntun, so Margaret excused herself and went in search of Rammeg Elder to order toys for her nephew. Raymond said Mass the next morning. Margaret beamed at him the whole time and spoke the refrains and prayers by rote memory and no sense. At breaking their fasts, Raymond reported his plans.

"I will stay two more days, Sister dear, but I must depart Monday. I am for London and the first boat across the Narrow Sea

I can employ. I dare stay no longer; I must be in Cluny before the middle of next month."

"Would you could stay longer, but I understand. Let us spend our time together doing whatever you like. Choose and we will do it."

Teary eyed, Margaret and Raymond parted with hugs. Each promised the other to write to keep each informed of their lives, and never again to lose contact with each other. Margaret handed him a small bag of coins to make his journey more comfortable and told him of the King's Inn. She and three knights escorted him down the lane. At the king's road, Demetre accompanied Raymond as far as the King's Inn. At the turn in the road, Raymond stopped to wave at Margaret before he disappeared. To alleviate her sadness, Margaret rode to the practice field, dismounted, and demanded a practice sword. Poor Roulin was the object of her full attacks and mad charging for the rest of the morn.

Margaret returned to her routines, but when she was alone, she talked to herself. Weeding the garden, she mumbled until Scandy arrived to inquire what she wanted. After dismissing him, she pulled her lips between her teeth. That night she spoke her prayers in a cheerful voice. She ended with her gratitudes. *July as been wonderful month. It began with a wedding and there is another on Sunday. I have practiced in the morn and rested during the heat of the day. I swear, Oh Lord, I can hear the crops growing. I can hear the stalks groaning because the grain heads are so heavy. I love walking the fields and feeling the full heads of grain. I love riding before we sup and listening to the songs and stories of the men. The village is complete, all the huts white-washed, and all the thatching repaired or replaced. South of the village, the Saxons have even completed the bridge so the animals will no longer walk through the stream. Thank you for sending Raymond to me. If it be your will, Oh Lord, I will see Rammeg Younger and Willa wed on Sunday and see the harvest begin. Please see how grateful I am to you, Oh Lord, for all your blessings.*

Margaret crawled into bed.

34

※

Royal Arrival

The second day of August Rammeg and Willa were happily wed. Again the meadow filled with tables, food, villeins, and Normans; the meadow was alive with talk, laughter, song and dance. Children dashed about, and Margaret smiled at their antics. Margaret appeared as happy as she had for the three previous matchings; she dined, visited, and walked among the groups. She sat with Father Manntun, Gytha, and Linton Younger, who was now called just Linton.

"Four weddings this summer," observed Margaret as she nibbled a raw carrot. "We are indeed blessed by God's bounty toward us. The new grain bins are ready and the stable addition is complete. The barracks' roof is finished. What we need next is a successful harvest."

Father said, "God is rewarding our prayers and good behavior."

"The sun and rain have cooperated. Soon we will harvest the ripened grains."

Father added, "We will continue to pray for God's blessings upon our endeavors. Much might happen between now and Michaelmas."

Margaret only nodded. *Matilda will give birth within a fortnight and seal both our fates. Dear God, please give me the strength to bear whatever comes next.* Margaret appeared to carry no worries; but, despite her smiles and at looking to be at her ease, her heart felt heavy. Late that night, Margaret stood beside a window slit. She looked toward a sliver of stars.

Oh God, she thinks me froward. She attacked me before the Court; at Christmastide she refused to see me. I am abandoned and hated. I can do nothing to change any of it. God, I have but one Sunday, mayhap two, of freedom left. We both know mine future. Should she deliver a son, I have hope for a marriage. If she delivers another daughter, I must use mine hidden garments and flee into the forest. I will know not what the king does. If no one can find me, I will be no part of her downfall. Please God, give her a son, a healthy one, so we both may have a future. Margaret wiped away a tear. I know. I have no power over mine fate. Your will, oh God, in all things. But for both our sakes, please grant mine plea. Margaret crept back into her bed and stared at the canopy above her.

Wednesday Margaret was in the lane returning from her afternoon ride with Demetre, Cachier, and Giraud when she first heard the church bell. *How long it peals will reveal boy or girl.* The peals continued as Night's hooves pounded over the bailey bridge. She was so relieved she was about to cry. *We are saved! Thank you, God!* Then she worried. *Is he healthy? Have all the poisoners been caught and punished? Will others try to kill him too? How will they keep him safe? Oh God, please keep him safe.*

The villagers cleared a path for her. The bell was still ringing. Margaret fairly jumped off Night in her excitement. Caitlin sidled behind Margaret, put a hand on her shoulder and whispered, "Halt tears. Calm yourself. Overreact not. Be only as happy as the villagers. What you do will be reported. Act like the others, or the royals may punish you."

Margaret gave the barest nod. *Slow breaths. Half smile. Breathe. Breathe.* As she pet Ferrant to settle the excited dog and herself, she announced, "This day is for rejoicing. May the prince be healthy and live a long, happy life," Margaret announced. "May England prosper in peace under King Henry's reign." Then she looked for Father Manntun, "Father, have you a service to celebrate this long-awaited day?"

The priest motioned everyone to follow him into church. There he led his congregation in a series of prayers: for God's continued blessings, for King Henry, Queen Matilda and their new son, for England, for peace, and for a heavy harvest.

At supper Margaret's knights thanked her for ordering two additional rations of ale. "To honor the prince's birth," was all she dared say. *I could cry with relief, but not until I am alone.* She kept her smile casual, talked easily with Roussel, and appeared only as happy as the rest. But in her heart, Margaret was rejoicing. *She is safe as long as is their son. He will guard them well. Baptized Saturday? Sunday more likely. Too many important people to invite. Mayhap now I am free to marry, if they remember me. They will celebrate for at least a month. Married before mine seventeenth birth date? Pray for that.* Margaret watched her men talk and laugh. *I pray mine future lord will keep you all. Each of you is a good man, and I love you. I wonder how many of you will stay. All I pray.* That night Margaret hid her tears of relief in her pillow so no one below would hear her. After a long cry, she blew her nose into a rag and let it burn in the brazier's embers so no one would find it. She slipped out of bed and knelt. She was a long time expressing her relief and thanks to God.

Monday, the tenth day of August. Margaret had just finished breaking her fast when a royal messenger arrived in the company of four knights. They strode into the hall as if they were the royals they represented.

"Lady Margaret, His Royal Highness, Henry King of England, commands your immediate presence in Winchester. You are to report to Her Royal Highness, Queen Matilda, in all haste. They will provide for you. We leave anon."

"I will be ready at dawn," was Margaret's immediate reply. Then she asked, "Even a lady's maid?" Margaret considered propriety. "I will not have one on the way," she reported.

"Your sword should be sufficient," retorted the messenger. Then he ordered, "You will pack now, my lady, and leave anon. Her Royal Highness requires you bring your best clothes and your wedding rib. Pack. We must be eight miles from here and at King's Inn before dark."

I am trapped. Or am I? I still have my hidden garments. If he marries me to a man I hate, I will survive until I return and use them then. I still have a choice. So the king wants to be rid of me as soon as possible. I want to be rid of him as well. So be it.

Please God, let him be a good man. "Cormac, you had best take Ferrant to the barn and secure him, or he will try to follow me." She whispered whom she needed and finished aloud with, "I will meet with you and them in the keep." She told the king's men, "I will be ready anon." Margaret ordered ale and boards of bread and cheese for the messenger and his knights. She stepped off the dais, grasped Ferrant's collar, and passed him to Cormac. She looked at her men and nodded to them. She left for the bailey and met Syghelm.

As they took the keep steps, Syghelm said, "I will await your return, my lady. Go elsewhere and need me, you have but to send word by any Saxon, and I will appear."

At the keep ladder, Margaret turned and smiled. "I am the only woman in the realm whose guardian angel carries an axe."

Syghelm smiled back. "True." He left when he saw others in the bailey walking their way.

As Margaret splashed cold water on her face to clear her head, her thoughts roiled. *Show Caitlin where I hid the chest key. Remind Cormac to pay everyone so the chest holds only what mine future lord may have. If Henry tries to force me into a convent to keep me available, I will ask for a marriage. I no longer care to whom. I must be married to escape his plotting.* Margaret removed her shoes to slosh one foot at a time into the bucket. *If he refuses, I will stall and send for Syghelm. He could get me away, mayhap to his homeland. He would save me from the king, of that I am cert. Night comes with me; I will never leave him behind.* Toweling dry her second foot, Margaret nodded at Caitlin as she strode through the doorway.

"I heard." Caitlin examined what Margaret had placed on the bed. She picked up the traveling clothes and boots and placed them on a stool. "Now you have enough room in the satchels. Where is the marriage rib?" asked Caitlin, referring to the rib of fine linen Margaret began stitching on her seventh birth date. The border was a blue wavy line. The flowers were white daisies with yellow centers, a reference to her name, with greenery weaving through the blooms.

"I have been embroidering on that rib for so many years it is long enough to decorate two bliauts and mantles," commented Margaret. "Now where did I put it?"

"In the wedding chest you have been filling, atop the bed linens," Caitlin reminded her. Caitlin shook her head at Margaret's "Oh yes!" as she watched Margaret bolt for the corner. "Calm yourself, girl. Hand your band to me to pack it for you. Now don your socks and traveling clothes."

Margaret brushed her feet of rushes and dressed. She removed the chest key from its hiding place and held it for Cormac. Sitting upon a stool, she sighed deeply at the old ritual of Caitlin brushing her hair. Margaret's disheveled locks, once chopped to her nape, hung well past her shoulder blades.

"Dearest Margaret," Caitlin began, "If they marry you, you may first travel to his home to meet his family or to begin in his household. You needs make plans for this place in your absence."

"Reeve serves until January, so he will lead the harvest and supervise preparations for winter. Cormac will continue to keep the accounts book and will keep order in the bailey." Margaret thought more before she added, "Oh, no! King Henry will dismiss Sirs Roussel, Giraud and Cachier if I am married. Who shall lead the men? I promised to pay them early if I am married before Michaelmas; I must do that anon. When Cormac arrives, I must instruct him to pay them to Michaelmas, even though it is weeks away."

"I am pleased you have remembered," said Caitlin.

"And you. Cormac can better manage the hall if you and he sit at the head table with the knights' leader and Father when he chooses. Will you, Caitlin? In addition to supervising the kitchen. Please help keep order, for men behave better with a woman watching."

Caitlin had expected Margaret wanted something from her. "I agree to supervise the kitchen, to sit for meals and continue to heal. But I insist on sleeping in mine own bed with mine husband. That I

416

will not give up. We will meet your knights and the bailey staff each morning at Mass."

"Agreed." Margaret sent Alura to give instructions to her men to meet and vote to make one of them their leader should the king recall Roussel, Gaylord, and Cachier. *A very Saxon thing to do—vote for a leader rather than have me choose. Also, to protect their pay and to give them the freedom to leave should they want to do so, I needs give the men their coins. I have no time; Cormac must do that after I leave.*

Cormac walked in carrying the accounts book. Margaret handed Cormac the chest key and showed him two places where he might hide it. "You must pay the knight who leaves with me immediately. I want not he should have to return here for his pay if he will not serve mine lord, should I get one. Please make everyone take their pay from the chest, even you two. I want not a greedy lord to cheat you. If I am gone long, remember to pay the tithe and taxes at Michaelmas. I expect I will have a lord when I return, and he will demand an accounting. "

"Of course, my lady. I promise he will be satisfied with mine work."

"Good. I want him to keep you, Cormac."

Caitlin handed the two packed satchels to her husband and cocked her head toward the door; he left.

"Oh no. I forgot. The toys for Charles Younger. And mine sewn gifts."

"I will see to them. Father Manntun will write a letter in your name. I will have the package delivered for you."

Margaret gave Caitlin a quick hug. "Thank you, Caitlin. What else have I forgot."

417

Caitlin held Margaret close. In a calming tone, she said, "Worry not. I will see to whatever needs be done. Fetch your mantle, dear girl."

Margaret donned her mantle and fastened the brooch. She hugged Caitlin hard. "I am more grateful than I have words. You have been with me since mine first breath; I will miss you terribly. Whatever happens, wherever I may go, remember I love you and pray for your wellbeing and happiness."

Caitlin placed her hands upon Margaret's shoulders and kissed her forehead. "I give you mine blessing. Were your mother here, she would give hers as well. Remember your mother's pride in you. May our blessings comfort you, whatever may come, whoever he may be."

Margaret sent Caitlin ahead. At the doorway she turned to commit the room to memory before she stepped onto the landing. *I am closing a part of mine life with this door. Please God, may mine new days be as good as this part has been.* On the main floor, she nodded recognition to the line of serving girls before the fireplace. Margaret thanked Sirs Roussel, Gailard, and Cachier for keeping her safe. "His Royal Highness is wise to have sent each of you into his special troop." At their smiles and nods, Margaret smiled back. "I know not how much longer you stay, but please remember you will always be in mine prayers. I pray you safe from injury, successful in your endeavors, and happy in your life after your service to His Royal Highness."

Roussel spoke for them all. "Serving you was our pleasure, my lady. You worked hard and made this estate successful. You will keep well any estate your new lord owns. We will tell anyone who asks what a good woman you are." The three knights bowed in unison and left for the hall.

Margaret spoke with Sir Verel and Felamaere about their continuing their duties. She informed them of Cormac and Caitlin's parts in maintaining the estate. She concluded, "No matter how long I am absent, I expect you to do well. If I get a lord, I want him impressed at what we have accomplished. Seventeen months ago I rode onto empty, wrecked land with starving villeins. Four couples have married, and I suspect we will see babes next year. Today I leave a safe, prosperous estate ready to fill the grain bins, and we have healthy, hard-working villeins."

"We will not disappoint you, my lady," promised Felamaere.

"I vow we knights will keep your estate and your people safe," Verel promised.

"Sir Verel, I have a special delivery for Her Royal Highness; I cannot carry it. Garwig has it. Might you send one knight with me to deliver it? At his nod, he turned and spoke to Cyne, who left the line and disappeared down the ladder.

Margaret drew her reeve aside and whispered, "Can you send word to the housekeeper of Lord Cai's home in Winchester? If the house is available, I want to wash off the dirt of the journey before I see the queen."

"Consider it done, my lady. If it is not available, I will have her hire you a safe home to fill your need."

"Thank you, Felamaere." Margaret and he returned to the group and formed a close circle with the others. *I dare not hug them. Try words.* "You are the best of friends, the best of knights, and the best of villeins I and this estate could have. I am proud of each of you, and I am so grateful to you. I am sad to leave you, and I will return as soon as I am able. Please repeat these words to mine men and mine villeins."

Margaret turned. Verel preceded her and held the ladder for her. At the keep gate, Margaret set her hand upon his left forearm as she strode toward the king's party already on their horses in the center of the bailey. Masselin was with them with two heavy sacks behind his saddle. Her knights stood at attention as she passed them. She startled Sauville when she stopped and extended her hand as she thanked him for all he had done for her. He shook her hand and wished Margaret a safe journey and a good end. Each man down the line also shook her hand and offered kind words as she spoke her farewell. Last was Syghelm who whispered, "If he is not worthy, remember mine axe is yours." Margaret succumbed to her desire and hugged the old man before she quickly walked away.

Night wore twin satchels on his flanks, and Jorgon held his head. *Now only he and I and Charles know. What can I say?* Margaret placed her hand over his. She smiled as she squeezed and whispered, "I am glad you are mine brother." Jorgon smiled back and nodded. At Margaret's familiarity with her hostler, the king's men scowled at her. Margaret scowled back. *I care not what you think. I will love mine brother all mine days.* "Please say fare thee well to Dena for me."

Jorgon offered his cupped hands and lifted Margaret to her saddle. The bailey staff stood in parallel lines near the gate as they watched their lady. Margaret tied herself to her saddle and sat tall. She took up reins she did not need because Night had felt her turn her head toward the gate and had turned himself. Margaret nodded left and right as Night walked between her people. She smiled at Duone as he waved and called, "Fare thee well, my lady." Margaret forced herself to smile left and right at her villeins lining the path. After leaving them, she gazed at her fields; she deeply inhaled the smells of the ripening crops. *Would that I could see you harvested.* She saw boys guarding the meadow of sheep and other livestock as the animals grazed in peace. When they waved to her, she waved back. The messenger and two knights rode ahead of Margaret with the other pair and Masselin following her.

Oh, William, he will not be you. A year and again a half. Too long to wait for a husband, and now I leave too soon for our harvest. I will ache for home. Mine, soon you will be mine no more. I pray their choice is worthy of all our work and worry. She knows I was Henry's alternative if she birthed another girl. Not mine doing. Not mine fault. What will she do to me when I arrive? To whom will she marry me off? She plots against me. Of that I am cert. Margaret stiffened her spine. *Look not back or I will cry.* Margaret lifted her eyes and blinked. She gazed at the beautiful arched canopy of deep-green leaves the oaks created over the lane they were entering. As the first shadow darkened Night's head, Margaret thought, *Now comes her revenge.*

Author's Notes

Henry is thrilled his heir, Prince William Adelin, is strong and healthy. The king is certain he will hold England and pass the crown to his son. King Henry feels more secure.

After charging Lord Robert de Belleme with breaking forty-five laws including treason, Henry chased him throughout England. He successfully stripped de Belleme of his allies and his lands. Defeated, Lord de Belleme fled to his estate in Normandy, but he kept the remains of his army with him. Robert Curthose still wants his brother's crown, but he remains on his Normandy estates and is quiet for now. Anselm, Archbishop of Canterbury, remains in self-imposed exile. He refuses to support Henry until the king agrees to permit the archbishop to choose the nation's bishops. Henry cares not because he thinks he does not need the archbishop.

Queen Matilda's position is safe now that she birthed Prince William. Exercising her newfound power, Matilda is making changes at Court.

The royals summoned Lady Margaret to Court and told her to bring her marriage clothes with her. She fears what will become of her.

About Early 12th Century England

Ale

In the 12th century and for centuries later, knowledge of germs was non-existent. Twelfth century practices of sanitation were few. Across Europe and England, animals drank, walked through, and eliminated in the streams in which people washed their clothes and from which people drank. People knew that drinking water was hazardous, but they did not understand why.

They had learned turning water into ale made the liquid safe to drink. In this era, ale was usually 1-2 percent alcohol, enough to kill the pathogens, but not strong enough to cause inebriation. One had to quaff pitchers of ale to become drunk, as Sir Andre did in this story.

To learn how the potency of 12th century ale tasted, I watered down one quarter of a cup of American beer from 5% alcohol using distilled water until the liquid was 1.5% alcohol by content. Yuk! It was lightly flavored water with no distinctive taste. A super-pale liquid, this beverage did save lives 1,000 years ago.

Flints

In 2018, while researching for this series in Winchester, I picked up a stone like the ones cemented into the outside of the wall encircling the city. At home, I consulted a geologist, who informed me it was flint. He reported flint could be found everywhere in the England.

I had my answer to a question that arose as I wrote *Lady Margaret's Escape.* If city dwellers were required to extinguish all candles and fires every night to prevent burning down the town, how did they restart their fires in the morning?

Striking one flint against another over a bit of fluff or loose wool would create a spark and fire needed to ignite a stick to start the fireplace or to light a candle.

Weather

Because weather affects everything from clothing to crops to prosperity and more, I researched the environment and the weather in England before beginning Margaret's story,

I learned historical climatologists agreed about weather conditions but not the dates. They reported a 300-year span of mild weather for northern Europe and the British isles. Longer growing seasons, milder winters, and fewer major storms enabled people to grow more food and to prosper. The population increased, ate better, and was healthier than in the previous era.

One expert dated the period from 900 to 1200 C.E. Another said the dates were from 950 to 1250 C.E. Either way, Lady Margaret's story (1099-1112) occurs in the middle of this warm spell. In this trilogy, you read about the Saxons' and Normans' successes in feeding people, and you found few references to severe weather because of what I had learned.

Languages

During this time, England was rife with assorted languages and many dialects. In the Danelaw in northeastern England, the languages included what we now call Old Norse, and Old Danish plus several dialects. Speakers of Old Saxon in southern England could not understand their cousins in the north, who had combined elements of Old Saxon, dialects, and Scottish. The Normans, who arrived from the area we now call Normandy, spoke Old Norman-French.

The common standard across the country was Latin. The Church and its clergy said Mass in Latin. At this time, priests wrote the country's laws and history in Latin because few were literate, even among the nobles. What words to use?

I included elements of Old Norman-French, the language the conquerors spoke, and Old Saxon, the major language of the conquered people of southern England. Most of us are unaware 20 to 25 percent of modern English is Old-Saxon based. Almost every one-syllable English word is Saxon in origin as are many two-syllable words. "Thaet" became *that*, "waes" is *was* and bitan (long "i") became *bite*. Think, *run, stop, go, want*, and several thousands more words. Compound Old Saxon words include *husband* (hoosbond) and *housewife* (hoos-weef-ah). A few of our modern spellings are the remainders of Old Saxon spellings, the most famous of which are *knight, knife, night*, which were pronounced "Ka-nicked," "Ka- niff-ah," and "nicked." Another antiquated use is A.D. (Anno Domini), which was used for two thousand years. In the twenty-first century, Americans switched to C.E. (Common Era). Within the stories I use A.D., and I use C.E. when I am writing to directly to you.

Sometimes I used word choice to hint at the language spoken. For example, *wed* and *cow* are Saxon. *Marriage* and *cattle* are Norman.

I had Margaret and Alfred use *shall* when they spoke Saxon and *will* when they spoke Norman. Within these stories, I sometimes stated who was speaking which language. King Henry required everyone speak Norman in his Court; I say so once in each book. This is how I played with words. Perhaps, none of my word choices matters. For you, Margaret's story does matter, for which I am glad. (glaed is another Old Saxon word.)

Preview

Lady Margaret's Future
Henry's Spare Queen Trilogy, Book 3

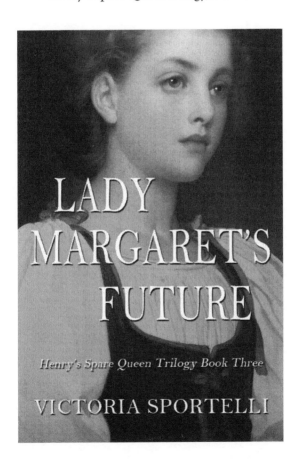

An excerpt

1

※

A Riddle

12 August 1103 A.D.

As Margaret rode beyond her estate, she worried. *What did that evil Lady Claire put into Her Royal Highness's head? Why does she not know I never wanted to replace her? Would she believe me if I told her so? What will the queen do to me when I arrive as the king commanded? Something bad. Something vengeful. Of that I am cert.*

At King Henry's messenger's order, Lady Margaret had packed and skipped her midday meal. The four king's guardsmen and the messenger hastened Lady Margaret and Sir Masselin eight miles to the King's Inn near the junction of two royal roads.

No sleeping in royal quarters and dining like one. I will eat in the great room at the women's table, but I will ask to have a room to myself or at least mine own bed. As the king ordered me here, he can pay for it. I will not.

The men supped at their own table and slept a few hours before the messenger awakened Margaret and ordered her to rise. *Two days*

428

more. We shall arrive Wednesday, late I hope. I will refuse to seek Her Royal Highness until the next morn. She frets and angers easily when she is tired. Margaret rose, dressed and descended the two flights of circular stone stairs to the Great Room. After breaking their fasts in haste, the party rode south toward Winchester. Nine miles later, the group broke their travels at a roadside inn after Lady Margaret complained they were driving her too fast for her old gelding. *Am I using Night as an excuse to delay my arrival? Yes. No, his head droops, and his gait is getting wobbly. I do well to rest him now, for the morrow will be an even longer day of riding.*

The twelfth day in August was dry and hot. By getting off Night herself or with Masselin's aid, Margaret twice forced the party to stop to water and rest her gelding. *You tire more easily than I remembered. You are getting old. Twenty-two? Twenty-three? Rest, my friend. I am in no hurry to meet the queen. I fear her.* Margaret remembered the Half Moon Inn was two hours from the city. As she passed the opened gates, she veered left and urged Night across the road.

"Stop not! My lady, we must reach the city this eventide," called a man behind her. As two knights and Masselin followed her into the yard, the messenger and the other two knights, who had already passed the gate, returned.

Ask not. Act like a lord, no, the king. Order. Here he comes.

"YOU! Innkeeper. See you the royal banner of King Henry's messenger and his knights? We are on His Royal Highness's business, and you will perform every task I order." Seated on Night well above the fellow, Margaret scowled at him as if he had already failed her. "Produce your best hostler. I expect excellent care for my steed and excellent meals and wine for ourselves. The king's men will tell you where they want to sleep. I choose the women's room." After hearing the man order a boy to the stables, Margaret untied herself from her riding platform. Climbing down unaided, she landed hard and kicked up dirt. She cupped Night's drooped head in the curve of her arm and stroked his cheek as she cooed, "There, there, boy. You will soon feel better with water and food. You will rest well this night, I promise." Night lifted his weary head toward her and nickered as if he understood.

"My lady, you must not. . ." began the messenger.

"NO!" I will hear it not. If you push Night for two more hours, he will die on the way. I will not have it! We stay the night. Ride ahead if you will. Night and I sleep here."

"I am at your service, my lady," said a young man who had skidded to her side. His brown hair bobbed into his face. He pulled his forelock and dropped his chin. He was so tall Margaret had to crane her neck to meet his eyes.

"He is Night. Walk him slowly until he cools. Wipe him down with soft cloths. In small portions, give him first water, then a mixture of alfalfa, oats and hay. Make him wait. Let his stomach settle. If he shivers, cover him with a blanket. Do not let him founder with too much too soon. When you think him ready, again give him small portions of water then food. Wait until you hear his gut rumbling and add a third time if you think he still hungers. Stay close to him all night and watch. Summon me at once if he acts unwell in any manner."

"Yes, my lady, said the boy as he nodded twice. "As you command."

"Best you do. Your life depends on Night being in good health and well rested in the morn." *Fear in his eyes. Good.* Margaret watched the boy shudder before he took up Night's reins. Speaking softly and kindly, he led Night toward the stables. *Two hours before sundown, a good time to stop, longer to sleep.* Margret turned. "Innkeeper, we will take half the great room and I will sit at mine own table." Margaret gestured over her shoulder and behind. "They will inform you of their desires. We wait here while I count ten. Be ready when we enter." The innkeeper, a man with a sallow complexion and of middling years and girth, dashed inside. Margaret turned and crossed her arms over her chest. She stared at the men still on their horses. "Messenger, I have something to tell you when you are ready to learn it. Four…five…six…seven…eight…nine…ten." Margaret turned away. As Margaret grasped the door latch, behind her she heard saddles creaking.

Seated alone at a large round table, Margaret ignored those in the other half of the great room. Several mumbled about being forced to share tables or to sup standing while holding bowls. *See them not. Ignore them.* Margaret finished her meal, pushed her soup bowl and bread board toward the center of the table, and refilled her mug. She looked toward the men's table to see the messenger frowning at her. Margaret cocked her head as if asking a question as she raised the bottle and tilted it as if she was about to pour wine into the air. The messenger took up his mug and left his table."

"Sir, if it please you, join me."

After the messenger sat, Margaret filled his mug and set the bottle near him.

"You are a froward girl."

"True." Margaret ignored his insult. "Sir, Night needs rest, as do I. Also, I choose not to face Her Royal Highness in dirty traveling clothes. I have let a house in which to wash and change into more suitable clothes before I present myself."

431

"We sleep but a few hours. The city gates will op to us no matter the hour. You will be quick in your preparations and be at the castle by dawn."

"Sir, have you learned nothing of royals? I approach them not until their bellies are full, and they have drunk at least one goblet of ale or wine. Time it as you will, but I will not go to Her Royal Highness until after she has attended Mass, broken her fast, and is at her ease."

"You are impossible!"

"True again! *I might as well say what he already knows.* I displeased her Royal Highness." Margaret snorted. "More than displeased." Margaret shuddered involuntarily. "I am unwilling to face her until I am at least presentable. I pray she will be in a favorable mood, but I will risk neither my horse nor my life to disturb her morning routine." When the man said nothing, Margaret added, "Please take the rest of the wine for yourself or the knights. I am for bed. Knock on the women's door at dawn. I will be ready anon." As she strode toward the stairs, Margaret nodded to Masselin, who had also sat alone at a table with the sacks at his feet. Masselin smiled at her as he nodded in return. *Good man. Glad he came with me. To bed. I am not sleepy; what tires me is fear.*

Margaret chose a straw pad on the floor and pulled it nearest to the door. *Do not pretend I have any rank as a girl. Avoid trouble.* She lay with her back to the wall with her sword atop its sheath between her and the room. Even though the sun still streamed into the room through a slit of window, Margaret tried to sleep. A single, fat candle with three wicks sat on its own tall table and illumined the darkest corner. Others entered and disturbed Margaret's efforts to nod off. As they prepared for bed and settled, Margaret lowered her lids to slits so she could observe unnoticed a pair who had drawn her attention. A mother and daughter wearing rich, fur-trimmed clothes had taken one of the beds. They appeared to be at odds over something. Margaret guessed the girl to be of an age to be married. *Mayhap the contract is already signed. Mayhap she is being taken to her husband's family and wants not to go.* The daughter refused to look at her mother, gave curt one-word answers when spoken to, and insisted on sleeping in her chemise and on the side of the bed toward the room. The room quieted as the candle sputtered and re-settled to a steady burn. The setting sun shifted and lit the room no more.

Margaret was almost asleep when a movement caught her eye. Through slits, Margaret saw the girl slip out of bed and move through shadow toward her. The girl bent and extended her hand. At her last step she reached. In a single fluid movement, Margaret rose to her knees and grabbed the girl's right wrist. Margaret's right hand held her sword.

"I just wanted to touch it!" yelped the girl.

The girl's mother sat up and begged, "Please God, no! I beg you. Harm her not!"

Other women woke, but moved not from their pads. They stared at the pair frozen in a tableau.

Margaret slowly pulled; the girl struggled to be released. Margaret remained silent until the girl was on her knees before her and trapped. She set her sword on the rushes between them and stared into the girl's eyes.

"You want to touch it?" Margaret asked in a steady, soft voice. In the silence, the girl nodded. *Silly girl, you know not the cost. I will teach you.*

"Before you touch my sword, solve a riddle. What can a woman do that a man cannot?"

433

Coming Late January 2021

Lady Margaret's Future
Henry's Spare Queen Trilogy, Book 3

Queen Matilda of England has just borne King Henry his heir,
Prince William.
King Henry no longer needs a spare queen or does he?
Lady Margaret fears the queen's plans for her
even more than she fears the king's.

**If you would like to be notified
when this book is available, please visit**
www.victoriasportelli.com
and submit your first name and email address.

**Please read my privacy policy. I do not spam my readers.
After you confirm you want to join V.C.S. Readers,
I will send you a free short story about Lady Margaret.
Occasionally I will send you updates about the
book's completion, launch date, and other information.
Thank you.**

V. C. Sportelli

You may go to

Author Website: *http://www.vcsportelli.com*
https://facebook.com/vcsportelli/
Pinterest: *victoriasportelli*
Twitter: *@SportelliVic*
for more information about me and my books.

Acknowledgments

Without T. M. Evenson's encouragement and support, I would not be an author. The trilogy and the prequel, which will follow, would never have been more than ideas rolling around in my head and stories I told her. She is an accomplished writer and computer expert, who introduced me to the program National Novel Writing Month (*NaNoWriMo.org*). She read the first draft of *Lady Margaret Escapes,* Henry's Spare Queen Trilogy Book One. After she helped me edit it, she taught me about how to be published. Dear Sister, I am forever grateful for all you have taught me and for your help while you launched *Emergence: The Journey Begins,* the prequel to *The Destiny Saga* and your first books in the series, *Providence: A New Home, A New Life,* and *Diffidence: An Unforgiving Journey.*

Any "horse sense" in this story comes from my friend Joyce sharing her equine knowledge and my meeting her American saddlebred Gizmo.

Thank you, T. Wiering, for helping me locate Creazzo Publishing.

I can not do without your computer expertise and good advice, Olivia, and I am so grateful for the many times you have come to my aid

E. Pagone helped me select the cover image. Well done, my friend.

Thank you Becky P. for supporting me by telling others about my novels.

Kathy Carlson listens to me read via long distance. I asked her if the novel flowed well; she said it did and made several suggestions. From Kathy I learned good editing only improves my work. She has encouraged me each step of the way and taken every late-night call when I wanted to discuss my writing. Kathy has always been a true friend and my sister-of-the heart. I consult her about my writing at least weekly.

Dick Carlson is part of my inspiration for all my heroes. Thank you for your patience while Kathy and I worked together.

I have praise and am most grateful for the "big three" in my writing career: Margaret Diehl, my editor; Doug of *wordzworth.com*, my book formatter, and Jenny of Historical Fiction Book Covers. Because of your expertise and dedication to excellence, I love how my books look. I look forward to working with you on my next book, *The Songbird of Venice.*

Glossary

Advent. A time of prayer and fasting from the fourth Sunday before Christmas to midnight Mass on Christmas eve.

Ancients/Giants. The names the English gave the unknown persons who built the North Wall (Hadrian's Wall) and left behind parts of villas and mosaic floors of villas. Actually, they were the Romans who ruled England from about 65 A.D. until 450 A.D. During this time, no one remembered who they were.

Anno Domini. (A.D.): Latin for "in the year of Our Lord." We now use C. E. (Common Era).

anon. Immediately.

Ash Wednesday. The start of **Lent** forty days before Easter excluding Sundays. One had ashes put on one's forehead in the shape of a cross as a sign of one's need to repent sinfulness.

bailey. A large area, usually protected by a dry or wet moat, surrounded by a tall wooden or stone wall called a palisade, which encircles the Hall, **Keep,** kitchen, garrison, chapel, and other buildings where a lord, his family and his retainers reside. Part of an early Norman castle.

barbican. A fortified entrance to a castle or to a town, of towers on either side of a passageway to enable guards to shoot arrows or to drop rocks or hot water over invaders. It often contains a portcullis, dropped it will stop an invasion.

bed and board. Bed is the right to have a table top, bench, cot, or bed to sleep upon as part as one's service. Board is the right to be fed.

bliaut (a). A Norman-French word. A Norman woman's outer garment to the wrists and ankles, fitted to the elbows for fashion, then flared to the wrist. Also flared from the hips for easy walking, usually wool in winter and linen in summer.

board. The right to be fed.

boon. A gift or favor granted by one person to another.

C. E. Common Era is the modern term used to describe years. It replaced "A.D." (Anno Domini): Latin for "in the year of Our Lord."

cert. The medieval word for certain. The opposite is uncert.

chatelaine. Usually the landholder's wife; she is responsible for everything on the estate except its safety and men's hunting practices.

chemise. A soft undergarment of linen or wool slightly smaller than a **bliaut** woman by Norman women to protect their skin from chaffing. Called a **shift** in Saxon.

Christmastide. The days from Midnight Mass on December 24 through the Epiphany on January 6.

Church. The one, catholic, true religion taught by Jesus the Christ and practiced throughout Western Europe; the pope in Rome is its head; also called the Christian Church.

Church ranks. In 12th century England, there were only three ranks of priests. They are:

archbishop, head of a great area within a country or the whole country. In 1100 A.D. England had two, Canterbury and York, both of whom answered to the pope in Roma, Italy

bishop. Holder of a section within an archbishop's responsibility. He often received estates and wealth from donations and wills, which he managed for the Church. He answered to the archbishop for his actions. Many created the position of **warrior priest** after King William II grabbed church lands and threatened bishops.

priest. He was responsible for the religious wellbeing and obedience to the Church's teachings and practices of the persons, both Norman and Saxon, in his territory, estate, village, or town. He answered to his assigned bishop.

Confession. A requirement to state one's sins to a priest, receive absolution and to do penance before being permitted to receive **Holy Communion.** What is said there can never be revealed.

constable. Man who is in charge of all the aspects of a castle compound outside the individual buildings.

corps d' elite. A group of especially trustworthy fighters, who are members of an inner circle within a larger army.

courses. The monthly cycle of a woman losing blood because she is not with child.. While a girl may be contracted to a marriage, the wedding may not be blessed and she may not be bedded until her courses arrive.

dais. In a **hall**, a platform two to four steps high upon which sits a table and benches, stools or chairs and from which the lord of the estate and his family dine and rule.

Danelaw. The region in northeast England where the Danes invaded and settled late in the 9th century. In the 12th century, they were ruled by the English king but kept their own language and customs.

ditch woman. A girl/woman whose father/husband has thrown her out of her family for unacceptable behavior, such as disobedience, having sexual relations outside marriage, running away, etc. She lives in fear of her life because anyone can do anything to her; she is a pariah.

dowry. The money, goods, and other items a woman's family agrees to give so she can bring it to her husband or her husband's family at her marriage; the amount of wealth she brings often determines her value as a wife

dram. A unit of liquid equal to 1/8 of an ounce or 3/4th of a U. S. teaspoon.

Epiphany (January 6). The twelfth day after Christmas, believed to be the day the Magi visited the Christ child and gave him gifts; a time of gift giving and feasting.

excommunicate. To issue the severe penalty for a gross offense to the **Church** that results in a person's inability to receive the sacraments or to be buried in holy ground. One must still attend Mass. The penalty is reversible if one repents, goes to **Confession**, completes a penance and changes one's ways. One is then readmitted to the Body of Christ's followers and to His **Church**.

farthing. A coin equal to one/fourth of a penny. The obverse side was scored so a penny could be broken in half, a **hapenny** and then again into a farthing (a fourth thing.)

fasting/fasting season. The time during **Lent** or **Advent** when one ate sparingly or the restriction of certain foods, especially as part of religious practices.

flagon. A portable corked leather pouch that transports a liquid.

feudalism. All of England was owned by the king. He portioned out some of it to be held by those beneath him, who worked and protected it on his behalf. A baron held vast tracts of land and answered directly to the king. With royal permission, a baron could separate his lands into baronies or earldoms and raise a lord or knight to that station. In turn, either the earl or lord could then assign land within the property he held to a knight who could then marry because he was a landholder. Each rank owed military service and taxes to the station directly above his.

First Day. January 1.

fletching. Feathers in a pattern at the back of an arrow to help it fly straight.

fortnight. A shortened form of "fourteen nights," a two-week time period.

foster. Giving or receiving parental care and special training from one who is not a blood relative.

freeman. A man who was born free or legally given his freedom.

freewoman. A woman who was born free or legally given her freedom.

froward. An insult referring to a person who steps beyond her/his station. The modern form is forward.

geld. Money, especially money owed to pay a debt.

gelding. A castrated male animal, this term often refers to a horse.

Giants/Ancients. The names the English gave the unknown persons who built the North Wall (Hadrian's Wall) and left behind parts of villas and mosaic floors of villas. Actually, they were the Romans who ruled England from about 65 C.E. until 450 C.E.During this time, no one remembered who they were.

girdle. A belt of leather or stiff fabric, decorated or not, women wear around their waists. They hang their personal dagger, a scissors, household keys, etc. from it. We now call is a belt.

girl. Any unmarried female, no matter her age.

Grand Crusade. In 1095 Pope Urban II called all of Christendom to a crusade to free Eastern Christians from Turkish rule and to take possession of the Holy City of Jerusalem. When Jerusalem fell to the Turks in

1147, a second Crusade was called and the custom of numbering the Crusades began; this one was then renamed the First Crusade.

grub. To dig in anticipation of planting.

gruit. A mixture of local herbs used to flavor ale. Each aleman made his own secret recipe. In the 12th century, hops were wild in England; some alemen included them in their gruit when they could find them. By the 14th century, hops was a crop in Europe grown especially to be a part of the product called beer. In 14th century England, a man wrote that a true Englishman drank only ale.

gunna. A Saxon word for a long-sleeved woolen dress worn to the ankles and fastened to the body with a belt. Most Saxon women owned only one, which they wore until they were annually given cloth by their lord to make another one in preparation for Easter. Similar to a **bliaut,** but straight from shoulder to hem.

hall. The building where the Norman members of an estate dine and conduct business.

hapenny. A half of a penny that was scored on the obverse side and then cut.

High Mass. A regular religious service lead by a priest or higher member of the Christian Church for a special occasion to which is added additional elements such as a procession, special prayers and the use of incense.

hide. A unit of land comprising about 120 acres.

Holy Communion. A piece of bread and a sip of wine transformed into the body and blood of Jesus the Christ by a priest during Mass. The ceremony unites all of Christendom, and only those in good standing with the **Church** may partake in it.

hostler. A person who takes trains, works, and takes care of horses.

Hure e Crie. Old Norman French term of warning. It means "See/Observe and Cry." The Saxon form was **Seon and Heour.** In modern English, the French form became "Hue and Cry."

Iberia. The Medieval name for the countries of modern Spain and Portugal. The land area is still called the Iberian Peninsula.

Keep. A square building usually of stone, sometimes of wood, where the Norman lord and his family may flee for safety if his estate is attacked and his bailey is breached; generally they live there.

knight errant. Designates a fighter in arms who serves or is hired by one of rank without his being given land and is called "Sir" out of politeness but bears no rank.

knight landed or just **knight.** A knight errant who has been given land and who may now marry; he serves a man of a noble rank above his; his is the lowest noble title during these times (See **titles**).

Lent. The 40 days of fasting and prayer in anticipation of the religious holiday of Easter.

mantle. A hoodless, sleeveless warm outer covering worn by women. We call it a cape.

marriage chest/wedding chest. A wooden chest, carved or plain, into which a girl places the linens she has hemmed and all manner of clothing, fabrics, household goods and items she has made or acquired and will take with her to her new home as part of her dowry. In the 20th century United States, it was called a "hope chest."

marriage rib/wedding rib. A strip of woven, lightweight cloth 3 to 6 inches wide used as decorative trim on clothing or is wrapped around a married woman's long hair when she wears it in two braids. Thin ribs are often woven into braids for decoration. We now call them ribbons.

Mass. A religious service lead by a priest or higher member of the **Church** in which all Christians attend and those in good standing with the Church receive **Holy Communion** as a way of uniting all Christendom and keeping its members faithful.

May Day. May 1.

merchet. The marriage tax a couple pays to their lord.

merlin. The solid part of the top of a wall that is separated by spaces called crenels, part of the battlement of a castle.

Michaelmas. September 29.

midden. A dunghill or refuse heap

Midsummer. The summer solstice, usually June 21 or 22, depending on the moon cycles in that year.

morrow. The next day. The medieval word for "tomorrow."

motte. A mound topped with a tower called a **Keep**, which is within a **bailey,** the whole of which comprised an early Norman castle.

mortal sin. A misdeed that will cause your soul be sent to Hell if it is not forgiven and more serious than a venial sin, which is a misdeed and a minor offense against God and/or the **Church**.

Norman. Both the name of the group and the language the Normans of England and Normandy spoke during the twelfth century. We now call the language Old Norman-French.

op/opt. (sounds like oap/oapt) the medieval words for "open" and "opened."

palfrey. A female horse only women and priests ride. Most often, English priests rode donkeys.

palisade. The wall of wooden timbers or of stone which surrounds the **bailey** and all within; usually has either a dry or wet moat around it for further protection and only one gate for entrance.

parchment. Sheep skin that has been pounded thin and stretched and upon which records are written.

penance. Prayers and good deeds that must be completed before one's sins are expunged and before one can receive **Holy Communion** during **Mass.**

pence. Another word for a penny; the word is sometimes used for a single coin or a number of coins, as in six pence.

people/s. A group of persons related by common elements such as descent, heredity, history, language, cultural traits, social norms or geography. In the early Medieval period, the chief determiners of a peoples were language and geography, so they were: Saxon, Norman, Scot, Irish, etc. One of the most shocking of King Henry I's policies was the marriage between Saxons and Normans to create a new people—English. In the sixteen century, the word became "race."

Percheron. A horse, usually black but sometimes gray, from Perche, a region which is now in northwestern France.

Picardy shepherd. An ancient dog breed from the Picard region now in France. It is known to be an intelligent, agile, lively animal who guards sheep, cows, goats, other farm animals and is an excellent guard dog.

pottage. Soaked grains, into which can be thrown leftover vegetables and meats, that is cooked and turned into a soup/stew served in the morning. This word was later changed to porridge.

pound. A unit of money in silver pennies/pence. In this era 240 pence
equaled 1 pound.

pull one's chin. Before the Norman invasion of 1066 C.E., Saxon men
swore they were telling the truth by pulling on their beard hairs and
swearing an oath of honesty. Norman law forbade them from wearing beards because "All bearded Saxons look alike." No longer able
to have beards, the clean-faced Saxons then pulled on their chins
when swearing to tell the truth.

rank. See **titles**. Within each title, men are ranked according to how
much land they hold, their level of wealth, and how the royals favor
them. Wives, sons, and daughters hold the same rank as the head of
their household.

reeve. On an estate, a man who has been elected each January by his
fellow Saxons to oversee all the assigning of land, planting, growing,
and harvesting of crops. Traditionally, he may elected only three
times before another man must be chosen.

rib. Any narrow strip of cloth. See also **wedding rib**.

riding platform. An early medieval woman's saddle, upon which she sat
sideways with her legs on one side of a horse and a sandbag counterweight the other side behind her. No self respecting or honorable
woman spread her legs around a horse's back.

roundseys. Icelandic/Norwegian horses who were the size of large
modern ponies. Not only could they carry heavy weights, their
five-gaited walk was much desired. In addition to walk, trot, canter
and gallop, they ambled, a gait they could maintain for hours. This
created easy riding for humans because it was so smooth. They still
exist and are now called Icelandic ponies.

Saxon. Both the people of England who were invaded in 1066 A.D. by
King William I (the Conqueror) and the language they spoke. We
now call their language Old Saxon.

scabbard. A sheath for a sword, usually of leather or cloth-covered
wood.

Seon and Heour. Saxon for "See and announce," a warning of danger.
Hure e Crie. was the Old Norman-French term of warning, which
became Hue and Cry in English.

seneschal. The man in charge of the estate who follows his lord's orders and the **chatelaine's** instructions; like the foreman of a ranch.

scribe. One who writes documents and makes copies of documents in an era before the invention of printing. Most likely a priest because they had been taught to read and most nobles had not.

serfs (see **villeins**). Term for the persons tied to the land owned by the king, earls, barons, and lords, as part of the **feudalism** system common on the European continent. Usually they are not free, but they are not bought or sold as if they were slaves. This term was used on the European continent, not England.

shift (a). A soft undergarment of linen or wool slightly smaller than a **gunna** worn by Saxon women to protect their skin from chaffing. Also called a **chemise** in Old Norman-French.

shilling. The term for 12 pence (pennies), a form of counting coins in bulk.

shriven. To confess one's sins to a priest and be given absolution and to perform the penance the priest assigned so one may receive the sacraments of the **Church**.

shroud. A cloth or sheet in which a corpse is wrapped for burial.

Shrove Tuesday. The day before **Ash Wednesday.** The last day one may feast on all the foods and drinks one desires before **fasting** for **Lent.**

Sign of the Cross. Touching one's right-hand finger tips together and making the shape of the Christian cross by touching one's forehead, heart, left then right shoulders.

simples. Ointments, creams, powders, and other simple remedies for a variety of illnesses and ailments; most use pig fat as a base.

slavery time. In Saxon England, slavery was a temporary punishment of labor when one could not pay a debt. The work done was given a value. (See **Geld**) Once the debt was paid, the person was again free.

sokeman. While he is more than a **villein**, he is not a **freeman**, However, he may purchase land and make contracts, which is usually to the lord of the estate in which he resides. He lives there and pays in rent or services rather than in crops or animals. In Norman times, such individuals were rare.

stone (a). A unit of weight equal to 14 U.S. pounds.

Te Deum. Literally "To God," it is a prayer or song to The Lord.

thrice. Three times or triple.

ticking. Cloth case of a mattress or pillow into which is stuffed hair, feathers, straw or the like.

tithe. Literally "tenth." Ten percent of one's goods, animals, or income paid as a tax in support of the **Church**.

titles, Royal: King/Queen

Prince/Princess

Noble* — Baron/Baroness (called Lady)

Earl/Countess (called Lady)

Lord (sometimes addressed as Sir/Sirrah)/Lady

Sir(Sirrah)/Lady (a knight who owns land)

*During these years, titles of address were fluid. All the nobles except for knights landed could be—and often were—addressed as "Lord"— even the earls—and many times the barons/earls and lords were informally addressed as "Sir."

treble. Threefold or tripple.

trestle tables. A table composed of a top of boards set upon a wooden, triangular A-frame (think sawhorse).

tuppence. Two pennies.

uisgebah. A 12th century word developed from the Celtic "uise" or "usque" for the Irish drink called "uisge beatha." In Scottish it means "water of life." These days we call it "Scotch whisky" or "whiskey." In the 14th century, a historian called the Scotch version "undrink-able" because it was much stronger than the Irish version.

uncert. The medieval word for certain. The opposite is **cert.**

unshriven. To die without first have been to **Confession** and com-pleting any **Penance.** Without these, one cannot be buried by the Church in holy ground.

vassal. Under the feudal system, any person who holds land and owes taxes and homage, fealty and/or military service to an individual of higher rank; in England all nobles and royals are vassals to the king.

Vespers. The Christian ceremony of prayers and/or singing that ended the day and after which the people went to bed.

villeins (see **serfs**). Term used in England for those tied to the land, and who are not free, but they are not bought or sold as if they were slaves.

walkway. Structure attached behind the **palisade** upon which guards may stand and defend the **bailey**.

marriage chest/wedding chest. A wooden chest, carved or plain, into which a girl places the linens she has hemmed and all manner of clothing, fabrics, household goods and items she has made or acquired and will take with her to her new home as part of her dowry. In the 20th century United States, it was called a "hope chest."

wedding rib/marriage rib. A strip of woven, lightweight cloth 3 to 6 inches wide used as decorative trim on clothing or is wrapped around a married woman's long hair when she wears it in two braids. Thin ribs are often woven into braids for decoration. We now call them ribbons.

warrior priest. A priest who has been trained as a swordsman and fighter and who guards the **Church**'s property. After King William II prevented Archbishop Anselm from appointing bishops and took their lands for the income, several bishops created these men to protect themselves and their bishoprics.

wattle and daub. A form of construction using softened sticks woven together (wattle) and a mud of dirt, straw and other debris (daub) to form walls of a hut that is then roofed with thatch. A common home for Saxons during this era. Fences and room screens were often made of wattle.

wench. A female servant, whether girl or woman.

wimple. A woman's head-cloth drawn in folds about the head and around the neck; it usually covered the forehead as well. Originally worn out of doors, it later became popular for covering one's hair indoors. Nuns started wearing it to cover their hair from being seen by men. A form of scarf with folds.

wort. The infusion of malted grains or meal to turn water into beer. Then is a small portion is used to start the next batch; the remainder is discarded and fed to animals, usually pigs.

About the Author

Ms. Sportelli is a life-long Anglophile, who loves British history, culture, manners, folklore, customs, and humor. How women worked and struggled, what they wore and ate, and how their families survived are the focus of her novels.

She has been to the places she writes about. One of her exciting finds is in the hall to the Queen's Wing of the Great Hall, which is all that remains of the large castle in Winchester. Hanging there is a photograph of a royal treasury chest King Henry I used.

During 25 years of reading and research, Ms. Sportelli concluded that Henry I of England was an under-rated king. She found compelling King Henry's struggles, and the dangers he faced amid the conflicts between the Normans and the Saxons.

In college, she majored in English with a special interest in the Anglo-Saxon and the early Medieval periods. She learned to read, write and speak basic Anglo-Saxon.

After Ms. Sportelli finishes this trilogy, she is off to Italy to research her next historical fiction novel, which is set in Venice.

Find Victoria online and on social media:

Author Website: *www.victoriasportelli.com*
Facebook: victoriasportelli
Pinterest: VictoriaSportelli
Twitter: *@SportelliVic*

Dear Reader

The author will be grateful if you leave an honest review online.
Thank you!

Made in the USA
Monee, IL
27 December 2022